For Guy Barker, Michael Brandon and Ian Shaw

SIGNAL RED

ROBERT RYAN

headline
review

First published in 2010 by HEADLINE REVIEW

An imprint of HEADLINE PUBLISHING GROUP

First published in paperback in 2010 by HEADLINE REVIEW

4

Cataloguing in Publication Data is available from the British Library

ISBN 978 0 7553 5820 5

Typeset in Janson Text by Palimpsest Book Production Limited,
Falkirk, Stirlingshire

Printed and bound in Great Britain by
Clays Ltd, St Ives plc

Headline's policy is to use papers that are natural, renewable and
recyclable products and made from wood grown in sustainable forests.
The logging and manufacturing processes are expected to conform
to the environmental regulations of the country of origin.

HEADLINE PUBLISHING GROUP
An Hachette UK Company
338 Euston Road
London NW1 3BH

www.headline.co.uk
www.hachette.co.uk

Although *Signal Red* was inspired by and based on real figures and events, the narrative is essentially fiction. Therefore the thoughts, feelings, dialogue and action ascribed to the characters are the author's invention, and *Signal Red* should be understood to be a fictional account, not history. The narrative contains many characters on both sides of the law who are entirely the creation of the writer, and any resemblance to real people, living or dead, in those cases is entirely coincidental.

A broad definition of crime in England is that it is any lower-class activity that is displeasing to the upper classes.

David Frost and Anthony Jay, *To England with Love*

Extract from *An Honest Citizen's Guide to the Criminal Classes* by Colin MacInnes

Which is the criminal aristocracy?
Safe-blowers, accomplished breakers and enterers, robbery with violence men and reliable 'get-away' drivers.

Have professionals characteristics in common?
To generalise, they are above average intelligence, with good nerves, loyalty (they have to be – to 'grass' is the only real criminal crime), cheerful and humorous and not particularly vicious, outside the job.

Why are there fewer women criminals?
The girls (and women) participate all right but as an informant put it – 'they make the tea while the men get on with the job'.

Are there criminal areas of London?
Yes, just as Marylebone is for doctors, Mayfair for advertisers and Holborn for lawyers. South London has, traditionally, a greater criminal concentration than the North.

Are the crimes masterminded?
The notion of there being one individual who sits like a spider in his web and plans it all, but does not participate, is quite unreal. On the other hand, there are many 'jobs' – and big ones – in which the initial information that makes them possible comes from a man or men with a considerable front of respectability, and whose role is to supply vital facts, but not do the actual job.

ROBERT RYAN

What are the relations between criminals and the police?
Intimate. They are enemies, yes, but in relation to anyone who is neither
a villain nor a copper, they form a closed society, rather like soldiers of
two warring armies in relation to the larger mass of civilians.

Sunday Times Magazine, 1963

Prologue

Blackheath, South London, May 1992

I was aware of the blue flashes on the bedroom ceiling even before the telephone rang. I felt a cold cramp grip my insides, although my brain told me I was being ridiculous. How could they have come for you? I asked myself. After all this time? Christ, Tony, even your VAT is up to date these days. And they don't do raids in the wee small hours for VAT anyway. Do they?

I listened to the sounds from outside, muffled by the double-glazing. There was the bark of a police controller on the radio, the distorted voice interrupted by stabs of static; a motor was still running, at idle, but hunting slightly. I thought the Met was meant to look after their vehicles?

Maybe they had privatised their maintenance departments, outsourced to the lowest bidder. And look at what you got. Revs that rose and fell at random.

The bedside phone chirruped the annoying tone set by my wife, Jane, jolting me out of my ruminations on free market forces. It sounded like a sparrow being strangled. She claimed it was less of a shock to the system than an ordinary ringing tone if a call came while you were asleep. Not when police lights were raking the room it wasn't.

'Hello?'

I heard a throat being cleared on the other end of the line. 'Tony? Tony Fortune?'

'Who's this?'

'Bill Naughton.'

I swung my feet out of bed and squinted at the clock. Past one in the morning. My head was clouded by the residual fuzz of the late-night brandy I had downed after taking in part of the Burt Lancaster season at the cinema in Greenwich. I had seen a strange movie called *The Swimmer* and John Huston's *The Unforgiven*. Maybe that last title applied to me, too. Perhaps they hadn't forgiven me my youthful misdemeanours. I was aware of Jane stirring behind me, pushing back the duvet, releasing a few stray molecules of last night's perfume. I held out a hand to stop her saying anything.

'Mr Naughton.' Or, more correctly, DC Billy – not Bill

– Naughton. At least, that had been his rank when I had known him. 'Been a while. How are you?'

'Retired, Tony. Have been for a few years now.'

I looked up at the lights strobing through the curtains. 'Pleased to hear it. So the fact that my bedroom looks like the last dance at the Policeman's Ball is nothing to do with you then?'

He gave the feeble joke an appropriately dismissive snort. 'Well, Tony, I am afraid it is. I'm back, as they say, for one night only, by public demand. Or at least, some Deputy Commander's request.'

I spoke slowly and carefully. Was it time to run, at last? At every house and flat I had lived in for the past thirty years I had rehearsed it. My escape route. Out the back, over the garden wall, or onto the roof, along to the neighbour's yard. But now I was too old for that. My running days were over. 'New evidence come to light has it, Mr Naughton?'

'Not about you, Tony.' Was that regret I could hear? 'Fact is, they dragged me from my bed, too. Youngsters are all fresh out of ideas. Need a couple of old hands.'

'Tony? Who—?' Jane began, but I shushed her.

'Sorry to disturb you and the missus, Tony.'

'What can I do for you exactly, Mr Naughton?'

'It's Roy. He's in a spot of bother.'

Jesus, I thought, so it is the VAT after all. I might have dropped out of the life, but even I knew that a few of the old lads were playing silly buggers with importing/exporting gold Krugerrands and running VAT scams on the deals. 'It isn't my area of expertise.'

'What isn't?'

'Whatever Roy has been up to. I haven't seen him in . . . must be ten or more years. Silverstone, it was.'

'He's shot someone.'

Now I was fully awake. The words, though, didn't make sense. 'Hold up. We are talking about Roy James?'

'Yes.'

'Roy James shot someone?' It was so ridiculous I laughed at the very notion. 'Come on, Mr Naughton. That can't be right. He was never—'

I almost heard the twang of Naughton's patience snapping. 'He shot his father-in-law, then hit the wife with the gun-butt.'

I was quiet for a moment while I took that in. Roy was never a violent man. He'd made sure he'd stayed away from all that business. The coshings that were sometimes a part of the job had always vexed him. And guns? He'd run a mile from them. 'I'll be damned.'

'And he'll be shot dead if you don't help. And then, no doubt, he'll be damned. The one and sevens are here.'

'Who?'

'PT Seventeen,' he explained carefully, as if only just remembering I wasn't up on the latest jargon. 'Tactical Firearms Squad – the boys with the Heckler and Kochs and what have you. Roy's barricaded himself in the house. So they want friendly voices to talk some sense into him before they are forced to go in guns blazing. And believe you me, these lads don't take much forcing.'

'How's the father-in-law?'

'How do you think? In a lot of pain. But he'll live.'

That was something. If it had been murder, the armed police would be even more trigger-happy. 'So the idea is for you and me to talk Roy down?'

'Yeah. Police and thieves,' he chortled. 'Working together for once.'

'Now, now, Mr Naughton,' I protested.

'Figure of speech, Tony. Forget it. Right – the car is outside, ready to take you to the scene.'

It was then I remembered I had tickets for the FA Cup replay the next day. Arsenal versus Sheffield Wednesday at Wembley, courtesy of BMW corporate hospitality. 'Is there nobody else?' I felt a prickle of shame as I said it.

It was nerves, I told myself. The nagging feeling that Billy Naughton might really have unfinished business with me, not Roy. 'What about Bruce?'

Naughton let out a sigh. 'Bruce Reynolds is too busy with his bloody memoirs, so he says. Which puts Roy's life in your hands, Tony. *Our* hands, that is. I hate to play this card after what, thirty years, but you owe me one. A big one, at that.'

I did. I owed him my freedom, even though he knew, deep down, I was a wrong 'un. He had an overdeveloped sense of fair play, our Mr Naughton, to ever be a real, hard, bastard copper. As I had found out to my benefit. 'So, payback at last.'

But sparring was over. 'You gonna help or what?'

I was already pulling on my clothes, so I supposed I had decided to go along with his plan. 'All right then, Mr Naughton, for old times' sake.'

His voice softened once more. 'Good man. Be nice to see you again, Tony. As you say, been a long time.'

'Yeah.' Not long enough, part of my brain protested as I struggled with my socks, using my free hand. 'I'll see you there.'

I cradled the receiver and explained to a bleary Jane that I had to go out to help an old friend. Jane was my second wife, younger than me, a different generation almost. She knew next to nothing of the old Tony Fortune, the one whose wife left him because of his misadventures in the underworld.

'Who is he?' she asked.

'A bloke called Roy James.'

I saw her brow furrow. Like most people she could recall the names of Roy's better-known associates, the celebrity thieves. To Jane, and most of the British public, Roy was a vague memory, a half-forgotten name. *Wasn't he the fella who played the trumpet?* they might ask. No, that was Roy Castle. *Or the quiz-show host?* Roy Walker. *Desert Island Discs?* Roy Plomley. If only he'd gone over the wall and ended up in Brazil doing crappy punk songs, they'd remember him then. 'Who?'

'He was a thief,' I went on. 'Cat burglar. First-floor man.'

She was awake now, eyes wide. 'How on earth do you know him, Tony?'

'It's a long story.'

One I had a feeling that Billy Naughton, Roy James and I were going to be chewing over for the rest of what was shaping up to be a very peculiar night.

'Try me.'

As I leaned over and kissed her forehead, I didn't actually say the sentence that formed on my lips. I thought it best to let it die a lonely, unloved death. *Roy was a Great Train Robber. And, come to that, so was I.*

Instead I whispered, 'I'll be as quick as I can. Go back to sleep.'

He backed away, muttering, and Dancey stood up behind him.

'Here, Vita ...'

'Kowalczyk?' Hammond Cox laughed. 'A killer, yes. She was quite nervy ... if you reckon you could take him, Tony?'

'You're ... person?'

'One that's saying that fully? I suppose not by my own ... I were going to be ... flowing over me ... in a sort of what a stranger asked a year people what rage.'

'...by me ...'

'And I found one upon another ... to road. I didn't realise all ... the remaining man beyond we all him ... I thought, then won't it was a long ... utilised ... within us not ... Then Within the ... me to put down.'

'...all between ...' I'll be around ... also ... Go back to sleep.'

Part One
POLICE & THIEVES

One

Warren Street, Central London, October 1962

Tony Fortune was polishing the bonnet of a signal-red AC
Ace Roadster when the big Rover purred to a halt outside
his rented showroom. It was a P5, the imperious political
barge much loved by government ministers. Except this one
was the newer coupé, with a raffish and rakish roofline. It
gave just a hint of flash to what could be perceived as a very
staid motor. Tony stopped applying the Super Hard Shell
Turtle Wax and waited to see who emerged from it.

Recognising the spindly figure unfolding itself out of the
car like a cobra emerging from a basket, he shouted to
Paddy, his mechanic, who was out the back: 'Put the kettle
on, mate. The poncy stuff.'

Then Tony returned to polishing, grabbing a few more

minutes, hoping to give the Ace the high lustre it deserved before his visitor came inside. He had loved cars all his life. He still had the first one he had ever owned, although it was now scratched and battered and missing a wheel. It was a maroon Series 30 Daimler, magically unearthed by his mum for a birthday during the war and treasured until peace came and Dinky Toys production resumed.

Bruce Reynolds – the man from the P5 – beamed as he saw Tony glance up at him through the plate glass. As tall, dapper and bespectacled as ever, Bruce adjusted the collar of his cashmere topcoat, smoothed down the front, with its concealed buttons, and strode into the display area. He stood and appraised the stock with an expert eye, dismissing most of it, before nodding at the Ace.

'That's nice.'

Bruce had an appetite for sports cars. Last time Tony had seen him he'd been squiring his young wife Franny in a sleek Austin Sprite. 'More up your street than the Rover, Bruce.'

Bruce looked out into the street at the P5. 'That? It's Charlie's, not mine.' No surname was needed. He meant Charlie Wilson, one of Bruce's childhood friends who had grown into a formidable blagger and hard man. 'He likes the leg room. My Aston's playing up again, so he lent it to me. You're right about the Rover, though. Bit too Reggie Maudling for my liking.'

Tony smiled and held out his hand. Bruce made him

laugh, always had. Tony's love of cars had progressed to 'borrowing' them when he was a young teenager. Which in turn had led to a meeting in borstal with an ambitious thief called Bruce Reynolds, who had a sideline in equally ambitious daydreaming. The slightly older lad used to describe in tedious detail The Good Life he would be acquiring for himself, once he pulled off The Big Job. It was a lengthy litany of quality cars, bespoke clothes, young attractive women, the finest booze and the best of mates, all to the accompaniment of the Modern Jazz Quartet and George Shearing. Even then, Tony had known it was a remarkably mature ragbag of aspirations for a young buck. And judging by the expensive sliver of a gold watch on his wrist, plus the fact that he had apparently acquired an Aston Martin, Bruce had ticked off at least some of his wish list. But Tony knew keeping up appearances was all part of the game. Bruce would walk and talk the high life even if he only had a half-a-crown in his Post Office Savings book.

'You doin' all right?' he asked Tony.

'Can't complain. There's more competition now, of course.'

Since the war, when it had been Spiv Alley, Warren Street had become car dealers' row. Initially it had been pavement jobs, cash only, no questions asked about such things as logbooks. But in the past few years, the ground floors of the office blocks had been opened up into showrooms and most of the dealing was more or less legitimate. It was still buyer beware, though, and you couldn't be sure that the name of the dealers – or the salesman – would be the same from one week to the next.

'How's the wife?' Bruce asked.

'Fine. Franny?'

'Good, thanks.'

'You workin'?'

Bruce's bony shoulders moved towards his ears in a noncommittal shrug. 'This and that.'

The role model for Bruce might be Cary Grant in *To Catch a Thief*, but the 'work' sometimes fell short of that. One week it might be a safe full of cash or jewels, but the next it could easily be a few dozen packs of Navy Cut from a tobacconists or a shipment of 30-denier stockings. If there was good information and a margin to be had, you went at it. Even a thief with ambitions like Bruce couldn't go after the Crown Jewels or the Bank of England every day.

Paddy emerged with the Darjeeling, the 'poncy' tea that Bruce liked. Bruce took the Castrol mug with a murmured thank you, sipped and smacked his lips appreciatively. 'The Champagne of Teas? You remembered.'

'You banged on about it so much inside, how could I forget?' Bruce stared at him, a slight smirk on his face, until Tony admitted the truth. 'All right, I have this guy who buys Mercs who likes it.'

'I thought it was a bit odd, keeping a caddy just on the off-chance I turn up.'

'Thanks, Paddy,' Tony said.

Paddy, a weather-beaten Dubliner of uncertain vintage, gave a smile that showed just how few teeth he had and retreated back to the workshop. 'Any more trouble from Mammie Jolson?' Bruce asked, the pleasantries over.

'No. I meant to say thanks.'

'You already did.' Tony had sent over a case of Chivas Regal. 'But it was Gordy really what put the word in. I mean, nobody's frightened of me, are they?' Hugh 'Mammie' Jolson had tried to collect pensions – protection money – from the dealers in the street. Most had paid up; Tony had called Bruce who had said he'd 'have a word', even though north of the river was no-man's land to him and 'having a word' wasn't his true calling.

Bruce was a thief, an opportunist, from smash and grab to safe-breaking, but he wasn't a strong-arm man. Not for him mixing it with the likes of the Krays, Richardsons, Frasers, Foremans or Hills. He enjoyed his elegant clothes and his good looks too much to get his hands dirty that way. Besides, as he said, nobody was ever scared of him; you wouldn't use Bruce to put the frighteners on anyone. But he knew men who *were* skilled at that kind of thing – men like Charlie Wilson or Gordon Goody.

Charlie was your down-the-line London chancer, not stupid by any means, but he conformed to type. As Bruce said of him, he was 'a hard worker, reliable and a very funny fucker when he wanted to be'. Gordy, though, struck Tony as a strange mix – a handsome face on a thug's body, a hair-dresser with a taste for Jermyn Street finery and thick gold bracelets, who was also capable of sudden violence.

A Tony Curtis haircut and two broken arms, please, Gordon.

Anyway, however it had been achieved – and often Gordy's trademark growl and daunting physical presence were enough to generate results – Mammie Jolson was off his back.

'You need some better stock.' Bruce pointed at a split-rear-windowed left-hand-drive Beetle. 'Not bloody German bombers.'

'What can I do for you, Bruce?' There was a price to be paid for unleashing Gordy, they both knew that. Bruce didn't stray far from his normal South London patch of the Elephant and Castle, Wandsworth, Battersea, Camberwell and Peckham without good reason – unless it involved Bobby Tambling and Chelsea. He was here to collect.

'Jags,' he said, peering inside the Ace. 'This one straight?'

'Had a prang,' Tony admitted. 'Insurance write-off. Drives OK. Well, pulls to the left a little when you brake. Can't seem to sort that out.'

'Chassis?'

'Maybe. Have to put it back on the rig. Or sell it to some chinless wonder. I thought you used Yul for cars?'

John 'Yul' Jones was a slap-headed chiseller whose only resemblance to his namesake, Mr Brynner, was the absence of hair. 'That bald cunt is currently chatting to Tommy

Butler about a little job he pulled in Penge that he neglected to mention to me. So we might not see him for a while.'

He said the policeman's name with a mix of disdain and admiration. The CID's Tommy Butler, who relished his nickname of 'the Grey Fox', had a way of getting confessions and convictions from even the tightest-lipped villains. And Yul's mouth was not that firmly zipped.

'What kind of Jags?' Tony asked casually. 'And how many?'

'The usual kind.' Nicked, he meant, and untraceable. 'Two.'

Tony hesitated. He knew that to ask any more questions would pull him deeper into whatever scheme Bruce Reynolds had in mind – and not necessarily to his benefit. Like the futile escape Bruce had organised from the Gaynes Hall borstal, which had ended with them doing a jolt at the much harsher Wandsworth unit. This time around, he didn't want to end up having a 'chat' with Tommy Butler like Yul. But Bruce was right: he needed better stock. A bit of cash to inject into the cars would come in handy, plus there was that Jolson business to square. 'Anything special? The Jags, I mean.'

'Well, perhaps. I'd like you to talk to my man about it. He's particular, he is.'

Tony didn't like the sound of that. Some wheel-men were so superstitious they insisted on the same colour upholstery in their getaway vehicle each time, let alone whether the motor was booted with crossplys or radials. You could waste days trying to find or create exactly the right spec. 'Send him along.'

Reynolds grimaced. 'Let's not do it here. What you doin' Saturday?'

Tony shrugged. 'I was going to see *Lawrence of Arabia*.'

'He's busy.' Bruce took off his glasses and polished them with a spotless handkerchief before replacing them. 'We'll go up to the Midlands and watch my driver race.'

'Race? Who is it – Graham Hill?'

They both laughed but then Reynolds looked serious. 'One day, he could be. Mark my words. His name is Roy James. Pick you up here at about nine?'

As soon as he nodded, Tony Fortune knew that Bruce had snared him once again.

Franny Reynolds was behind the counter of the antique shop when he walked in. She was playing 'Let's Twist Again' on the HMV record player, her eyes closed, lost in the swinging motion of the dance.

Charlie Wilson stood and watched her for a while. It was a gaze of appreciation, rather than lust. She was married to one of his oldest friends; he had known Bruce since 1943, when they had shared an Anderson shelter. Bruce was the man who had once saved him from a chivving at the hands of a razor gang outside the Wimbledon Palais. Charlie had been all for taking them on, but Bruce reckoned that fourteen to one – he didn't count himself as a fighter – was not good odds, even for a little maniac like Charlie. Bruce, already tall for his age, had towered over Stevie Pyle, the leader, and talked them out of striping young Chas. Bruce had even ended up discussing *Catcher in the Rye, The Naked Lunch* and *The Manchurian Candidate* with one of the tearaways later, at the coffee stall on Battersea Bridge.

It was why Charlie trusted Bruce, though: he didn't think like the rest of them. Charlie, Buster Edwards, another South London thief, and to some extent Gordon Goody ran on tramtracks. You knew where you got on and got off with them. Bruce had a series of branch lines, which meant his mind went in different directions.

Chubby Checker was nearing the end of his invitation to the dance when Charlie finally spoke, his voice an imitation of Bruce's lighter cockney accent. 'What do you think this is? The Scotch Club?'

Franny nearly leaped out of her skin. Charlie began to laugh at her flustered fumbling with the arm of the record player. It made a loud scratching noise as the needle ripped across the grooves. She turned and faced him. 'Chas! You bastard!'

Charlie smiled at her. She was lovely all right, even devoid of make-up as she was now. Bruce had once dated her older sister but it was Franny who had written to him while he was inside, sixteen-year-old Franny who was waiting, all grown up, when he got out. Today, in slacks and a stripy top, she could still pass for a schoolgirl.

'You ought to get a bell on that door,' he told her. 'Anyone could sneak up on you.'

'We don't get that many customers.'

Charlie looked around the store. It was called *Milestones* and it was meant to be an antique shop, although most of it was tat. There were bentwood chairs piled high, a pair of old joannas, a couple of oak tables, bed headboards, a wall of wardrobes, chrome fireside sets made redundant by High Speed Gas, and canteens of cutlery in velvet-lined boxes. But nothing you might call an heirloom. It was hard to imagine anything in the shop being a milestone in anyone's life. That wasn't the point; its job was to give Bruce a respectable front, like Charlie's work at the fruit and veg market or Gordy's hairdressing. 'Anything new in?'

'This record player,' she said, sliding an LP of Nina Simone out of its sleeve and putting it on the turntable. That would be Bruce's influence, of course. He loved all that American jazzy stuff. She changed the speed with a flick of the dial. 'And some Clarice Cliff stuff Bruce is excited about.'

'She a singer too?'

Franny hesitated, unsure whether he was pulling her leg. 'Pottery. It's out the back if you want to see.'

'Just in Time' came out of the HMV's speaker, the voice cool yet brittle, giving the song a slightly menacing edge.

'Nah. Only making conversation,' Charlie said. 'Bruce about?' She shook her head. 'Know where he's gone?'

'Didn't say.'

Charlie put his hand in his pocket and brought out a handkerchief, which he placed on the counter. He flipped it open to reveal a ladies' timepiece. 'Put that in your display, will you, Franny? We'll go fifty-fifty on it.'

Franny picked it up. It was a Cartier gold bracelet watch, probably from just after the war judging the patina on it. It caught the light beautifully as she draped it over her wrist.

'Where'd you get this?' she asked.

'I know and you don't have to. Looks good on you, Fran.'

She smiled at him. There were plenty of people frightened of Chas Wilson and those steely blue eyes of his. Bruce had taught her not to be. Charlie, he explained, had watched his father squander any money the family had, then had suffered the belt when the last of it had gone and his dad couldn't afford the pub. Charlie's aims in life were simple: never to be poor and scrabbling like his father, and never to let anyone get the upper hand, at least physically, ever again. Charlie had worked hard to earn his reputation, Bruce said, and now that rep did most of the work for him.

'It's pretty,' she said. 'Classy, too.'

Charlie gave an exaggerated sigh, as if he had just been browbeaten into a decision against his will. 'Oh go on, you can have it.'

Her jaw dropped and she gave a little squeak. 'Charlie, I couldn't.'

'I only got it in payment for a debt.' This was true. Although the man would be in deep shit once his wife found out how he had settled the loan. 'You must have a birthday coming up.'

'Not for months.'

'Early present, then.'

'No. Bruce'll—'

'I'll square it with Bruce. I'll tap him for twenty sovs, so he'll know it was business.' She had already fastened the catch. 'Although seeing it on you gives me a certain amount of pleasure.'

She looked flustered, not sure if he was flirting or not. It made her momentarily uncomfortable. 'Charlie . . .'

'Rather than the fat cow who owned it, I mean. You couldn't see it in the folds of her flesh at all.'

'What about Pat? Wouldn't she like it?'

Charlie smiled. 'Pat's got enough tom to start her own shop.'

Franny unclipped the bracelet and laid it down on the white cotton square once more. She admired it for a few moments. 'I'll ask Bruce before I wear it. Just in case.'

'Very wise,' he said, with studied solemnity.

Franny sighed. 'This all right, is it – this work he's doing with you? Whatever it is.'

Charlie shrugged. 'Be fine.'

'But you're worried about something, aren't you? Is that why you came to see him?'

Very perceptive, he thought. She wasn't just a pretty, well-scrubbed face. 'Nothing serious. Just a little problem with one of the boys, is all. Tell Bruce I'll be at the Lambeth later.'

'I will.' She scribbled a note to remind herself. 'And thanks for this.'

'You're welcome. I like things to go to a good home.'

He turned to leave and Franny asked: 'Charlie, how bad is the problem?'

He smiled and his ice-blue eyes seemed to darken. Franny remembered some of the stories she had heard about Chas from his younger days and suppressed a shudder.

'Nothing I can't take care of,' he said.

They drove up the M1 in the Rover, with the lanky form of Gordon Goody behind the wheel. Bruce Reynolds had turned up dressed in flat-fronted checked trousers and a Lanvin sweater over a pastel Dare & Dolphin shirt, managing to make both Tony – in his Dunn's sheepskin, and Goody, in his trademark long black coat – look dowdy.

The Rover's V8 happily pulled them to 90mph, effortlessly passing the Hillmans, A30s and Morris Minors plodding up the middle lane. The Rover had a Smith's Radiomobile that was audible even over the tyre noise the big car generated at close to the ton. *Saturday Club* was on, with Eden Kane, but Bruce switched to the Home Service.

'"Forget Me Not", indeed,' he said, naming the singer's

signature tune. 'Chance'd be a fine thing.' He swivelled round in the front seat. 'You seen that film *Too Late Blues*?'

Tony said he hadn't.

'Good movie. About a jazz man. Bobby Darin's in it and . . . that little fella, you know who I mean. Played Johnny Staccato on the box.'

'John Cassavetes,' grunted Gordy.

'Blimey,' said Bruce, looking across at the big man with a puzzled expression. 'When did you turn into Dilys Powell?'

Gordy just grinned.

'Anyway, that's who Roy reminds me of. He's not a big bloke, but intense. Committed. Know what I mean?'

'Yeah.' Although Tony had no real idea what he was talking about.

The M1, touted as the Highway to Birmingham, actually fell short of the city, ending in Northamptonshire. Their speed dropped as they came off the motorway and hit the A road, and Tony settled down in the leather of the rear seat and nodded off, just as Bruce retuned to Eamonn Andrews and *Sports Parade* and began to fret about Chelsea's new season in the second division, hoping they could bounce back up. As an Arsenal fan, Tony was used to disappointing Saturdays, although it hadn't yet come down to the ignominy of relegation. But the Gunners had never been the same since Tom Whittaker died in 1956. Now *there* was a manager . . .

'Oi, Tony – Sleepy Bollocks. We're here.'

24

He pushed himself up the seat, unmussed his hair and rubbed his eyes clear. He looked at the clock on the dashboard. Out for almost an hour. They were on a B road now, in a short queue behind an MGA, a Morris Oxford and one of the brand new Ford Cortinas, which Tony hadn't had a chance to drive yet.

At the head of this line, a young lad in a duffel coat was collecting the five shillings entry and parking fee. Next to him was a large sign telling them they were about to enter War Department property. Then a board proclaiming that this was RAF Hemswell, home to No 97 (SM) Squadron. Someone had scrawled the letters CND across the sign and underneath *Yanks Go Home*. There was, indeed, an American flag fluttering over the gate, indicating that USAAF personnel were deployed on the base. Tony had done his miserable National Service in the RAF. He knew what all this meant.

'I thought we were going to see a race?' he said.

'We are,' Bruce replied.

'What, an arms race?'

Gordy edged forward in the line as the Cortina drove into the site and then turned to look at Tony. 'What you mean?'

'Don't you two ever read the front of the papers? This is a bloody nuclear missile base.'

Two

Holland's Gym, Elephant and Castle, South London, September 1962

Charlie Wilson counted the repetitions as he crunched his biceps with the twenty-pound dumbbells. He'd been doing the same routine for six months now, and although he wasn't yet Steve Reeves, he could see the difference in his physique. It was harder, leaner. Old Man Levy had been forced to let out the chest of his latest suit jacket, and allow more material in the sleeves so Charlie could flex his arms. Now, when he walked into the Mayflower or Donovan's, he could feel the dip in the volume of the conversation as the mugs looked him over. He'd always had a reputation, usually backed up with blades or a revolver. Now he didn't feel he needed anything other than his bare hands to make his point.

He was even fitter than when he'd fought bare-knuckle with the pikeys in Barnet, and he'd been bloody hard to put down then.

Lately, he had built a fitness room in the shed at home in Clapham. His wife Pat joked he must be training for the Tokyo Olympics. He was training, that was true, but not for any athletics. With a new house, three kids and a wife, never mind the cars, clubs and the clothes to support, he needed more money than ever. That's what he was in training for.

Although he had the home gym, it did him good to get out from under Pat's feet during the day and he liked Danny Holland's place. Danny had the best equipment, some of it Jack LaLanne from the States, as well as the standard punchbags and speedballs of boxing. Charlie relished the satisfying smack of leather on leather when they were used by a pro, loved the smell of liniment and sweat that was missing from his domestic set-up. But when he put down the dumbbells and wiped his face, all was quiet. There were no grunts, groans or thrown punches because there were no other clients. Danny had booked him an hour clear, all to himself.

He heard the thud of footfall on the stairs. The heavier tread would be Ray Cauli, so-called because of the pair of misshapen ears bracketing his head that testified to a long but not very illustrious boxing career, sometimes in the ring but mostly in the field at the gash fights at Epsom and

Epping Forest. The softer sound would be Derek, the lad Ray was 'escorting' to the meeting.

Charlie stood up off the bench, put his foot on it, retied his Lonsdales and fetched himself a glass of water from the sink. At their meeting at the Lambeth Walk pub, Bruce had given him a free hand on this. It was Charlie who had brought the job to Bruce, but, as always, it was Bruce who had taken it and shaped it from crude concept to a workable plan. When, over pints of bitter, Charlie had told Bruce about Derek, however, he had deferred to him. 'Do what you think is appropriate,' Bruce had said. *Just do it when I am not around* was the second, unspoken part of the sentence.

The two men entered the second-floor gym puffing and wheezing. Derek had on a shiny Levy Tonik mohair suit and Cecil Gee Italian suede shoes. They all did now. The first bit of money in their pockets, they copied the boss and went to Levy in Whitechapel for their first taste of Dormeuil. That was why, on Bruce's advice, Charlie had decided to take his custom from Levy to Dougie Millings on Old Compton Street, Soho. Dougie dressed pop stars like Billy Fury and Wee Willie Harris, making silly stage outfits, but he could also produce the genuine article. And Charlie wasn't going to shout about who made his stuff this time. Let them find their own bleedin' tailors.

'Charlie,' Derek squeaked when he had his breath back, nerves taking his voice up the octaves. 'Ray here said you wanted to see me.'

Charlie rose to his full height. He had on a black Everlast vest and shorts. When he crossed his arms, he knew the biceps bulged impressively. He crossed his arms.

'Nice to see you suited and booted. I approve. But a bit out of condition, aren't you, Derek? Too many Woodbines?'

'No, I'm all right, Charlie. Straight up.' Derek had just turned twenty, making him a decade younger than Charlie, and he still had the pipe-cleaner thinness of a teenager. He was from that generation who were lucky enough to have just missed National Service. Or unlucky. Charlie had met some who claimed they had learned all they ever needed to know about thieving in the Army.

Charlie slapped the wooden bench. 'Stamina, that's what you need. Lie down here. No, no, serious. Don't worry, you won't mess up your whistle. Here, let me take the jacket. Nice shirt. Turnbull and Asser? Oh, Woodall's. Nice, that is. 'Ere, lie down.'

He threw the jacket across the room and it landed in a heap near the entrance.

Ray Cauli stood and watched impassively as Charlie laid the youngster prone on the padded wooden bench. Derek had begun sweating, moisture glistening on his upper lip. 'What 'ave I done, Charlie?'

'Nothing. Yet. But we'll sort you out. Ray, give us a hand, will you? Pass me that barbell and the weights.' He looked back down at a parchment-pale Derek. 'We'll work the chest first.'

Between them Ray and Charlie made a pyramid of the various weights that could be slid onto the steel shaft of the barbell.

'What's on it now?' Charlie asked himself. 'Sixty pounds. There you are. Take it. Go on, my son, take it. Arms straight. There we are. How's that feel?'

Derek grunted.

'I'll loosen your tie for you. There. How's that?'

'Fine.'

'Good. Now bend the arms and push it up again. Go on, like that. Let's do ten.' A tremor ran through Derek's arms as he lowered the bar to his chest then straightened them again. They all knew it wasn't the weight that was causing the shaking. 'Come on, nine to go.'

Charlie stood back and appraised him, as if he were a genuine protégé. 'Three, two . . . one. Easy? OK, let's put a few more pounds on. Keep the arms locked.' He nodded to Ray and they selected a forty-pound disc each and slid it onto the stock. Derek let out something between a groan and a squeal.

'Ten.'

'I can't, Charlie—'

'TEN!'

As Derek struggled with the raises, his eyes screwed shut, Charlie leaned in close and bent at the waist. 'You know what I hate most in this life, Derek?'

'No, Charlie.'

30

'Yes, you do. Think. Seven to go.'

'Coppers?'

Charlie jutted out his lower lip in approval. 'Not a bad guess. Bent coppers, that is. How can you respect a man who'll turn a blind eye for a fiver or a tenner? Why are they better than us?' He paused, as if thinking what tortures should befall such people. 'But no, that's not what I hate most. Not coppers, bent or otherwise. Three . . . two . . . one more, you can do it, me old china. Right, keep it up. I said keep it UP. Arms straight, you fuckin' cunt.'

Derek's arms wobbled even more at this last spittle-rich outburst, but he managed to lock the elbows, although the barbell began to swing in an arc, like an inverted pendulum.

'No, Derek, what I hate most in this world is a grass.'

Charlie could tell from the whimper that escaped Derek's mouth, and the fact that he now had the complexion of a maggot, that he was going to piss himself or worse any minute. Turkish Delight, all over his nice new Bowl of Fruit.

'Charlie, I ain't—'

'Even worse than greasy coppers.' He indicated to Ray and they loaded up another disc each and slotted them onto the shaft. It was nudging two hundred pounds now. Charlie could have taken it; the lad couldn't. 'Grasses are scum. Wouldn't you say so?'

There were stains spreading under the arms of the Woodall's shirt, so big and dark that Charlie doubted you'd ever get the stink of fear from it. The barbell was clattering as the unsecured weights banged against each other.

'Yes, Charlie, you're right but I ain't no grass.'

Charlie stared down at him. Derek had forced himself to open his eyes so he could plead with them.

Charlie silently counted to ten. 'No, Derek. You're no grass. 'Cause grasses are Judases. They should be drowned at birth. If I thought you were a grass, I would have just wrung your fuckin' neck, here and now, and have done with it.'

The relief at hearing this was so great that Derek's poor, tortured muscles gave out. Charlie caught the barbell just before it cracked into the lad's sternum. He held onto it and rolled it over the chest until it rested against Derek's throat. 'What you are, you sack of shit, is a loudmouth.'

Derek's windpipe was being crushed so he couldn't really reply. He did manage to shake his head a fraction of an inch either way.

'Oh yes you are, Derek. A fuckin' big cakehole on legs – isn't he, Ray? Ray just nodded, Derek. I could get Sid the Coalman to put a hundredweight of nutty slack down that black hole of a gob and there'd still be room for me to reach in and pull your lungs out.'

Charlie lifted the barbell slightly, easing the pressure. When Derek spoke, the voice was raw, sandpapered. 'I swear I ain't said anything out of turn.'

'Oh no? Look, I know what it's like. You walk in an' they know you're with me, so you get served first, before the mugs. You get an extra on the house. You get the girls too, don't you? Works wonders. Well, maybe not in your case, you skinny little fucker. But even you would get a half-hour with the Gobble Twins, once they knew you were my boy. I accept that. We all start as privates, don't we? And we take whatever perks we can. I mean, what does Bruce say? We're in it for the three Cs: cars, cunt and cash, but not always in that order. But you, Derek, had to go one further. You tell people you don't just know Charlie Wilson, do a bit of work for him on the fruit at Covent Garden or Spitalfields now and then, but more than that, you *know* what Charlie is up to. Can't say too much, eh? Nod and wink. *But it involves an airport.*'

Charlie let the full weight of the barbell fall onto the throat, holding it there for a second while Derek struggled to push it away. The cold-sick colour of his face darkened as his oxygen supply plummeted. He coughed when Charlie finally lifted the steel away from his bruised flesh.

'Now, Charlie is doing a bank, OK? Well, not OK but not a disaster. A Post Office. Fine as far as it goes. I mean, nobody knows *which* Post Office, do they? But how many London airports are there, Derek? I mean real airports that handle gold and money and freight?'

Derek replied in a tremulous voice. 'One.'

'ONE! Fuckin' right. One. That narrows it down for any grasses earwiggin', doesn't it? One. Take the money or open the box, Derek?'

Derek's pupils darted left and right nervously. He didn't know what to say.

'What's that? Box thirteen, you say? Let's see what's in Box thirteen. Oh dear. The booby prize.' Charlie changed his tone, letting some more menace creep into it as he lifted the barbell off Derek. 'You are going to fuck off out of my sight. And I mean out of it. No more suits from my tailors. No more suck-offs from the Gobble Twins. If I walk into a boozer and you're there, you walk out. You don't even finish your drink. Understand?'

'Yes, Charlie—'

'Mr Wilson!' he barked.

'Yes, Mr Wilson.'

'And if, after a year, I haven't seen your face or heard your name, then maybe we'll think again. Won't we?'

'Yes, Mr Wilson.'

'Get him out of here, Ray. I'm going to do some punchbag work.'

Ray yanked Derek to his feet. The youth made to say something, but Ray clipped him smartly around the back of his head. Charlie was busy tying on the gloves, no longer even aware that Derek was in the room. It was over. And as Ray would tell Derek later, he'd got off very lightly indeed. The guv'nor must be going soft.

Three

RAF Hemswell, Lincolnshire, October 1962

The three-minute warning siren sounded, its hideous cry carried, appropriately enough, by the wind from the east that came across the North Sea and then blew unimpeded over the flatlands of Lincolnshire. Every man and woman on the base momentarily froze as the wail gathered its breath, rising to a full scream. All but the very youngest had the sound of sirens cauterised into their brains, either from the early days of the Blitz, the later, more insidious threats of V1s and V2s, or, in recent years, the pointless Civil Defence exercises.

Roy James scanned the sky, hoping, if these were indeed the final minutes of his life, to see the sleek silver English Electric Lightnings of the RAF powering north to meet the bombers, intent on revenge for the millions who would die.

The sky remained unsullied, however, apart from a lone Vickers Viscount rowing between the thin cumulus. Instead, the siren faltered and died. A test.

What a place to stage a race, he thought. But there was a keen karting club on the base, run by a kid called Mike Lawrence, and driving between missile silos did, Roy had to admit, add a certain sense of extra danger to the proceedings.

He folded his slender frame into his kart, checking straps and connections as he did so. There was a tap on his helmet and he looked up into the grinning face of little Mickey Ball.

'Your fan club is here,' Mickey said, pointing at the sparse crowd of spectators.

Roy picked out the towering shape of Gordon Goody, in his long leather Gestapo-style coat; next to him the willowy Bruce Reynolds, aka the Colonel, fussing with his shirt collar, as dandy-ish as ever. Completing the trio was a third man Roy didn't recognise. He wasn't short, being five ten or eleven, but he looked it next to the other two. The stranger was about Roy's age – younger than Bruce and Gordy – with fairish hair and a frown, as if he wasn't quite sure what he was doing there.

A distorted voice came over the Tannoy system. *'Engines, gentlemen, please.'*

Roy knew what the visit from Bruce and Goody meant. About half a million quid, with a bit of luck.

Goodbye Italkart, hello Brabham.

Strapping himself in, Roy lowered his visor and gave the signal for Mickey to kick the Bultaco into life.

Four

Comet House, Heathrow Airport, West London, October 1962

As he washed his hands for the fifth time, Ronald 'Buster' Edwards wondered why he had ever agreed to get involved with this malarkey. Sometimes you did it for the laugh, for the buzz, for the sheer hell of it. And sometimes it was just for the money. But he didn't need money, not at that moment. The club was doing OK. However, when they were putting a firm together, it was hard to say no to that little wave of excitement – euphoria, even – that swept through your brain and made your stomach fizz like it was filled with best bubbly. And there was always the fear that next time, they wouldn't ask you at all. What's more, he had to be honest with himself. Running a drinking den was fine – but it was also on the dreary side, a life oddly becalmed, waiting for a seductive wind to fill its sails. And right now Bruce, Charlie and Gordy were blowing a gale through his rigging.

A tall, thin-faced man in a pinstriped suit came into the Gents, gave him a sharp glance and Buster smiled. 'Mornin'.'

'Good morning,' came the frosty reply. The man hesitated, as if he was going to ask Buster what his business was on the third floor, but his bowels got the better of him. He slipped into a cubicle, and Buster heard the lock slide across and the ping of braces.

Buster looked out of the window at the graceful Air France Caravelle coming in to land. It made him think he'd like to be on one of the sleek jetliners, heading to Paris or Cannes. Bruce had told him so much about Monte Carlo and Nice, he felt as if he'd been there already, experienced the Mediterranean sun on his face. The way the Colonel told it, it'd been like Cary Grant in *To Catch A Thief* down there, with Roy and Mickey as his sidekicks. Except, unlike Cary's character, Bruce hadn't retired.

Buster realised he had been so distracted by thoughts of the Riviera, he hadn't noticed the blue armoured van that had left the Barclays Bank that was just visible down the road and was now heading for the entrance to the airport and on to Comet House.

Quickly rolling down the sleeves of the pinstriped suit he was wearing, he checked his appearance in the mirror – putting on a bit of weight round the chin there, Ronald – and slotted the bowler hat onto his head. He almost burst out laughing, thinking he looked more like Bernie Winters in a sketch than a City gent. The lavatory flushed in the closet behind him and Buster grabbed the folded umbrella he had left dangling from one of the sinks and hurried out to the lift, almost knocking over the lavatory attendant, who had been on his break, as he did so.

At first, Buster thought he'd bollocked it with his daydreaming: the entrance lobby to Comet House was empty, but two receptionists were behind the desk. It was a shift changeover, the blazered young man taking over from the woman in the blue blouse. Good, he'd prefer it to be a man. No qualms about a little touch of cosh action there. Buster could see the dark shape of the van parked outside, but no sign of the bank guards. Perhaps, he fretted, they had already passed through.

Also outside, thirty feet back from the van that had travelled from Barclays, was a Ford Zephyr 6 police car, its roof light flashing lazily.

He remembered what Charlie had told him, not to break step no matter what happened. As he approached the conventional exit to the left of the revolving door, he was relieved to see two men emerge from the far side of the van. Each was carrying a metal strongbox, which they heaved onto a steel trolley. Their actions were observed by a supervisor with a clipboard. The men repeated this procedure, so there were four hefty boxes in place. Then they looked around, nodded to the waiting policemen to show all seemed in order, and wheeled the conveyance towards the lobby. Buster hesitated as he came face to face with the guards, with the glass door between them.

He grabbed the handle, jerked the door open and said loudly in his best, mellifluous Leslie Phillips voice: 'After you, gentlemen.'

One of the security men muttered his thanks and the duo trundled the trolley through en route to the BOAC vault in the basement. Buster could tell from the effort it took to overcome the inertia of the steel cart that the metal boxes must be full. Maybe the old bastard who was their informant had been right. Perhaps there was half a million quid in there. He felt the Moët gurgling in his stomach already as he strode through the door to the outside.

As he left the building, he raised his bowler to the policemen in the Zephyr pulling away from the kerb. The fact that one of them saluted him almost caused Buster Edwards to wet himself with laughter. They're just asking for it, he thought. Just asking for it.

Five

RAF Hemswell, Lincolnshire, October 1962

Tony Fortune had always thought Go-Karts faintly ridiculous, like dodgems freed from their overhead electric grid and sent round the track. That day at the missile base changed his mind for good. As the flag dropped on Roy James's race, the field of cars seemed to bunch together like a flock of starlings, and began to weave in the same way, as if one organic unit. The noise of the 200cc engines and the stench of oil, rubber and petrol was exhilarating. Unlike at Goodwood or Silverstone, the drivers – alarmingly vulnerable on their tiny chariots – flashed by feet away from the spectators. The physicality of wrestling with such a small yet potent machine was all too apparent as they approached the first bend.

'Those Go-Karts got limited slip diffs?' he shouted to Bruce.

'Don't let Roy hear you call them that. They're karts, not Go-Karts.'

'Why?'

'He says it's like calling every racing car a Vanwall or a Cooper. Go-Kart is just another make, so he reckons. Anyway, it upsets him – and I don't want him upset. There are no diffs at all though, not limited or otherwise. If you want to corner tight, you have to lift one of the rear wheels. If you get it wrong . . .'

As if to demonstrate his point, one of the karts drifted wide, catching the rear of another; it spun out in a cloud of dust and an explosion of hay as it crashed into the bales.

The mass of men and machines began to pull apart as they came into the second lap, with four drivers breaking away from the pack. Tony didn't have to ask which one was Roy. He was the one in third place throwing the machine into the dogleg between the missile silos with one rear tyre spinning in thin air. There looked to be a good ten inches of space between rubber and track.

'Jesus, he's going to overcook it, isn't he?' Tony muttered.

'Wouldn't be the first time, mate,' said Gordy.

'How many laps?'

'Ten,' replied Bruce.

The field began to stretch out, the initial solid wall of engine noise devolving into the buzz of individual machines.

Roy was still third, but he was slipstreaming the kart in front, so close that Tony thought they must be touching. It was a risky strategy, because if Roy didn't match his opponent's braking exactly, he could end up going over the top of the man in front.

Gordy detached himself and came back with three teas, all of them heavily sugared, and a Mars Bar each.

Roy made his move on the fourth lap, just as he approached their position, seemingly moving directly sideways, and taking not only the second man, but rejoining his line in front of number one. The former leader braked as he saw Roy was about to tangle with his front wheels, and the number two and three made contact. The pair of them pirouetted together, off into the grass on the inside of the track. Angry, frustrated fists were raised as the dust-cloud settled, but the damage was done. Roy James was now in the lead, where he looked set to remain.

Bruce put his tea in the crook of his arm and applauded. 'See, stunts like that may not be what you always want in a racing driver.' He shook his head in admiration. 'But in a wheel-man . . . fuckin' gold dust.'

Roy was examining his silver trophy as he walked up to Bruce, Gordy and Tony. He held it up to show them. 'I could knock out a better one than this during the fuckin' potter's wheel interlude,' he sneered.

'I didn't say', said Bruce to Tony, 'that Roy here fancies

himself as a regular whatsisname. The one who made the eggs.'

'Fabergé,' said Roy.

'Yeah, Fabergé. Roy's clever, see. When he did his borstal he learned silversmithing. Not like the rest of us. We learned fuck all.' Bruce looked at Gordy. 'Well, how to blow a peter maybe.' Then he stood back and pointed at each man in turn. 'Tony Fortune. Roy James.'

They shook hands. 'Nice driving,' said Tony, and meant it. Roy grunted his thanks.

'Tony here can get us what we want,' Bruce went on.

'Oh yeah?' Roy asked, his voice laced with disbelief. 'Mark Twos?'

Tony nodded. 'Any preference on what model?'

'The three point four,' Roy said firmly, accepting a fresh tea off Gordy and taking a sip. 'Bloody hell, Gordy, how much Harry Tate you spoon in there?'

'Put hairs on your chest.'

'And on my tongue.' He looked over his shoulder, where the Class 1s were about to begin a rolling start.

'Why the three point four?' Tony asked. 'The three point eight is faster.'

'Yeah, 'course it is. And it's the same lump, just with a bigger rad and oil cooler. But somehow, the balance is all wrong. And the power output isn't as even; there's a good chance of wheelspin, especially on those Dunlops they fit. The three point four is a sweeter engine, gets the power down much more smoothly.' He shrugged. 'That's what I think anyway.'

'Well, you'll be the one driving it,' Tony said. 'Anything else?'

'I really like the metallic blue that Jaguar does,' said Roy with a smile. 'One of them in that colour would be handy.'

Tony nodded again. 'OK, Roy, a three point four Mark Two Jaguar in metallic blue. Leave it to me.'

The Class 1 karts came up to the start line, the flag dropped and, in a cloud of two-stroke, the angry buzzing of competition began again. 'I got another race after this, boys,' Roy told them. 'See you later.'

After Roy had left, Bruce said, 'I told you he was particular. There's one other thing he doesn't know about though, another mod.'

'What's that?' asked Gordy. 'A gun turret?'

Bruce stroked his chin as if he were actually considering it before breaking into a grin. 'No, more's the pity.' He turned to Tony. 'Just make sure you lose the back seats.'

Six

From the Daily Sketch, *16 October 1962*

ACTOR LAMENTS LOSS OF
'PRIDE AND JOY'

TV's Peter Gunn, the American actor Craig Stevens, last night appealed for the return of his metallic-blue 3.4 Mk 2 Jaguar. The luxury saloon was taken from outside his home on Eaton Square, where he is renting a house with his wife Alexis, on Tuesday night. 'The car was a welcome-to-London present from Lew Grade,' said the actor. 'I have only had it a few weeks and it is my pride and joy.' Mr Stevens, who played private detective Peter Gunn for a hundred episodes of the series, is in England to film *Man of the World*, his new thriller programme, for Mr Grade. A reward of a hundred pounds has been offered for the safe recovery of the Jaguar.

Seven

Detective Constable William Naughton never did
discover who put his name in the Flying Squad's 'book'
at Scotland Yard. Whenever their peripatetic approach
to crime took them to an outlying district, the Squad
detectives were encouraged to keep an eye out for any
likely prospects among the officers there. Names were
logged back at New Scotland Yard – The Big House – and
enquiries then made of DIs as to the subject's suitability
for moving up a league.

Billy Naughton, like every other plainclothes copper,
knew this. So whenever a unit of the Squad came to his
station at Lucan Place, Chelsea, the young DC made sure

47

he helped wherever he could, from taking fingerprints to pointing the blokes to the right pub for an after-hours drink. He'd been stuck as an Aide to CID for two years when he was called in to see his DI. 'Whose arse have you had your tongue up?' the latter had enquired with a grin. 'Some fucking blind and deaf idiot on the Flying Squad has asked for you.'

Whoever had written in the book that he 'showed promise', Naughton thanked him every time he walked into the shabby Squad room at New Scotland Yard on the Embankment. The rectangular space was dominated by the rows of desks where the eight teams did their paperwork. Along one wall was a bank of telephone booths. The air was rich with cigarette smoke, stale sweat, foul language and jokes in questionable taste. But to Billy it smelled sweeter than roses.

Naughton's first task was to check in with the Duty Sergeant, see what was in the message book and which outstanding warrants needed typing up. But there was always a small pause after he entered where he looked around the smoke-filled room – much of it Old Holborn generated by a couple of dedicated pipe-puffers – at the group of men, The Big House's finest, and almost pinched himself, unable to believe he was one of the elite. The tricky part, he knew, was staying in it.

DS Len 'Duke' Haslam, his face all sharp lines and widow's peak, threw a thumbs-up in greeting. He'd earned his nickname from his spot-on impersonation of John Wayne. He was able to nail it all, from the lazy drawl to the rolling gait, and he claimed to have seen *The Alamo* six times. Duke was the senior partner in their two-man team, assigned to show Billy the ropes. Unlike many others clobbered with a rookie, Duke didn't mind having a fledgling to nurse. Although only in his early thirties, Len believed in traditional coppering – and that included being free with your knowledge.

'DC Naughton! Line Four.'

The operator's deep baritone boomed over the hubbub of conversation. Naughton raised a hand in acknowledgement and crossed to the battered booth. Like all of them, its walls were defaced by hastily scribbled numbers and names, some of them going back twenty years, and the cubicle not only stank of fags, but there seemed to be lingering undertones of whisky-breath too. He wondered if Bill Cunningham, a DS notorious for his DTs, had been using the telephone before him.

'Naughton, Flying Squad.'

'You love saying that, don't you, you smug cunt? Naughton, Flying Squad, oh and possessor of the biggest cock in Scotland Yard. And the biggest head.'

Naughton laughed. 'Hello, Stanley, what got your goat?'

Harold 'Stanley' Matthews had gone through police training at Hendon with Billy Naughton. They had boxed together and played football, later on opposing teams when they ended up in different districts. Naughton though, had slipped ahead in the promotion race, with Matthews trailing behind. Stanley was now an Aide to CID at Chelsea, his old job. Billy Naughton had never let on that he had recommended him to his DI before he left Chelsea, was the one who had got him out of uniform, away from the dullness of Brentford.

'Been on Early Turn. Got here at five-thirty. You lads swan in at . . . what time is it? Bleedin' nine o'clock gone. You lot think villains punch-in those hours?'

Naughton laughed. 'Most of the villains I know don't get up till midday – don't even know there are two eleven o'clocks in a day. How's Chelsea?'

Stanley dropped the pretence of irritation. 'Good. I'm on the footie team already. And bagged a police flat off Holland Park. Hayley is well chuffed. Well, mostly.'

Billy Naughton knew Hayley, Stanley's young wife, and liked her, but like most non-Force wives, she didn't fully understand The Job. He was glad he hadn't been saddled with a missus yet. He had quickly discovered what a hindrance they were to ambitious Squad officers.

'Hayley will have to get used to the fact that there's a bit more to do after-hours than Brentford,' he said. Whereas the suburbs had very little nightlife, Chelsea was full of pubs, clubs, not to mention celebrities. You couldn't throw a stone down the King's Road without hitting an actor or an artist or a pop star.

'Just a little. And it's more interesting. We had this bird in yesterday,' Stanley went on. 'She was a bit of a looker, demanding we arrest her boyfriend for pulling out her pubic hair. To prove it—'

Naughton laughed as he interrupted. 'She hoiked up her dress and showed you the evidence. They sent her to you, did they?'

There was a heartbeat of a pause before realisation dawned at the other end of the line. 'Oh, fuck.'

'Don't worry, she'll come round again and you can point some other green sod at her and snigger as he writes up the report.'

There was a tap on his shoulder from Duke. He mouthed the words 'Boss wants to see you,' and Naughton felt his stomach cramp.

Ernie Millen, the head of the Squad, always found time to keep an eye on the new lads. Rumour had it he gave you three months to show you had what it took – perseverance, an instinct for villainy and a decent sense of humour – to stay with the Squad. Millen and his trap-faced deputy Frank Williams were the ones who decided which new bloods should get a permanent place in the room. There was one trait that Williams prized above all else: the ability to 'bring in the work' by being proactive, using informants or dangling bait in front of suspected villains. And as it was common knowledge that Williams had the casting vote as to whether an apprentice had made his number and stayed in the Squad or was quietly transferred out, it was a good idea to 'get some in', as they said.

'I gotta go, Stanley. Glad it's all tickety-boo.'

'That's not why I called, mate. I remembered what you said, about keeping a note of villains' favourite wheels. Well, yesterday we went to Eaton Square. Car been nicked. We made a fuss 'cause of whose it was, this actor bloke. A Yank. But anyway, the car they took was a three point four Jag. Metallic blue. Only about a thousand miles on the clock. You always said to follow the motors, didn't you?'

Naughton found himself nodding, even though he had borrowed the phrase from a DI at Acton.

'Billy? You there?'

'Yeah. Sorry, I was just thinking.' Just thinking that according to the OB – the Occurrences Book – another Jag had been taken in Savile Row, just down the road from West End Central police station, the cheeky buggers. Some poor bastard – well, not cash-poor obviously – being measured up at Anderson & Shepherd had come out to find his wheels missing. A 3.4 Mark 2. Burgundy. Also showroom-fresh. 'Thanks, Stanley.'

'Well, just returning the favour, mate.'

'Yeah. Cheers.' What favour? He must have found out about him putting a word in. Maybe Stanley wanted Naughton to repeat the exercise at the Squad. Well, it was too early for that. Naughton hadn't got his own feet under the table yet, and here he was being summoned to see Millen. He rang off, thanked the operator in his cubbyhole, and threaded between the desks, thinking he might just have a bone for The Boss to chew on.

Eight

Fortess Road, North London, October 1962

'What the fuckin' hell are these?'

Tony Fortune looked up from his cornflakes, sucking a stray one off his lip as he did so. Marie was standing in the doorway to the kitchen of the flat they rented in Tufnell Park, dangling his set of twirlers.

He shrugged. 'Just some bunch of keys from the garage.'

She tossed them onto the pine table.

'Oi. You'll scratch it.' He moved the keys onto the *Daily Mirror*, with its cover photograph of Oswald Mosley, who had caused a riot addressing his Union Movement. Nasty old fascist.

Marie walked in and leaned over the table. She was dressed in the dark jacket and skirt she wore to work at the Midland

Bank. She stabbed at the enormous ring of keys of various shapes and sizes.

'Twirlers.'

Well, it was true there were some skeleton keys among them, but most were legitimate. 'You know what it's like. People always losing their keys and need the car opening.'

'And people always need cars "opening" when the owner's not about.' She blew out her cheeks, making the freckles stand out even more. Marie had long red hair and the palest of skins that betrayed her Irish roots. Her enormous, extended family was in the business – the ducking and diving business – working the north-west of England. She had deliberately distanced herself from them – apart from her brother Geoff, who turned up like a bad penny every few months for a handout – but she had been around enough car thieves to recognise a professional key-set when she saw one.

When they had met, at a dance in Kilburn, she had known who Tony was and what he was. A ringer. A man who took stolen cars and turned them into something else: unrecognisable, untraceable stolen cars. In order to move the relationship on, he had been forced to renounce the ringing game. It was something he had never regretted, not really. But it had its moments, which you couldn't say about running a showroom in Warren Street.

Marie had her hands on her hips, her 'fierce' pose. 'There are coppers who would arrest you just for having those things.'

'There are coppers who will arrest you for being in possession of a tongue in your head,' Tony shot back. 'It's a regular tool of the trade.'

'What are you up to, Tony?'

'What do you think I'm up to?'

'What am I supposed to think when you come home at all hours stinking of thinners?'

He laughed at that. The splashes of cellulose thinners on him were legit. He'd been respraying a Standard van for a local joinery firm. 'I'm not at it,' he said with all the conviction he could muster.

'Because I have a job in a bank now,' she reminded him. 'But how long do you think I'd keep it if they thought my old man had friends who were partial to the balaclava.' She rubbed her stomach. 'Look what you've done.'

She walked over to the old-fashioned metal kitchen unit, pulled down the drawer and rummaged for some Alka-Seltzer. 'You give me indigestion. I shouldn't wonder if I've an ulcer.'

He stood up, crossed over and put his arms around her. She let a hand rest on his crotch, saying, 'I swear if you go bogey on me I'll pull it off.'

He turned away from her slightly, just in case she was considering a warning shot across the bollocks. 'You really know how to win a man's heart.' He kissed her neck.

'I can still smell the thinners.'

'I'll cover it up with a splash of Old Spice.'

'Not now, Tony.' She moved his arms aside with that practised combination of sharp elbows and a quick wiggle that women perfected at an early age. 'One of us has a real job.'

'So have I.'

'How many cars you sold recently?'

Tony bristled. 'As it goes . . .' He pulled the roll of notes from his pocket, undid the elastic band, and let the cash flutter onto the linoleum floor.

'What's all this?' She knelt down and he could see her stocking-tops. He didn't bother to help as she gathered up the five-pound notes. She was laughing as she did so, until she realised how much there was. The laughter died and the smile faded soon after. 'What's this from, Tony? It's a—'

He waited for her to make a joke on their surname. None came. This was no laughing matter.

'A quick turnaround yesterday,' he lied. 'Car came in, gave him a ton for it. Customer walks in half an hour later. Cash on the nose.'

'What car?'

He hesitated, sticking as close to the truth as he dared. 'Some nice old Jag.'

She stood up and handed him the sheaf of notes. He wrapped the band around it again. 'Can't have been that old. There's a hundred and fifty quid profit there.'

'Give or take.'

Her eyes flashed with amusement. 'A hundred and fifty dead. I count that stuff all day long, remember. You sure it's bona?'

'As my dick is long.'

She slapped his shoulder. 'Don't be crude.' He could see she was already thinking about what the cash could buy. A refrigerator. A decent television. A holiday.

'Sure we can squeeze a meal at the Carousel out of it.'

She smoothed down her skirt and straightened her jacket. In one deft movement she tied her hair back and became every inch the severe bank cashier. 'I have to go. Love you.'

'When I give you money.'

A smirk. 'Take it or leave it.'

The guilt at lying only kicked in after she had gone, while Tony made himself a fresh pot of tea. Well, it was a one-off. Just repaying a favour. There was no way on God's earth that Tony Fortune was going to get involved in any tickle for Bruce Reynolds, that was for sure.

They had ringed the two Jags in part of a disused bus garage in Camden, not far from the Met's Stolen Car Squad at Chalk Farm. Tony didn't do much apart from changing the plates and swapping the vehicle ID plates over. He also put a Webasto sunroof in the burgundy model, which would throw anyone looking for the original car, and changed the wire wheels on the metallic-blue one for regular steel disc wheels. He could sell on the wires, no problem.

Mickey Ball ventured up north to help drive the cars south from Camden to where Roy wanted them – in Battersea, within walking distance of his garage and the shop where he sold antique silverware. He and Tony took different routes. It didn't do to be going around in convoy, just in case some copper put Mk 2 and Mk 2 together and got a sniff of something.

Tony went via Westminster Bridge and made it there first, and as he bumped down the track that punctured a scruffy row of terraced houses, he spotted Roy waiting at the garages, with the doors to both open. He chose the nearest one, waited until he had cleared the rutted access alley and accelerated. He roared past the lock-up, slammed on the brakes, engaged reverse and propelled the Jag into the dark interior, stopping it with an inch to spare before the bumper engaged with the tool rack at the rear.

As Tony squeezed out of the driver's door Roy was making exaggerated waves in the air to clear the dirt the tyres had kicked up. 'Done that before, have you?' he smirked.

'Once or twice.'

'Wait till you see Mickey. He goes in like a mum trying to park her pram.' He closed the garage doors and engaged the clasp lock. 'You done any driving?'

Tony knew what kind of driving he was talking about. 'Not the way you mean. Not serious.' A couple of high-speed chases after he had been spotted in a wrong 'un was the closest he had ever come to being a wheel-man. And that was six, seven years ago.

'Stoppin' for a drink?' Roy asked.

'Best get back,' said Tony.

'Give you a lift somewhere?'

'The Tube. Cheers.'

'Just wait for Mickey.'

'Right.' He offered Roy one of the new Embassy Filters, which Marie had started buying, saying they were better for you than unfiltered.

'Nah. I don't. Stopped the booze, too.'

'Why?'

'Slows you down. For the racetrack.'

Well, Bruce had said he was serious about his racing. Tony lit his cigarette from a Colibri lighter. He smoked in silence for a while.

'Bruce wondered if you wanted to stay on.'

Tony looked down at Roy, who was a good four inches shorter than him. 'Stay on?'

'Get involved, like. In the job. It needs a sizeable firm. Room for one more on top, as they say.'

The next step was, he would have to ask what exactly the job was. That was as good as saying 'Yes, count me in'. You didn't tyre-kick with these lads. If you said you were interested, it meant you were interested. Not merely curious. Curious was bad.

He was flattered. Roy would only have asked if both Bruce

60

and Goody had given the say-so. But he could hear two things. One was the familiar thrum of a Jaguar 3.4 as it changed down a gear, ready to turn into the lock-ups. The second was his scream as Marie twisted his testicles off and toasted them on an open fire.

'Tell Bruce thanks all the same, but I got a lot on at the moment. Wouldn't want to let you all down at the last minute.'

Roy swung back the doors of the second garage to their full extent, ready to receive the Jag that was bouncing towards them. 'Sure. Don't worry. There's always a next time, eh?'

'Yeah,' said Tony. 'Maybe next time.'

Nine

Bruce always supplied the music. Even if the meet was held at someone else's house, he would still turn up with a selection of his LPs. The first real gathering for this job was held in Buster's flat in St Margaret's Road, Twickenham. Bruce liked Buster, but he had a tendency to musicals: *My Fair Lady* and *The King and I* and, even worse, after a drink or two, Flanagan and Allen. Underneath the fuckin' Arches, indeed.

So once he arrived and shrugged off his coat, Bruce took charge of the Pye radiogram. June, as always, had made sandwiches and put out some sausage rolls. As far as she was concerned, this was a gathering of a betting syndicate, and she would never question that. It was best the girls

62

knew as little as possible about what really went on at these meets. After all, the rule about grasses didn't apply to wives; they weren't expected to be able to hold up under pressure from people like Tommy Butler or the Flying Squad's Frank Williams. So it was best they kept their heads in the sand, emerging only to make the sarnies.

It was just the core members of the team present, it being prudent to keep things tight in the early stages. All jobs bled information, it was inevitable. Who was doing what – and how much it was worth – was as much the fuel of conversation in the pubs, clubs and spielers such men frequented as the usual mix of football, cricket and the horses. It was essential to make sure that the leak, the whisper that something big was on, came late in the day, when the police were left with crumbs, not the whole cake.

So today, it was just Bruce, Buster, Gordy, Charlie, Roy and Mickey. Only Mickey looked ill at ease, thought Bruce. Jittery. But he was all right, Mickey, he just got a lot of gyp from his mum about the sort of company he kept.

Most of them were chatting, apart from Charlie, who was staring at the ceiling, lost in thought. Bruce noticed the tightness of his shirt over his chest. Charlie's bulked out, he thought.

Bruce turned off *Z Cars* on the TV and selected Ahmad Jamal's *But Not For Me* from his stack of records. He ran a finger over the stylus and groaned.

'Buster, when did you last change your needle? You've got enough fluff for Cyril Lord on the end of this.'

'"This is luxury you can afford by Cy-ril Lord".' Buster sang the carpet ad as he handed out the beers. 'Dunno. You have to change them, do you?'

'See you later, love. Off to Bingo.' It was June leaving. They all shouted their goodbyes.

Bruce bent down and examined the end of the diamond-tipped stylus. It still looked good and sharp, not like some of the chisels he saw in people's homes. Probably all the muck had protected it. He plucked it clean then lowered it onto the record, listening to the familiar rhythm of the drummer's mallets as the beat began, soft yet insistent, with the accent from the hiss of the hi-hat. Beautiful.

'I am using these to show the perimeter,' said Buster, waving a plastic cow at the group to get their attention. He pointed at the fencing that he had used to create a circle on the coffee table. It was from a Britain's farmyard animals set. 'This is my niece's birthday present, so be careful.'

He placed a barn next to one of the lengths of plastic fence. 'This is Comet House.' Next he positioned the farmhouse down the road. 'Barclays Bank. I haven't got any aeroplanes. We'll take it you know they'll be taking off and landing in the middle there. We have the armoured car.' He produced a Massey Ferguson tractor.

'Bloody hell, Buster, who's pulling this job?' murmured Charlie. 'The Archers?'

Gordy nearly choked on his Shippam's fish-paste sandwich and it was a few moments before order was restored.
Bruce put the record arm back to the beginning of the Jamal
album. He loved the opening number, 'Poinciana'. The
dynamic always made him think of the tempo of a good
tickle. Soft and tentative at first, a theme stated, then developed, becoming more sure and intricate – but not too tricksy
– building to a solid crescendo with an inventive climax,
then the slow release, the feel of a job well done. Villainy
or sex, 'Poinciana' stood as a fine metaphor for both.

Buster had at least got a couple of Corgi diecasts to
stand in as the getaway cars – neither of them Jags though
– and the farmer and his various farmhands represented
the security guards.

'Right, gentlemen,' Bruce said. 'Any thoughts so far?'

'I'd give the milkmaid one,' offered Charlie, pointing at
the overly voluptuous figurine.

'That's enough,' said Bruce, adopting his best stentorian
tones. 'OK. Listen, please. Let's run it down.'

Over the next forty-five minutes beer gave way to scotch
and the air filled with smoke. After each of the principals
had spoken, Bruce asked if there were any questions.

'We're still short-handed,' said Gordy. 'A couple of extra
bodies wouldn't go amiss.'

'We could bring in Ronnie,' suggested Bruce. 'Ronnie Biggs.'

Foreheads were collectively furrowed as they tried to place
the name. 'Who?'

'Biggsy. Good worker. Reliable.' Bruce had met him in borstal and been impressed with his loyalty and tenacity. But he didn't feel as if he could force any more of his own opinions on the group. After all, Charlie had got the tip-off, which made it his job really. 'Charlie?'

'Not this time, Bruce,' he said softly. 'I'll have some names in the frame for our next meeting.' The odd quip aside, Charlie never said much in these sessions, not unless he had a point to make, but Bruce always took account of his opinion.

'Fair enough. Anything else?' Bruce asked.

There was a collective groan as the lights were snuffed out and the music slowed and then stopped completely. 'Bloody hell, Buster.'

'Hold on.' Buster went out into the hall and fed some shillings into the meter. The record wowed up to speed again and the lights flickered on. 'Sorry about that.'

'Where were we?' asked Bruce.

'At any questions,' said Gordy.

'Yes,' said Roy, leaning forward and pointing to the perimeter fence. 'I'd like to take a look at the gate we'll be driving out of. Which way it opens, that kind of thing.'

Gordy shrugged. 'It's chained shut. Opens inwards, which is a shame. But I reckon I can get a decent pair of bolt-cutters. And make it so nobody'll notice the cut.'

'All right,' said Roy, knowing that if Gordy said he could take care of it, he would. 'We should also look for a changeover spot. The Jags'll be all over the police radio within five minutes.' He looked at Bruce. 'And somewhere to lay up the cash.'

'Got just the place,' said Charlie. 'Norbury. I'll get it sorted out.' He meant so that a group of them could hole up for a week or more if need be. Mattresses, blankets, food, booze, reading matter – books for some, magazines and comics for others – cards and board games would all be needed.

'Right,' said Bruce. 'We all got a bit extra to do. Next meet in a week's time.'

'I ain't here,' said Buster. 'Brighton. Missus.'

Bruce didn't want any details. It would be a birthday or anniversary. Buster never forgot those things. Not for him the last-minute dash to the florists or the box of Black Magic from a corner shop. 'Ten days then. At my place.'

The men stood as one, stubbing out cigarettes and picking up the empties. They might be villains, thought Buster, but they were house-trained villains. 'Hold up, one last thing,' he said, brandishing a lined exercise pad and a Bic. He had forgotten about Bruce's little suggestion. 'Before you go, I need all your hat-sizes.'

The Flying Squad detectives could smell the stink of prison on John 'Yul' Jones as he was led into the interview room at Wormwood Scrubs. Piss, cheap soap and fear hung about him. Billy thought of the ad: 'Even your best friend won't tell you about BO.' In the Scrubs that was because everyone smelled the same: Old Nick.

Yul was younger than Billy Naughton had expected, not yet twenty-five, with a totally bald pate and a round, boyish face that suggested a happy, over-fed baby. The effect was marred, however, by dark half-moons under his eyes that told of too many sleepless nights.

The barrel-chested warder pulled back the chair for him and Yul slumped down at the metal table. He was on remand, so he had on a nice blue cotton shirt and jeans. When he spoke, the voice that came out shocked Billy. It was that of a far older man, coarse and raspy. 'Gentlemen. What can I do for you?'

'Tommy Butler sent us.'

'Did he? You got a cigarette?'

Len Haslam glanced at the warder, who nodded. Billy handed over a pack of five Woodbines and a box of Swan Vestas. Yul took his time lighting the cigarette, never taking his eyes from them, wondering how he should play this.

'You should be honoured, you know,' Len said eventually.

'Why's that then?'

'Being collared by Tommy Butler. He doesn't do much thief-taking these days. Not personally. You've been nicked by royalty.'

Yul gave a smile that showed a chipped front tooth. 'I should ask for some whatsit then on my chamber pot. That fur.'

'Ermine,' offered Billy.

'Yeah. I'd like an ermine piss pot.'

'I think we might be able to do something for you. But that might be pushing it, Yul. Other cons might get jealous. They'd be wanting silk pyjamas next.'

Duke let it sink in that 'something' might be on the table. He looked around the room at the bare walls, the bricks painted a lurid, glossy green up to waist-height, then dirty cream above that. You'd do a lot to get out of this place.

'You're Butler's boys, are you?' Yul asked.

'Not exactly.'

'C Eight?' This was the section that contained the Robbery and Flying Squads, as opposed to C5, the CID. It meant Yul knew his coppers.

'Yup.'

'Sweeney?' A nod acknowledged this. 'All right then.' He seemed satisfied that he was dealing with men with some clout at least. 'So what we going to talk about?'

'Motors,' said Billy.

Yul stuck out his lower lip, as if pleased. He was on safe ground here. Nothing about his cellmates or any of the more outlandish plans to go over the wall. Outside. Talking about the outside was safer than discussing the inside. 'What kind of motors?'

'Fast. Four-door,' said Len. 'That kind.'

'Mr Butler suggested to us,' added Billy, 'that you might know where a man who wanted a particular type of Jaguar might go, were you not available to source it for him.'

Yul's jaw tightened and he looked from one policeman to another. 'I don't know what all that means.'

Duke laughed suddenly, a violent explosion of mirth that made Yul flinch. 'Don't be ridiculous. My friend here might have made it a little too convoluted, but you know what we're saying. You want a car for a job, you come to you, Yul. Everyone knows that.' He pointed a finger as the prisoner made to speak. 'Shut up. All we want to know is: with you out of the picture, where would someone go? If they were in the market for a couple of fast Jags.'

Yul considered, smoking his Woodbine for a minute. 'They'd go to the Old Kent Road or Warren Street, wouldn't they? I can't give you names.'

'No?' Len asked quietly. 'Shame. 'Cause we can't do anything without a name, can we?'

'Well, we haven't discussed that yet, have we? What you can do for me?'

Len shot forward over the desk and Billy thought he was going to strike Yul for a moment and so did the prisoner, because he scraped the chair back out of arm's reach very sharpish indeed. The warder stood by, his face implacable. He'd seen it all before.

'Look,' Len said, 'you don't have to be a cunt all your life. You can take a day off. Today, for instance. You know how this works. Two Jags, stolen to order: who is doing the stealing and who is doing the ordering?'

It might seem a ridiculous idea, that one man would

70

know about two cars in a city of thousands of them, would have knowledge of a particular criminal in its vast underclass. Except it wasn't that vast. Not once you took out all the petty chancers. When it came down to it, the hardcore blaggers constituted a small close-knit community.

Yul shrugged. 'If I hadn't been put on remand, I could've helped you.'

'If you weren't on remand, we wouldn't be having this little chat at all, would we?'

Yul accepted this truth with a nod. 'All I can tell you is which firms it might be doing the ordering.'

'And the drivers?'

Yul shook his head. 'You know them as well as I do.' Again, there were no more than ten or twelve top-class wheel-men in the capital.

'So, what've you heard? Who might be the market for a three point four?'

Yul moved his chair back in and drummed his fingers on the table. He glanced over his shoulder. 'This'll be worth my while?'

Len Haslam looked up at the warder and, with an inclination of his head, pointed him at the door. Once the big man had left, Billy told Yul, 'Tommy Butler said we could make it worth your while. Said you had his word.'

'I see.' The prisoner started on another cigarette, his tongue worrying his teeth. 'Well, before we get into that, there is one thing you can do for me straight off.'

Len relaxed, feeling the fish wriggling on the hook. 'What's that, Yul?'

'Have a word with the MO. Get me on the asthma list.'

'Asthma?' Billy asked.

'Wheeze something dreadful, I do. Ask Stevie James, who I share a flowery with.'

A flowery dell, Billy automatically translated, a cell. He winked at him. 'I think you need an inhaler. Is that what you are saying?'

'A Benzedrex one, yeah.'

A supply of Benzedrex inhalers would make Yul a prince of the block, able to exchange hits of the amphetamine – usually boiled up as a soup – for fags or favours. At Chelsea Billy had come across plenty of lads marked for borstal who suddenly developed bad lungs and tight airways. Never mind that the inhaler was mainly a decongestant that had little effect on asthma or that the only way to get a kick from it was to dissolve the drug-soaked strips of blotting paper inside, which meant taking in a nasty dose of menthol as well. The result was the 'minty-burp', which plagued users for days afterwards. The ragged high, they claimed, was worth the continuous taste of too-good-to-hurry-mints.

'Used to be a Teddy Boy, did we, Yul?' asked Billy. The Teds liked their inhalers and their pep pills as much as their bicycle chains and cut-throat razors.

'For a bit, yeah, when I was like, fourteen. When I still

had hair I could get into a Duck's Arse.' He stroked his naked scalp, as if remembering a dear, departed friend. 'But the asthma's real, straight up.' He made a noise like a pair of bellows.

'I'll see to it,' said Len.

Yul fell silent as if gearing himself for the last sprint to the finish line. 'Um . . .' he began, then thought better of it.

'Well?' asked Billy at last.

When Yul spoke, both the policemen knew why he had been so hesitant, why his voice shook slightly as he said, 'I did hear, before I got banged up, that Charlie Wilson wanted to see me about a bit of business.'

Once the firm had dispersed, Buster washed up the glasses and the saucers that had doubled as ashtrays. He liked to keep busy. It was too early to go to the club, and June wouldn't be back from Bingo for an hour at least. All that was on TV was *Compact* and *This Is Your bleedin' Life*.

It was at times like this Buster felt vulnerable to a strange melancholy. It blew through him like an east wind, cutting into his very heart, almost making him physically shiver. He wasn't sure what caused it, but for the time it had him in its grip, there were no jokes that could crack a smile, no drink that could cheer him. A half-bottle of Bell's wouldn't even take the edge off it; if anything, it made it worse. So he had to keep active, prevent the black mood from forming.

The washing-up done, Buster turned on the radio section of the Pye and as he waited for the valves to warm, he took all the hat-sizes and placed them in an envelope to deliver to Frank Rossman at his breaker's yard in New Cross. He must remember to take a brolly along, just in case. Frank, who was half-gypsy and worked in a vest in all weathers, probably didn't have an umbrella anything like the ones the City gents favoured.

The radiogram burst into life. The Northern Dance Orchestra and Bernard Herrmann came on, so he switched to *Whack-O!* with Jimmy Edwards, hoping for a lift in his spirits.

'*Sir, sir. I am being punished for something I didn't do.*'

'*That's outrageous, young Carter. What didn't you do?*'

'*My homework, sir.*'

'*You cheeky blighter. You know what you need, young man?*'

What the young man needed, Buster knew, was six of the best and sure enough there soon came the sound of a cane swishing through the air and making contact with buttocks, followed by a yelp of pain. Buster wasn't sure why it was amusing. It wasn't when it had happened to him at school, which it did with tedious regularity.

The thought of the beatings reminded him of something. Buster went back to the kitchen and from under the sink fetched his new toy. It was a length of pipe-spring, used by plumbers to bend copper pipes without crimping them. He'd spotted it in a builders' merchants. He'd filled it with lead shot and then bound it with thick tape. In its new role, as a 'persuader', it would work a treat. He mimed beating it around one of the guards' heads. Charlie had a cosh he had bought from a Guardia Civil in Madrid, but Buster reckoned the flexiness of his pipe made it even more effective. Plus if the Old Bill found it on you, you could always claim you were doing City & Guilds plumbing at night school and had made a few modifications. Much harder to explain why you had a Spanish police baton down your trouser leg.

He gave it a few more strokes and then smiled when he heard the key in the door. June was back. He'd done it. He'd kept that angry black dog at bay. He'd be all right now.

The pub was on the South Circular Road, not far from St Dunstan's, the posh boys' school that seemed out of place in working-class Catford. 'A rose on a turd,' is how Len put it, then changed his mind as he looked around at streets still bomb-marked from the war. 'Or on a bloody great cowpat.'

Billy parked the Vauxhall outside while Len counted out fifty pounds in a mixture of one- and five-pound notes. Then he put an extra fiver on top. 'This is from the information fund. Use the five to pay for any drinks. Give him a score to keep him sweet near the start, then the thirty at the end. With the promise of more to come.'

'And the change from a fiver?'

'What change?' Len raised an eyebrow towards his black widow's peak. 'There won't be any change. God's sake. Nobody ever bothers putting anything back into the information fund. It's one-way traffic. OK, off you go. He'll be by himself, reading the *Sporting Life*. Just ready for pluckin'.'

Billy hesitated. 'Aren't you coming?'

'The hell I am,' Duke drawled, before switching back to his normal, non-Wayne voice. 'You can't run a snitch mob-handed. It's a one-to-one relationship.'

'But—'

Len gripped his arm, tight. 'If you're going to mention the new bloody guidelines, I'll beat you to death with this gearstick. Now get in there. Public Bar. Pick you up in an hour.'

'What will you do?'

Len growled. 'Pick you up in an hour.'

Billy opened the door and got out of the car. The DS winked at him, restarted the engine and left him standing on the South Circular. He looked over at the pub – or 'tavern' as it styled itself – and took a deep breath. Time to meet their new snout.

His legs wobbled slightly as he crossed the two lanes of sluggish traffic. Just like when he went up on stage on school prize day to collect his reward. Why was he so nervous? This was what he had wanted from day one at Hendon. And it was hardly his first snitch. But it was his first as a

Squad man. So, bizarrely, he felt like that young man shaking hands with the headmaster as the man handed over the award for most original English essay. It had been *The Boy's Book of Modern Marvels*, full of cutaways like the ones that appeared in the *Eagle* comic. Billy still had it, was still fascinated by the detail exposed when you stripped the skin off a Lancaster Bomber or a Hawker Hunter or a nuclear power station.

Inside the pub, he clocked the nark immediately. Young, spotty, cocky from the way he flexed his shoulders, as if trying to get the chip on it to shift. He was indeed reading the *Sporting Life*, but then so were half the other customers. The walls of the tavern were covered in sporting pictures: a few boxers, the odd golfer, but the rest was heavy on the gee-gees, with portraits of Scobie Breasley and Lester Piggott dominating.

There was, he had noted, a Jack Swift bookmakers next door. A year ago, no doubt, bets would have been taken in this very bar. Now, with close to fifty new betting shops opening each week across the country, the tradition of the pub bookie and his runners would probably die out.

Billy bought himself a pint of Guinness, moved to the snout's table and sat down. He held out his hand. 'Billy Naughton.'

The young man didn't move to take it. 'Yeah?'

His sort hated the police even when they were going to deal with them. Billy was used to it. He had lost half of his schoolmates when he told them about Hendon. They all had older brothers or sisters who had had run-ins with the law, usually during the dance-hall fights that had flashed across Britain in an epidemic from the late 1940s onwards. None of them had any respect for coppers. Their heroes were Niven Craig – The Velvet Kid – and later his brother Christopher, who famously told Derek Bentley to 'Let him have it'. For months his former chums had hummed the theme from the radio series *The Adventures of PC 49* at him. He was only grateful that he had left school before that irritating whistling from *Dixon of Dock Green* became popular. 'Mr Haslam sent me.'

'Did he now?' Several pair of eyes had glanced over, so the nark took Billy's hand and gave it a perfunctory shake.

Billy looked the youngster up and down. He had a scarf wrapped round his throat, but it couldn't quite hide the yellowing of old bruising. Duke had said that the lad had a grudge. He had turned him up after Yul had admitted that Charlie Wilson had expressed some interest in acquiring stolen Jags. 'Said you was interested in a bit of work. Digging.'

'Might be.'

'Can I get you a drink?'

The kid pointed at his glass, which was still a third full. 'Double Diamond.'

'Coming right up.'

'And a Teacher's,' the lad added quickly.

Another one with a sudden attack of nerves, Billy thought.

No doubt his throat was drying and his palms sweating as he realised what he was about to do. The enormity of it. The finality. Billy didn't blame him. No matter what he had done to him, it took some balls to grass up Charlie Wilson.

'All right, Derek,' Billy said, as if granting a condemned man his last wishes. 'Whatever you want.'

Ten

Red Lion pub, Derby Gate, November 1962

'There's something going down at the airport!' Billy Naughton wanted to yell as he walked into the Red Lion. 'And we're fuckin' on to it!'

The Lion was the Squad's designated pub, an act of apartheid that was respected by lesser coppers, who tended to use the Gate or the King Edward. It was also acknowledged by Squad chief Ernest Millen, who might come in to celebrate a good collar with a half, but generally left the Lion as somewhere for his team to let off a bit of steam.

Billy began to push through to the bar, where it looked as if a session was beginning. A fug of blue smoke hovered over the three-deep crowd. Someone was singing 'Diamonds Are a Girl's Best Friend' in a terrible falsetto. There was a television, tuned to a Brian London fight, but nobody seemed to be watching. The rough-edged but brave heavyweight had lost his crown as British boxing's favourite son to the more polished Henry Cooper. London, though, was staking his resurrection on a forthcoming bout with Ingemar Johansson. By the look of it the contest on the television was a warm-up for that, because London was hammering an opponent who seemed unable to come back at him, despite London's famously lax defence. Cannon fodder, Billy decided, and looked away.

'How's it going, son?' someone asked.

Billy turned. It was DI Jack Slipper, a tall, erect, military-looking man who had come through a similar path to Billy – Hendon then the suburbs, then CID – a decade earlier. He was known as a diligent detective who, belying his clipped, stuffy appearance, was prepared to bend rules and take the odd risk. Although, like Butler, not strictly part of the Squad, he had been given a floating role by the Yard's chief, Commander George Hatherill, which was why he was tolerated in the Red Lion. 'Fine, Skip.'

Slipper's moustache twitched, like some insect's antenna. 'Have you got something on the boil?'

How could he know that? 'I might have.'

Slipper nudged him and Billy caught a clove-heavy whiff of Bay Rum cologne. 'Now, now. I bumped into Duke. He said you'd been busy. Wouldn't tell me what. Said it's your shout.'

Nothing got past Slipper. What they had gleaned from Derek Anderson meant putting a team together to watch the airport. It was a big number, tying up a lot of manpower, and calling on many elements of C Division. Soon it would be Billy's baby no more, but orchestrated by Commander Hatherill and Tommy Butler with someone, perhaps even Jack Slipper, in charge on the ground. He might as well enjoy the feeling of power while he could. 'Once I write it up.'

'Please y'self, son. What you having?' Slipper asked. Well past the six-foot mark, the DI towered over the crush at the bar and could easily attract the barmaid's attention. He fetched Billy a pint of bitter and they moved to the side of the mêlée, up against the panelled wall, beneath the old *Punch* cartoon of Churchill clinging to Big Ben, swatting Messerschmitts from the sky, like King Kong on the Empire State.

Billy raised his dimpled glass. 'Thanks, Skip.'

'How's Duke?'

'Yeah,' Billy said. 'Magic.'

'Be careful, son. Good copper is Duke,' Slipper said, 'but not perfect.'

Billy supped his pint. 'Who is, Skip? Apart from you?'

Slipper grinned. 'Tommy Butler.'

'Oh yeah.'

'Although even he . . .' Slipper stopped, as if talking out of turn. Then he lowered his voice. 'The word is Tommy might be moving into Millen's seat. He's a different animal. He'd rather a verbal than a fingerprint. Old-fashioned, methodical policework, that's what he likes. Nothing involving a microscope or men with little brushes. Not sure he even trusts something as modern as photographs.' They both laughed. Butler was certainly an odd one. Still lived with his mum. But he could catch a thief, that was for sure. 'So what is it you've got?'

Billy decided he could afford to give Slipper a taster. 'It's just a snout with a score to settle.'

Slipper downed his whisky. 'Promising. I like it when thieves fall out. Right – got to get back. I'm on SPECRIMS.' This meant he had to return to the Yard and check the Serious Crime reports on the internal police communication system before he could call it a night. If he found anything important enough he might well return to clear the pubs with an all-hands-to-the-pumps order. 'You come and see me tomorrow, eh? We'll tidy up whatever you've got before we pass it along to your Guv'nor.'

An old CID hand helping a green Flying Squad boy write his report? Unheard of. But he would be a fool to turn it down. 'Right, Skip, thanks. I will.'

Another singer started up with 'I Wanna Be Loved By You'. The drinkers at the bar joined in the *boo-boo-be-doo* chorus.

Billy looked up at Jack, puzzled.

'Haven't you heard, son?' the older man said. 'Roy Foster is starting the Marilyn Monroe Memorial Drinking Club.'

* * *

At Ronnie Scott's Club in the basement of 39 Gerrard Street, Stan Tracey and the band were mining a piece by Thelonious Monk, excavating the quirky chord sequences with a dogged invention that had Scott himself – the co-owner – nodding from his place at the bar. The club being the size it was – it had been a bolthole for gypsy cabbies to have coffee and cigarettes between fares – this meant Ronnie was virtually on the stage with the players.

Although Zoot Sims, Dexter Gordon and a talented but cantankerous sax-player called Lucky Thompson had all graced the tiny venue in the past few months, there were no big names on the bill that night, just homegrown talent. This meant the club was relatively quiet, which suited Bruce, who had called the meet, just fine.

He sat at the rear, at one of only two rough tables, alternating watching the band with admiring the woman sitting on a stool next to Ronnie in her black, sleeveless and mostly backless dress, smoking a cigarette as if it were an erotic act. Actually, the way Janie Riley smoked a Sobranie *was* an erotic act. She could get a slot at Raymond's Revue Bar, just by lighting up and blowing smoke, any night of the week.

Charlie Wilson came and sat down next to Bruce and ordered a beer. He listened to the band for a few moments with his face screwed into concentration. 'When does the tune start?'

'About one a.m. usually,' said Bruce. The club was only

licensed until eleven – for the first few months of its life the strongest drinks on offer were coffee or a lemon tea – but musicians often gathered after-hours, especially tyros looking for impromptu tuition and false-fingering tips from Ronnie.

'I had to join to get in,' Charlie complained. 'Never had to join a club in me life.'

'It's in a good cause.' Bruce had often spoken to the guv'nor, as they called Ronnie, and knew how precarious it was running a jazz club. Ronnie claimed he and his partner got together on Sunday afternoon every week and decided whether they could afford to reopen on Monday or if they should just hand back the keys. Their hunger for cash meant that getting past Pete King on the door without shelling out for membership was a feat in itself, even for a hard man like Charlie. 'Besides, there's one thing you never get in here.'

Charlie cocked an ear to the spiky runs coming from the stage. 'Melody?' he offered.

Bruce had to smile. 'Old Bill.'

Charlie grunted. It was true that most of the clip joints, strip clubs and drinking dens in Soho were subject to random visits by coppers, either looking for information or a few quid. Some of the West End Central boys were regulars at the Flamingo, Murray's Cabaret and the Kismet. So were various politicians, judges, hacks, and even members of the clergy, the hypocritical bastards. But the kind of real jazz played at Ronnie's kept most of them away.

'Where've you been?' Bruce asked.

There was no reply. Charlie had clocked Janie Riley and was craning his neck. Bruce was well aware that Charlie was a fervent family man, doting on Pat and his daughters, but once in Soho he would take a run at anything that didn't have a dick between its legs.

'Oi. Get your eyes off her. Where've you been?'

'Geisha Club.'

That was round the corner in Old Compton Street, a mix of a cabaret and a hostess bar that, like Murray's, turned a blind eye to how the girls earned a little extra on the side. Charlie, of course, never paid for any of the 'specials'.

'Anything happening?'

'New act called Ding Dong Belle,' said Charlie, taking a slug of his drink. 'Covered in these little bells. She lets you ring them as they come off. Ends up with just three. You can guess where.' He was looking at Janie Riley again, his eyes glistening with lust. 'She's really nice. Classy. Looks like Audrey Hepburn – only after a good feed-up.'

Roy was the last of the three to enter the club, just as Stan Tracey gave his final two-fisted flurry of Monk. Ronnie grabbed the microphone and waited for the applause to fade. 'That was Stan Tracey, the thinking man's Winifred Atwell, with Tony Crombie on drums and Mr Jeff Clyne on bass. There will be a short break now while we give the piano the kiss of life. We'll be back in fifteen minutes when we will be auditioning a young saxophone-player called Ronnie Scott. Please treat him kindly as he only got his horn out of hock today. If any of you blokes want something to eat after the show, there's a new German-Chinese place over the road. Food's great, but an hour after you've eaten you're hungry for power.' He flashed a lopsided grin at the baffled audience and walked off.

Ronnie nodded to Bruce as he strolled by and climbed the rickety stairs. Ronnie liked to gamble, which meant he knew some of the same Soho faces as Bruce. 'There's a lot in common between jazz and what you do,' the guv'nor often said. 'Insecurity, never knowing where the next payday is coming from and the hours are bleedin' awful.'

Roy got himself a Heineken from the bar and sat down as the drums of Art Blakey snapped out from the PA. 'All right, gents?' He gestured back up the stairs. 'I had to join to get in.'

'Apparently it's all in a good cause,' said Charlie, pointing at Ronnie's back. 'They're saving up to buy the owner a joke book.'

Roy looked around at the dingy basement. 'I was talking to Dave Hill at the Steering Wheel Club up Shepherds Market. Dave bloody Hill, eh.' He was clearly disappointed to be pulled away from a chat with a Ferrari driver to a subterranean dive in Soho playing jittery bebop.

'Steve there?' Bruce said casually. They had seen McQueen take a credible third, behind Christabel Carlisle, in a Mini at Brands Hatch. No doubt the American was annoyed to be beaten by a woman, albeit one that Roy considered a great driver regardless of sex. The actor had spun out in the next race, although he had shown great control not flipping the tiny car. Unfortunately, despite Roy pulling a few strings, he hadn't managed to engineer a meeting between Bruce and the actor. The thief had hidden his disappointment, although not well.

'Nah, he's gone back over to Germany. He's filming some prisoner-of-war movie.'

'How'd it go with the gates?' Bruce asked, getting down to business.

'Gordy has bought the biggest pair of bolt-cutters I have ever seen. Honest. He could slice through Tower Bridge with them. He's going to cut the chain the night before. By the look of it, nobody ever goes near it, so it should be all right.'

Bruce didn't like that. In his experience 'should be all right' often came back to bite you on the arse. 'I'll have a word with him.'

'How is it with you two?' Roy asked, looking from one to the other.

'All in hand,' said Bruce. 'Harry, Ian and Tiny Dave are coming along as muscle.' Dave's nickname was ironic; he was an ex-weightlifter who looked as if he had accidentally left a set of barbells in the sleeves of his jacket. 'They'll be on a drink.' Which meant the heavies would get a fixed fee, not a share.

'Good.' Roy drank his beer, wondering why Bruce had called the meet. There didn't seem much to discuss. Especially as there was no Gordy or Buster. He felt a little trickle of fear and ran back over the last few weeks. Had he done anything wrong? Upset somebody? 'Is everything all right, Bruce?'

Bruce moved his head from side to side and sucked air through his teeth. He then rubbed one side of his mouth, as if he was suffering from a bad attack of nerves, something he was usually immune to. Charlie took a swig from his bottle and shot Roy a quizzical glance. With relief, Roy realised that Charlie Wilson had no idea what was coming either.

'I got a favour to ask, Roy.' He turned to Charlie. 'And as the tickle was your find, I thought you ought to hear it.'

Charlie nodded to show he appreciated the respect.

'What is it?' asked Roy

'Bit late in the day, I know, but I want to bring someone new in. Not part of any of our firms.'

Roy began to peel the label off the Heineken. 'Well, that's down to you, Bruce, isn't it?'

'Thing is, I'd like them to ride with you. In the Jag.'

Roy tore another strip from the gummed label and rolled it into a ball. Someone to keep an eye on him, perhaps? Had they lost faith in him – or in Mickey Ball? 'Who is it?'

Bruce looked up and snapped his fingers to get her attention above Wayne Shorter's tenor sax. Janie Riley slid off her stool and walked over towards the three men, a mischievous smile plastered over her pretty face.

Eleven

Headley, Surrey, May 1992

The police had brought in one of those long white squared-off caravans to use as an incident room and parked it up at the gates to the driveway that led to Roy's house. It was an impressive pile, 1930s by the look of it, the front door boastfully porticoed, the green tiles of the roof glowing verdigris in the moonlight. I couldn't help wondering who, or what, had paid for it. This was the stockbroker belt, but Roy was no stockbroker or rock star, the other cashed-up profession that had moved into the area.

Neither of the two coppers in the front of the Panda car had spoken during the trip, which was fine by me. I needed time to get my brain into some kind of gear.

I stepped out and examined the road. It was the kind lined

ROBERT RYAN

with high walls and hedges, and the driveways came with
solid wooden gates to deter prying eyes; this was an area
where an Englishman's home was his castle, and the residents wished they still came with moats. And boiling oil.

Bill Naughton was waiting for me outside the caravan,
older, stouter, greyer, a cigarette in his mouth, rubbing his
hands against the chill of the small hours. As I stepped out,
I wished I'd brought more than a thin jacket. It was heading
for 3 a.m. Wasn't that meant to be the hour when your
metabolism was at its lowest, the perfect time for Gestapo
raids and interrogations?

'Tony, thanks for coming. Cup of tea?'

'Why not?' We went inside the caravan. There were three
uniforms and two detectives already in there, plus one bloke
in black fatigues with body armour and a soft cap on his head.
He also had a pistol on his belt. That would be PT 17.

'This is Tony Fortune – he's come to help us out. Get
him a brew will you, Dave?' He turned to the Milk Tray
Man. 'Give us five minutes, eh, John?' When John had
gone, he explained to Tony, 'They've got their own van
down the street. For the moment, they're staying in it.
We want to keep it that way.' He indicated one of the
plainclothes. 'This is Detective Inspector Reed. It's his
situation.'

'Can we speak to him?' I asked. 'Have you got the GPO
in?'

'BT, Tony, BT,' said Naughton. 'Got to move with the times.

92

Jesus, hasn't been GPO since . . .' He furrowed his brow, trying to remember when the Post Office lost the phones, but gave up. 'Anyway, yes, we have a line to him.'

'Want to tell me what happened?'

DI Reed took my tea from the Constable and passed it to me. The Inspector looked tired. Perhaps we all did in that stark over-white light.

'Roy had the two kids for a long weekend—' Reed began.

'Hold on. You said on the phone about a wife. When did Roy get married?'

'A while back,' Reed said. 'You didn't hear?'

'No.'

Billy turned to Reed. 'Tony here runs a BMW franchise near Blackheath. Doesn't mix with the old crowd much.'

'Well,' continued Reed. 'Married, yes. Much younger girl.'

That was no surprise. They all liked their girls young. Franny was barely sixteen when Bruce proposed. Most of the hostesses they tapped in Soho had just turned eighteen. But Roy had never really been part of that back then. For him, the racing was the thing; he didn't seem attracted to the girls in the clubs. Not queer, just not interested.

'It didn't last. His wife was picking the daughters up last night. With her father. Once they had the kids in the car they announced that they would be taking them to Spain for the summer, so Roy wouldn't see them for six weeks or more. Thing is, he loves those girls. He tried to get the kids back in the house, as a bargaining tool. The wife and father-in-law went to stop him. That's when it all went off. At least, the gun did.'

'What do you want me to do?'

'He's still in the excitable phase of the proceedings. Hyper. Bring him down, Tony. Talk about the old days. Make him see some sense, eh?'

'I don't know,' I said. 'We weren't that close.'

Billy gave a small grunt of disbelief.

'OK, for a few months maybe.'

'Look, PT Seventeen is itching to kick the door down and go in with the flashbangs like it's the bleedin' Iranian Embassy,' Bill said. He pointed at Reed. 'We've both done hostage and siege courses. DI Reed here went to bloody Quantico. You know – FBI. But we both agree, a friend trumps any pro negotiator in a domestic. That's all this is for the moment, a domestic.'

He let me ponder on the 'for the moment'. If Roy started shooting at an armed Met policeman, the chances were he wouldn't be coming out of that house vertical.

'I'll get him on the line, shall I?' Billy said.

I nodded.

Bill Naughton lifted up the receiver and pressed one button on the keypad. After a long minute, he said: 'Roy? Bill Naughton again. Got someone here who wants to speak with you.'

He handed the receiver across and picked up a second handset so he could listen in. 'Roy? Tony Fortune.'

I thought it was static on the line, but it was Roy laughing. 'Fuck me. Talk about scraping the barrel.'

'Thanks.'

'No offence, mate. I meant about dragging you out of bed. How you doing?'

Better than you, I thought. 'Can't complain. Except when some plod turns up in the middle of the night. I thought they'd come for me at last, I really did.'

Roy gave a more considered, rueful laugh. 'Well, they never stopped coming for me, Tony, that's the truth.'

The voice was full of self-pity, not a quality I associated with Roy. You didn't get to be his kind of driver – a genuine, exciting, God-given talent – by wallowing in what-might-have-beens. I guessed he'd had a few knocks over the past decade or so. I wondered how he must feel when he saw Nigel Mansell or John Watson or Graham Hill's son – what was his name? – Damon. What went through his mind when he saw those British drivers take on the world or when he saw Jackie Stewart, the elder statesmen of the sport, pontificating on TV? *It should've been me*, no doubt.

'This is not good, though – is it, Roy?'

'Not good at all, Tony.'

'Why don't I come in?'

'In here?' I felt a hand on my bicep, squeezing it. A signal to back off.

'Yeah. We can talk properly then.' The grip tightened

and I shrugged it away by twisting my body. 'Without this lot earwiggin'.'

'That would be good.'

'Tony—' hissed Billy.

'I'll be right over. Anything you need?'

'Packet of Rich Tea?'

'See what I can do.'

I put the phone down. I felt everyone in the room glaring at me. 'You've just given him a hostage,' said Billy.

'What, me? Leave it out, Billy. You got any biscuits?'

'I can't let you go,' said Reed. But I had spotted some milk chocolate digestives. I scooped them up and put them in my pocket, then turned my collar up for the short walk across the street to Roy's house.

'Call yourself coppers?' I asked the room. 'You don't see it, do you?'

'See what?'

'What's wrong with him.'

Billy scratched his head and sniffed. 'Oh aye. I know what's up with Roy James. We're all agreed on that. Off you go. Dave, walk him to the gate, will you?'

The young uniform followed me down the steps and across the cordoned-off section of the road, our footsteps unnaturally loud. I caught sight of a few neighbours, standing back in the gloom, curiosity strong enough for them to leave their fortresses.

The air felt like treacle; I found every step an increasing effort until, finally, I ground to a halt.

The only sound seemed to be my breath, coming harsh.

'You OK?'

Sort of, I thought. Only sort of.

'What's wrong with him then, mate?' the copper asked softly. 'The bloke in there.'

But I didn't answer. I took another step forward. Then another. Keen to get there now, speeding up. It was obvious what was wrong with him. Roy James, once a celebrity thief, was now just a lonely, mixed-up, middle-aged man.

Twelve

London, November 1962

As he stood smoking a cigarette in the shade of a stores hangar, the smoke mixing with his breath in the cold morning air, Billy Naughton reflected that, although he had never really thought about it, it made perfect sense that the bulbs in airport landing lights sometimes needed changing. And it seemed silly to shut down a whole airport just so you could screw in a new Osram.

They worked in four-man teams, in constant touch with the tower. If a bulb failed, the tower radioed the appropriate team – there were three, covering different parts of the airport – and the quartet that made up the specified Illumination Replacement Unit moved into action in their Austin Champ jeep.

It was, to the uninitiated at least, hair-raising stuff. They drove into position at one side of the runway or taxiway and waited while the tower relayed details of aircraft movements. When there was deemed to be sufficient space between landings or take-offs, the Champ drove onto the flight path.

The driver stayed in radio contact. One man, the gangmaster, located the faulty light and undid the restraining clips. A second then removed the housing, and the 'bulb man' – that was Billy's assigned role – twisted out the dud and put in the new one.

The very first time, he had fumbled, unable to get the old bulb out at first, and then having trouble with the replacement and the heavy-duty bayonet mechanism. Meanwhile, a Dan-Air Ambassador was on its final approach, its lights glaring down on them.

'Abort!' the gangmaster had shouted and they had sprinted for the Austin and spun out of the way as the old prop plane – the same sort that had crashed at Munich, killing Manchester United's Busby Babes – roared in for touchdown. He had been glad of the wads of Handy Andy tissues shoved in his ears then.

Since that first morning, almost a week ago, he had acquired some dexterity at the operation and a proper pair of foam earplugs. Mind you, he had had time to practise. The police ambush team had worked for two mornings, waiting for the robbery to take place. They were scattered across the airport, disguised as everything from baggage loaders to aircraft fitters. All were in radio contact because, although Derek Anderson knew the vague details of the plan – early Tuesday or Wednesday morning, within a week or two using a six- or eight-man firm, and promised to be the legendary Big One – the score that set them up for life – he couldn't be sure of the exact day. He was no longer in the inner circle, he was merely picking up crumbs from the periphery. It was a dangerous place to be. But then, should the raid be foiled, he was in line for a substantial payment from the intended victim. Not that they knew who that was either. Hence the dispersal of the Squad. But they had enough manpower to be all over any crime scene at the entire complex within minutes and, as an extra precaution, three high-speed pursuit vehicles were located just outside the perimeter fence. And this time they were equipped with stripped-out 3.8 Jaguars. Just the kind of thing the villains liked. Only better.

Sometimes, Naughton felt his stomach dissolve when he thought about Operation Icarus, as they had christened the airside stakeout. It was all on him, this deployment of the Squad's finest. Billy and the snout. As Frank Williams had said, if he got this one right, then he could start thinking about DS. *Detective Sergeant Naughton, Flying Squad.*

He liked the sound of that. And if it went tits up?

Don't even think about it.

A British Caledonian jet came in to land, the reverse thrust screaming as it touched down, its following plume of grit, rubber and jet fuel obscuring the pale, ineffectual sun still climbing clear of the control tower. Almost seven o'clock. *Soon*, something told him. If it was going to happen, it would be soon. And he felt it in his bones that this day, this Tuesday morning, was when it would all go off.

'Hey, Billy.'

It was Frank Jordan, the amiable gangmaster in charge of his Illumination Replacement Unit. 'We got two out at Holding Four. You want to do this one?'

Billy stubbed out the cigarette then rubbed his chilled hands together. The pale sun had been swallowed by a tin-coloured ceiling of cloud and the temperature had dropped once more. He checked his police radio was still live, and then went off to join his IRU. If need be, there was a real IRU member on standby in the canteen, but Billy preferred to be out here in the open and looking like he belonged at the airport, just in case the raiders had an inside man or two scoping the staff. And he might as well do something useful while he was waiting for this Big One to go down.

Bruce Reynolds glanced at his Patek Philippe watch. It was seven-twenty in the morning. Charlie had just phoned to tell them the severed chain on the gate was still in place, Gordy's tampering apparently undetected. Bruce had heard the excitement in his voice, a fizz like a fresh Alka-Seltzer in it. Good. That was how he liked Charlie.

Buster was still polishing his Oxfords, trying to get that

City gent style. Bruce's black Berlutis – perhaps a little continental in style for a worker in the Square Mile, but Bruce doubted anyone would be looking at his footwear – already had a fine sheen on them. He selected his bowler and tried it on, admiring himself in the mirror that hung above the mantelpiece in Buster's place. He had on a navy pinstriped suit, a white shirt and, for the tie, the blue, maroon and thin white stripes of the 1st Queen's Dragoon Guards. He turned left, then right, checking the reflection. Not bad.

'What do you reckon?'

He heard Buster burst out laughing. Gordon Goody had changed in Buster's bedroom – he had wisely shunted his wife to the mother-in-law – and was sporting a ridiculous handlebar moustache. Bruce smirked at him. But, on second glance, it was so outlandish it didn't seem at all fake. 'Got this at the theatrical shop on St Martin's,' he said. 'Here, take your pick.'

From his jacket pocket he unloaded half a dozen packets with face furniture of a variety of hues and sizes. Bruce sorted through them, trying to find an example that struck the right note. He took one out of the cellophane and held it on his top lip. 'Bit Terry-Thomas,' said Buster.

He tried another, but it was too bushy and eccentric for a man with a military background. The Guards tie suggested something more clipped. He found one that, although a little dark in shade, was the perfect shape. 'Alec Guinness,' he said. 'What do you think?'

'That's the one, Colonel,' said Buster, saluting.

There was the parp of a horn outside and Gordy pulled the net curtains aside. In the street was a lorry with the legend *Co-operative Removals Ltd* stencilled on the side. 'It's Mickey. In the van.' The Jags had been left at the changeover point in Hounslow the previous night, safely tucked away in a garage. Roy had stayed in a B&B nearby and would rendezvous with Harry, Tiny Dave and Ian, the muscle later.

'Tell him to go round the back,' said Buster.

Gordy indicated that Mickey should drive around to the rear access alley. It wouldn't do for three City gents to be seen climbing into a workers' van. Someone might notice. Or worse, remember.

Bruce ripped the backing from the adhesive strip on the phony 'tache and positioned it on his top lip. It was the perfect finishing touch. *Colonel Reynolds, at your service*. He grabbed his brolly, surprised yet again by the weight of it, and looked at his watch once more. *Seven thirty-five*.

He scooped up the gloves he would not remove again until this was over, one way or another. 'Right, let's go.'

'This is Icarus One-Seven. Over.'

That was Len, thought Billy Naughton. 'Icarus One-Five receiving you. Over.'

'Anything happening there? Over.'

Billy looked down the runway at the unnaturally bright strips of light. 'You'd be surprised how often those bloody bulbs fail.'

'That's not what I meant, Billy. Over.'

Billy could hear the impatience in Duke's voice. 'I know. What do you want me to do? Rob something myself? Over.'

'I think I will if this goes on much longer. That little toe-rag better hadn't be leading you up the proverbial garden path.'

'Say Over.'

'Fuckin' Over.'

Leading *me*? he thought. He was *your* snout. I get dropped in the shit, you're just one flush behind. 'He's kosher,' is what Billy actually said, as convincingly as he could. 'Over.'

'I'm only winding you up. Over.' There was a silence across the airwaves, filled by the hiss of static, then: 'What time is it, Billy? My watch must have stopped. Over.'

'Just gone eight. Over.'

'That's what it says. Watch hasn't stopped. Time's just slowed down to a crawl. Tea break? Over.'

'I reckon must be due. Canteen B? Over.'

'Canteen B it is. Let's hope the other side are havin' a cuppa too, eh? Over.'

'Cheers.' Bruce took the cup of tea that Janie Riley poured from the flask. He was careful not to get his moustache wet as he sipped. Last thing he needed was to find it floating in the mug, like a drowned hairy caterpillar.

It was a few minutes past eight and they were in the large, empty warehouse in which they had stored the Jags overnight, and where they would be dumped after the job. In one corner, Roy kicked into life the little BSA motorbike he had brought along, checking it started first time. Mickey was in the back of the van, changing into his chauffeur's uniform, joshing with Harry, Tiny Dave and Ian, the three most unlikely City bankers he had ever seen. Dave's jacket, in particular, was stretched as tight as tarpaulin over his barrel chest. Once he was satisfied with the motorbike, Roy killed it, washed his hands and went to join them.

'You all remember the address of the rendezvous in case we get split up?' Bruce asked everyone.

Gordy repeated it back, parrot fashion.

'Nobody's been stupid enough to write it down anywhere – like on the back of their hand? Good.'

Janie came over with a Nice biscuit. 'No thanks, love,' said Bruce. 'Don't want to get crumbs in the 'tash.'

'Thanks for letting me come along for the ride, Bruce.'

'Think nothing of it.'

Anyone who had been in Ronnie Scott's the night she was accepted by Roy wouldn't have recognised her. Gone was the Louise Brooks vamp-ish look, replaced by a smart grey Jaeger suit. Her face was devoid of all make-up, apart from a delicate black line around the eyes and a pale lipstick. She still looked impressive though, albeit more in a Grace Kelly Ice Queen fashion. If Grace Kelly had been a brunette.

Bruce saw Gordy look over and wink. Like all of them,

Bruce strayed now and then. It was, depending on how you looked at it, one of the risks or the perks of their chosen profession. You found yourself in the Flamingo or the Gargoyle or Esmeralda's with a pretty – and willing – girl on your arm, what were you meant to do? The same as the MPs, lords, ladies, actors and barristers, photographers and pop stars who frequented those places did. Live a little.

Janie was around thirty, a little older than he liked them, but he just enjoyed the pleasure she derived from hanging around with his sort. She wasn't alone. There were plenty of people, including many showbiz stars such as Stanley Baker and Diana Dors, who hankered after the occasional stroll on the left side of the street. Mostly you found the hangers-on in Esmeralda's Barn, the Kray twins' club in Wilton Place, perhaps the Black Gardenia in Soho's Dean Street or the nearby Establishment in Greek Street.

Bruce and Charlie generally avoided the limelight of such places, but they had picked up a few fans of their own – the criminal equivalent of Sinatra's bobbysoxers, he supposed, or Tommy Steele's hand-jivers. Sometimes these girls provided nothing more than a few drinks, sometimes an alibi, occasionally a lift out of town, no questions asked. They were, thought Bruce, a bit like Dracula's willing helpers in those Christopher Lee movies, drawn to the thrill of the night.

Janie claimed her motivation was simple: Bruce & Co made a change from Mr Riley who, she said, was a dull civil servant whose idea of excitement was having sex with the 60-watt left on.

Bruce touched her hair absentmindedly, letting some of the strands fall through his fingers.

'You know, you are a very gentle man for a thief.'

Bruce thought she was being sarcastic, but her face was a picture of innocence.

He nodded over to indicate the man with the incongruous handlebar moustache who was fencing the air with his umbrella. 'Well, when you have friends like Gordy and Charlie, you don't need to come the hard man.'

'Oh, I'm sure you can come the hard man when you want to.'

Bruce smirked at the innuendo. 'Right. But Janie, we get caught, this is no laughing matter, you know. It'll mean doing time. Even if you are just a passenger.'

'I'll say you forced me.'

Bruce laughed. 'I never forced a woman in my life.'

'Never had to, I'll bet.'

Bruce wagged an admonishing finger at her. 'Behave yourself.'

Janie pouted at him. 'Why should I?'

He consulted his watch again. This was work; the saucy banter could wait. 'Because we've got a job to do.'

Roy emerged fully uniformed, grey double-breasted jacket

and trousers, with a matching peaked cap. He saluted smartly and Bruce threw him a thumbs-up.

'Gentlemen,' Bruce said. 'Start your engines.' He looked at his watch for the tenth time in less than a minute.

8.20 a.m.

Thirteen

Heathrow Airport, November 1962

At 9.35 a.m. precisely, Buster Edwards walked into the Gents on the third floor of Comet House, swinging his briefcase. He had been in there so many times, he thought, it was beginning to feel like a home from home. Or a khazi from khazi. Behind him was Charlie, umbrella over his arm, looking, if you stared too hard, a shade too beefy to be a convincing City gent. Both men were relaxed and calm. The jitters, if any came, always hit before kick-off. Once everything was underway, every fibre was concentrated on playing your part, not letting your mates down and, above all, not screwing up the score. There was no place for nerves.

Buster nodded to the lavatory attendant in cubicle two. The old boy, happy to see a familiar face, returned the gesture and carried on sprinkling Vim into one of the lavatory bowls.

Charlie put down his umbrella, removed his gloves and took up position at the urinal, slowly undoing his fly buttons. Buster decided to stand next to the window and wash his hands, once he had put down his nice new briefcase. He began to whistle a Frank Ifield tune. From his position he could see the turning from the bank perfectly.

'Beautiful morning,' came the voice from the cubicle.

'Marvellous,' said Buster, in his plummiest accent. 'Makes one glad to be alive.'

Charlie craned his neck and looked out of the window. Beautiful? It was a grey November day, the sky sullen and featureless. Ah well, just making conversation, he supposed.

The attendant came out. 'Follow the football, do you, sir?'

Charlie realised he was talking to him. 'No,' he said, not wanting to be drawn. 'I'm a rugby man.'

The attendant sniffed. 'Right.' He moved to the next cubicle with his brush and powders.

Buster turned to Charlie and gave the slightest inclination of the head, just to let him know all outside was as it should be. He could see his watch now he had rolled up his shirtsleeves. It was 9.37 a.m. Things should be moving at the bank.

Inside Barclays Bank (Bath Road Branch) the second hand of the enormous Wessex wall clock swept round and the

110

minute hand jerked to show 9.38 p.m. Cecil Cochrane, the Manager, waited an extra minute before he gave the signal for the vault to be opened. His deputy and his assistant then inserted their keys while he himself dialled the combination lock.

Behind him came the security guards with their trolley, ready to collect the strongboxes sitting within. The BOAC wages had been sorted and packaged up the night before. Once they were loaded and left the premises they were no longer Cochrane's concern.

The door opened and Cochrane pulled it back. He gave a last glance at the wall clock before entering the vault: *9.40 p.m.*

Just to the side of the runway, Billy Naughton lit another cigarette, his fingers cold and sore from a shift of changing bulbs. It had been a novelty at first – exciting, even. Now though, the noise, the frantic rushing, the broken fingernails as he struggled to free a stubborn housing, had all taken the shine off it. His back was also giving him gyp from all the crouching and bending over. One muscle was going into spasm every now and then, dancing to its own internal rhythm. And he was a young man. Some of the gangers were in their fifties. How did they manage it in all weathers?

Winter was already beginning in earnest, the metal housings cold and painful to the touch first thing in the morning. He didn't want to do too many more days of this.

He found himself willing the thieves to show themselves, to make their play. Come on, fellas, he thought. Get a bloody move on.

It was close to quarter to ten when Roy, looking splendid in his grey chauffeur's uniform, swung the Mk 2 off the M4 and towards the airport access road. Behind him, Janie and Tiny Dave Thompson balanced on folding stools, placed where the back seats should have been. 'Telstar' by the Tornados was twanging out of the Jag's radio. Tiny Dave – whose gym-pumped frame filled most of the back window – was tapping his armrest in time to the instrumental. Janie was smoking a cigarette, slightly nervy. She looked every inch the smart businesswoman, right down to a briefcase, but the fag was somehow wrong.

As they approached the main entrance, she wound down the window and tossed the stub out. Good girl, thought Roy. Don't do anything that makes you seem ill-at-ease, like smoking too aggressively.

Janie leaned forward and tapped him on the shoulder. 'Thanks for agreeing to this.'

'That's OK, Janie,' Roy said. 'What's an extra passenger?'

'Always wanted to see Bruce and you lads work up-close.'

Roy chuckled. Those on the receiving end wouldn't share that sentiment, he thought. He checked his mirror. Mickey Ball was right on his tail. He could make out the silhouette of Ian in the rear of the following car, his bowler hat in place.

'Dave?'

'Yup?'

'Hat on.'

Dave slotted the bowler onto his head. Roy looked away before he started giggling. For some reason he couldn't stop thinking of Bernard Breslaw.

He checked the Smiths clock on the dash. Almost ten minutes to ten. Right on time.

At Barclays Bank, the security guards loaded the four steel boxes into the rear of their armoured security Bedford van. They were observed by two policemen, parked a few yards away in a Wolseley 6/110 area car. The driver's fingers were thrumming on the wheel. His colleague suppressed a yawn.

Cochrane, the Manager, stood on the pavement, looking to right and left, feeling himself to be more alert than the two coppers, who seemed bored silly. They wouldn't be quite so sanguine if an ammonia gang suddenly heaved up.

The door to the Bedford slammed shut. 'All done,' said the security supervisor.

'Sign it off, please,' said Cochrane, indicating for his deputy to step forward with the paperwork.

A signature was scribbled.

'And add the time, please,' said Cochrane, looking at his wrist. 'I have nine fifty-two.'

*   *   *

Charlie was still at the urinal and he had been there long enough for the attendant to take notice. Charlie realised he must think he had problems with his plumbing. He and Buster exchanged glances and swapped places, Charlie moving to the sink to wash his hands, Buster to empty his bladder.

The attendant, finished in the cubicles, came out to make conversation when the door opened. Bruce stepped in, followed by Harry.

'The thing about Pritchard', said Bruce, 'is he just doesn't understand figures. Show him an accounts book and he goes cross-eyed.'

Harry grunted.

'I think you would do a much better job in the wages department.'

'Tea break,' announced the attendant as the new arrivals manoeuvred around him. One of them was large enough to make the place seem overcrowded. 'See you later, gents.'

Bruce checked his false moustache in the mirror. It was still there, despite the sweat trickling down from under the brim of his heavy, modified bowler. As soon as the attendant had gone, Bruce turned to Charlie and the window. 'Well?'

'Where's Gordy?'

'Tying his shoelaces down the hall. See anything?'

There was a pause before Charlie said, 'The van has just come into view. Followed by the police car.'

'Right,' said Bruce. 'Places, everyone.'

Billy Naughton's radio crackled and he pressed the button to receive it, giving his call sign.

'Anything that end?' It was Len. 'Over.'

'No. Over.'

'Well, keep sharp. Something tells me today's the day. Over.'

Billy laughted. 'You said that yesterday. Over.'

'And I won thirty bob on the horses. I was right about something happening.'

'Over.'

'Yes, yes, over. Hold up.' Len went off-air for a moment. 'Apparently, there's a suspicious car over at your end. Registration Bravo, Mike, Alpha seven two three. Can you check it out, Billy?'

'On my way. Over.'

The passes that Gordy had sourced worked a treat. As soon as Roy had flashed his to the uniform at the gate, the barrier arced skywards. He had hardly slowed. The guard threw Janie a salute and she raised an imperious hand. Christ, they think we're royalty, thought Roy. He watched as Mickey came through behind him and together they turned onto the perimeter road. Roy put his hand out of the window, waving it up and down to tell Mickey to slow down to 15mph. It had just gone ten o'clock. They didn't want to get there too early.

A Comet 4B roared in overhead, trailing a dirty brown cloud of burned fuel. Noisy bugger, thought Roy.

As Buster and Charlie waited for the lift to arrive, Buster began to whistle 'Colonel Bogey'. Meanwhile, Bruce, Gordy and Harry took the stairs down to the ground floor, the stairwell echoing with the sound of metal Blakeys on bare concrete.

'Stop that,' said Charlie. 'I hated that film.'

'Fair enough. Got any requests?'

'Yes.'

'What?'

Charlie winked at him. 'Don't whistle.'

Buster felt the pouch of the briefcase that held the cosh. A little spark of anticipation shot through him and he let the adrenaline flow, enjoying the thump of his heart.

A bell pinged and the doors slid back. Both men stepped smartly into the empty lift. Charlie looked at his watch and jammed his umbrella against one of the doors. 'Two minutes, yet. Don't want to be too early.'

Buster eased the cosh from his case and put his right hand behind his back to keep it out of sight. Anyone entered and made a fuss about a jammed lift, he'd take care of them.

* * *

Outside Comet House, the Bedford security van had pulled to a stop in front of the revolving door and the hinged glass double doors beside it. The police Wolseley slotted into place behind the armoured vehicle, allowing enough room for the guards to gain access to the rear of the Bedford. The supervisor came round from the front seat, banged on the door and the two guards inside opened up. The trolley was manhandled out and the four boxes quickly placed on it. The door was slammed shut again.

In the police car, one of the officers was surreptitiously reading the sports pages of the *Herald*, spread out on his knee. 'You know what? I wouldn't mind doing some breast-stroke with that Anita Lonsbrough.'

The driver shook his head, more in pity than disgust. 'You wouldn't mind doing some breaststroke with Dorothy in the canteen.'

'Leave it out. I do have some standards.'

'Yeah. Low ones.'

The lead Jaguar, driven by Roy, rolled to a smooth halt in the parking bay ten yards behind the police Wolseley. Roy feigned disinterest, but from the corner of his eye he watched as the two security guards started to push the trolley towards Comet House and the basement vault. A third man appeared to be riding shotgun. But without the shotgun, just a baton dangling at his belt.

'Seats,' Roy said quietly.

Janie exited the rear and moved quickly to the passenger seat next to Roy. Tiny Dave quickly collapsed the two folding seats and remained crouching, his powerful thigh muscles able to take the strain for as long as need be.

Roy again looked in his mirror. He could tell that Ian, the other heavy in the back of Mickey's Jag, was also dismantling his stool. Excellent. Ten past ten and all was well.

Still crouching, Tiny Dave reached into his inside pocket. From it he extracted a new quarter-inch chisel and removed the red plastic cover protecting the tip. He gripped the handle like a knife, careful not to catch anything with the unused, factory-sharp business end.

At eleven minutes past ten, the two guards plus the supervisor entered the foyer.

'Morning!' the supervisor shouted to the male receptionist. One of the guards pressed the lift button. Nothing happened. The supervisor stepped in and stabbed it repeatedly. 'Come on, come on,' he grumbled. 'Is this lift OK?' he yelled at the receptionist.

The lad shrugged. 'As far as I know. Could be someone holding it while they load stuff in. It happens.'

The supervisor muttered a curse under his breath.

Somewhere in the shaft above them a distant bell pinged and an arrow above the metal doors illuminated, showing that the lift was on its way down.

'About bloody time.'

'Bacon butty after this,' said one guard.

'Starvin',' agreed the other.

The supervisor tapped his foot impatiently.

Billy Naughton approached the suspicious car at a crouch. There was a driver in the front, he could see the silhouette, but no passengers. He moved towards the rear so he could check the registration on the plate. It was the right car. A Morris Oxford.

Another aircraft came in low over his head, the screech of jet engines swirling around him, and his walkie-talkie squawked. He ignored it. What was this one up to? he wondered as he sprinted round and yanked the driver's door open.

Gordy, Bruce and Harry had reached the bottom of the stairs some minutes ago and watched the trio of security men waiting for the lift to arrive.

'Now?' asked Harry.

'Not yet,' said Bruce. The word had barely left his lips when the doors to the elevator began to separate and a louder bell sounded. *'Now!'*

Gordy was out first, his long legs closing the distance between stairwell and reception desk in a few lengthy strides. He looked at the duty receptionist, a young man with bad spots, and decided he would give them no trouble. At the same time, a second internal voice told him it was always best to play it safe. Kid might be a black belt in karate, after all. Behind him he could hear Bruce and Harry crossing to the guards, the metal tips on Harry's shoes ringing on the parquet.

A puzzled look on his face, as if he wasn't certain what was occurring, the receptionist automatically reached for the internal telephone. Gordy whipped off his hat and brought it down on the kid's hand. It made a dull clang as metal hit bone. The lad, his expression transformed into a mask of shock and pain, buckled at the knee and he went down, disappearing from view.

Not a black belt after all, thought Gordy.

The driver of the car shrank into his seat as the door was pulled open and a wild-eyed figure lunged in at him.

'Who the fuck are you?' yelled Billy as he grabbed at a lapel and pulled the lad close to him.

'Who the fuck are *you*?' retorted the young man, raising his hands to cover his face.

'Flying Squad.'

'What? I ain't done anything. Honest.'

It sounded as if he was about to cry. Either he was a very convincing actor, or he really wasn't up to no good. Billy relaxed his grip. 'What are you doing here?'

The lad fumbled in his pocket and produced his airside pass. 'I work over there. Just showing the car to a mate. He might buy it.'

'Here? At the airport?'

'Perimeter road, it's a good place to try a motor out. Straight up.'

'Shit,' said Billy, letting him go and stepping back. His walkie-talkie crackled once more. This time he answered it.

Unaware as yet of the commotion at the reception desk, the guards stepped aside as the lift doors opened, intending to let the smart gentlemen within pass out.

The supervisor felt a thump on the side of his head and stumbled. He'd been fetched a tremendous blow with an umbrella from Harry.

One of the guards, realising a snatch was in progress, whipped out a baton and smacked it down hard on Bruce's head. Bruce staggered a little, but recovered. The guard, puzzled, raised the baton again. As he did so, Buster swung his cosh and caught the guard in the jaw. There was a sickly cracking sound. He did it again and the man crumpled into a heap. Buster leaned over for a *coup de grâce* when he felt Gordy's hand on his arm. Gordy indicated three prone men, all with blood on their faces, each groaning and out of the game. Charlie, Gordy and Harry were all panting from the short, sharp skirmish. Bruce was pulling the laden trolley clear of the fallen men. The first part of the snatch was over.

'What the bloody hell's going on in there?' shouted the police driver, trying to make sense of the mêlée through the distortion of the glass windows.

121

His partner looked up reluctantly from the newspaper and his tawdry fantasies. 'Jesus Christ, someone's havin' it.'

He scrambled to leave the car, extracting his truncheon as he did so, while the driver reached for the radio handset to call it in.

As the copper left the car, Tiny Dave and Ian bent down and stabbed the rear tyres of the police car with the chisels. The Dunlops exploded in a rush of fetid air.

When the policeman turned to investigate this new occurrence, Tiny Dave swung at him repeatedly with his phony umbrella. Under the rain of blows, the copper fell back; two more sharp raps on the head and he was on the deck. Ian, meanwhile, had jerked the driver out of the car and felled him with a blow from the steel bowler.

Tiny Dave gave Roy and Mickey the thumbs-up.

The two Jags swung around the police cars and reversed up to the entrance in a cloud of exhaust smoke, slotting neatly either side of the Bedford armoured car.

The apron outside Comet House was quickly full of men, some of them carrying strongboxes.

'Get the doors!' yelled Bruce.

The rear doors of the Jaguars were yanked open.

They had rehearsed this dozens of times, but Bruce knew amnesia could strike even the most well-prepared team. So he carried on with the instructions. 'Put the boxes where the back seats were.'

The strongboxes, two per Jaguar, were slotted in to form new rear seats.

'Blankets.'

A cover was thrown over the boxes.

'Get in. Move it.'

Three men clambered in and sat on top of each of them. The doors were pulled shut.

Mickey was first away, tyres squealing and smoking, heading west away from Comet House towards the exit gate.

Please God, let them not have replaced the chain, thought Roy as he accelerated after him.

The young receptionist, sure that the robbers had fled, reached over and pressed the alarm button with his undamaged but unsteady hand. A siren screeched around the hallway; he knew a similar sound would be torturing the ears of those down in the strongroom and at the local police station. Then he slumped back down and cupped his good hand over his nose as his palms filled with the blood streaming out of his nostrils. Fear had burst the vessels in his nose.

The felled driver of the police car, his vision still blurred from the blow, managed to crawl back inside the Wolseley and grab his handset. He pressed the transmit button. When he spoke, his voice was thick, the words slurred. It was as if brain and jaw muscles were no longer in sync. But he was certain he could make himself understood. 'Hello, control. Hello, control. This is Romeo Romeo Alpha. Robbery in progress . . .'

Mickey slithered the Jag to a halt next to the exit gate in the perimeter fence. Gordy, primed for action, was out of the car while it was still rolling. He ran to the gate, lifted the chain and pulled at the phony link.

Nothing happened. The chain held.

Roy heard his anguished shout of 'Fuck!' even over the idling engine. As he braked to a full stop, he wondered how long it would take before Gordy abandoned the trick linkage and fetched the cutters. Time was ticking away.

But Gordy held his ground, tugging at another link, then a third and finally, on the fourth, it pulled apart. He turned, a grin slapped across his face, like he was a turn on *Sunday Night at the London Palladium*.

'Fuck's sake,' yelled Roy to nobody in particular. 'Get a move on.'

He checked the mirrors. All was still quiet behind them, although he had no doubt the alarm had been raised. They were still in the stunned phase of the blag, when the victims couldn't quite believe what had befallen them, but that wouldn't last much longer.

Gordy pulled open the left-hand gate fully and pushed the right one partly back, giving just enough room for the cars. Mickey took the Jag through, pausing only for Gordy, who had reconnected the phony chain-link, to throw himself into the rear. Roy ducktailed out into the Bath Road traffic after them. He floored the accelerator, feeling the wheels spin. Careful, he reminded himself. Wheelspin was a sign of nerves, of too much right foot, not enough finesse.

The little Austin A40 came from nowhere, reversing with speed and precision, powering at him like a tiny green rocket, ready to cut off his escape.

Roy used the little drift he had got into with the wheelspin and allowed the back to come round, blipping the throttle and going onto opposite lock. He could see the face of the other driver, flat cap, a mask of hate beneath it. Some do-gooder hero, no doubt, out for a headline.

The cars made contact, the Mk 2's rear panel smacking into the A40, but side on, lessening the impact. Both cars rocked to a halt, engines still burbling. Roy hoped the wheel arches had held. He didn't want torn metal to shred a tyre on the A4.

In the rear, Bruce raised his brolly like a rifle at the Good Samaritan. The man ducked. Roy gave the Jag a tentative press of the throttle and snapped the light embrace of the Austin. With one last wiggle as the power went down, the Jag, its pride only slightly crumpled, leaped away from the encounter and weaved its way through the traffic, heading for Hounslow.

As Roy dropped the car's speed to blend in with the regular folk, a whoop of joy and relief came from the rear.

Janie lurched across at him. Roy felt the wetness of her mouth on his cheek and allowed himself a little smile of victory. *Done it.*

10.45 a.m. Billy gave his call sign and waited for a reply. There was just a stream of profanity, spat out over the airwaves.

'Say again?'

It was Duke on the radio, his voice full of anger and fear in equal measure. 'Fuckin' hell, Billy, there's been a wages snatch.'

Billy's mind couldn't quite grasp what was being said, distracted by the failure of protocol. 'Over?'

'Fuck "over", you silly cunt. A wages snatch at Comet House. At the airport.'

Billy felt a surge of acid into his windpipe and his bowels loosened. 'I don't—'

'London Central Airport. At Heathrow.' Billy stared up at the sign that said *Gatwick Airport: Authorised Personnel Only.* 'Don't you get it, Billy?' The voice was almost a falsetto now. 'You've been sold a pup. We're at the wrong bloody airport. O-fuckin'-ver.'

Fourteen

From the Daily Sketch, *28 November 1962*

In a daring raid yesterday, members of a gang wearing bowler hats, false moustaches and carrying briefcases to make it appear they were businessmen carried out a cosh raid on wages clerks at Comet House, London Airport, and stole in excess of £50,000. The money had been transported from a nearby Barclays Bank and was destined for the BOAC pay-roll.

The robbers fled the scene in two high-powered Jaguar saloon cars, later found abandoned. Detective-Inspector Hugh Jarvis who will be leading the investigation said yesterday that they were looking for a criminal gang of: 'At least six men and one woman. We are appealing to any witnesses who saw the cars being driven to the airport or anyone who saw suspicious activity there in recent weeks. This a well-organised gang, and the raid took careful planning, but I would remind the public these are dangerous men.'

ROBERT RYAN

Police believe that very few criminals in the capital have the audacity and skill to carry out such a raid. 'It is only a matter of time before we learn their names,' a Scotland Yard spokesman said, although he did not dismiss the conjecture that there might have been 'foreign elements' involved completely. 'Crime is an international business now,' he added.

All airports and ports are being watched.

DI Jarvis said anyone with information should not approach the men, but call WHItehall 1212. A reward is expected to be offered.

Fifteen

London, December 1962

The highlight of the week following the airport job was its appearance on Shaw Taylor's *Police 5*, which Roy watched in his flat above the Battersea garage. The police had discovered the Jags eventually, abandoned in Hounslow. They had also found the BSA motorbike, because the little bastard machine had failed to start for Roy. He had been forced to leave the area by bus, while Tiny Dave had driven the Co-operative furniture van to Norbury with the cashboxes and Mickey and Buster in the rear. The others had taken Tubes, trains and taxis.

Still, finding the cars had yielded nothing, because everything had been very well wiped down. Roy had used T-Cut abrasive cream on the doors and handles of the Jags to take off the top layer of paint, turpentine and thinner elsewhere. Those handling brollies and hats had been careful to wear gloves. So there were no latent dabs there. If there had been, they wouldn't all have been sitting in their respective homes or hangouts, watching *Police 5*.

'*And did anyone see these two cars? Very smart Jaguars. Both stolen a few weeks before their use as getaway vehicles. They must have been stored somewhere.*' Shaw Taylor adjusted his trademark thick-framed black glasses as he stared at the camera. '*Perhaps in that lock-up down the road? That disused factory? Were there any strange comings and goings in the middle of the night? If so, call the number I shall give you at the end of the show.*'

Shaw Taylor moved to the rear of the Jaguar, hands in his sheepskin jacket, breath clouding the air in front of his face. Must have filmed this early in the morning, thought Roy. Taylor fished out one of the steel umbrellas and the metal bowlers from the boot. '*And look at this.*' He clashed them together. '*Solid metal, painted to look like the real thing and used to inflict –*' he shuddered – '*horrible injuries on innocent men. Make no mistake, these are not Robin Hoods or William Tells, fighting the Sheriff of Nottingham or Landburgher Gessler. These are vicious greedy crooks who have stolen the wages of hard-working men and women.*'

Yeah, yeah, thought Roy as he turned off the TV and watched the image implode to a white dot. Not that many wages. When they had opened the cashboxes it was found that each contained around £15,000, rather than the £150,000 they had hoped for. Once the expenses were covered, Tiny Dave, Ian and Harry bunged a few grand, The Frenchman – one of the underworld's financiers who had laid out a few thousand quid to help with set-up expenses – reimbursed and given his whack, there was only a pittance left each. And Bruce had insisted on 'taxing' that, creaming off enough to create a fund for the next job. The next 'Big One'.

It was a crying shame. It had been slick, daring and fast, and nobody got hurt. Well, a few headaches, but not much more. Certainly not the 'horrible injuries' Taylor had mentioned. No thanks to Buster though, who complained he never got to use his homemade cosh in real anger.

Still, with the sale of his kart and his share he had enough, just, for that Brabham. Let Bruce and Charlie spunk their share away on bespoke suits and tarts, Buster on that Sunbeam Alpine he claimed he'd always fancied and Gordy on . . . nobody was sure what Gordy spent his money on. Bigger and better hair-crimpers and driers, maybe. Or a new salon. Perhaps he wanted to be the new Mr Teasy Weasy demonstrating modern hairstyles to Cliff Michelmore on telly.

Roy picked up the current issue of *Autosport*, which had a Mark X Jaguar on the cover. He flicked through the technical articles on gas flow and came upon a beautiful cutaway drawing of the F1 Brabham, the one in which Jack Brabham himself, no less, had come fourth in the US Grand Prix, the first ever GP driver to score points in a car of his own design. It was built by Brabham and fellow Aussie Ron Tauranac at their workshops in Byfleet. This was the goal: Coventry-Climax powered, sitting on fat 13-inch front and 15-inch rears, twin Lukey Muffler exhausts, 174bhp at 8,300rpm. But that was walking before he could run. Karts to F1 in a single bound was unheard of. He'd have to prove himself in Formula Junior first.

The phone rang and he tossed the magazine aside. He knew who it would be. One of the lads to wind him up about Shaw Taylor. Roy 'Vicious Crook' James they would call him from now on. Made a change from *Le Furet*, the nickname his crimes in France had earned him. *Les Flics* had announced that the thief was able to scale drainpipes as if he had run up inside them, like *Le Furet*. Funny, it sounded better in French. 'The Ferret' didn't have quite the same ring.

He picked up the receiver. 'Yeah?'

'Roy?' It was Bruce.

'Yup. I saw it—'

Bruce cut him dead. 'They've picked up Mickey Ball.'

It was at that moment the doorbell rang.

Tony Fortune watched the two policemen enter the Warren Street showroom and start appraising his stock. The younger one clearly didn't know much, but the older guy, he went straight to an MGA that had the wrong grill on it. This was one of the Chalk Farmies, Tony thought, an MVE – Motor Vehicle Examiner – from the Stolen Car Squad. They were good, as he knew to his cost. Sharp enough to know when mileage and condition didn't match.

Paddy emerged from the workshop at the rear, an oily rag in his hands. He moved phlegm around his throat at the sight of the coppers, as if he was going to hawk over them but merely glared at the pair instead as they circled the MGA like carrion, and went back to cleaning spark plugs.

'I couldn't match the right year to that one,' Tony said to the MVE, explaining why the style of grill – it had too many vertical bars – didn't quite sit right with the body. 'Well I could, but you know how much they want for a new one?'

The younger man flashed his warrant card. 'Mr Fortune?' When Tony nodded, he carried on. 'Detective Constable Naughton. Flying Squad.'

Maybe, said a voice inside Billy's head, *but for how much longer?* After Gatwick, he had been savaged by Ernie Millen and Frank Williams, the heads of Flying Squad. It reminded him of the way you saw the lions at London Zoo tucking into a leg of lamb – with him playing the role of the dead sheep. Then the piss-taking had started, about him being in the wrong place at the right time. Every time he gave a destination or address someone would tell him to make sure that wasn't Oxford Street, Aberdeen. Ha-fucking-ha. Unless

133

he got a result on the City gents, his days at the Squad were numbered and his copybook permanently covered in blue-black Quink.

'This is Constable Rowe, of the Stolen Car Squad.'

'How can I help you gentlemen?' Tony asked. Rowe was examining the sticker on the MGA. It was up for £375, not a bad price. 'It's not an insurance write-off,' Tony assured him. 'Legitimate repair. Just you know what some people are like. Once they scratch their pride and joy . . .'

'It's not about that,' said Billy Naughton. 'It's about Mark Two Jags.'

Tony sighed. 'I'm right out, I'm afraid. Can't help you. Lot of demand for them, but we don't see many of them at this end of the market.'

'That's not what we heard.' What they had heard were names: Ball and James, drivers. And the cars? Word was they definitely came from Warren Street. Six grand reward from BOAC, it jogged a lot of memories.

For the next five minutes the two coppers walked around the showroom. Tony knew the game. They would find something pony and use it as leverage to prise him open. Except there was not a hooky or pony item in the show-room, apart from the odd wind-back on the mileage, and nothing there was too greedy. After the Mk 2s he had made sure of that, just in case a day like this came around. He had been over it dozens of times; there was zero to connect him to the stolen vehicles, no physical evidence.

Only if someone grassed would they be able to pin him to them.

'Can we see the log books for all these vehicles?'

'Of course,' said Tony. 'All except the Goggomobil.' This was a German microcar, once fashionable but made redundant by the better-performing and more spacious Mini. 'That's in the post.'

He went out the back and fetched the stack of documents from the safe and watched while they began painstakingly matching car to book. He made himself a tea while they did so.

'What do they want?' Paddy asked.

'Routine.'

Paddy shot him a look that conveyed his disbelief. 'You been doing something behind my back?'

'No.'

Paddy pointed his wire brush at him. 'You know I did some time once. Never again, Tony. It's not fun.'

Tony poured his PG Tips and a second cup for Paddy. 'Don't worry, nobody is doing any time.'

Back in the showroom, Rowe was still lifting bonnets to crosscheck numbers with documents.

Tony sipped the tea. 'Doing this to everyone on the street, are you,' he asked, 'or did my number just come up?'

They didn't answer, just carried on with their whispered deliberations.

The phone rang. It was his wife Marie, sounding jittery

and almost teary, so he didn't mention the police. She immediately sensed something was wrong from the stiffness of his
replies and quickly signed off. More grief when he got home.

As he came out of the office, Billy handed the fat pile of
log books back. 'That all seems to be in order.'

'Good. Is this about that airport job?'

Billy pursed his lips and looked baffled. 'Can't say, sir.
But what would make you think that?'

'Shaw Taylor. He's interested in Mark Twos as well, as I
recall.'

Billy smiled. 'Oh yes.' He picked some fluff off his overcoat. 'Well, as you brought it up, and just to avoid any
confusion, can you tell me where you were on the morning
of the seventeenth, the day of the robbery?'

'At my sister's house in Reading. A christening. I'm the
godfather. I'm pretty sure the vicar would remember.'

Billy had to admit that, as alibis went, it wasn't bad. 'I'm
sure he will. Well, sorry to trouble you.' Billy turned to go
then hesitated. He took out a photograph and held it at
eye-level, so Tony could see it. 'Ring any bells?'

Tony looked at the picture of a young man leaning in a
doorway, a cocky smile on his thin face. 'No. Who is it?'

'Name's Derek Anderson.'

'What you want him for?'

To wring his bloody neck, thought Billy Naughton, then
said, 'Just some routine questions.'

*   *   *

136

Charlie Wilson counted out the five-pound notes in the snug bar of the Two Kings in Clapham. Colin, the barman, made sure the two men weren't disturbed. Charlie stopped when he got to £500. Then he put two more notes on top, and then a third, pushed them over the table, and took a gulp of his beer. 'There you go. That should keep you all right for a while. But I'd leave it for a year till you show your face in London again. So if you are short, let me know, eh?'

'Yes, Mr Wilson.'

'Charlie.'

Derek Anderson beamed at him. 'Thanks, Charlie.'

'You did well to come to me when they tapped you on the shoulder. A stupider person might have...' he hesitated, '... been tempted. But you'd never get that much from the police kitty.'

'The money's not why I did it, Charlie.'

'I know.' Charlie took another gulp of beer. Derek had been desperate to get back into the family fold, to make amends. That was why he had risked coming to Charlie with a story about the Robbery Squad trying to squeeze him. He should have been angry with the kid, because it was his initial loudmouth act about them doing a job at the airport that had drawn the Old Bill in the first place. That and his drunken, disgruntled sulks once he had been banished. But when Charlie had told Bruce the police had been sniffing about, the Colonel had come up with the

137

brilliant idea of a diversion, a dummy job. 'Just like D-Day,' he'd said. 'Hitler thinks we are coming ashore at Calais, but no, wallop, we do the beaches at Normandy.'

So they had put out enough hints that they were going to turn over cargo at Gatwick to keep the police's eyes looking the wrong way, enabling them to do the Comet House job. Had there been a sniff of new faces or a stake-out at Heathrow, Charlie would have pulled them. When they did the job they were 90 per cent certain the cosspots had bought the dummy. It made it doubly sweet: a successful blag *and* red faces at the Yard. Shame the boxes weren't full. Still, the shortfall in cash wasn't down to Degsy. He'd earned his little bung.

As the young man reached for the cash, Charlie grabbed his scrawny wrist. 'And you aren't tempted by the reward?'

Derek tried his hardest to look shocked at the very thought. His hand was shaking and he could feel the pulse. It reminded Charlie of a hamster's heart hammering away when you picked it up. 'No, Charlie. Never.'

'Six grand?'

With his free hand, Derek tapped his stack of newfound wealth. 'At least I'll live to spend this.'

'That's right, my son,' Charlie agreed, releasing his grip. 'Go on, fuck off, see you in twelve months. Sure I'll have something for you then.'

Derek wrapped the money with an elastic band, folded

it into his inside pocket and left. Charlie was still sitting in the snug, drinking, when Len Haslam, sporting a face like a sack of hammers, and two uniforms came in to arrest him.

Sixteen

London, December 1962

The steam in the sudatorium at the Savoy Baths on Jermyn Street was so thick, it was as if super-heated cumulus had fallen to earth and been manhandled into a cupboard. Through the swirling clouds, Bruce Reynolds couldn't tell whether there was anybody already in the room. He sat down on the hot, wet marble bench and waited while Buster made himself comfortable opposite. Neither spoke for a while, letting the vapour scour their lungs.

Eventually, when they were sure they were alone, Buster spoke. 'Fuck, eh?'

'Yeah. Fuck.' Bruce thought about the relatively poor haul. A few months' grace, that was all it would give him, before they would have to do it all again. 'On the bright side, it worked, didn't it?'

Buster laughed. Bloody optimist, he thought. Bruce could be a regular Pollyanna. 'Yeah, it worked.'

'Shows what can be done with a little planning. Good, tight teamwork.'

'Yeah. True enough.' Buster took three deep breaths, feeling his airways burn and almost enjoying it. 'Didn't really do it for the camaraderie, Bruce.'

'No?'

'Nice though it is. A bit more cash wouldn't have gone amiss.'

'Yeah.' Sweat began to trickle into his eyes, and Bruce leaned forward. The moisture gathered on his nose and dropped onto the floor with a loud plop. 'Any news on Roy and Mickey?'

'Identity parades,' said Bruce. 'But they only pulled them because of who they are. You know that. Anyone drives a bit handily, there are only six names on the Squad's list. Roy and Mickey are at three and four. Might have even been promoted to one and two.'

'You heard from Charlie?'

'Nah.' Bruce wasn't worried. Charlie often went to earth after a job. 'Probably taken Pat off to Jersey.'

Buster grunted. 'Been there once – never again. Full of stuck-up rich gits. Everyone seemed to be over sixty. Give me Brighton any day.'

They sucked more hot air for a minute, lost in their thoughts. 'Where do you think you'll be when you're sixty, Buster?'

Buster wiped his forehead. It was slippery with sweat. He was already looking forward to a cold shower. Bruce had a bit more stamina for this kind of thing than him. Man must have been a lobster in a former life. 'Parkhurst at this rate.'

'You miserable cunt,' Bruce said affectionately. He didn't understand the gloom that could afflict Buster. It was a mystery. Buster hated the idea of prison and he suffered deep bouts of melancholy about it, even on the outside. 'It might never happen.'

Bruce accepted pokey as part of the deal, the same way that life and death were intertwined; you couldn't have one without the certainty of the other. For him, his chosen path – the criminal way, some might call it – was a state of mind. It moved life to an intensity that was only rarely achievable in other ways. A film might do it, a few bars of Bill Evans, sex, of course, but nothing else sustained that feeling of being larger than life, beyond its quotidian dullness, like being in the midst of a great take-down. Quotidian. That wasn't a word you heard every day. He had read that in JP Donleavy. He'd had to look it up, but he liked it. The Quotidian Life. It was what they all kicked against, some harder than others. Like Dangerfield in Donleavy's novel, or Marlon Brando in *The Wild One*, which Bruce had seen in France, he wanted to live these

142

few years on earth at full tilt, not succumb to an anaes-thetised greyness.

'And where will you be?' asked Buster, interrupting his thoughts.

'Me? Saint Tropez. Acapulco. Watching Frank at The Sands in Vegas and flying over to see Terry Downes fight and Rod Laver play.' He leaned forward and tapped Buster's knee. 'You got to have ambition.'

'My ambition is for Gordy to hurry up so I can get out of here.' Through a gap in the steam, Bruce could see Buster's pudgy face, red and glistening, with rivulets of sweat gathering at his chin. 'You thought about that other thing – for the next tickle?'

'Tickle? More like a belly laugh, Buster.'

'Is that a yes?'

Bruce shook his head, even though he doubted Buster could see the gesture. 'I'd love to do the Bank of England,' he said, 'but come on.'

Buster had been approached by an ex-messenger at the Old Lady of Threadneedle Street, who had given him details of the Watch. This was the system by which a rotating roster of staff members stayed the night at the Bank of England. Every employee gave up one night a month plus four weekends and a Bank Holiday a year. Each night at 6 p.m., every bank key – a hundred in all – had to be checked in and the bank secured. A convivial supper and rooms were provided. The odd guest was allowed in, but males only.

The source had told them that the men-only rule was subtly undermined by smuggled mistresses in tuxedos or even kilts.

'You got to be able to hide in a place that size,' said Buster. 'My bloke says there's a dozen hidey-holes that could avoid the Sweep.'

At 10.45 each night patrols reported to the Bank's Security Control that every corner of the Old Lady had been swept and was free of stowaways intent on mischief.

'And the Guards? Just our luck we'd get the fuckin' Gurkhas.' The various Guards regiments took it in turns to supply the military presence overnight at the bank; but the Gurkhas occasionally did a stint. Bruce could imagine being gutted by one of those little bastards with his *kukri*.

'Who's being negative now?' Buster asked petulantly.

And what, thought Bruce, was the jolt for trying to rob the Bank of England? Ten years? Fifteen? Christ, a hanging judge might go as high as twenty. For a man who was bird-averse, like Buster, it didn't bear thinking about. But banged up they would be, because there was no way on God's earth Prime Minister Macmillan and Co would let anyone get away with tickling the Old Lady. Only politicians got to rob the country blind.

Bruce, not wanting to encourage his friend into despondency, said: 'You're right. Set up a meet with your man. It's worth dropping a bit of cash to see if he's on the level, if he can get us plans and the like.'

'Will do.' Buster made a blowing sound, like a whale breaching. 'I've got to get out of here, Bruce.'

Buster stood, just as the door opened, allowing steam to billow out into what suddenly seemed like an icy corridor. Standing there was Mannie, one of the attendants at the baths.

'Mr Reynolds. Mr Edwards. Sorry to interrupt your steam but there're a couple of gentlemen here to see you. When you are ready, they said. And not to worry about Mr Goody, they said. They have dealt with him already.'

A couple of gentlemen? Buster looked down at Bruce. 'Fuck.'

'Yeah. Fuck.'

'It doesn't look much like a villain's drum,' said Billy as he walked into Gordon Goody's neat, clean flat. There was G-Plan furniture, a Bush TV, Axminster carpets – none of that Cyril Lord tat – a well-stocked drinks cabinet and a sideboard containing some fancy Wedgwood tableware. In the kitchen was a nice new stove and the biggest refrigerator Billy had ever seen, taller than him, but that was probably the flashiest item in the place. What kind of villain spends his ill-gotten gains on a fridge? he wondered.

'That's because his mum lives here, too,' said Len. 'WPC Waring has taken her off to tea and Bingo.'

Billy and Duke stood and watched as the mostly uniformed team went methodically through the place, unzipping cushions and carefully lifting carpets. Billy was impressed. On too many of the warrants he'd witnessed being served, the searching officers had acted like Desperate Dans. Big and oafish. These lads had finesse.

'Nothing so far, guv,' said the DC from the local nick to Duke.

'Fair enough. He's the careful sort, is Gordy. Why don't you go and get a cup of tea as well?'

'Tea?' the DC asked, as if he never touched the filthy stuff. 'We've only the bedrooms and the loft to do.'

'And I want them done properly. Not the sudden spurt at the end when everyone thinks it's time for a cuppa. Come back refreshed.' He pointed at Billy. 'We'll hold the fort till you get back.'

The DC pointed down to the nylon sports bag Duke had brought along. 'Off to the gym?'

'Oh aye. Judo. Couple of throws on the mat. Nothing like it at the end of the day.'

The DC looked sceptical, but he waved his uniforms out.

Duke took out a fiver. 'Get them a sandwich, too.' The DC hesitated before he took it.

After they had left, Duke crossed to the cocktail cabinet and opened it. 'Bird's eye maple, this. Pricy. Oh, looky here. Nice drop of Laphroaig. Fancy some?'

'Nah.'

'Come on.' He examined the bottle. 'It's not like he's marked it. Bent bastard isn't going to miss two snifters.

Probably swag anyway.' He splashed out a generous measure into each of two cut-glass tumblers. 'Secret with this is, a drop of water.'

He returned from the kitchen beaming and handed Billy one of the glasses. 'Cheers.'

Billy just gave a tight smile. He wasn't sure he felt like toasting with the guy who had dropped him in this particular pile of shit. He sipped his drink, his eyes watering at the rich, peaty aroma released by the few drops of water.

Duke grabbed an arm, steered him over to the sofa and pushed him down. He stood over him, a lopsided grin slapped onto his face. Billy felt an urge to punch it. 'Now look, Billy boy, I know you are pissed off. Black mark and everything. But just imagine if that little shit's tip-off hadn't been moody. The power and the fuckin' glory you would have got. Would you be sharin' that with me now? Would you fuck. But listen, old Millen is sayin' to George Hatherill, "Well, he's a new boy. Happens to us all. Give him some slack." More than they would for me. "Cocky cunt," they'd have said about me; "should have seen it comin'. Should have smelled it".' He sniffed his drink to emphasise the point and the grin returned. 'But all that could be water under the bridge if we make this stick on someone. That's all they care about. Arrests have been made – that's good. But what have we got so far?'

'A couple of IDs.'

'Right.'

'And the bolt-cutters.'

'Also correct. We have a man who fits Gordon Goody's description down to a T buying a massive pair of bolt-cutters. Now, Gordy will claim they were for home dentistry. And by the time we come to court, the hardware bloke will have changed his mind.'

'What makes you say that?'

'Oh, I'd put a few bob on it. He'll get a visit from the chaps. Then he'll contract terminal amnesia. I know the type. He just wants to go back to his brown coat and his pound of nails. Not all of them will roll over, mind. But for Gordy . . . we need more than his word against a witness.'

'Such as?'

'Such as you going to take a peek under the bed?'

'He doesn't seem like the kind of man to put his loot under the mattress.'

'You'd be surprised. Go and have a butcher's.'

Curious, Billy went to the bedroom, got down on his hands and knees onto the soft cream carpet and peered at the space under the bed. Empty. Not so much as a dust ball. He got up and went back out, bored with Duke's games.

'There's nothing th—'

The bowler hat came flying across the room at him, spinning almost at face level. Billy reached up to pluck it from the air and felt his fingers pushed back and a stab of pain in his wrist. 'Ow. Shit.'

The hat made a dull thump as it hit the carpet.

'There will be if you slide that under.'

It was one of the steel bowlers recovered from the scene. No prints, no indication who made them. Useless. 'Why?'

'I checked,' said Duke. 'Seven and three-eighths, give or take. Have a look at the trilby in the hall. Same size.'

Billy felt his stomach shrink when he realised what the DS was suggesting. 'Duke—'

'You know and I know that Gordon Goody is right for this. All we have to do is convince a jury of that. He bought the cutters three miles from the airport and he has previous. Oh, and guess where his neighbour used to work?'

He knew – the bloke had been a janitor at Comet House, but the neighbour had insisted it was mere coincidence.

'Circumstantial.'

Billy's face darkened. 'So is your career in the Squad at this moment. The hat puts him at the scene. The hat saves your skinny arse. Because we get a result and it isn't a fuckin' fiasco. You live to fight another day.' He finished his whisky. 'Up to you, son. No, really. I can put it back in the bag here and have it returned to the shelf where it will lie gathering dust because it is of no use to us. Or we can make it count.'

Billy's mouth went dry and he was worried that, if he spoke, his voice would betray the tears he felt welling up inside. It wasn't the way he wanted to catch crooks, not what he envisioned at all. Oh, he knew it went on, the verbalising, the fit-up, but not him, he had always thought. Not Billy Naughton.

149

Against that, he had to stack the cloud he felt oppressing him every day, the looks and the mumbles in the Squad room. The new dread of showing his face at work at all. A work he loved. Perhaps Duke was right. It was better to live and fight another day. He left the room to find a spot under the bed where the local DS would discover the steel bowler.

Tony Fortune didn't like the atmosphere in the flat when he got home that evening. Marie had come back early from work at the bank and had made shepherd's pie. But she wouldn't catch Tony's eye as she laid the table. He opened the cupboard to fetch the sauce and found himself staring at a dozen bottles of HP.

'We'll be all right for sauce when the bomb drops then,' he said.

'They were on special offer. Just the peas to do. Want a beer?'

'All right.' He sat and flicked through the *Evening News*, to see if there was any more on the Heathrow job. He also wondered if Shaw Taylor's appeal had generated any leads. He hadn't had the Jags for long and had worked on them well away from Warren Street. Everyone involved had been paid handsomely, so there was nobody disgruntled. But there was the reward, that insidious cancer which might eat away at the cash-strapped. Tony determined to do a quick ring around, make sure everyone was sound.

150

Marie opened a brown ale for him, and then delivered the bowl of peas and the pie to the table. He sat up and stared across at her as she ladled out the food. She gave a thin smile. She looked tired, her brown hair needed a wash and she still had on one of those cheap synthetic drip-dry blouses she wore to work. Still, he felt a sudden burst of affection, possibly tinged with lust, for her. He didn't speak until he had tasted the pie and nodded his approval. 'Lovely. You all right?'

She pushed the hair away from her face. 'Yes, love. Except . . . well, you know I had those pains the last couple of weeks?'

Tony recalled something about stomach cramps and ulcers, but he had been too distracted by his own concerns to pay much attention. 'Of course.'

'I went to the doctor, Tony.'

He felt a stab of nervousness. His mother had died of some female cancer. Cervical, that was it. He put down his knife and fork and gave her his full attention. 'And what did he say?'

'He says we're going to need a bigger flat.'

She burst into tears, and it was a good few seconds before he made the connection. The realisation hit him like a sack of wet sand. He was going to be a father.

Seventeen

Cannon Row police station, December 1962

The young copper popped his head into the interview room. 'Be ready for you in about fifteen minutes, Mr Reynolds.' The lad nodded towards the empty mug on the table. 'Need a top-up?'

'No, thanks,' said Bruce. 'Tell you what though, wouldn't mind a paper. *News* or *Standard*. Might put a bet on later.' He tossed a shilling over.

The uniform frowned as he caught the coin. For a few seconds Bruce thought he had been rumbled. He was just about to give an it-was-worth-a-punt smile when the youngster said, 'I'll see what I can do.'

'I'd appreciate it.'

The door closed and he heard the bolt slide home with

a clang that echoed around the bare, stuffy room. They were fishing. No, they were trawling, pulling in every one of the chaps they could. Roy James had warned him that humiliating the Flying Squad by selling them a dummy was not a good idea, that wounded pride made the detectives dangerous and reckless, much more likely to fit up whoever they fancied for the job. But Charlie especially had thought it too good an opportunity to miss, sending the coppers down to Gatwick while the firm did Heathrow. Priceless.

As Roy had predicted, they did react in the fevered way they had whenever a policeman got shot. And in their Old-Bill-in-a-China-Shop routine they had scooped up Bruce, Charlie, Gordy, Roy and Mickey.

Bruce had no idea what they had on him and acted as if there was nothing *to* be had. He was merely helping police with their enquiries. He hadn't even contacted a solicitor. Best be nonchalant, as if he really was giving every assistance, as if he was certain of his own innocence.

An ID parade. But who was going to eyeball him? The lavatory attendant? Surely he had seen Buster more times than Bruce. The security guards? The receptionist? None had got a decent look at him.

The young copper came back with an *Evening Standard*. Bruce flicked through it after he had gone, but the City gent gang was already old news. Kennedy had declared a blockade on Cuba, because he believed nuclear missiles were there. Four hundred people had been killed by a flash flood in Barcelona. China and India were going to war over a border dispute. What was a few grand lifted at Heathrow compared with that lot?

'OK, Mr Reynolds. I'm DS Haslam.' The young copper had been replaced by a plainclothes, older, rougher, baggier about the eyes. They were Flying Squad eyes, reddened and veined from booze and smoke. 'You know the score, I'm sure.' Bruce didn't bother disputing that it wasn't his first parade. 'Would you mind putting these on?'

It was a pinstriped jacket and a bowler hat. Bruce did as he was asked, irritated that the jacket was a size too big and came down to his knuckles and the hat-band was tight. 'If you'll come this way.'

As he left, Bruce grabbed the *Standard*, rolled it up and slotted it into the jacket pocket. 'Let's get it over with. My mum is expecting me for tea.'

Len 'Duke' Haslam smiled. 'I hope she hasn't baked special, Mr Reynolds.'

'Oh, she will have. My mum makes the best scones.'

'Let's hope you don't let her down then,' the detective said, in a tone that hoped for just that.

There were seven others in the open yard at the rear of the station. This less than magnificent group were already in a loose line, all in dark suits and hats, ready for the few bob they would pick up as concerned citizens doing their bit. They ranged from five-eight to six-four, with Bruce somewhere in the middle, and half had moustaches. The outside

154

air stung, needle-sharp on his face, only just above zero. Bruce shivered, hoping this wouldn't take long. 'It's freezing out here,' he said.

'Shut it.'

'Why do you always have to do these things in midwinter?' he asked.

'We're hoping your bollocks drop off.'

Haslam positioned Bruce third from the end – he felt those bookending him move away slightly – and inspected the group, like an RSM on parade. He swapped a couple around and straightened the line, making sure the gap between Bruce and the others was closed up. Then he produced four fake moustaches, and pressed them onto the cleanshaven faces. He stepped back, then adjusted Bruce's 'tache. 'That tickles, DS Haslam,' he complained. 'I hope I don't sneeze.'

Duke Haslam said nothing.

When he was satisfied with his charges, he clicked his fingers and out came another detective, younger, with the witness. Bruce kept his face impassive as he recognised him. It was the old bastard from the Austin A40, the one who had backed across the gates to try and block them in. The one Bruce had taken careful aim at with his fake umbrella.

'Take your time now, sir,' the new copper said to the witness.

You could usually smell the nerves and fear on the poor sod who had to walk the line-up. It was no small thing, to face the suspected villain head-on and place the incriminating hand on the shoulder. He had seen plenty bottle it before. Not this one.

The old man – in truth he was probably no more than fifty, flat cap, bad dentures – strode down the line, pausing before each of the potential robbers, looking him up and down and peering into the eyes. 'Can you ask this man to squint?'

'Squint, sir?'

'Yes. Screw up his eyes.'

'Number three, would you mind screwing up your eyes? Thanking you.'

A shake of the head and the witness moved on, until he came level with Bruce. Stay impassive. No smiles. No attempt to either ingratiate or intimidate. Neutral. Bored. Want to get back to your desk.

He watched as the eyes flicked down to the newspaper in his pocket. His brain would be processing that little prop. Why would a prisoner have a newly rolled-up newspaper in his jacket? Surely this was more likely to be one of the makeweights, pulled off the street, who had hastily pocketed his *Standard*.

Go on, you old bastard, put two and two together.

The witness moved on and Bruce saw a flash of irritation cloud Haslam's face. Bruce Reynolds didn't move a muscle, just let a slow stream of air – an extended sigh of relief – bleed from the corner of his mouth.

He would have warm scones for tea after all.

* * *

Jack Brabham's place was in Byfleet, Surrey. Although the racing cars with their Coventry-Climax engines bore Jack's name, the machines were principally designed by Ron Tauranac, and the company was officially Motor Racing Developments, MRD for short. It wasn't until the first race of one of the new cars in France that they realised a drawback with the initials, when the announcer introduced Team MRD and the crowd tittered. Team MRD. Team *Merde*. Team Shit. The cars were hastily rebadged as Brabhams.

Roy James discovered the workshops were shuttered and locked. Yet he could hear the sound of car builders at work inside, the clatter of tools, the hiss of hydraulic and airlines. It didn't surprise him. Formula One teams disliked casual visitors who might just be coming to see how the monocoque or the water-cooling was configured.

He found a side door, with a bell, and pressed it. A feeble ringing sounded somewhere deep within the unit.

As he waited, Roy put his case down and wondered how Mickey was doing. Mickey fucking idiot Ball. It was a few weeks since they had all been lifted. Both Roy and Mickey passed the ID parade, but Mickey had left part of his chauffeur's uniform at home. A pair of grey trousers. How stupid was it to go down for a pair of strides?

They earned Mickey a second ID parade and one of the barrier operators at Heathrow placed him at the scene.

On the positive side, Bruce had walked away, but Gordy was in trouble. False moustaches had been found in his flat,

157

along with a bowler hat. Planted, of course, so Gordy said, although it was pointless saying that. He was going down the Fancy Dress Party defence route. Juries must think dressing up in silly costumes was an essential part of the villainous life. And there was an ID from the hardware-shop owner, saying it was Gordy who had bought the cutters, and another from a security guard. Charlie, too, had been fingered, in his case by the lavatory attendant.

The initial hearing was set for three weeks' time. It wasn't long to sort something out for the two lads. They wouldn't grass, that was for sure, which meant they were looking at a decent stretch.

'Yes?' The metal door swung open and a knotted face with hefty sideburns was staring at him.

'Ron in?' Roy asked.

'Busy.' From his accent, this was another Antipodean.

'Can you tell him Roy James is here?'

'What for?'

Roy suddenly put a name to the face. 'You're Denny Hulme, aren't you?'

The man relaxed a little. Belligerence softened into merely prickly. 'Yeah. That's right.'

'I saw you race at Aintree. A second. You picking up a car?'

He shook his head. 'No. I'm the Service Manager here now.'

Well, it was hardly service with a smile. 'You're not racing?'

A shrug. 'Can't afford it, mate.'

'Tell me about it,' said Roy sympathetically. 'Rich man's game.' Hulme nodded. 'Shame though. You're bloody good. Can I see Ron?'

'Really, he's under the cosh, working on the cars for South Africa.'

'Yeah, right. 'Course he is.'

The South African would be the final GP of the year and would decide whether Graham Hill or Jim Clark would be World Champion. Although Brabham weren't in contention for the top two places, with Stirling Moss out of action after a hideous crash, Bruce McLaren, who had won at Monaco, just had to be in the points to stay ahead of Surtees and take third. It would be a real boost for the Brabham-Climax team.

'Just that I want to order a car.'

'A car?'

'To race,' he added redundantly.

Hulme looked down at the case at Roy's feet. 'You one of those rich men we were just talking about?'

'Had a bit of luck on the Spot-the-Ball competition.'

'Congratulations. What you after?'

'Formula Junior. A BT6.'

'You done much racing?'

'Karts. British team. Ron can vouch for me.' *I know what I am doing*, is what he really meant.

'A BT6 is five and a half thousand, including Purchase Tax. You must be good at spotting those balls.'

Roy picked up the case. It was most of what he had earned from the job. Affording the running costs for any car he bought was going to be tricky, but he would worry about that later. 'I am. Think Ron'll take cash?'

For the first time Denny Hulme smiled, and when Roy left two hours later, he had a single-seat racing car specced up, a delivery date and a chassis number: FJ-13-62. He was on his way.

Eighteen

London, January 1963

The council of war was held at the Trat – the Trattoria
Terrazza in Romilly Street – on another bitterly cold day.
A series of angry storms had lashed the British Isles and
there had been four days of fog in London. Now the temperature was down in the basement. So the men who entered
the Italian restaurant were bundled up in coats, scarves,
gloves and hats and took several minutes to disrobe as Alvaro,
the manager, fussed around them, ordering *vino rosso* before
they had even sat down, and listing the day's specials.

Alvaro had selected a circular table at the rear of the
room. There was Bruce, back from the South of France
where he had gone immediately after the identity parade.
He was in the clear now. Fifteen hundred pounds, spread

around liberally, meant his name was no longer associated with the Heathrow job. Roy was present, as were Gordy, Buster and a young solicitor, Brian Field.

Gordy was only there because of Brian, who had secured him bail, which had been refused for Charlie and Mickey. Bruce, a tanned and relaxed figure among wan winter-struck faces, ordered some antipasto for the table and said: 'Well, gentlemen, who is going fill me in? How's Charlie?'

'Quiet,' said Buster, who had visited him on remand. 'But calm.'

'What do they have on him?'

'The lavatory attendant,' said Brian. 'Good ID.'

'Is that all?' Bruce asked. 'Can we get to him?'

The solicitor shook his head. 'No.'

'Is he solid?'

'He's an old bloke. A good brief'll make him wobble,' said Buster.

'And Brian has an idea,' said Gordy with something close to admiration. Theirs was not a normal client-counsel relationship. In fact, Bruce sometimes thought the angel-faced Brian, with his short hair, neat suits and sensible shirts, was the most bent out of all of them. He had, after all, a glamorous German wife with expensive tastes to support.

Bruce turned to look at the young man, not yet out of his twenties. He could almost pass for a teenager, albeit a particularly harmless, suburban one, apart from the flinty eyes. Bruce glimpsed a greedy venality in there.

'Well, there is a lad works at the airport – has done for two years. Never been on a plane, even though he has to watch them all day. That kid would love to catch a jet to New York or Rio.'

'Yeah? Go on.'

Brian hesitated as a large platter of ham, artichokes, olives and tomatoes was placed in the centre of the table, along with a stack of hot, crisp bread. 'So he'll say that he saw Charlie at exactly the same time as the robbery was taking place – but over with the plane-spotters.'

'Plane-spotters?' Bruce asked incredulously. 'Charlie? He can't tell a 707 from the hole in his arse.'

'I'll slip him a copy of the *Observer's Book of Jet Airliners*,' said Brian with a smirk. 'Come the trial, he'll be an expert.'

Buster took a sliver of translucent ham and folded it into his mouth. 'OK, fair enough, that's confusing the attendant's evidence – can't be in two places at once,' he said eventually. 'But is that enough?'

Roy waved away the offer of wine and asked for lemonade. 'What about a juror?'

Brian nodded. 'Likely we can get us one. We'll have to wait on that, obviously.'

'How much for the kid at the airport?' Bruce asked.

'Two grand should do it.'

Two grand. The money from the score was dwindling fast. 'I'll get it to you,' said Bruce. 'What about Mickey?'

What he really meant was: would he go QE? 'He's holding

up,' said Roy, knowing Mickey would never take the Queen's Evidence route. 'Saw him last week.'

'And what do they have on him?'

'Two witnesses who put him in Comet House.'

'What?' He looked at Brian. 'He wasn't inside.'

'They think it's me,' said Buster. 'Same sort of height, you see.'

'Bollocks,' said Bruce.

Brian supped his wine. 'He could cop a plea. If they do him for the violence inside, he could be looking at a cockle, maybe more.'

'And Mickey can't do ten years standing,' said Roy glumly. They all appreciated that Mickey wasn't made of the same stuff as Charlie, Gordy or Bruce.

They finished the antipasto in silence. Bruce indicated that the table be cleared.

'What if he does cop a plea?'

Brian sniffed. 'A handful, maybe.' Five years. 'They have the chauffeur's trousers from his drum, so it isn't hard to convince them he wasn't inside but behind the wheel. He might even get away with a lagging. Three and out in two.'

'But he won't roll over?' asked Buster, suddenly concerned for his own skin.

'Mickey? Nah,' insisted Roy. 'He knows which side his bread is buttered on.' He also knew what would happen if he did give them Charlie or any of the others. Life inside wouldn't be safe. 'I'll have a word. See if I can get him to change his mind and do a Not Guilty.'

A small bowl of ravioli each – on the house, the waiter informed them – was set before them and more wine taken by all but Roy. Then Bruce turned to Gordy. 'What about you?'

Brian answered for him, mischievousness in his voice. Bruce was reminded yet again that the solicitor often treated all this as a game. Brian v the Bogeys. 'Now Gordon has an idea.'

Gordy quickly outlined his plan, which clearly appealed to his sense of humour. Bruce wasn't so sure.

'That's it? Bit Tommy Cooper, isn't it?'

'And a juror or two, of course,' said Brian reassuringly. 'And we can get to the bolt-cutter man, I'm certain. There's the security guard, but I'm not sure he's enough on his own. It all happened so fast.'

Bruce still wasn't sure about the wisdom of the whole set-up, which had elements of farce about it. There was a time and place for clowning around, and the Central Criminal Court wasn't it. However, the others seemed up for it. 'OK, give it a whirl. But you'll need someone on the inside at AD.' This was the police slang for Alpha Delta, Cannon Row's designation, a term that had been picked up by the other side.

'I could ask the Twins,' said Gordy.

Bruce shook his head vigorously at the thought of

involving the heavy-handed Krays. 'No. Keep it tight. And you best stay out of it, too, Gordy. Me and Buster, we'll see what we can do.' He signalled to Alvaro. 'Ready for the mains now.'

Alvaro put on his most flamboyant act, waving his arms and gesticulating, as if a time bomb was about to go off. '*Sí*, of course, Signor Reynolds. Gilberto, *cinque secundi piatti, tavola uno, presto, presto.*'

He might be an old ham, thought Bruce, but Alvaro was the best host in London, excepting perhaps Mario at Tiberio, the sister restaurant in Queen Street, who had the edge when it came to the ladies. Mario made them all feel like Gina Lollobrigida.

Brian glanced at his watch and stood up. 'Not for me, chaps, sorry. Got work to do. Believe it or not, some of my clients are actually innocent.'

The young solicitor left them laughing at that one.

Nineteen

London, March 1963

Charlie knew enough to wear a royal-blue shirt to the Old Bailey, rather than a white one. The public areas of the Central Criminal Court might have been vacuumed, washed, polished and waxed daily, but downstairs some of the grime dated from the eighteenth century. He'd seen too many in the dock with smudged white shirts, looking like they'd just delivered a hundredweight of coal. Dark colours, they were best.

Charlie was led by one of the Brixton screws who did turns at the Bailey, past the squalid and crowded 'on bail' cells. One of the steel doors was open, a guard bellowing a name. Charlie glanced in, hoping for a glimpse of Gordy, but couldn't see beyond the swaying youth blocking the doorway. He'd worn a white shirt and tie, like a good boy. The effect was rather spoiled by a nose that had been split like a ripe tomato. Charlie shook his head. That would make a good impression on the jury. Still, the kid might be a nonce or a rapist and deserved it. The young offender glanced over his shoulder, back into the cell. He wasn't more than nineteen and his legs bowed and shook as he was pulled towards his moment in the dock. Nah, thought Charlie, he probably just looked at someone the wrong way.

As they approached the 'kennels' one of the prison officers unlocked the closest door and bowed, as if welcoming him to his hotel suite. Charlie remained impassive. Fuck them. The kennels – cells reserved for those on remand brought from prisons – were often worse than the 'on bails' – scorching in summer, cold in winter, no windows, just a series of holes drilled high in the wall for ventilation. No lavatory, of course, just a bucket. One shower on request, should your day drag on and your clothes and hair and skin grow rank as they absorbed the stench of your own, and everyone else's, sweat. But one shower for sixty or seventy meant you might not get a turn and if you did, the slimy, mould-tinged cubicle was hardly inviting.

'Mr Wilson,' said the screw with exaggerated politeness. 'We'll be calling you shortly.'

Charlie gave the man a thin smile, and imagined punching him hard, right between the eyes. He preferred it when they didn't speak to him. He did them that courtesy, why couldn't they just return it and keep their mouths shut? They all knew what this was: a risk of the life he had chosen. As such, he thought of it now more like an athlete thought of a pulled tendon or a pilot his plane crashing. It can happen. It had happened.

The cell held only six other people, and one chair, occupied. The others sat on the filthy floor, cross-legged. He scanned the faces as they looked up at him. No sign of Mickey. He didn't recognise any of them. No friends here. Not much warmth either, with the winter that still ruled the country bleeding in through the ventilation holes.

The door closed behind him with a resounding clang and Charlie looked around at walls covered in graffiti and food slops and not a little blood. There was no way on God's earth he was going to lean against that. And the floor was covered in a film of dirt and piss. He looked at the man in the chair. Forty-ish, with the pallor of a life in pokey about him. Flabby upper arms, crude, homemade tattoos. Not in shape at all. Charlie had a hand on his own biceps. They were good and hard. He'd done push-ups and sit-ups morning and evening, hundreds of them, a way of numbing the pain of being separated from Pat. That was the only hard thing about being inside. Everything else was easy. The thought of five or ten years away from the family, though . . . but that wasn't the problem right now.

The man in the chair was reading a paper. Charlie scanned the second lead story. A 'freelance model' called Christine

Keeler had failed to appear in court as a witness to a shooting by a 'coloured' man, John Arthur Edgecombe. Charlie knew Christine, vaguely, from the clubs. Hard-faced but soft-hearted. He wondered how long before the hacks really joined up the dots. Everyone knew who else hung out at Murray's Cabaret, and that the group treated Cliveden as its country branch.

But the man in the chair wasn't reading that. He was groaning about how the West Indies had beaten England by ten wickets in Barbados. 'Can you believe those nig-nogs?'

Those nig-nogs included players like Sobers and Gibbs, the best off-spinner in the game, thought Charlie. Ignorant cunt. He took a step forward and sniffed loudly.

In the confined space, it sounded like a bull snorting. The long-termer in the chair looked up, then returned to his paper. Charlie took a step closer, folding his arms, feeling his worked muscles press against the fabric of his clothes. The man put down his *Mirror* once more. He opened his mouth to speak, saw the expression in Charlie's eyes and the honed shape of his torso, and thought better of it. He stood and stepped aside.

Charlie shot his trousers from the knee as he sat, then nodded his thanks as he held out his hand. The man hesitated and passed over the newspaper. Charlie snapped it open at an article claiming that the police needed an extra £25 million a year to fight the underworld. A White Paper called *Crime in the Sixties* was claiming that every aspect of law enforcement, from the probation service to the courts, was 'clearly inadequately funded' with the ever-present risk of 'crime going unpunished'.

Charlie laughed to himself. That's handy, he thought. Crime going unpunished. Maybe the day would work out all right, after all.

Twenty

From The Times, *12 March 1963*

MAN ACQUITTED ON
£62,000 CHARGE

At the close of the case for the prosecution at the trial of the three men accused of being concerned in a £62,000 wages robbery at London Airport last November, Sir Anthony Hawke, the Recorder at the Central Criminal Court, directed the jury yesterday to acquit one of the accused on the grounds that there was insufficient evidence to justify proceeding further against him. A witness who placed the accused at the site was deemed 'unreliable', especially as another witness had insisted he was elsewhere at the time.

Charles Frederick Wilson, aged 30, bookmaker of Crescent Lane, S.W., was then found Not Guilty of robbing Arthur Henry Grey and Donald William Harris of boxes containing £62,599, the property of BOAC, while armed with offensive weapons. Wilson was formally discharged.

CONFESSION DENIED

Addressing the jury, the Judge said that the evidence against Wilson was of such doubtful character that it did not justify proceeding against him further.

The trial then proceeded against Michael John Ball, aged 26, credit agent of Lambrook Terrace, Fulham, S.W., and Douglas Gordon Goody, aged 32, hairdresser, of Commondale, Putney, S.W. Mr Ball denied that he originally admitted his role in the robbery in a verbal confession and said that he intended to plead Not Guilty. The trial was adjourned for two weeks.

Twenty-one

London, March 1963

As happened every weekday except holidays, at six that morning the Billingsgate bell gave its sonorous clang, echoing around Fish Hill and Pudding Lane. Within the great hall and its satellite lock-ups, the market roared into life. Prices were shouted between buyers and sellers in an impenetrable piscine argot. As deals were made, the wooden-hatted porters stacked boxes of lobsters from Whitby, eels from Holland, mackerel from Newlyn or whiting from Fleetwood on their heads. The market's chimney began to belch its plume of black smoke into the slowly lightening sky.

Bruce took in the scene from the edge of the pandemonium, outside the entrance to the market hall, his etiolated form positioned under a street-light as he waited to be noticed.

He was wearing a thick Aquascutum overcoat and a Hermès scarf, but still felt the bitter early-morning chill. The place, of course, also stank. It was a fish market, after all.

Alf Flowers was busy instructing his lads when he caught sight of Bruce. Like Charlie, who had a stake in a Covent Garden firm, Alf had a history – was 'known to the police', as they said. He had been up the steps a few times, although after the last stretch he had sworn to the missus that the only fishy business he would do was at the market. Which was mostly true. Except his chosen business now was not blowing peters but trading information and contacts. For half the villains in London, Alf was like dialling Directory Enquiries. One advantage of using Alf's services was you could get a nice Dungerness crab or two while you were at it. You never got that from the GPO.

'All right, Bruce? Sparrowfart's a bit early for you, isn't it?'

Bruce stifled a yawn. 'Hello, Alf.'

'Got some lovely halibut if you're interested.'

'Fancy a drink?'

Alf knew full well this wasn't about that night's supper. 'Rum and coffee over at the Wheatsheaf?' he asked, throwing a thumb to indicate across the river towards Borough Market. The pub opened at six, serving the porters from the local vicinity. Billingsgate had its own early licensed boozers, but Alf clearly wanted to do business away from under the gaze of his co-workers. Very wise.

'Perfect.'

'See you in thirty?'

'Fine.'

Alf lowered his voice. 'Give me an idea what you after?'

'A copper.'

The fishmonger didn't seem surprised by this. It couldn't have been any old bogey though, because he knew Bruce was on nodding terms with a few of them down at the Marlborough in Chelsea. But then, Bruce was clever enough not to shit on his own doorstep. 'What kind of copper?'

'The kind who likes a flutter at Crockford's or the Pair of Shoes. Preferably one from AD.'

Alf smiled, as if certain this was unlikely to be a taxing assignment. 'I'll see you over there. Order me the FEB.'

'One Full English Breakfast coming up.'

It was Roy and Buster who made the drop. Buster chose Postman's Park, the churchyard of St Botolph's-Without-Aldersgate, famous for its monument to ordinary men and women who turned out to be heroes and heroines. The tiny space was just behind St Bart's Hospital, next to the GPO Headquarters.

There was snow in the air, small flurries presaging a full shower to come. While Roy paced back and forth in front of the park's narrow entrance, looking for suspicious activity and trying to keep warm, Buster put down the Derry & Tom's bag and read the glazed porcelain plaques in the little cloister.

He stopped before a plaque that commemorated a brave cozzer.

> *George Stephen* FUNNELL
> *Police Constable*
> *December 22nd, 1899.*
> *In a fire at the Elephant and Castle,*
> *Wick Road, Hackney Wick, after rescuing*
> *2 lives, went back into the flames, saving*
> *a barmaid at the risk of his own life.*

Good man, thought Buster. He knew a few barmaids he'd like to save. Not that he would run into a burning pub for them – although doubtless this one was very grateful to Constable Funnel. He wondered if the Elephant and Castle public house was still there.

A piercing whistle from Roy reached him and he turned around. A figure was heading towards him – a man in his thirties, with thinning blond hair, trailing clouds of cigarette smoke as if he was steam-powered. Buster waited for him to approach then turned back to the plaques.

'Look at this,' he said, reading from one of the other commemorations. '"Frederick Mills, A. Rutter, Robert Durrant and F.D. Jones who lost their lives in bravely striving to save a comrade who had fallen into the sewage pumping works. East Ham, July the eighteenth, 1895".'

The detective kept mute.

'Now that's what I call being in the shit,' Buster growled. 'Know what I mean?'

The policeman looked down at the carrier bag. 'That it?'

Buster indicated it was. He looked for Roy, but he had gone. Fetching the car, he hoped. 'You know what to do?'

'You want to go over it again?' the copper asked.

Buster suddenly felt nervous. 'No, I fuckin' don't.' He seized the man's overcoat and started pulling it open.

'Hey, hey, what the fuck—'

Buster grabbed the man's face, squeezing the cheeks together. He had little respect for coppers anyway, zero for bent ones. 'What's your game?' Buster hissed.

'Relax. Jesus, I was just winding you up. I know what to do.'

Buster let him go and the man readjusted his clothing. Buster felt a sour taste rise in his mouth as he said, 'It's all in there – the item and the money. If it goes right . . .'

'Look, I've got no say in that.'

'If it goes right, there's a bonus, as agreed. Now fuck off and piss it away at some spieler.'

Buster turned and strode off, hands in pockets, head down, alert for any lurking strangers. He reached the ornate gates and Roy pulled up in front of him, leaned over and opened the door of the Mini. Buster jumped in, banging his head as he did so. Roy gunned the little engine, releasing a satisfyingly deep note from the stainless-steel sports exhaust and they pulled away. Roy navigated them down to

Fleet Street, past the Black Lubyanka – the *Daily Express* building – and onto the Strand, heading west and keeping one eye on the mirror.

He took a last-minute, tyre-squealing left turn onto Waterloo Bridge, towards the Festival Hall and the remnants of the Festival of Britain, now being reworked into some concrete monstrosity. Once on the bridge, he checked the wing mirrors. At the far end, he took the roundabout and drove back north again. Nobody followed. 'Where to?' he asked.

'The Marlborough,' Buster said, needing a drink and knowing Bruce would be there. He banged the dashboard of the diminutive machine. 'And don't spare the fuckin' ponies.'

Twenty-two

From The Times, 26 March 1963

For his part in the £62,599 wages robbery at London Airport last November, Michael John Ball, aged 26, credit agent, of Lambrook Terrace, Fulham, S.W., was sentenced at the Criminal Crown Court yesterday to five years' imprisonment.

Ball had changed his plea from Not Guilty to Guilty of robbing Arthur Henry Gray and John Anthony Doyle of boxes containing £62,500, the property of BOAC, while armed with offensive weapons.

The jury was unable to agree on their verdict in the case of Douglas Gordon Goody, aged 32, hairdresser, of Commondale, Putney, S.W., who had pleaded Not Guilty to the same charge. After the foreman had said there was no prospect of reaching a decision so far as Goody was concerned, Sir Anthony Hawke, the Recorder, discharged the jury from giving a verdict. Goody was then released on £15,000 bail pending a retrial.

Twenty-three

Old Bailey, London, April 1963

Sir Donald Harris, the prosecution counsel, approached the witness, one of the men who had transferred the strong-boxes at the airport. A fresh trial needed a fresh approach. But the security guard who had seen Goody, who had originally picked him out in an identity parade, was now wavering even more than the last time. Sir Donald wondered if he had been nobbled.

'So, is the man who coshed you the man in this court or not?'

'I think so.'

'You *think* so?' He let a sneer play around the word 'think'.

'I can't be sure, sir.'

'Can't be sure?' Sir Donald barked.

The security guard swallowed hard. 'No, sir.'

'Yet you were sure in an identity parade.'

'They had hats on then, sir.'

'Hats?' asked the judge. 'What kind of hats?'

The witness looked over and addressed the judge directly. 'Bowler hats, like they wore in the robbery, Your Honour.'

'I see,' came the reply.

'It so happens we have a bowler hat recovered from Mr Goody's premises,' Sir Donald said affably. 'A steel hat, no less. Is this the type of hat he was wearing?'

'I believe so.'

The heavy metal bowler was passed to the witness, then the judge, and finally displayed to the jury. 'And if you saw him in this hat, do you think your memory might suddenly improve?'

'Objection!'

Sir Donald inclined his head and rephrased. 'Excuse me, do you think it might aid in identification?'

'I am sure it would, sir.'

'Very well. If the defence has no objection, I would like to invite Mr Goody to place this bowler hat on his head.'

'No objection, m'lud.'

Gordon Goody leaned over and took the bowler by the brim, spinning it round and round, as if selecting the correct alignment.

He stared over at the witness, an accommodating smile on his face, while he raised his arms above his head. He brought the hat down to the crown and hesitated, as if pausing for effect. When he let go, the oversized bowler – at least three hat-sizes too large – fell down around his ears, swallowing them and covering his eyes. 'Hold on,' he said. 'The lights have gone out. Someone got a shilling for the meter?'

The courtroom dissolved into laughter and Sir Donald's jowly face sagged further. He could hear the verdict already: Not Guilty.

'Did you see that cocky cunt?' Len Haslam spat beer and phlegm across the bar of Ye Olde Cheshire Cheese pub in Fleet Street.

'You win some, you lose some,' said Billy. 'You know that.'

Len shook his head. 'Not like that. Not like it's some bloody variety show and he's Max bloody Miller.' He thumped the wooden bar top. 'Someone was got at.'

Len was in such an agitated state that the majority of the other early-evening customers – mostly journalists – were giving him a wide berth. He stank of trouble.

He was taking the Not Guilty worse than most, but Billy, too, was disappointed. Not only that, they had missed a trick. Once the verdict had come in, Gordy had walked across to where the chain and lock from the airport gate were sitting and pulled at it. A phony link had given way, showing how the robbers had opened the gate so quickly. He must have rejoined it at the scene and none of the so-called experts who had examined it had spotted that.

All had assumed a key had been used, and the clasp reclosed.

'We got one for it though, didn't we?'

'Mickey Ball? Yeah, right. We lose Wilson then Goody and we're left with him? Nose-pickings.'

Len downed his pint and signalled for another, the anger still twisting his features. 'Let me tell you this, Billy boy.' He tapped the rim of the empty pint pot against the young man's chest. 'One day, I'm going to have that Douglas Gordon Goody by the short and curlies, whatever it takes.'

Twenty-four

London, April 1963

The celebrations kicked off with champagne cocktails at the Ritz. They cost a whopping eleven bob each, but Bruce insisted that they were the best in town and well worth every penny.

'A lump of sugar in the bottom of the glass, one drop of Angostura bitters—'

'Anger what?' asked Buster.

Bruce ignored him. 'A dash of brandy, not too much or you kill the champagne stone fuckin' dead, ice-cold bubbly and an orange peel. Lovely.'

Buster sipped his drink. 'Very nice.' He winked at Bruce. 'If a little poncy.'

The small group, all but one suited and booted, sat in a corner of the bar. Roy thought its green and gold décor could do with refreshing, but then he was drinking orange juice. Judging from his friends' reactions, the cocktails packed quite a kick; you wouldn't worry about the state of the wallpaper after two of them.

They were celebrating first Charlie and then Gordy getting off. The steel bowler had been replaced by the larger one that Buster had slipped the bent bogey in Postman's Park. Somehow, he had switched them in the evidence room at Cannon Row.

Roy watched as Gordy and Charlie toasted each other. Brian, taking his due for his machinations behind the scenes, was there as well as Bruce, Buster and, looking dangerously glamorous next to the Colonel, Janie Riley in a black sheath dress.

'One more and we'll have dinner at Madame Prunier's and a drink at the A and R club. Then maybe catch the Blue Flames at the Flamingo. All on the emergency fund.'

The cash from the robbery had been divvied up so each of the principals got around seven grand each, and what was left was split into two pots, the emergency fund, for things like bail, and the investment fund. A few drinks and a slap-up French meal on St James's plus a few rounds at boxer Freddie Mills' club and watching Georgie Fame would empty out the emergency fund. That left ten thousand in the investment pot. And that had to kick-start the next job.

'I'd like to make a toast,' said Roy. 'Gentlemen?'

The others fell silent.

'A toast to Gordy and Charlie, of course.'

There were some grunts, but nobody raised their glasses. There was more to come.

'And Brian. Nice one.'

Nodding heads all round.

'But we shouldn't forget we lost a soldier.' Roy looked at Bruce, who clearly approved of the military analogy. 'Tonight, we are a man down. Gentlemen, I give you Mickey Ball.'

'Mickey Ball,' the others said in unison, before drinking, all of them thinking of the five years he had pulled down. It was on the high side because he refused to name any accomplices.

Bruce came over and sat down next to Roy. 'You know we'll see him all right, don't you?'

'Yes, I know. Be nice to have something for him to come out to.'

'True.' Bruce thought of the empty coffers. 'Well, while he was inside, Charlie heard about something interesting that might be right up our street. Mickey will get a drink out of it. Absent friends and all that.'

'What sort of thing?'

Bruce leaned in. He hadn't been going to say anything until he learned more, but he felt he should show Roy he was thinking ahead, and of Mickey.

'A train, my son.'

'What kind of train?'

Bruce looked surprised. There was only one sort of train that would interest him. 'The money kind.'

Part Two
CASH & CARRY

Twenty-five

Headley, Surrey, May 1992

My legs wobbled slightly as I opened the gate at the bottom of the path and stepped towards the siege house. Nerves, I guessed. The young copper had turned back; I was on my own. No light shone from within. I wasn't sure what the form was. Did I go up and knock? Wait until the door opened?

In the end I strode up the gravel as if I was just popping round for a chat – which, in a way, I was. Apart from the fact that one of us had a gun and was probably unhinged by recent events. I walked up the three marble steps between the pillars, rang the bell and waited.

An indistinct voice answered. 'It's open.'

I pushed the door and it swung back. The Yale lock

had been clicked into the withdrawn position. It was dark inside.

'Come in and close it behind you,' said the disembodied voice.

I did as I was told.

'Release the catch so it locks.' I had him now. He was sitting at the bottom of the stairs in the cold, black hallway. As my eyes adjusted I could see the shape of Roy James, looking shrunken, no bigger than a child. I could also make out the faint glint of metal. The gun.

I pulled the button down and heard the latch snick into place. 'Hello, Roy. Long time.'

'Yeah. A very long time.'

I rubbed my hands together. 'Christ, it's cold in here.'

'Is it?'

'Yes, it is. You got any heating?'

'The boiler's broken. There's a gas fire in the kitchen.' He gave a loud, self-pitying sniff. 'They coming to get me, Tony?'

I shivered again, not from the chill in the air this time, but from the odd dispassion in the words he spoke. They were colder than the house. 'Eventually, Roy.'

He stood. 'Fancy some tea?'

'I do, Roy. I have biscuits.'

'You go and light the fire. I'll put the kettle on. Matches are on the mantelpiece.'

It was a huge kitchen, stone-flagged, with a fireplace large enough to roast an ox in. Much of it had been boarded up, leaving a triple-element gas fire. While he fussed with the kettle I lit it, almost singeing my eyebrows.

The sole illumination was a 100-watt bulb hanging above the table with no lampshade and it made his skin look waxy and accentuated the shadows under his eyes. Once I had unloaded the biscuits onto a plate, I stood near the now-glowing fire, letting it warm my legs. He sat at the table, the pistol – a Browning automatic – in front of him.

'You remember that winter?' Roy asked. 'Sixty-two and three? That was fuckin' cold.'

It had been beyond cold into absolutely freezing, the sort of temperature that made your very bones ache. Trains shut down, there were power cuts, blizzards. The days and weeks of ice and snow and grim, low skies had been very bad for the car business, and me with a baby on the way. Roy, too, had suffered disappointments as more and more race meets were cancelled. Had he got consistent early practice in, he would have progressed to International Formula Junior more quickly, which would have meant the chance of sponsorship, which meant . . . well, it could have changed everything for him.

'It's all turned to shit, hasn't it, Tony? For me, anyway.' He paused. 'Fuck, I've given that speech too many times. But I was good.'

'We all knew it, Roy.'

'I hope he fuckin' dies.'

'Your father-in-law? No, you don't.'

He took a deep breath. 'No. I don't. But sometimes I think I was happier in nick.'

'Don't say that.'

'Well, you know, in one way it's a lot less aggro. Just do your time. Out here, fuck, it's a battle, isn't it? Every day a battle. I saw Buster the other week on his flower stall. Says the same. Gets him down.'

'Buster always had a black streak,' I said carefully. 'You know that. Things just look bad now. Nobody's died. It's a bit of a domestic that got out of hand, that's all. I think we should go outside, Roy.'

'Why?'

'Before they come inside.'

He suddenly looked up at me, his eyes suspicious. 'Why did you say yes?'

'To coming here?'

'No. That day I came to the showroom and asked you to drive for us on the train job. Why did you say yes?'

It had been April, winter easing its terrible, almost malevolent grip at last. Nobody who lived through those months would ever forget it. Britain was thrust back to the Middle Ages – cold enough for Frost Fairs, almost. I had said yes for the same reason they all had: the money. I had no ready cash, too many cars nobody wanted to buy – the only people doing well in the motor business were the makers of antifreeze and snow chains – and a wife who was pregnant. A wife who suddenly wanted a bigger house and things for the baby. Nice things. Expensive things.

Roy had come asking for two more Jags and I'd said no, not with the Chalk Farm boys looking my way. So he had asked whether, if they sourced the cars from elsewhere, I would take the second wheel. For good money. Buy-you-a-nice-flat kind of cash. Yes, I'd said, even though I knew what had happened to Mickey Ball. Five years.

I told myself I wouldn't ever make that kind of mistake. Yeah, right.

Twenty-six

London, May 1963

Billy Naughton thought the girl would pull away as he came, but she kept her mouth clamped over the end of his cock until the last spasm had passed through it. When he had finished, she stood up and crossed the dingy room to the sink where she spat loudly while the detective buttoned himself up.

They were in a grey cubicle above the Hat Trick on Berwick Street. It was one of those come-on places with a hawker at the door who promised punters no end of delights but, in the end, sent them to a grim basement in Rupert Court where they were fleeced all over again. Its real business happened in the warren of tawdry rooms above it: a bed with a mattress that didn't bear thinking about, a dresser,

196

a sink and a sharp smell that a gallon of Dettol couldn't hide.

The girl rinsed her mouth and looked at him with a disarmingly direct gaze. Billy felt himself blush. She was barely in her twenties, skinny, with a black Helen Shapiro semi-beehive that was in need of fresh backcombing. She spoke with an accent he couldn't place, apart from it originating north of the Watford Gap. 'You been eating spicy food, have you?' she asked, smacking her lips.

Buckling his belt, he checked the front of his trousers for stains. He recalled that the team had been for a curry at some place off Regent Street the night before. When he admitted he had never had an Indian before, Len had made him order vindaloo. Bastard. 'You can tell that?'

She gave a grin that dimpled her cheeks, softening the hard lines around her mouth. 'Look, love, after two years of this I can tell whether the customers prefer fruit gums or fruit pastilles.'

Two years? He thought briefly of all the cocks she had sucked in that time and shuddered. She had offered more, but now he was glad he just went for the oral.

There was a banging on the door and he heard Duke's voice through the thin chipboard and ply. 'You finished, lover boy? Come on, wipe your dick on the curtains and let's be havin' you.'

Billy gave a shrug and reached into his pocket, pulling out a crumpled pound note. The girl arched an eyebrow.

'Blimey, a copper who leaves a tip. Is that a pig with wings I can see?'

He threw it onto the lurid shiny bedspread, then felt he had to say something as he put on his jacket. 'Look, Paulette, wasn't it?'

She nodded. 'Well, Pauline as was. But the punters like a French name. Among other things.'

'I don't normally do that . . . you know.'

'Do what?' She was teasing.

'Take advantage.' It wasn't strictly true. Len Haslam had nobbled him out for a similar 'treat' to drown their sorrows at Gordon Goody slipping through their fingers. It was a 'stag do' after a lock-in at a pub in Bermondsey. There had been blue films and a couple of willing girls high on, appropriately enough, blueys.

'"Course not,' she sneered as she sat on the bed. Its over-worked springs gave a tired groan. He went to continue but she held up a hand to silence him. 'Look, darling, one of your lot comes round for a free gobble every week or so. Happy to oblige. GTP, eh?'

It stood for Good To Police and described anywhere that gave discounts or free samples to the Force. 'But I don't want to listen to any speeches. Some of you coppers, the fresh ones like you, get sucked off and turn into Sir Galahad. Start suggesting I'm special, tell me how they'd like to help. But you are no different from the bastards that run this place, sonny. Or the punters. At least they pay decent.'

She picked up the note and tossed it back at him. He let it flutter to the floor. 'Go on, fuck off, there's probably someone with real cash downstairs waiting for a good time. Types like you ruin the business, you do.'

He opened the door. She had folded her arms across her bony chest. He stepped out into the narrow corridor, leaving the pound note where it had fallen onto the greasy carpet.

Despite the occasional visit to the working girls, Soho wasn't their patch, not really. The Flying Squad left it to Vice and West End Central, who had it carved up like a very fat, filling meat pie. But Duke had a few contacts he liked to keep sweet, ones he had known before they had gravitated like bluebottles to the shit-heap of Old Compton Street and environs. And besides, as he was fond of saying, a free quickie never did anyone any harm. A perk of the job.

In the division of spoils at the Big House they had caught two cases, one a jewellery lift in Hatton Garden, the other a vicious Post Office raid in Islington, and spent the rest of the day flitting between the two locales, achieving very little that Billy could see, except winding up the local coppers and sinking a few pints.

They finished their shift at the Lamb and Flag, where Billy felt a cloud of gloom descend around him as he lit what would be the first of many fags. Duke sensed his mood at once. 'You think we've been wasting our fuckin' time, don't you?'

'Nooo . . .' Billy said, drawing out the word to breaking-point.

'Look, get over the idea that we have to be Sherlock Holmes and Doctor Whatsit,' said Duke, supping his eighth beer of the day. 'Sooner or later it'll fall in our lap, just like that tom of yours earlier.'

Billy smirked along with him, but there was no humour in it. His dick had been itching for the last couple of hours, even though he'd washed it in various scabrous Gents' sinks since the encounter. He was beginning to wonder if you could catch the clap from blowjobs.

'The thing you have to remember about villains is they are either stupid or overconfident or both. Some of them have intelligence, or rather rat-like cunning. A few have imagination, but not many. Which is why they stick to their patches. Territorial, see, like any animals. Yet we think of them as some kind of Raffles. You know, gentlemen thieves backed by a criminal mastermind. Now there's a fuckin' contradiction in terms. Criminal bleedin' masterminds. I tell you, if they were so mastermindy, you think they'd do the same thing over and over again? Do you? Does the team think, eh? I don't fuckin' think so.'

He was shouting now, and Billy looked around. The pub was almost empty, just a few woozy stragglers, and they weren't paying much attention. A buzzer went for last orders, but it didn't register with Duke. Billy knew that coppers were conditioned to ignore such sounds, like the opposite of Pavlov's dogs. At the sound of the bell, act like fuck-all has happened and it's got nothing to do with you. Which, with a flash of a warrant card, it rarely did.

'Well, does the team think?' Duke said, savouring the phrase. 'Not much, Y'Honour. Can't teach an old slag new tricks. Can you, Billy?'

A slyness had crept into Duke's voice and Billy realised he wasn't as pissed as he was pretending to be. He punched the older man on the shoulder. 'You cunt.'

Duke took that as a compliment and flashed his nicotine-stained teeth. 'You know this place used to be called the Bucket of Blood? Because of all the bare-knuckle fights outside. Back in . . .'

But Billy wasn't having any of that old flannel. 'Spare me the history lesson, Len. There'll be more blood on the floor if you don't tell me what you picked up.'

Duke reached into his pocket and took out a small square of paper which he unfolded and laid on the bar towel in front of them. There were two registration numbers on it. 'Bingo,' he said. 'All the three point fours, nickety-nick.'

Billy picked up the scrap and stared at it. 'What you on about?'

'Last weekend, just gone. Two Jags go missing within half a day of each other. And not any old Jags. Three point fours again. What does that tell you?'

Billy didn't need to think too hard. 'The Comet House boys?'

'Precisely. The City gents. Old fuckin' habits, see? Jaguar three point fours. The motor of choice for the discerning wheel-man everywhere.' His eyes were suddenly sober, the glassy stare replaced by something altogether more steely. 'They took the piss, didn't they? So now we take a good, long look at Roy James, Buster Edwards and especially Gordon "Big Head" Goody, and this time we catch them doing a bit more than scratching their bollocks.' He pointed at Billy's empty glass. 'Fancy another, son?'

Twenty-seven

London, May 1963

Tony's stomach was burning as he parked the Hillman in a side street lined with tall Edwardian houses, a ten-minute walk from the lock-ups at Lee where Jimmy White had stashed the two Jaguars. The idea was to move them closer to the job, which was scheduled for that night. A train. Robbing a bleeding train. It was like the Wild West, with Bruce Reynolds as Cheyenne Bodie. No, he was a good guy. Paladin, that was the bloke, a gunfighter with a dark streak in him. *Have Gun, Will Travel* it said on his calling card. Except Bruce said no guns. Using a shooter was like *Double Your Money*, he had told them, only here it was called *Double Your Jolt*.

Marie had sensed there was something up. She had never

stopped asking questions. *Where are you going? What are you doing? Why are you staying the night? Is it a woman?*

No, it's not a woman. Well, she believed that. Because it was the truth. If only. No woman would churn his insides like this. His cover story – alibi, he supposed – was that he was going to buy a Ford Zodiac and a Zephyr in Southampton and would be staying over before driving one of them back, with his new pal Jimmy White chauffeuring the second. (Who the hell is Jimmy White? she had asked.) He had already ordered them to be delivered by low-loader, so should she check in the showroom over the next few weeks, they would be there. He would probably sell them, too. *Z-Cars* had just swapped their Ford Consuls for the newer models, and sales had received a boost.

He walked quickly down towards the parade of shops and two pubs – the Old Tiger's Head and the New Tiger's Head – that faced off against each other and formed the heart of Lee, which for most people was little more than a cross-roads on the A20 to Lewisham. He glanced at the pubs, suddenly thirsty, but kept his head down and continued across the lights.

Tony lit a cigarette as he went. He'd started smoking more, a pack a day. Marie could smell it on him and complained that he was stinking the flat out, even though he never lit up indoors. It was hormones that made her hysterical, he supposed. Everything for the good of the baby. Well, why did she think he was doing this?

And then those strange words when he had left. *'Make sure it's worth our while, Tony.'*

He could see Jimmy up ahead, waiting for him, also smoking but leaning against a lamp-post, loose and relaxed. An old pro, Bruce had said. Best key-man in London. He raised a hand as he recognised Tony, who tossed his cigarette away. Before he reached him, Jimmy detached himself from his post and walked up the track that led to the lockups, where the Jags were stored.

Tony watched Jimmy's back as he strode down the lane between the houses and turned left towards the row of garages, disappearing from view. If Tony took one step onto the rough driveway, he was committed. He could just walk on now if he wanted. Say the Old Bill had spotted him and he'd become spooked. Say his bowels had turned to liquid. Say he had a feeling Marie needed him. Say anything.

Make sure it's worth our while.

She knew. Marie knew he was up to no good, as she used to say, and she didn't care. Just as long as the risk was worth the reward. Well, Bruce was talking fifteen, twenty each. They could live in Hampstead for that.

Jimmy's head reappeared, followed by an arm beckoning him on, a gesture ripe with impatience. They had two ringed Jags to deliver to Bruce & Co for their tickle. A train, so he had heard. But he was just a delivery boy, Tony told himself. Drop off the Jaguars and you're done. Take the fee and walk away. Tony realised he had stopped walking, his legs suddenly leaden. Jimmy waved at him again.

Tony sniffed nervously and took his first, heavy step on the road to robbery.

The observation van, a scruffy old Ford, stank of long-eaten Wimpys, greasy chips, sweat and ripe farts. It was a potent combination that always resisted even the steam hose deployed at the end of a particularly long stint.

The tatty Ford had been moved into position three days ago, when Roy James had been spotted at a disused bus garage in South London. Through the ventilation grills on the side, a policeman with binoculars could keep a log of the comings and goings at the depot.

That morning it was all comings. Bruce Reynolds – in some flash motor as always, this time one of the new Lotus Cortinas – Roy James, Buster Edwards and three men that Duke didn't recognise. No Goody or Wilson, which was disappointing. But something was definitely up. There was no way that lot was thinking of going into the public transport business. They had already brought in a Bedford van, sliding back the big main doors to allow it in, and then slamming them shut again. Duke could only imagine what was inside, but he'd wager his arse-hole it involved pickaxe handles and masks or something similar.

A couple of streets away were two Flying Squad drivers

with two detectives, ready to either move in or follow, depending on what Duke decided.

'I need a piss,' said Billy Naughton.

'Go in that bucket.'

'I can get out quietly.'

'Fuck off. You'll be spotted. Who's to say they're not clocking us from the top floor now.' He moved the binoculars up to the shattered panes of the metal Crittall windows and refocused them. There was no movement, but that didn't signify anything. 'You can go out when you need a shit. Before that, use the bucket. Hold up.'

Billy moved close to Duke, but he couldn't see much through the grill. 'What is it?'

'Someone's coming out.'

The small access door cut within the larger gates opened and Bruce Reynolds stepped through into the feeble sunlight. Even so, Duke could see him squint at the unaccustomed glare. Must be dark within the old garage, Duke figured. Reynolds glanced at his watch – some fuck-off Swiss one, Duke didn't doubt – then looked right and left. He's waiting for someone, thought Duke. It's going down. He stared at the radio, the one he could use to call in reinforcements. Did they break it up now, or try and catch them red-handed?

He heard the sonorous ringing of the bucket as Billy relieved himself.

'Here, keep the bloody noise down, will you? It's like Big Ben going off.'

'Sorry. Christ, I needed that.'

Duke wrinkled his nose. 'Put the cover on it, will you?' There was another clang as Billy dropped the tea tray that acted as a lid onto the receptacle. 'Quietly!'

'Let's have a look.'

Len handed the bins over to Billy, and helped himself to some stewed tea from the Thermos, trying to ignore the smell of hot piss still wafting from the bucket, despite its lid.

So, Duke continued to muse, do we go in whenever the consignment or vehicle Reynolds is waiting for arrives, or see what develops? Jam today or tomorrow? There were times when he wished they had a bloody Whirlybird, a heli-copter to track the buggers from the air.

'He's gone back in, Len,' said Billy.

'How did he look?'

'Very smart. Nice suit.'

Duke sighed. 'His face, you prick. What was his expression?'

Billy smirked to let him know he'd been pulling his plonker. 'Didn't give much away. Concerned, maybe.'

'Like he was expecting something?'

'Yeah.'

Charlie Wilson and Gordon Goody, perhaps. That would be a result. Duke picked up the radio. It was time to wake up the others. However it went down, here or at some as-yet-unknown tickle, Bruce Reynolds and his mates were going to be spending some time at a not-so-friendly nick that day.

Opportunity fuckin' Knocks, he thought, and the clapometer swings to 100 per cent.

Jimmy White waited until Tony caught up with him. He put out his hand and they shook. 'All right?'

'Yeah,' replied Tony, with a confidence he didn't feel.

'Where you parked?'

'Effingham Road.'

'Good. OK, they are in the end ones,' he said, indicating along the row of multi-coloured, up-and-over metal doors. Jimmy gave Tony a sidelong glance, something in the new boy's demeanour unsettling him. 'You sure you are all right?'

Tony shrugged. 'You know . . .'

Jimmy put a hand on his shoulder. 'Yeah, I know. Be all right. You're with the big boys now.'

'Don't worry about me, I'll do my bit.'

'Sure. Here. Take the green one.' Jimmy handed over a set of keys with a Jaguar leather fob, the metal disc featuring a close-up of the snarling cat. Tony took them, hoping Jimmy wouldn't see how sweaty his palms were.

'And this is for the garage. Number thirty-one. The one on the right.' He produced a second set of keys and tossed them to Tony.

They lined up in front of their respective metal doors, bent down and turned the keys in the locks, then twisted the handles. 'One, two, three,' said Jimmy, as if they were waiters about to lift their cloches in unison.

There was a rattle and rumble as the concrete counter-weights slid down their runners, and the doors yawned open, to reveal the space within. And that was all there was. Space. No Jaguars. Just the empty, oil-stained cement floors where they had once stood.

Tony turned to Jimmy, open-mouthed, a baffled shock mixed with a cowardly streak of relief. White had already seen the hole in the roof where the robbers had gained initial access and discovered the cars. As a key-man, he knew how easy it was to start a Jag, almost as simple as picking and then resetting the locks in the garage doors' handles.

'They've gone,' said Tony.

Jimmy's face darkened, his lips twisting, but then, unexpectedly, he laughed. It was a coarse, frightening sound, although there might have been a hint of admiration in there as he shook his head in amazement. 'The thievin' bastards.'

Twenty-eight

New Scotland Yard, May 1963

Frank Williams, Ernie Millen's deputy, barely glanced at the reports on his desk before he looked up at Duke and Billy. He ran a hand over his thinning hair, his expression like someone sucking on a lemon. 'Fuckin' shambles,' he said quietly. 'A right fuckin' shambles.'

Len Haslam shifted his weight from leg to leg uncomfortably. 'We were sure they were at it . . .'

Williams's face closed like a fist. 'Of course they were bloody at it. But *what* were they at, Lennie boy?'

Duke shrugged. Williams reached over and took a sip of his tea. 'You are lucky Ernie or Hatherill haven't seen this, or they'd be having you back on the Big Hats. You know that, don't you?' No response was required.

Williams leaned back in his chair and put his hands behind his head. His jacket flapped open to reveal a spreading gut – one of the hazards of the job at his level; there was desk work and there was boozer time and little in between. Frank still believed the best way to catch villains was to mix it up with them, to spend time in the spielers and drinking clubs. He knew Ernie Millen distrusted this method of thief-taking, but he wasn't changing it now, not after all these years. He had too many valuable contacts.

'I'm not sure I shouldn't move young Billy here to the guidance of someone with more of a future in the Squad.'

Both junior officers remained mute. They jumped when Williams came forward with a crash. 'The thing is, it was Surrey.'

'What was?' asked Len.

'Whatever your lads were up to. Down Surrey way. No idea what. Not yet.'

Williams was enjoying this, thought Duke, the smug bastard. He still had a good network of snouts out there, and guarded them like an attack dog.

He let his revelation – that he was one step ahead of Duke – hang in the air while he fixed himself a cigarette. He didn't offer them around.

'But what we do know is that Charlie Wilson is running around like a bull with its bollocks in a vice.'

'Wilson?' asked Billy. 'We didn't see him.'

'No. As I said, down Surrey way, apparently,' Williams

told them, with all the deliberation of a primary school teacher. 'He was at the business end – unlike you two. Now, Charlie is knocking heads together to try and find out who might have come into the possession of two nice three point four Jags, and when he finds them, he's going to fuck them in the ear then take them out on one of the Bovril boats and dump them in the North Sea.'

Bovril boats were the slurry ships that sailed from Beckton, full of London's human waste, reduced to a thick oil-like liquid. It was released somewhere away from the English coast, in designated dumping grounds. Rumour had it that, for a consideration, some of the crews wouldn't mind taking a little extra waste – suitably weighted – and disposing of it.

'I don't get it,' said Billy.

Now, for the first time Frank Williams smiled, creasing his face into deep furrows, and Len Haslam allowed himself a little smirk.

'It means,' Duke said to his young apprentice, 'that some cheeky fuckers went and half-inched the motors our lads had nicked to do their job in Surrey.' Now he began to laugh. 'Which is why Reynolds was standing there looking like someone who'd just put his finger through the lavatory paper.'

Williams chortled at that.

'Fuck me,' said Len, 'what I wouldn't have given to see the faces on the boys who discovered someone had robbed the robbers.'

'Priceless,' Williams agreed. 'Absolutely priceless.' Then his face resumed its previous seriousness. 'But look, lads, it's Keystone Cops and Ealing bloody Comedies all round, isn't it? Meanwhile, N Division is wondering what happened to their support from the Yard. We are not the Don't Give A Flying Fuck Squad. I know you were pissed off about the airport fiasco. Who wasn't?' He picked up a pencil and pointed it at each in turn. 'Let it go. They'll pop up again. They're thieves. Stand on me, Len, we haven't heard the last of them. All right?'

'Yes, skipper,' said Duke.

'All right, then.' Williams seemed to relax a little. 'Then fuck off and catch me some real villains.'

Bruce Reynolds downed the last of his pint and said quietly, 'Leave it out, Charlie.'

Charlie Wilson ground his teeth at the thought of leaving anything out. 'We look like cunts.'

'We'll live. Two more here, love.' They were in the Angelsey Arms in Chelsea, a nice boozer with a dartboard and well-kept beer. It was true there were some sniggers when the story got out, but Bruce didn't mind. It was just one more tall story that would get taller over the years. Charlie, however, and to a lesser extent Buster and Gordy, had taken it as a personal affront. But Bruce knew the cars were fair game, as long as it was some firm he didn't know. Now if it had been mates, *then* he'd be angry. But he was pretty sure it wasn't. So, like a colonel after a skirmish that had gone badly, he was ready to regroup his men and plan the next part of the campaign.

Bruce paid for the fresh pints and waited till the young girl in the scandalously short skirt moved away from their section of the bar. 'It's a shame,' he said. 'It was a nice one.' It had been a train from Bournemouth, fingered by a BR porter, with money unloaded at Weybridge. Roy had been looking forward to it because the getaway route took in part of the old Brooklands circuit, spiritual home of the monied toffs known as the Bentley Boys. The idea of taking a hot Jag stuffed with money round there had tickled him.

It had been a simple plan: wait till the cash bags were unloaded, then use numbers and brute force to overwhelm the police and security guards and have it away in the 3.4s.

'Do you believe in fate, Charlie?'

Charlie shrugged. 'I know what fate's got in store for those monkeys who nicked the cars if I ever find them.'

'I'm sure.' Bruce raised his glass to a DS at the far end of the bar and indicated to the barmaid that the cosspot's drink was on him. Neutral ground, after all. 'But I mean, you know, that some things are pre-ordained. Meant to be. We should have been able to live off Heathrow for years, shouldn't we?' Charlie nodded. 'And Weybridge looked like a steal.'

Charlie pursed his lips. 'It still could be.'

'Nah. It's gone.' Bruce knew there was too much specu-lation out there, too many whispers about what the Jags had been for. He doubted anyone could pinpoint the exact job, but he would steer clear of Surrey for the foreseeable future. And Jaguars. 'Fate, see? Wasn't written in the stars.'

Charlie spluttered into his pint. 'What are you now? Nostra-fuckin'-damus?'

Bruce was impressed that Charlie knew who Nostradamus was, but let it pass. 'It's almost like we were waiting for the real one, the genuine article.' He indicated the dartboard with his glass. 'Game of arrows?'

Charlie collected two pouches of darts from behind the bar and moved over to the corner. Bruce rubbed the board clean and chalked 301 at the top of two columns. 'Double to start.'

Charlie weighed the Unicorn darts in his hand and fussed with the flights, licking finger and thumb and smoothing them out. Then he stepped up and threw a double top.

'Bollocks,' said Bruce. But Charlie's next two throws only added forty-one. He wrote in the opening score and took his place at the line.

'Thing is, Gordy and Brian have come with something else. Something better.'

'What's that?' Charlie wasn't keen on Brian Field, the bent solicitor. Oh, he had his uses all right, but at the other end of the business, some way down the line, when it came to briefs and bail. He didn't like the idea of him becoming active in the actual thievery.

Bruce's first effort went home into the fibre of the board with a satisfying thunk. 'Double eighteen.'

'Yeah, yeah. What's better?'

The jukebox kicked into life and Bruce frowned over at the greaser type who had fed money into the machine. Leather jacket, enough oil on his hair to run a fair-sized chippy and stiletto-thin winkle pickers. It was a style rapidly going out of fashion, replaced by something neater, smarter, of which Bruce approved. He heard the whirr of the Wurlitzer's mechanism. What had the kid selected? Looking at him, he was likely to be a Gene Vincent or Johnny Kidd and the Pirates boy.

The Beatles came from the speakers – 'Ask Me Why', the B-side of 'Please Please Me'. Bruce relaxed; he quite liked the group. They might be gobby Scousers with long hair, but they were just a bunch of working-class kids trying to make some money. Mind you, they had started using Dougie Millings, his and Charlie's favourite tailor, and now you couldn't get into the shop for screaming kids or pop groups wanting to get the Beatles look. They would have to move on again.

He threw a triple twenty and stepped to one side to give himself a decent line of sight.

'So what is it?' asked Charlie once more. 'What's better?'

Bruce winked at him, and Charlie could sense his excitement. He had already left Weybridge behind. That's why he didn't give a toss about the Jags and who took them.

They were history. Bruce felt it was no good letting a slight fester or harbouring a grudge if it got in the way of future business. Charlie, he knew, didn't let go of an insult quite so easily. Bruce had to refocus him.

'I don't know what, exactly.' Bruce hesitated with his last dart poised in mid-air. 'But Gordy said how much.' He let fly. 'There you go. One hundred and eighty.'

'Bruce,' snapped Charlie. 'What's the griff? How fucking much?'

The Colonel dangled the same bait that had been used to snare his interest. He was guessing until he met the inside man up at Finsbury Park with Gordy and Brian Field, but it was a nice, round juicy plum to dangle in front of Charlie. 'Big money.'

'How big?'

'How does a full million quid sound?'

'Big.' Charlie thought for a minute, imagining the noise one million pounds' worth of fivers might make. He gave a dreamy smile. 'Big like bleedin' Beethoven.'

'So forget about the Jags?'

Charlie gathered up the glasses for a refill. 'What Jags?'

'You can call me Jock. That'll do for now. Not even Brian Field or the man you were introduced to as Mark know my real name, so let's leave it like that, eh, Mr Reynolds? Yes, a tea would be lovely, thank you. One sugar.

'Now, what I am proposing concerns the Night Mail from

218

Glasgow to Euston. You know that film? And the poem? The one about the Night Mail, crossing the border and bringing the cheque and the postal order? W.H. Auden. Well, gentlemen, the train doesn't always bring cheques and postal orders. It also carries good old-fashioned money, of the paper kind. If banks in Scotland have surplus cash, then it is parcelled up and sent to London in an HVP. That's a High Value Packet carriage. It's a separate section of a TPO – a Travelling Post Office – locked and secured from inside. Five or six workers are in there, sorting the mail. In the sacks is the excess cash from the banks plus there's worn notes to be destroyed, too. Untraceable notes. How much in all? Well, I'll come to that.

'The thing is, gentlemen, the Night Mail has been running for one hundred years, give or take, and nobody has ever even tried a blag. Not once and why not? Well, there are lots of coppers at every station along the route, you see – at Glasgow, at Euston and all six or seven stops in between. Yes, it picks up as it travels towards London, so the nearer to Euston it gets the more cash there is on board. The bags are piled on platforms, but there is always a Transport Police guard, so the stations are too risky. You have to stop the train between them. How isn't my problem. The service runs both ways, but I would go for the "up", the one bringing cash down here to the central banks.

'The other problem you have is that, although there is only a handful of staff on the HVP, there might be eighty other sorters on that train, sorting those letters for the penni-less and the stinking rich, as the poet had it. Now I know you lot are a bit handy, but eighty is a big opposition. You have to think of that. I can see what you want to know. I do believe Mr Field here mentioned a sum of one million. That's a minimum. And I have to say that if that is the case, my associates and I want a hundred thousand pounds. But, choose the right day, just after a Bank Holiday when money has backed up in the system, for instance, and it could be a lot more. But if it is more, my amount increases propor-tionally. I know I can trust Mr Field to look after that side for me. There will also need to be something for Mark, who was instrumental in forming this plan and introducing me to Brian. So, shall we say forty for Mark? And we have some expenses of our own.

'One more thing. British Rail has ordered three new HVPs for the Glasgow service. They are steel-lined, triple-locked, like mobile safes. You would have to cut into them. Now, they are due into service later this year. So, choose a Bank Holiday – a Scottish Bank Holiday, mind. And you'd better look carefully at your Letts Desk Diary, and do it sooner rather than later, before these Wells Fargo jobs come on line.

'Well, that is the proposition. I appreciate you would like to discuss this matter further. Perhaps you'll let me know your decision within the week? Perfect. Nice meeting you, gentlemen.'

Twenty-nine

Glasgow Central station, May 1963

Spring had yet to make much of a mark on Glasgow and, as he felt a creeping dampness invade his bones, Buster Edwards cursed that he had drawn the short straw of coming north. Bruce had given him detailed instructions, and after a few drinks in the station bar, he had spent the last half-hour acting like any commuter waiting for his stopping service home, pacing up and down to keep warm. The mail train had been there as he had been told to expect, platform 6. He had watched stacks of mailbags being transported onto the platform by red Post Office vans and unloaded under the beady gaze of uniformed policemen. A team of porters then conveyed them, by trolley, to the appropriate carriages. He couldn't actually see the HVP, thanks to the curve of the track obscuring the front portion of the train, but certainly some sacks – the bright crimson ones – were treated with more respect than others.

Now the doors had been slammed, the porters dispersed and the transport cozzers were standing, hands folded, eyes on their watches and their hopes on an early-evening pint. Which didn't sound too bad to Buster. He was booked on the sleeper back down south, which gave him a couple of hours to kill in the city.

The train gave a single powerful jerk, there was a synchronised clanking as couplings took up the slack, and the Night Mail moved forward, taking its haul of letters, postcards, coupons and cash to London. *Cash*. Bruce hadn't said how much, but those initials, HVP, caused Buster's heart to flutter and his palms to sweat. There were a lot of readies in this one, he could feel it, smell it. He knew people who had been stopping trains on the Brighton line – Roger Cordrey, Bobby Welch from the Elephant – netting a few good grand at a time. But this was different, this was clearly big money. Life-changing money. That had been promised at Weybridge, but he had never believed in that the way he did in this.

Buster Edwards rewrapped the scarf around his neck as he watched the rear lights of the Travelling Post Office disappear around the curved track of Central station.

Godspeed, my son, he thought. For tonight, anyway.

*   *   *

At Euston, two hours later, Roy James watched the West Coast Postal, a second Night Mail, again with an HVP as the second coach, prepare to slide out of number 3 platform and head north. Sorters had been arriving for the best part of ninety minutes, and work had already begun inside each carriage, placing letters and parcels in the appropriate pigeonholes. There were no passengers. Apart from the train crew, every man aboard was a Post Office employee.

Roy, situated at the end of platforms 1 and 2, was loaded down with the railway books he had bought at Euston's Collector's Corner and was scribbling in a notebook. His platform ticket had permitted him to walk right out adjacent to the Travelling Post Office, enabling him to examine the great brute of a slab-faced loco, the parcel carriage and, behind that, the HVP. He scribbled down the number on the engine: D326/40126.

'English Electric Class Forty,' said the voice over his shoulder.

'What?'

It was a young lad, sixteen or seventeen, but a good head taller than Roy. A good-looking boy, marred by his skin: his face was positively ablaze with spots, mini-volcanoes all, some already erupted. He was wearing a school blazer, scarf and grey flannel trousers. The boy held up his own notebook, filled with dense writing in different coloured inks. 'You should do columns. Date. Station. Platform. Engine Type. Number. Makes it easier.'

223

Roy smiled at him. 'Yeah, thanks. I'm new to all this. I mean, I used to do it when I was your age but I'm out of practice.'

'You'll get ribbed for it. Specially a grown-up. People will take the mickey.'

'That what your mates do?'

'Sometimes.'

'Fuck 'em.'

The lad grinned. 'Yeah. Fuck 'em.' He said it as if he was trying the obscenity for the first time. It can't be easy, thought Roy. Blighted by acne and out trainspotting, when he should be chasing girls. He pointed at the pages in the lad's book. 'What do the colours mean?'

'Steam, diesel or electric,' he replied. 'I'll show you.'

The sudden burst of enthusiasm, and the wild look in the lad's eyes at finding a fellow spotter, unnerved Roy, and he recalled Bruce's warning about not getting yourself noticed. 'No – no, thanks,' he said hastily. 'I only do diesel, me.'

'Diesel?' The kid's blotchy face twisted with scorn. 'That's really boring. A lot of them don't even have names.'

'Yeah, well,' said Roy with a shrug, shuffling away. 'Takes all sorts, eh?'

Jimmy White poured a cup of Bovril and passed it to Tony Fortune, who was behind the wheel of a Vauxhall Velox, sitting in the overflow parking area just off Mill Road.

This asphalted area was higher than the main car park, affording them a better view of the activities on some of the over-lit platforms of Rugby railway station. Unfortunately, most of the activity seemed to be happening beneath the cantilevered canopies that blocked their view. Still, they weren't worried about that.

It was coming up to two o'clock in the morning, stars pin-sharp in a clear sky, and both men were sleepy. Jimmy was supposed to do this by himself, but he had felt sorry for Tony after the Jag foul-up. He had expected a decent drink and what did he get? An empty garage. And, apparently, an earful from his missus about missing paydays.

Jimmy had cleared bringing Tony along with Bruce, of course, and Bruce had said OK. They might still need a driver for the job he had in mind, and Roy had told him that Tony could handle a motor.

'Thanks,' said Tony as he took the Bovril.

Jimmy poured himself a second cup. He held it in both hands and blew across the surface. 'Love this stuff. Bloody Army marches on it. Well, the Paras do. You all right?'

Tony had only been lending half an ear. He felt more at ease with Jimmy than he did many of the others. Certainly more than Gordy and Charlie. With them, he felt that the least wrong word would land him a right hook or worse. There was always an air of crackling tension about them, as if an electrical storm could break out at any moment. 'What? Yeah. Just thinking. You don't want to buy a Hillman Husky, do you?'

Jimmy laughed. 'Nah. I like Land Rovers, me. They go on for ever.'

'Husky's got a heater.'

'You poof,' chuckled White. 'A heater? Only sissies need a heater in their car. You'll be telling me it has suspension next.'

'And you don't need an airfield to turn it round in.'

'Greengrocer's car,' sneered Jimmy. 'Not your sort, I would have thought.'

'Brother-in-law's,' Tony admitted.

'Ah.'

Marie had beseeched him – there was no other word – to take the Hillman Husky off her brother, Geoff, who was boracic. He'd done so, and paid him cash, over the odds. Now it was stuck at the back of the showroom, embarrassing him. 'I got myself right stitched up. Wife's up the duff, you see. Hard to say no to her.'

'Congratulations. First one?' Tony nodded. That explained why she had been disappointed in him, Jimmy thought. Broody women have big plans. 'This'll come in handy then.'

'What will?'

'The tickle. This train thing, whatever it is.'

Bruce had been very tight-lipped, insisting this was simply a reconnaissance mission, just to confirm certain facts. They were not to let their minds run away with them.

'I don't know if I'm in yet, do I? I mean, if they need a driver. And it's not really my thing.'

'What isn't?'

'Robbery with violence, I think they call it.'

Jimmy chortled. 'Nor me, son. This is not going to be just some smash and grab. I don't like the rough stuff either.'

Tony was surprised. Jimmy had a reputation. 'You were a Para.'

'We're not all Sergeant bloody Hurricane. We had a bit of finesse. So does Bruce. I wouldn't be here if I thought we was just the heavy mob. Hold up.'

They heard the whistle of an approaching train and squinted into darkness broken only by what appeared to be a random pattern of red and green lights. The powerful loco of the Night Mail appeared, its twin beams glaring like jaundiced eyes, and above them the duller glow of the tripartite screen. Tony knew people were sentimental about steam, but he had to admire the monstrous brutality of the diesel that shouldered its way under the station lamps and disappeared from view. It was all solid muscle and attitude, like a steel-clad bull terrier.

They wound the Vauxhall's windows down and listened. The TPO sat, obscured by the station buildings and roof, its engine thrumming at idle, for another ten minutes. Then came a coarse whistle, the low grunt of the engine taking the strain, and the money train pulled out. Next stop, Euston.

Jimmy White slapped Tony's thigh, making him jump. 'Best go out and buy that baby the biggest fuckin' cot you can find. If I know Bruce, and he's thinkin' what I *think* he's thinkin' – then we're in the money. Fortune by name . . .'

Tony smiled as if he hadn't heard that one.

Jimmy was still whistling the tune 'We're in the Money' when they pulled out of the car park and headed back to London on empty roads, each lost in their own thoughts of untold riches.

Thirty

South-east England, June 1963

It seemed appropriate for Bruce to catch the train down to Brighton, rather than take the Lotus. It meant breakfast in one of the Pullman carriages, after all, and they had the place nearly to themselves, as most morning traffic was 'up' to the city. He had taken Janie Riley along, now dressed as a prosperous middle-class housewife in twin-set and pillbox hat. He would park her at the Grand or let her do some shopping while he met the Flowerpot Man. Bruce didn't like to bring in outsiders, but the more he thought about it, the more he needed particular expertise. After all, this was a moving target. He had heard – from Buster – that the Flowerpot Man could take care of that. Buster had told him about the train jobs on the South Coast Line, engineered by a pretty solid team. Small beer, Buster had said, but the principle was sound.

'Looks like summer is finally here,' said Janie, making conversation with the white-jacketed steward as he fussed around them with the tea and toast.

'About time, miss.'

Bruce glanced out of the window. London had fallen away and Janie was right, the countryside was bathed in a diffuse pale yellow and the sheep were sunbathing rather than shivering. The winter and spluttering spring had played havoc with the country. The football league was still in disarray, with dozens of postponed matches yet to be played, and race cards had been scratched for weeks on end. It had been the coldest year since 1740, so the *Express* said. Bruce didn't know about that, but he remembered the one of 1947 – the bombsites, suddenly pretty under the thick crust of snow, but even more dangerous than before. His mate Jimmy Standing had jumped into what looked like a harmless snowdrift and fallen into one of the firefighters' emergency water tanks from the Blitz and broken his leg. Bruce still remembered the sight of the red-streaked bone poking through flesh and the sound of the poor sod's whimpering.

'Bruce.' Janie brought him back to the attentions of the steward. 'Full breakfast?'

Bruce could still feel an echo of the queasiness that the wound had brought on. 'Bacon, sausage, scrambled eggs,' he said. 'Hold the tomatoes and black pudding.'

'Very good, sir.'

Janie concentrated on lighting a cigarette and Bruce went back to thinking about trains. The team so far was himself, Charlie, Gordy, Buster and Roy. Good men all, but just not enough. He would add Jimmy White to that and, for sheer muscle, Tommy Wisbey. Old Tommy would make both Frank Nitti and Elliot Ness shit their pants. Bruce loved the TV series *The Untouchables*, and often wondered if he should give the gang a moniker like that. That, and a sound-track by Nelson Riddle. Although he already had a tune for the job. Of late he had been playing Charles Mingus's *Ah Um* and the track 'Boogie Stop Shuffle'. Just the right tempo for a great heist sequence with sudden dramatic stabs from the horns and the wah-wah of plunged trumpets. He could see the title sequence, designed by the guy who did *Anatomy of a Murder* or John Cassavetes's *Johnny Staccato*.

That train of thought took him from Waldo's, the Greenwich Village jazz club that featured in the Cassavetes TV series, to Bobby Welch. Bobby also ran a drinking club, but it was not as classy as Waldo's, being an after-hours dive popular with the better kind of toms and their punters – and Bobby himself was always short of cash, being the type of gambler that bookies put out bunting for. Buster said he had done some very handy work with the Flowerpot Man on this very line. If Bruce brought in Bobby and Jim Hussey – a painter and decorator with a sideline in being very handy in a ruck – then he would have a formidable group of intimidators in

Gordy, Bobby, Tommy and the two Jims. That was real muscle power. It was spreading the net wider than he liked by going beyond the Comet House team, but even Charles Atlas would think twice about kicking sand in those faces. *The Intimidators.* Was that a suitable name? It was for the heavy section of the firm, at least. Bruce chuckled to himself.

'Bruce?' Janie finished her cigarette with a deep inhalation and let the smoke stream from the side of her mouth. 'I have something to ask you.'

Bruce leaned back as the breakfast arrived and was placed before him. 'What's that, luv?'

Janie fixed him with a very direct stare, in case he should drift off again. She stubbed out the cigarette in the Brighton Belle ashtray and switched on a blinder of a smile. 'I wondered if you would talk to a friend of mine. As a favour.'

Bruce didn't like the sound of that. Favours could lead to all sorts of trouble. 'What kind of friend?'

The Queen and Artichoke was close to Victoria Park in Bethnal Green. A grubby little boozer, known to its regulars as the Q&A, it had an unusual mix of clientèle, comprising East End locals and students from the hostels on Victoria Road which were part of the Sir John Cass Foundation. The two groups had co-existed well enough in a kind of uneasy truce until recently, when the students had become more self-consciously bohemian, or 'beatnicky' as Frank, the Q&A's guv'nor, preferred to call them.

Sunday lunchtime though was for the fellas only, with arty types told to drink elsewhere. There was sometimes a stripper, but always cockles and crisps on the bar and Marion, the guv'nor's missus, pulling pints. Marion Castle was a Diana Dors type, an ex-beauty queen (albeit from Butlin's in Clacton), who kept the boys' attention with her Jayne Mansfield-like stretch tops.

Charlie Wilson arrived a little after one, and the Q&A was already soupy with cigarette smoke. He pushed his way to the bar and helped himself to snacks. Marion fetched him a mild and bitter and as he paid her he said, 'Frank in?'

Marion took a long, hard look at him and he knew she was weighing up whether he was Old Bill. The turned-up corner of her scarlet lips suggested she was reaching that conclusion.

'Charlie Wilson,' he answered. 'Friend of Andy Turner.'

Marion's face relaxed. She pulled one more pint and went out back. Frank appeared when Charlie was halfway through his drink. He was a squat, red-faced little fucker who only came up to Marion's shoulders. Both cheeks sported a flower of broken capillaries and one eye was AWOL, darting all over the shop. He could only assume he provided for Marion in departments other than looks.

His wife nodded over to indicate Charlie, and Frank positioned himself behind the pumps. 'Charlie, is it?'

'Yeah.' They shook hands. 'Andy said I could have a word.'

'Did he?'

'Said you could get me a motor.'

Frank blew his florid cheeks out. This wasn't the time or the place. 'It's fuckin' Sunday, mate. Day of rest.'

Charlie took a sup of his pint. 'No rest for the wicked.'

'Yeah, well, there is for this one.' Frank turned to go. Charlie looked at the clock. It was quarter past. He reached over and grabbed the landlord's shirtsleeve. There was a tearing sound from the shoulder and the man swore.

'Don't go, Frank,' Charlie beseeched him. 'You'll miss the show.'

The landlord glanced over at the stage, but the girl was still sitting at the table next to it, talking to her minder.

'Not that one.'

Charlie was aware of the character next to him taking an interest in what was occurring, but ignored him. The landlord pulled away. 'What the fuck is your game?'

'That your Jaguar in the street?'

Frank's brow furrowed like a ploughed field. 'Yeah—'

The Q&A's frame shook as the timer detonated the gelignite, which had been placed inside condoms, in a cut-open Duckhams tin filled with petrol. Every face turned liverish as a wall of yellow flame engulfed the Jaguar parked outside and the frosted window cracked with the sound of a whip snapping. There was a second blast as the petrol tank ignited and now all those nearest the street stampeded away as the inferno pumped heat through glass and brick into the pub.

Marion screamed, a noise that threatened to take out the rest of the windows.

Frank looked open-mouthed at Charlie. Then he pointed a loaded finger at him. 'You are dead, mate. You don't know who you are messin' with.'

As Frank leaned forward, his face like a bulldog with a boot up its arse, Charlie punched him. Then, just to be certain, he smacked the bloke next to him who had taken far too great an interest in his bit of business. The man staggered back, giving Charlie a bit of space to contemplate his predicament.

There was a dull thud that shook the floorboards under his feet and a long whooshing sound outside as the interior of the car began to burn. The pub's customers were recovering from their shock now, and he felt all eyes turn towards him. Most of them were nothing, no threat, but there were a couple of lads who might cause him trouble. Of course, even they wouldn't be sure what they might be getting into.

The Queen and Artichoke was within the Twins' sphere of influence. It would be a madman who didn't take that into account before mixing things up. Charlie was lots of things, but he wasn't insane. He wouldn't have fried the car or hit Frank unless he had taken tea with Reggie at Vallance Road. Frank, apparently, hadn't been telling the Kray brothers about all his activities. They knew nothing about his sideline in nicked motors, on which they had been due a little something. So it was fine by them if Charlie taught him a lesson on their behalf. They would sweep by and mop it up later.

As Charlie stepped away from the bar, Marion finally ran out of puff and, as her piercing racket subsided, he sensed the mood of the crowd change. Bewilderment turned to anger, not least because their Sunday session had been so comprehensively disrupted. The stripper certainly didn't look in the mood to disrobe any more. The crowd shuffled a step closer.

'Oi!'

Gordon Goody pushed himself to his full height at the rear of the pub, knocking one of the tables over as he rose up like Reptilicus. He waited until he had everyone's full attention then, from beneath his trademark full-length coat, he pulled a baseball bat and stepped towards the group, brandishing it in his right fist. The crowd couldn't have parted faster if he'd been Charlton Heston.

'Time to go,' Gordy said, pointing with his free hand towards the rear as he poked one of the customers in the chest with the bat. Gordy had been in place for thirty minutes before Charlie's arrival, and had already ascertained that the rear exit he had cased the day before was clear. This way they could make good their escape without being toasted by a burning Jag.

Charlie pushed through to Gordy's side and the two slowly backed out towards the pub's yard and the Rover waiting in the alley with Roy behind the wheel. Charlie wanted Roy driving, just in case there was any pursuit, but it looked like the lad had earned himself an easy drink.

The flames out in the street were angrier now, turning the interior of the Q&A a deep crimson. Frank had staggered to his feet, but he remained behind the bar, holding his shattered nose. Another pane of glass cracked, causing the customers to start, as if a pistol had gone off. Charlie knew then they didn't have the bottle to come at them.

'Fuck me,' said Gordy as they bundled out, a roar of ineffectual outrage at their heels. 'I hope that was worth it.'

Charlie laughed as he yanked open the wooden gate that accessed the rear alley. 'Well, those cunts won't be nickin' Jags off us again, will they?'

'Morning, sir. It's Detective Constable Rennie here, from the Stolen Car Squad. Yes. I have some good news for you. We have recovered your Jaguar. Yes, I know. We were surprised as well. Don't get to make too many of these calls, to be honest. No, it appears to be relatively unharmed. Perhaps a slight scratch on one wing, but that will T-Cut out. Not today, I am afraid. We just want to check it for fingerprints and fibres, but that will only take a day or two. You should have it back by the weekend. Where did we find it? Well, there's the strange thing. It was left outside a police station in Romford, with the keys in the ignition. No, I can't imagine why. Maybe some villain had a sudden attack of conscience, saw the error of his ways. Stranger things have

*happened. Although not many. You are very welcome, sir, nice to
have a result. Good day.'*

Bruce Reynolds didn't have time for distractions and favours.
He had a fucking great train robbery to plan. His brain was
revving like one of Roy's racing engines, a jumble of possibilities, all centred on the TPO that left Glasgow every night.

But, after some horizontal persuasion in the Grand at
Brighton, he had promised Janie he would take the meeting,
answer a few stupid questions. The guy had suggested a meet
in the Colony Rooms, but although he had drunk in the
place – George Melly had taken him a couple of times –
Bruce had never felt particularly comfortable there. Rude
bastards, he thought, and not half as clever as they clearly
thought they were. Being called 'cunty' a lot was not his
idea of entertainment.

Bruce had originally chosen the New Crown Club at the
Elephant and Castle, which was home turf, but knew just
how intimidating that crowd could be, so he had switched
to the Star, a flower-decked pub tucked down a mews in
Belgravia. It covered all bases from lords to layabouts. Roy
popped in now and then for a soda water because it had been
Mike Hawthorn's boozer and it still pulled a crowd of racing
drivers and their acolytes. It was also home to a hardcore
of very genuine criminals.

It was Friday lunchtime, with that fuck-it one-more-pint-
and-a-fag end of the working week feel. Although very few

of the patrons of the Star actually had a conventional working week, apart from the odd copper who wandered in. They caused no problem. You saw it on *Zoo Quest*, when herds of antelope allowed lions to stroll among them without getting too spooked. The animals sensed when the predator was on the hunt, otherwise they ignored them. So it was with the police who liked to think that getting pissed in places like the Star was all part of vital detective work.

Bruce had given a rough description of himself – tall, glasses, a copy of the *Daily Express*, light-blue shirt and navy-blue suit. There was a horseshoe-shaped bar on the right as you entered the pub, the rougher clientèle nearest the door, toffs at the far side. To the left, through an arch, were the seats, and Bruce had taken himself through this and to the far corner, past the fireplace, against the wooden wainscot. That nook, beneath the portraits of Regency jockeys and *Punch* cartoons, was as close to a 'snug' as the Star got.

Bruce ignored his newspaper and played with a beer mat while he waited. He had called together the entire crew – his boys and those with a Brighton connection – for a meeting in four days, and they were going to expect a plan. He was the Colonel, after all. Not quite Jack Hawkins – the meeting would be at Roy's place, rather than the Café Royal – but he was expected to lay it all out.

Timing, he was certain, was the key, not just the application of mindless brute force – although that, or the implied threat of it, would play its part. A timetable was needed, a realistic one that should be adhered to, no matter what. It helped that everything, right down to the schedule of the trains, was just as this 'Jock' character had said.

Except maybe he wasn't a Jock.

Gordy claimed he could hear Belfast in there. Was he an Ulsterman? No matter, the man clearly knew what he was talking about. Did he know too much too well, though? Was this a set-up by the cops? A bit of fishing with a very, very juicy worm? After all, he was sure the Squad had a hard-on for them now.

But no, it felt right, like the genuine article. It was all too elaborate for the Old Bill, anyway; he doubted they had the nous to set up such an operation, just to pull in a team of blaggers. And anyway, a million quid was worth circling the hook for. It was a little tinge of paranoia making him think the cosspots were behind it. But he shouldn't disregard the feeling. It kept you sharp, kept you out of some stinking flowery for ten years.

'Mr Allen, is it?'

Bruce looked up at the tall, slightly cadaverous-looking man who had addressed him. Just those few well-rounded words marked him out as posh, a man who would be right at home with the Lucky Lucans and Maxwell-Smiths who gathered under the Star's Smiths clock each evening. His suit was of a good pedigree, too, although it looked as if he had slept in it. It was his face that was remarkable – as if all the blood had been drained from it: deathly white, with thin bloodless lips and remarkably pale eyes. He was close to albino.

'Colin Thirkell.' He held out a hand and Bruce took it. Thirkell looked around as if he approved. 'I don't much care for pubs. They are like banks – never open when you need them. But I enjoy this one. Used to drink here . . . oh, must be ten years ago. With poor Tommy Carstairs.'

Bruce laughed. Poor Tommy Carstairs was doing a long one for murder. 'You aren't an ordinary journalist, are you?'

'No. And you, I hope, are no ordinary crook. Now, that lovely Godfrey Smith, my editor, was foolish enough to advance me some expenses. Would you care for a drink?'

Bruce examined his half-full glass of mild and bitter and said, 'A scotch would be very nice.'

'Very well.'

Bruce watched him walk away. Something in his manner suggested he batted and bowled, or at the very least fielded for the other side when they were a man short. Posh and a poof. Not that he minded either. Without posh there would be no Madame Prunier or Connaught Grill. As for poofs, well, they were on the wrong side of the law, too, poor buggers. He smiled at his choice of phrase. Where did Janie find this bloke? He knew she was a woman of many parts, but had never had her down for a literary type. A writer, she had said. Needs someone . . . what was the word she used? *Erudite*? 'Most of your mates can grunt and scratch their balls,' she said, 'and that's about it. And rarely both things at the same time.' Had a waspish streak, that Janie.

Thirkell came back with a scotch and a gin and tonic for himself. Bruce was impressed with how he had handled himself up there. It was a cliquey crowd; the writer, though, had an ease about him that suggested he was perfectly at home in any company.

'There.' He slid in opposite Bruce and raised his glass. 'Did Jane tell you what this was for?'

'You are writing an article.'

'For the *Sunday Times*, yes. About what you might call the underworld. Well, I'm sure you wouldn't, but my editor does. It is to be a plain man's guide to crime and criminals. No names, no direct quotes. Just a few thoughts. You see, I was lamenting to Jane – Janie as you call her – that my own contacts tend towards the pugilistic sort of criminal. Gangsters, should we say. I needed some light with that shade.'

Bruce looked at the table in front of them, empty but for the drinks. 'You take notes?'

'No, Mr Allen—'

'Bruce.' He had used Franny's maiden name just to be on the safe side. He had checked with Janie about what she had called him to the writer. 'My friend Bruce,' she had said. No surname. So it did no harm to invent one. And there were lots of Bruces around.

'It's all very impressionistic, if you know what I mean, Bruce. And, as I say, no names, no sly references that might establish who you are. You might be referred to as "an informant" or "a professional".'

'Fair enough. Fire away.'

Thirkell took a large mouthful of his G&T and leaned forward, elbows on the table. When the questions started, the man's voice took on a brittle tone. Sparring was over, this was somehow combative, needling even. 'Do you consider yourself a criminal?'

'Yes. Very much so.'

'And would you say that is a result of your upbringing?'

Bruce shook his head. 'Not in my case. My parents were straight. And I never said, "When I grow up I want to be a train driver, a fireman or a robber." It just happened. I was in the Army for a while, found it didn't suit me. Had a job, didn't like it. Met some blokes who showed me a different path, you might say. But that's me. I can't deny that certain conditions do breed criminals.'

'Such as?'

'Take a look around,' Bruce said, pointing through the archway to a group consisting of Little Caesar, Lance Kirby, Dickie M and Honest John Perry, together one of the Star's pair of dog-doping syndicates. 'Those four grew up within three streets of each other. Not here, not Belgravia. Those are Deptford boys, born and bred. And that's why they are at it.'

'So you mean specific areas of London create the environment? Like the Elephant?'

'Parts of every city. Liverpool, Manchester, Glasgow. Wherever there are poor people, I suppose, who aren't happy to stay where they've been put. The only way out has always been the military, sport – football or boxing, probably – and crime.'

'Or pop music. Look at Tommy Steele, Bermondsey lad made good.'

Bruce nodded. 'True. So now the kids are stealing guitars and amplifiers.'

'And do you consider yourself a particular type of criminal?'

He gave a shrug. 'A thief. That's what I am.'

'And would you ever go straight? I mean, are you a criminal for life?'

Bruce considered this. If you got a decent chunk of one million quid, pumped the cash into a business, had you gone straight? Or would the old Bruce Reynolds always be there, ear to the ground, his heart going all jittery when he heard of a nice tickle? 'You might drop out of the life for a while, but the instinct is still there. I'm pretty sure it's a case of once a villain . . .'

'And how much would you say you earn? On average?'

'I don't know,' he replied honestly. The money rarely hung around long enough to be counted. 'Straight up. If you are looking for an average, you have to take off any time inside, don't you? Unproductive years, we might say. I am guessing about the same as a bank clerk.'

'A bank clerk?' Thirkell's expression was disbelieving.

'Well, a bank manager then,' Bruce said with a smile. 'In a West End branch. Look around you. Every one of these blokes has been up for the big score at some time or another. Some of them been grafting at it for forty or fifty years. Still here though, aren't they, rather than Surrey or Spain? So, you make a living. If not an honest one.'

'I see. But you don't pay tax, do you?'

'No, but we put the money back into circulation pretty damn quick. You buy a motor, drinks, nice clothes.' He recalled how fast a few thousand could dwindle to nothing. 'Nobody can accuse us of hoarding.'

'Is there any form of criminality you wouldn't indulge in?'

'Poncing,' Bruce said quickly. 'I don't know why, I think that's pretty low. I don't like anything that is parasitic, you see. Blowing a peter or a wages snatch, a good clean job, that's what I enjoy. I always say, "Never steal from anyone who might go hungry". Well, I think Cary Grant said it first.'

Thirkell pursed his lips, thinking, before he framed the next question. 'And the police? What do you think of them?'

'I don't think about them. They have a job to do. I mean, you could argue that without us they would have no job, couldn't you? They need us more than we need them. To be frank with you, I don't mind them, I even get on with some of them. We're like pilots in the Battle of Britain, the RAF and the Luftwaffe. They had to shoot each other down, but there was a kind of respect there. I tell you, I'd rather have a drink with a copper than a member of the public. At least they understand us and we understand them. Ordinary people, well, they are like another species, aren't they?'

'And the violence that comes as part of your profession. How do you defend that?'

Bruce finished his pint, pushed the glass away and pulled the scotch towards him. He found his temper was rising. 'I don't have to defend it. I don't like it, but it has to be there sometimes. But I don't have to justify it. The thing is, it's never against outsiders, not if you can help it. Those kids that shoot or cosh members of the public? Scum. I don't like threatening shopkeepers or club owners or toms for money, although I admit I mix with those that do.' He pointed at the bar, just to make his point. 'But when you confront a bloke who has a bag of wages, it's part of the game and he has the choice. Give it up or take a whack. He knows that. Nine times out of ten he gives it up and we're all happy.'

'But you don't think it's wrong that you don't work for a living?'

Bruce had to laugh at that. 'Don't work? What you on about? You think being a thief is an easy choice?' He was tempted to explain what he had been doing for the past few

246

weeks, but held his tongue. 'There is a lot of effort goes into the job, a lot of risks, a lot of tension. And everyone thinks it's all about big scores – diamonds, wages snatches, banks. It pisses me off. Yeah, you try those sometimes, but you aren't above breaking open the odd cigarette machine or fronting some hooky Milk Tray. We work, all right. You know, Colin, thieving might even be a bit harder than writing for a living.'

That got him a wry grin from Thirkell. 'And what about guns?'

'Guns? Guns are for maniac kids. Scared kids who have seen too many movies. The thing is, you go up to someone with an iron bar or a cosh, then the other fella knows there's a good chance he'll get a tap if he doesn't do as he's told. With a gun, it's different; the psychology is different.'

There was a glint of excitement in Thirkell's eyes, as if he was close to the motherlode now. 'Go on.'

Bruce took a deep breath, gathering his thoughts. Some of the chaps thought his insistence on no firearms was a weakness. He rarely explained himself to them, just told them it was part of the Colonel's ground rules. Now he had to lay out his philosophy, and do it logically. 'It isn't just because you get longer sentences with a shooter, although that might be part of it for some people. I suppose I do take that into account. For me, though, it runs deeper than that. I pull a gun on you now, a few things will go through your mind. One, is it real? Two, am I man enough to pull the trigger? Three, if I do, will I hit you? So you start thinking the odds might be in your favour. So you do something stupid. And next thing we know, bang, you are dead. Now we are both fucked.'

'So there are no circumstances under which you would use a gun?'

Bruce thought about that HVP carriage, the sorters who would look up as they burst through the doors, the reaction if he were to pull a pistol or a pair of nostrils, otherwise known as a sawn-off shotgun. And he thought about one of them deciding Bruce didn't look like he had the bottle to use it. He spoke firmly. 'No. Never.'

Len Haslam was on his fourth pint, talking to a jobbing actor and stuntman called Beefy Bob Atkinson, who had just landed a role on *Z Cars* as a DS. Beefy Bob did have knowledge of the law, but it dated back ten years, when he was involved in chiselling the back off obsolete safes. Up till now his roles had involved wearing a stocking over his head or leaping from a burning car as it went over a cliff. This was his big break.

For a small fee and a bellyful of bitter, Len was meant to be briefing him on how to behave as a Detective Sergeant in the CID, to help him get 'the method', as Beefy Bob said. But Duke's eye kept wandering over towards where Bruce Reynolds was sitting. The thief's jaw was going thirteen to the dozen and the bloke opposite was listening intently, nodding now and then. Duke was well aware of what he had promised Frank Williams, but he was certain that Reynolds was at it. And at something pretty big, judging by the intensity of the pitch he was making and the hand gestures going on. But who was the bloke Reynolds was talking to? Not a face from the Elephant, Peckham or Camberwell, that was certain.

He told Beefy Bob to get him another drink and he would tell him how they really interrogated suspects, then headed for the Gents. As he crossed the room he rummaged in his pocket for coins for the phone box out there. He would call Billy Naughton and get him down to put a tail on the unknown man. Duke had promised to leave Reynolds and the others alone. That did not include new faces on the block that were clearly up to no good.

As he walked out of the Star pub and towards Hyde Park Corner, where he would catch a cab into Soho, Bruce Reynolds mused on what a very strange man Thirkell was. The conversation had begun as a straightforward interview, but after a while Bruce got the idea he was being auditioned. It was only towards the end of the session that he got an inkling of what the bloke really wanted. He wanted to steal part of the Elgin Marbles from the British Museum, as a show of outrage at the original looting from the Parthenon.

The writer had wanted him to put up a firm to rob something, not for money, but for a principle. He said he could pay expenses, not much else. But it would be righting a great wrong.

Bruce chuckled to himself. He could just imagine selling that one to the chaps. Had Janie said he might do it? Maybe she had. Perhaps it was time to move her a few paces back. Her putting his name in the frame for a bit of altruism, that just wasn't on. At the end of the day, Bruce Reynolds had just one favourite charity. Himself. Anyone who thought otherwise had lost another kind of marbles altogether.

Thirty-one

From Motoring News, *June 1963*

JAMES TRIUMPHS AT AINTREE

Driving a Brabham BT 6, rookie Roy James won the twenty-lap TJ Hughes Trophy at Aintree last Sunday, at a new record average speed for FJ of 89.4mph. James, whose car seems to have taken on a new lease of life – and pace – since its last outing, was followed home by Dennis Hulme in a second Brabham and Peter Proctor (Cooper). After an exciting race in which the lead changed hands no fewer than five times, there was less than six seconds between the final trio at the flag.

Further back in the field a fierce battle was waged between Jo Schlesser (Ford/France Brabham) and Bill Moss (Gemini), the two cars circulating nose to tail for much of the race, until Moss left his braking a little too late on the 90-degree Cottage Corner and lost some 15 seconds in the process.

The three-mile Aintree circuit was hailed as the 'Goodwood of the North' when it opened in 1954, but recently some drivers have complained (see Letters, page four) that the course, with its taxing bends such as Becher's, Anchor and Village, is too hard on man and machine. However, Stirling Moss won the British GP here in 1955, driving for Mercedes, and has always enjoyed and defended the track layout and Roy James, too, had no gripes, telling a cheering crowd that Liverpool has 'one of the best and most challenging circuits for single-seat racing in Europe'. Runner-up Hulme added to the young man's achievements by proclaiming James 'one of the most promising drivers of the 1963 season in any formula'. James, Hulme and the other Formula Juniors will be in action again at Oulton Park next weekend.

Thirty-two

Headley, Surrey, May 1992

I looked out through the heavy drapes in the living room at the eastern sky, hoping for a sliver of light, but there was none. Dawn was still a no-show. I replaced the curtains and walked back across the scuffed parquet and into the kitchen, where Roy was sat at the table. He looked up, his face troubled.

'Find it OK?'

I had been to the lavatory and taken a little tour while I was at it. 'Yeah. This is a nice house, Roy.'

'It's too big for me. Needs money to fix it up. Someone richer than me anyway. One of today's drivers – they're all loaded. I should've been a contender for that, you know,' he said morosely.

'Could've,' I corrected the quote before I could stop myself. 'Could've been a contender.'

'Should've, could've. It's all the same. After the win at Aintree, I should have dropped all the grifting, forgot about the train. Just concentrated on the car.'

'Hindsight,' was all I could think to offer by way of consolation. 'Wonderful thing, Roy.'

'So's foresight, Tony.' Roy looked down at the pistol in his hands. I wondered whether to make a lunge for it, but not for long. It wasn't only in movies that guns went off in tussles.

'We should go outside, Roy.'

'Not yet.' He looked up at me, tears in his eyes. 'They'll take the kids now, won't they?'

I didn't know what to say. Of course they would. Shooting and pistol-whipping rarely went down well in court. 'For a while, I dare say. Best thing to do is plead a temporary moment of madness.'

'It's all been a bleedin' temporary moment of madness.' He sniffed loudly. 'You know I split my life into BT and AT. Before the Train and After the Train. Like BC and AD. And just like Jesus, we got fuckin' crucified.'

'What about another cup of tea?' I asked, trying to shift the mood. 'Then we'll go out together.'

'Fair enough.'

There was a banging on the door, fist on wood, and Roy raised the gun, hands shaking slightly.

'Steady on,' I said. 'The Gun Squad tend not to knock.'

I crossed the gloomy hall, undid the latch and opened the door a crack. What I saw caused my chest to constrict, more in shock than anything else. For a second I had trouble speaking.

'Put the kettle on. It's bleedin' freezing out here.'

I stepped back. It was getting on for thirty years since I had last seen him in the flesh. Back then, he was in his element, dressed in SAS uniform, a swagger in his step and victory in his eyes. Now, he was gaunter and greyer, a little stooped perhaps, but the coat was cashmere and the spectacles Chanel. 'Hello, Bruce,' I managed to stammer.

'Hello, Tony,' replied Bruce Reynolds as he hurried inside. 'Drop of scotch would be nice, too.'

'Kitchen,' I muttered, pointing down the hallway. 'Past the stairs.'

As we entered the room, Roy struggled to his feet, looking every bit as nonplussed as I felt. I could see the new arrival staring at the gun in Roy's hand. I wondered then if Bruce remembered that thirty years ago he had blamed me for the whole fucking fiasco.

Thirty-three

Fulham, West London, June 1963

'Sir, sir, Mr Reynolds, sir. I have a question, sir.' Buster Edwards was bouncing up and down like Jimmy bloody Clitheroe, the eternal schoolboy.

Bruce turned away from the blackboard that was the source of the ribbing, to face the group of men, their faces shrouded in smoke from half-a-dozen cigarettes. 'Piss off, Buster.'

Bruce was tired. He had been living this for two weeks now, and he had become short-tempered. The previous night he had consumed a whole bottle of Veuve Cliquot and a third of Glenfiddich, and ended up chasing Franny around the house threatening her with a toilet brush.

It had taken a lot of making up that morning.

He tapped the board to get their attention and then found

himself smiling. 'Although you fuckers do look like the Bash Street Kids,' he said. He pointed his chalk at Buster. 'Which makes you Plug, you ugly bastard.'

Buster pulled a hideous face.

'OK, just some quick formalities. This is Roger, the Flowerpot Man.' Roger Cordrey nodded, although most had been introduced to him informally as the party had gathered at Roy's flat. 'He's worked with Buster.' This was the equivalent of references; 'worked with' meant he was a stand-up bloke. In truth, Roger didn't look like one of them. Small, self-effacing but with sly, shifty eyes, he reminded Bruce of a vicar with a guilty secret – embezzlement, perhaps – in an Ealing comedy.

'Tommy Wisbey, I think most of you know.' Tommy was a bookmaker who hired himself out as a frightener. 'Bonehead', they sometimes called him, because he was as daunting as the bloke who played that character on kids' TV. He wasn't anything like as daft, though.

'Jimmy White, same, and next to him that's Tony Fortune. Let's hope that's a lucky name, eh? Roy says he's almost as good a driver as him. Which, as you know, is like a blessing from the Pope. By the way, Charlie, you quite finished?'

Charlie looked puzzled. As usual he had said very little, just gazed at the ceiling while he waited for the proceedings to begin. 'With what?'

'That new hobby you have.' Bruce allowed a theatrical

pause to build. 'You know the one. Setting fire to cars in Bethnal Green.'

There were some sniggers, just like naughty schoolkids. Bruce should have been annoyed, but he had to be careful. He was the man at the front with the chalk. There had to be a leader in these situations but he mustn't overstep the mark. A lot of these chaps were in the game because they despised any form of authority. Even from a fellow villain.

Charlie's eyes narrowed. 'I think I might have got that out of my system, yes, Bruce.'

There was a steely undertow to the words, but Bruce ignored it. 'Good. Because from now on, we keep a low profile. Not get our names plastered over every pub and club. Nobody should be at it. I mean all of you. Whatever you are working on, ditch it. It'll be peanuts compared to this. Understood?'

A few nods.

'Still, now Charlie has laid down a few ground rules for them, I don't think we need worry about any other firm treading on our toes, eh?'

That seemed to placate Charlie, who took it as a compliment. Bruce didn't really object to Charlie's refusal to let the pricks who took the Jags go unpunished. After all, it was going to be hard to keep the train job quiet, but the thought of what Charlie might do to anyone who flapped his lips would help keep a lid on things.

'Now. Glasgow.' He tapped the top of the board, on which

was a primitive outline of the British Isles with a few key places chalked in. Now he pointed further south. 'And Euston. Our Man in the North seems to have steered us straight on this. Every evening at five past six, give or take ten minutes, the up Travelling Post Office leaves Glasgow, stopping at Carstairs, Carlisle, Preston, Crewe, Tamworth and Rugby. By the time it leaves Rugby it is fully loaded – next stop Euston. The train consists of twelve or thirteen coaches. The second coach is always the High Value Packet carriage. It's that we want. It will contain between seventy and two hundred bags, depending on how fortunate we are. You've all heard the figures, but we take those with a pinch of salt. We've all been there, eh?'

There were grunts as several of them remembered the disappointing haul from the Heathrow job.

'What we have to do is stop the train somewhere between Rugby and North London. That's where Roger comes in. The crucial thing is, *where* do we stop it? So this week's little task, gentlemen, is for some of us to scout the line from Watford northwards, looking for places where we have easy road access.'

'And a signal gantry,' said Roger.

'Roger will tell us what to look for in a moment. He and I will take one section, Gordy and Jimmy another, Roy and Tony a third. All right?' He pointed at Buster once more. 'The HVP and the rest of the Mail Train must be shunted somewhere during the day. I want to look inside it, see what we are up against. Buster, Jim Hussey, Tommy, I want you to look at all the shunting yards and sidings. Roger has a list. We also have to decide how big this firm will need to be. There are about eighty people on that train, but only five in the HVP. If we can isolate that HVP, we are quids in. On the other hand, moving a hundred mail-bags at double-quick time is going to need a lot of hands. I am open to suggestions for extra bodies, but, you know, keep it in the family, eh lads? Roger and Jimmy have some ideas.'

'Tiny Dave Thompson,' said Jimmy White. 'Another ex-Para.'

There were a few murmurs of agreement. Tiny Dave had kept his head when the arrests were happening after the London Airport job. Harry and Ian, the other two musclemen, had lost their bottle and left town.

Bruce said: 'Good idea. But I'll make the approaches – agreed? This has to be tighter than a duck's arsehole. That's me done for now. We meet again at the end of the week. Clapham Common, five-a-side. Bring your boots, your Dextrosol and your liniment. Any questions?'

Gordy asked: 'When are we aiming for, Bruce?'

'Our man tells us the most cash is carried after a Bank Holiday. The one that stands out is August the fifth. It's a Scottish one, before you ask. Now, we don't do it on August the fifth, 'cause the money is still in the banks. So we are looking at the night of Tuesday the sixth, morning of

Wednesday, August the seventh. A little over two and a half months away.'

Someone whistled. All they had so far was a vague idea of what they were going to do and when. Not *how*. And when it came to robbing trains, the how was the big ask. Ten weeks was no time at all when it came to planning that kind of job.

'So we best get to it.' Bruce stepped aside. 'Roger will now read from the *Big Chief I-Spy's Book of Train Signals*.'

Roger Cordrey, florist by profession, train robber by inclination, stood up. Next to some of the muscle gathered in the room, he looked just like a flower-seller. But he had specialist knowledge, which was always respected in the business, and most of the men carried on puffing their cigarettes and listening intently as he prepared to give them a chat about the difference between dwarf and home signals.

'Britain has seventy-three TPOs, Travelling Post Offices,' he began, just to show they weren't the first firm to have noticed all this money moving around the country on rails. 'They have been running since 1830 . . .'

Buster Edwards, suddenly transported back to school, began to roll up pieces of Rizla cigarette paper to flick at Gordon Goody's ears. Whatever the division of labour, Buster was fairly sure he wouldn't be part of any technical team. Not while he still had his spring-loaded cosh.

* * *

DC Billy Naughton arrived back at the section house tired and dishevelled. He had spent too many hours chasing after the man Duke was convinced was a criminal mastermind only to discover he was a bloody scribbler. Colin Thirkell. Waste of time.

Well, not entirely. On the bright side, he had been bunged a fiver by some guilty poof who had thought that he was going to run him in for gross indecency. The man had leaned over the porcelain dividing wall of the urinals to take a good look at his tackle. The Liberace had a neck like a bloody flamingo. Billy, outraged at this invasion of his privates, had slapped the man around a bit, then flashed his warrant card, and the terrified queer had reached for his wallet. Billy guessed it wasn't the first time he had bought his way out of scandal.

Maybe he shouldn't have settled for a fiver. The man was well-dressed – a City type or solicitor, perhaps. Probably married. Just like the plot of that Dirk Bogarde film, a man with VICTIM written right across his forehead. Billy had little against queers, other than the usual disgust at what they got up to, but the need to carry out their perversions in public toilets – what was that all about? Maybe if they had to hand enough fivers over to policemen they would start thinking twice. Which made 'fining' them a public service, didn't it?

In the tiny, overheated box room that he called home, Billy yanked off his tie and stripped off clothes that stank of booze and fags and threw them into the corner. Remembering what was in his pockets, he retrieved his trousers and fished out the fiver the pillow-chewer had bunged him. In only his underpants and socks now, he fetched the dented Oxo tin from the suitcase under the bed and opened it up, intending to simply stuff the fresh cash inside. Now, though, the assorted ten bob-, pound- and five-pound notes sprang out onto the swirly nylon carpet.

So much, he thought. How did it get to be so much in such a short time?

He stood up and turned on the Dynatron transistor radio that sat next to the bed. It was still tuned to Radio Luxembourg, trotting out the inevitable plug for Horace Batchelor's fail-safe Infra-Draw Pools method. Once the drone was over ('That's Keynsham: kay, ee, why . . .') on came *Rockin' To Dreamland* with Keith Fordyce, who announced he was playing the best new music from Britain and America, starting with the surf sound of the Beach Boys.

Billy upended the Oxo tin on the bed and began to sort the notes into piles according to denomination. He nodded his head to 'Surfin' Safari' as he did so, the harmonies interrupted periodically by the atmospheric whistling that was one of Radio Luxembourg's specialities.

He didn't notice the song end, or the next irritating advertisement break for the stupid pools system. He was busy looking at three hundred and thirty-three pounds and ten shillings. And that was just crumbs, picked up here and there.

He had more than three hundred pounds, yet he was still living in a station house, listening to music on a cheap transistor and eating meals in a police canteen.

Billy carefully repacked the cash, thinking about a better hiding-place, before deciding he should put it in the Post Office or a building society. It was, perhaps, time for Billy Naughton to move up in the world. And if the drinks, backhanders and tips weren't entirely legal, then so what? It wasn't as if he didn't put the hours in – and did anyone ever mention the word 'overtime'? Was there ever talk of time-and-a-half or double time? No. A fifteen-hour day got you twelve and sixpence subsistence pay. Subsistence if you ate at the Wimpy every day, that was.

The Dynatron's signal drifted to interference, white noise interspersed with the snap and crackle of ghostly voices captured from the radiosphere. It reminded Billy of an electronic séance when that happened, like he was eavesdropping on ancient wireless broadcasts. He half-expected an ethereal voice to emerge from the static: '*We are receiving reports that something has happened to the Titanic . . .*'

Billy reached up and switched the radio off, then placed the box back into the suitcase and pushed it deep under the bed. He resolved to ask Duke where the best place to keep his money was. It shouldn't be under the Dunlopillo mattress. Not in a room with no lock on the door, as was still the rule in London station houses. It should be somewhere secure and legit, somewhere it could grow. After all, it wasn't as if he had done anything wrong, was it?

'This is it, then?' Bruce asked Roger, as they sat on a locked toolbox in the shadow of the concrete hut and watched a passenger service rattle by on one of the four lines. It had been easy to hop over the fence and walk down the embankment to the little depot, with its hut and toolshed. Both men wore donkey jackets over blue boiler suits, and they looked like any team of gangers taking a break, watching trains go by in bright sunshine.

Roger Cordrey had the OS map spread out on his lap, while Bruce fussed with a flask of tea. They had been driving up and down their designated section of the line for several days now, but kept coming back to this spot. They had looked at the viaducts discovered by some of the other scouts, but one was far too high – a heavily laden bag tossed over could kill someone on the road below – and the other had no stop signals nearby.

'I reckon it is,' said Roger. He indicated towards Linslade, on his right, beyond the small bridge that crossed the line, giving access to Rowden Farm. 'Dwarf single down there, which will be switched to amber.' Then to his left. 'Home signal there has to be on red.'

Bruce hesitated while a goods train groaned past them at not much more than walking speed, drowning out the conversation. When it was clear he asked: 'All of which you can take care of?'

Roger grinned. He had done it on the Brighton line enough times, although they had never taken a decent haul, and some of the attempts had been fiascoes. But the false stop light part of the plan, that always worked a treat. 'Leave it to me. Never fails.' He took the tea. 'Cheers.'

'But how can you be in two places at once?'

'How do you mean?'

'Doing two signals? Shouldn't we have someone on the dwarf, another on the home gantry?'

Roger pursed his lips. Bruce knew what he was thinking. Tricks of the trade. Roger was valuable, would more than earn his whack, by interfering with the signals. If he spilled the beans on how to do that, if anyone with a couple of crocodile clips could switch the lights, then he became redundant.

'Look, I don't give a fuck how it's done, Roger. I'm not going to make a career out of nobbling the Royal Mail. I just want to make sure you aren't stretched too thin. I could put a man up there with you.' He had someone in mind – Ralph. A distant relative, not a hardened crim, but a good worker and, most of all, dependable.

'We'll see,' said Roger. He changed the subject and pointed across the tracks to the low buildings that constituted the inhabited part of Rowden Farm. 'That's a bit close.'

'It'll be three in the morning. I know farmers are early risers, but that'd be ridiculous.'

'Still, should cut the phone line to it.'

That made sense. Even if they did spot something, the owners wouldn't be able to raise the alarm. 'Good idea. Drink up. Mustn't hang about too long.'

Bruce's new Lotus Cortina – its side flash as green as Roy's envy when the driver saw it – was parked off the main road next to a farm entrance on the B488, which cut through quiet pasture and rolling woodland. He had pulled off onto such turnings many times in recent days and inevitably had left tyre-marks. He would have to get the boots on the car changed. The police used tyre-tracks like fingerprints now – both as evidence and a convenient way to place you at the scene. In fact, it was best if he retired the Lotus, just in case anyone had clocked it over the past week or even taken the licence-plate. He had read there was a DB5 due in September. It might be nice to go back to an Aston. The last one had cost him a fortune in garage bills, but that wouldn't be an issue this time around.

'Of course, you are still half a mile short,' said Roger. He gestured at the track behind them that led up to the elevated crossing. 'No way you can get the bags up this embankment and over to the main road. Not without giving everyone a hernia. It will have to be bridge 127.'

He pointed down the line to Bridego Bridge, which was, according to the plate on its side, BR's crossing number 127. It was a relatively low span over a narrow country lane, with easy access up the embankment at the side of the arch to the track itself. There was even a parking area for fishermen

267

who visited the small pond next to it. But it was, as Roger had said, a good half-mile away. Trotting up the track like pack mules was also out of the question.

'So once the train is stopped, we have to move it up to the bridge?' asked Bruce.

'Well, you don't have to move the whole train, do you? Just the HVP.'

Bruce sipped his tea. 'So we uncouple the business end and shunt it the half-mile.'

'That's right.' At Crossing 127 they would be dropping the bags down a slope to the roadway, not carrying them uphill to one, the only option where they were now. 'To where we can unload the bags straight down into the vehicles.'

They sat and thought about this for a minute. 'Roger?'
'Yes?'
'Can you drive a train?'
'No. I can stop them, that's usually enough.'

'So we need a driver then. Although they do tend to come complete with one, don't they? Trains, I mean.'

Roger screwed his face up. 'In my experience they are stroppy bastards, these BR types. If the fucker at the controls says you can go and fuck yourself – well, you're fucked, aren't you?'

That was true. *Drive the train or we'll beat your brains out. Go on, then.* The whole thing could come down around their ears because of one bolshie driver. 'OK, best have a think.'

Bruce stood up and threw the dregs of his tea towards the track. 'What's this place called again?'

'Sears Crossing.'

'Sears Crossing,' he repeated. 'Right. Sears Crossing is where we catch our train.'

Thirty-four

New Scotland Yard, June 1963

Len Haslam took one glance at Billy Naughton, sitting rigid at his desk in the Squad room, and knew something was wrong. 'Fuck me, lad, you look like someone who drank seven pints and three scotches last night.'

'Don't exaggerate. Five pints. Two scotches.' He did feel rough around the edges, his stomach burning from all the alcohol – celebrating the nicking of the Islington Post Office gang – and no food. But that wasn't why he felt queasy.

Duke, fresh-faced apart from a razor nick on his upper lip, grinned. 'Right. Must have been me who did the seven and three then – and I feel fine. So what's up with you, Junior? Need to see Dr Kildare?'

SIGNAL RED

Dr Kildare was the half-bottle of scotch that Duke kept handy in case a hair of the dog was needed.

'Leave it out. Got to see the TM.'

TM stood for Top Man: Commander George Hatherill, overall head of Scotland Yard's C Division, the business end, and a classic Old Sweat, who had been everywhere, seen everything.

'He asked for you?'

Billy said he had.

'Could be a good thing,' Haslam told him. 'You never know.'

Billy doubted it. He hadn't made much of an impression over the past few months, could hardly claim to have established himself as a thief-taker.

'By the way, I forgot to ask you last night. Did you turn up anything on that bloke who was with Bruce Reynolds?' Len clicked his fingers in front of Billy's eyes. 'Come on, boy, snap out of it.'

'He's a writer,' said Billy distantly.

'A what?'

'A writer,' he repeated.

'What kind of fuckin' writer? A signwriter?'

'Journalist. Author. Colin Thirkell.' Billy fetched one of the paperback novels he had bought at Foyles from his drawer and tossed it onto the desk.

Duke picked it up and read the title. '*Black and Blues*. What's this?'

'About the clashes between the coloureds and the police. In Notting Hill.'

'Is he a coon-lover then, this Thirkell?'

Billy shrugged. 'I haven't read it. He's queer though.'

'How do you know? Is it because he takes men's dicks up the arse? Is that the clue?' Len leered at him, making Billy feel even more nauseous.

'Drinks at the Moorhen off Tottenham Court Road.'

'Ah. Queers and nig-nogs.' Duke scanned the rear of the novel. It was a twin-strand story about Dexter, a Jamaican seaman who ends up as a pimp, and Stirrup, a Detective Inspector on the Vice Squad. 'Coon-lover,' he confirmed. 'As well as an arse-bandit. What time are you seeing the TM?'

'Eleven.'

'Well, don't get trapped by one of his bloody stories. If he mentions the Penn murder case, fake an epileptic fit. The big kind.' Duke handed the book back. 'Filth. But it means he might have just been trawling the gutter for background to one of his stories.'

'What shall we do about him then?'

Len Haslam thought for a moment. They had a lot on their plate. Millen was pressuring them to find Michael Morris, who had escaped from Lewes Prison swearing to kill the woman who had sent him a Dear John letter. There had been a dozen sightings over the past three weeks and it was known he had bought a Luger in Brighton. Some queer nig-nog lover in Notting Hill who liked to hang around with thieving toerags like Bruce Reynolds wasn't much of a priority.

Just then, the operator yelled out Duke's name, telling him he had a call. 'Pass his name along to the Vice,' he advised Billy. 'He gets caught cottaging, tell them to let us know. Otherwise, we'll save him for later.'

George Hatherill's nickname of Top Man wasn't just a respectful courtesy title. Billy stood before the man's desk in an office crammed with commemorative photographs and awards, going back to before the war. Hatherill was well past the age when he could have retired, but there was always one last little job for him. Right now, with the senior management laid low by a series of unforeseen deaths – three heart-attacks and a cancer that had spread with terrifying speed – and long-term illnesses, it was to supervise a reorganisation of the Yard. But everyone knew he was really sniffing around for the Last Big Case, the one that would seal his career.

Hatherill was portly and avuncular, smoked like the proverbial chimney, enjoyed a good glass of wine – thanks to his pre-war travels on the continent on police business, which also gave him his eight languages – and was always well turned-out. Today he had on a dark three-piece suit, with a white saw-toothed handkerchief in the top pocket, a finely pinstriped shirt, Windsor-knotted tie and, although Billy couldn't see them, doubtless mirror-finished shoes.

Billy was aware of the man's career and its scope. Hatherill had met Hitler and Himmler when he was investigating forgery of British fivers in Germany before the war. Which was ironic considering that during the war Hitler and Himmler went into the same forgery business. He had even been allowed to tour Gestapo headquarters and got a good sense of Nazi justice. He had also been responsible for the capture of Peter Griffiths, the so-called Beast of Blackburn. The latter had raped a three-year-old girl whom he had abducted from her hospital cot. It was said Hatherill stood virtually every officer in the Met a drink the day Griffiths had hanged.

In recent years he had gathered a reputation for long-windedness, for recapitulating highlights of his career, as if rehearsing for the memoirs he claimed to be writing. Some said he was only sticking around for the Last Big Case so he had a closing chapter for the book that wasn't entitled *My Twilight Years Behind a Desk*.

'I have been speaking to Mr Millen and a few of your colleagues,' said Hatherill, tapping Billy's file. 'They mostly have good things to say about you.'

Billy noted the 'mostly' and wondered what the caveats might be. 'Thank you, sir.'

'Of course, it is not easy fitting into the Flying Squad. They have their own way of doing things.' He arched an eyebrow.

He was referring to the informal way of recruiting. The Flying Squad liked to 'bring on their own', which helped foster the camaraderie and elitism for which it was known. It also meant that when officers were transferred out, they sometimes had trouble adjusting to a different regime. 'But it appears you have made a good job of it.'

'Yes, sir.'

'But I think you need a wider experience. You did ten weeks' Detective School?'

'I did.'

'Then how long in plainclothes before coming across?'

'Six months, give or take. But I was an Aide to CID as well. In and out of uniform.'

'Mainly in,' said Hatherill, showing he had read the file. 'Not enough, m'boy, not enough. Well, pack your bags. Mr Millen has released you to me. We are going on a trip.'

'Trip?'

'Cornwall – Newquay. You know it?'

'No, guv.'

'Actually a little place called Perranporth. Look it up.'

He thought about Len's reaction. It would be something along the lines of 'teacher's pet'. 'Sir, how long will we be gone? I mean, I have ongoing cases—'

'I know what you have. It's a pretty light caseload though, now Islington is sorted. DS Haslam can handle it on his own. And we'll be away as long as it takes.'

Hatherill lit up a cigarette from a burnished walnut box

with what could be a German eagle on it, picked out in silver. Almost as an after-thought he offered Billy one of the Senior Service. After a moment's hesitation, he took one. Hatherill lit both with an enormous desk lighter. 'Take a seat. Look, Billy, I'm long enough in the tooth to know that breadth of your experience will matter as much as its intensity. The Squad can't teach you everything. There is one investigation I recall that demonstrates that perfectly. Did you ever hear of the Penn murder case?'

Billy's heart sank. He remembered Duke's advice about feigning an epileptic fit if the guv'nor starting blahing. 'Rings a bell, sir.'

'Well, look it up, look it up. This one in Perranporth could be as interesting.'

Billy realised he had been spared a long walk down Memory Lane and brightened. 'What is it, sir? In Cornwall?'

'A headless corpse.'

Now the old windbag had his interest. *The Last Big Case*.

Bruce Reynolds had had enough. So had Franny. He hadn't told his wife exactly what he was up to, but she knew from the comings and goings, the phone calls, the drinking and the short temper that something big was on the cards and that Bruce was feeling the pressure.

So, on the night before the football match at Clapham Common, Bruce agreed to drive Franny down to Redhill to visit Charmian and Ronnie Biggs. The two girls could make dinner and have a good chinwag, while Ronnie and Bruce went to the local. It would do him good to talk about something other than trains. They parked their son Nick with Mary, a friend, and motored down in a TR4, borrowed from the garage that was reshodding and servicing the Lotus. Bruce took with him a copy of *Afro Blue Impressions* by John Coltrane, which he had picked up in Dobell's on Charing Cross Road. He presented it as a gift to Ronnie, the only one of his friends who would really appreciate it.

'I think you'll like it. Bit out there in places, if you know what I mean. It's got this mad twenty-one-minute version of "My Favourite Things",' Bruce explained as the two men left the house. 'Don't play it while Charmian's in the room. Drives Franny mental. She says he's just forgotten the tune, that's why it's so bleedin' long.'

The two men walked down to the Red Lion, which Ronnie said was his new favourite boozer. Bruce knew the beefy, affable Ronnie was a so-so thief but excellent company, and he was obviously popular: Biggsy was greeted by name by almost everyone in the place.

Having equipped themselves with mild and bitters, the two men found a table, away from the jukebox that was pumping out 'Foot Tapper' by the Shadows. A couple of burly would-be Hank Marvins at the bar were doing the Shadows' walk, swinging imaginary guitars.

'Look at those plonkers,' said Ronnie, speaking loudly so the men could hear. 'More Lee Marvin than Hank. I hope they lay bricks better than they mime guitar.' He laughed when that earned him synchronised V-signs. Satisfied, Ronnie turned to his old friend. 'You all right, Bruce? Look tired.'

'I've been busy.'

Ronnie cracked a smile. 'When were you never?'

'What about you?'

'Usual. Bit of painting here and there. How's that racing driver pal of yours, Roy?'

'Doing well.'

'No more sponsorship? Doesn't he need a nice Duckhams sign painted on his car?'

This train job goes off, Roy won't need to go cap in hand to Duckhams, Bruce thought. 'Not yet. But the cash will come once he gets his name in the paper a bit more. They'd be daft not to invest in him. He's going places.'

Ronnie sniffed, as if suddenly a little nervous. 'Talking of investing, I was wondering, Bruce – you know, if you were interested in helping me set something up.'

Bruce waited. The sentence was ambiguous. It could mean lots of things.

'I mean something on the straight and narrow.'

'Not motors, I hope?'

Ronnie's last three-year stretch had been for a bungled car theft. It had been a harsh sentence, Bruce thought. Cars were so easy to steal, he wondered why everyone didn't do it. You could make a key that worked out of tinfoil for older models; newer ones had the serial number written on the dashboard or on the collar of the ignition lock. And when you went to get a key made, nobody ever asked you if you actually owned the car you wanted it for. Which, of course, made it tragic that Ronnie was caught for something that should have been child's play. He just wasn't a born thief.

'No. Painting and decorating. I've been doing this bungalow in Eastbourne. Seems to me, those seaside places need painting more than any other, what with the wind and the salt. Lots of demand for painters, but most of the blokes do a terrible job. Slapdash. No stripping back to bare wood, no filling. It's criminal.'

They both laughed.

'Ronnie Biggs, the decorator you can trust?' Bruce asked.

'Well, as long as you don't leave too much lying around.'

'What do you need?'

'I reckon one or two grand. Enough to cover a van, leaflets, adverts in local papers and all that.'

Bruce drank while he thought. Part of the plan he had spent the week putting together involved lorries, which would need disguising, with new plates and new colour schemes. 'A few hundred is the best I could manage right now, mate. Had some expenses. We might have a painting job for you, though.'

'We? You mean you and Fran?'

'Nooooo.' He let the word draw out. 'Me and some of the chaps.'

Ronnie shook his head vigorously. 'Look, Bruce, if it's anything not quite on the level, best count me out. Charmian said she'd have my bollocks on the mantelpiece next time.'

'Fair enough. But I might be in a position to help you out in a couple of months.'

'A couple of months? That long? Must be a big one, eh?'

'Just being careful. You know how it is. I don't think Franny wants to see me across a metal table again.'

He could see curiosity in Ronnie's eyes, the conflict of a man who wants to know more but is scared to ask. It would be like describing a gourmet feast to a starving man, so Bruce just said, 'Another?'

When he returned with the refills, Bruce asked: 'You OK for the moment though?'

'Scrabbling a bit. Working for this old geezer. Hasn't got a lot of money. House is in a right state. He pays me half in cash and half in bloody kind at the yards. Actually, you should bring your Nick down. Both the boys could have a go. The two Nicks.'

Like Bruce, Ronnie had called his son after Nick Adams, the Hemingway character. A love of Papa was something else, along with the jazz, which they shared. Hemingway, Miles, Brubeck, Orwell, Jamal, Fitzgerald, Mingus, Cheever, Dexter, Capote – it was their common language.

'Have a go at what?' Bruce asked.

'Driving the train.'

Bruce slopped a mouthful of beer onto his slacks. 'Shit.'

He took out his handkerchief and blotted the mark on his thigh. 'What train?'

'That Stan Peters I was talking about – the bloke whose bungalow I'm doing up. Well, he's getting on a bit so he only does some of the shunting once or twice a week now. But he takes Nick along on the footplate sometimes. Lets him do the horn, everything.'

Bruce couldn't quite believe what he was hearing. 'Footplate?'

Ronnie was puzzled and slightly alarmed at how Bruce's demeanour had suddenly changed. His body had become taut, as if he'd received an electric shock, his eyes were bulging and a pulse was throbbing visibly in his temple.

'So this . . . Stan,' Bruce asked, leaning forward, the pressure in his chest meaning he could only take shallow breaths. 'He's what, exactly?'

'I told you. A train driver.'

Thirty-five

Cornwall, June 1963

The headless corpse had been transported to Truro and examined there by the local Home Office pathologist. In fact, as Billy Naughton discovered, it wasn't just headless, there was precious little of the rest of it left on the slab of the overlit mortuary. The internal organs had mostly disappeared as well as one arm, and the remaining limbs looked like sections of a barrage balloon, all bloated and blue.

It was so far from being the body of a young woman that Billy found he was almost able to distance himself from it as having once been human. He could look upon the remains dispassionately, as if it really were just flotsam, albeit of organic origin. Only the rich chemical brew that infused the room's atmosphere made him feel nauseous.

Norman Carter, the pathologist, was wearing a double-breasted suit with a hospital gown thrown carelessly over it, as if he had rushed in from lunch.

'Well, of course, if we had got it when it was first spotted, we might have had more luck,' said Carter, who had travelled from Bristol for a second time to go over his findings and was clearly none too pleased with having to venture so far from home again. 'As it is, the saltwater immersion has ruined the fingerprints. There is, of course, no face.'

'What do you mean, if you had got it when it was first spotted?' asked Hatherill. They had only arrived the night before and were billeted in a pub near the beach where the body had been washed up. He had read through the preliminary reports on the finding, but none had mentioned a delay in contacting the authorities.

'You don't know the background?' asked Carter, looking over his half-moon spectacles.

Hatherill ignored the slight sneer in Carter's voice. 'I thought we had better see our victim first, and get your reaction. I've read the report of PC Trellick who found her.'

'The bobby might have found her, but she was seen on that beach a good week before – when she still had two arms and, I'll wager, all her internal organs.'

'Bloody hell,' said Billy. 'So why wasn't she brought here then?'

'Good question, lad. She lay on that beach for eight days.'

'Where is the head?' asked Billy.

The pathologist shrugged. 'Missing in action. As I said in my notes, there appear to be saw-marks on the cervical vertebrae that remain.'

'Saw-marks?' Hatherill asked. 'You sure?'

'Well, there are striations. You want to take a look?'

Hatherill stepped forward and Carter swung a magnifying lens over the stump of the neck. Billy held back, not wanting to see the gore in any greater detail. Hatherill made grunting noises.

'Sir, isn't it an offence not to report a dead body?'

Carter looked up at him with pity in his eyes. 'Have you been to Cornwall before, son?'

'No.'

He gave a wan smile. 'You'll learn.'

Hatherill clapped his hands together. 'Right. Can you try and get us some dabs?'

'Off this?'

Hatherill gave a flattering smile. 'Well, you pathologists have your methods, I know.'

Carter thought for a few moments, stroking his chin as he did so. 'I could dissolve away some of the tissue on the fingertips, see if I can get an impression of the underlying ridges then – if you don't mind me removing the hands and taking them back to Bristol.'

'I don't, and I think she is past caring. Don't you, Detective?'

'Sir,' Billy agreed.

'And palm prints?' Hatherill asked.

Carter tossed one of the hands back and forth, like a flipper. 'They might be easier to obtain, yes.'

The Old Man turned to Billy. 'People forget palm prints. They're just as distinctive though, as any fingerprints. So, DC Naughton, any thoughts?'

Billy felt himself blush as the two older men stared at him. I wish I were back in London, he thought. Even turning over queers in public toilets is better than this. But that wouldn't do as an answer.

'That the head was sawn off to prevent identification.'

'Then why not the hands?'

'Because . . . well, if the woman had no criminal record, the murdered would know we wouldn't have anything on file.'

Hatherill shook his head. 'But once we have a list of missing women in the area we could dust those houses. The murderer, if there were one, wouldn't know how long the corpse would be immersed, would he? If it is a he.'

Billy tried to think of something pertinent to say, but nothing came.

'Let's get the list of everyone who might have seen the body during the week it was there. Dog-walkers, beach-combers, fishermen, holidaymakers. We'll interview them all, reinterview if they have already been done.' Hatherill took out his cigarette case and placed a Senior Service in his mouth. He was enjoying himself. 'Then I want you to phone the Met in London.'

Billy assumed he meant Scotland Yard. 'We need more men?'

'Not the Metropolitan Police, the Meteorological Office. We are at the seaside, remember. I want a weather forecast.'

It had been raining persistently for two days until that morning and the sky was still a flat pewter colour, threatening more of the same. Clapham Common was greasy underfoot, the grass beaten into submission and dotted with muddy patches the size of small ponds. Bruce Reynolds was concerned. He knew how competitive some of these men could be. He imagined Charlie going for Jimmy, or Buster taking on Gordy and it all ending in grief.

'I want you to think about what you are doing.' Bruce tapped his temple forcefully with his right index finger. 'Think why we are here. We don't need any broken legs now, do we?' he warned them as they gathered on the edge of the pitch. 'It's not Yugoslavia versus Russia. And I don't want any Mujics. Got it?'

Tito's lads and Khrushchev's boys had faced up to each other in Group One of the previous year's World Cup in Chile. It had been a scrappy match in all senses of the word, with on-pitch fighting and a broken leg sustained by Dubinski thanks to a heavy-footed tackle. The photo of the Russian's agony flashed around the world; Mujic was sent home in disgrace.

Bruce looked at the group of men gathered for a kick-about.

Some, like Roy, had gone to town with their kit. He looked like a pocket-sized Roy of the Rovers. Buster, on the other hand, in his long black gym shorts and vest, looked more like Alf Tupper, the Tough of the Track. Most were somewhere in between.

'Right, let's get the important bit over first. Gordy, pick your men. I'll have Roy and Tony.'

'Oh no, you don't,' said Gordy. 'Two fast wingers, I bet. You can have one of them.'

In the end, it was Bruce, Roy, Buster, Jimmy White and Charlie to take on Gordy, Tony, Ralph – a friend of Bruce's who would help with the signals if need be – Tommy and Roger. Brian Field, the solicitor, opted to stay on the sidelines. 'I'll peel the oranges at half-time,' he said with his cheeky grin.

'You can buy the pints at full-time,' said Buster, pointing towards the Plough.

'Before we get started,' said Bruce, looking at Roger. 'I may have solved the problem of moving the train.' He suddenly had their complete attention, and felt like Alf Ramsey giving a pep talk. 'Ronnie Biggs knows a driver.'

'Will he let us at him?' Roy asked.

'No. It's his shout. I said I'd bring Ronnie in.'

Buster gave a loud sniff. 'None of us have worked with him. Not really.'

'I told you. He's reliable,' said Bruce, with feeling. He'd seen Ronnie beaten by screws till his testicles were like purple rugby balls, and he hadn't given an inch. 'He's keen.' The truth was, once Ronnie had realised the scale of the job, all his concerns about upsetting Charmian went out of the window. She wouldn't be miffed when she saw a heap of fivers on the bed. When he and Franny had left, Biggsy had given him a clear message. No Ronnie, No Stan the Engine Driver.

'He can be very useful,' Bruce went on. 'Ronnie's a big strong lad. Once we get the train to that bridge, we are going to need to get the bags down to the lorries.'

'Lorries?' asked Roy, dismay in his voice.

'I'll come to that,' said Bruce. 'And besides, Tony has worked with him before, haven't you?'

All eyes turned on Tony, but Tony examined Bruce's face. He had never even met Ronnie Biggs, let alone worked with him. 'Yeah. He's all right.'

'I can drive the bleedin' train,' said Roy, with a hint of petulance.

'What? You bought a Hornby Dublo?'

Roy glared at Buster. He *had* bought a train set, but hadn't told anyone about it yet. Besides, it was a Triang. 'No, I haven't got a bloody Hornby, but I've got the *Railwayman's Handbook*. Looks easy enough. I drive a racing car – how hard can a train be?'

Bruce flicked from face to face, gauging the mood.

'It would be nicer to keep it tight,' said Gordy. 'And not bring in too many outsiders.'

Bruce knew that wasn't going to be an option. On paper

he had worked out they needed eighteen people to do this; sixteen at a stretch. They were still short. 'Well, we'll see if you can,' Bruce said to Roy.

'How do you mean?' asked the wheel-man.

'We'll go and find a train to drive. You lot have been doing the yards. You must know ways in.'

Several of them nodded. 'Security's piss poor,' added Gordy. 'Pair of overalls, you can walk right in and out, no questions asked.'

'And we've found the mail train,' said Buster with a grin, unable to keep the news to himself. 'Up near Wembley, in the sidings. As your man said, the HVP is not connected to the rest of the train by a door or corridor. It's self-contained.'

'Good. But I'll need to take a look for myself,' said Bruce. All they had to do then was figure out how to unhook it from the body of the train. But, as Roy would say, how hard could that be? Stan would know. If they brought Stan and Ronnie in, that is. 'And then we can let Roy play choo-choos.'

'Fuck that. Are we going to play football or what? It's going to rain soon.' It was Charlie who, as usual, had been listening without saying much. 'I paid two guineas for these.' He pointed down at his shiny new Puma Pele Signature boots.

Bruce picked up the ball. 'You're right. That's enough villainy for now. Twenty minutes, then half-time, another chat about the transportation we'll need, and change ends. OK? Right – my lads over here. I want to give you a proper talk without those dirty bastards overhearing.'

When Tony Fortune walked up the stairs to the flat, he was fully expecting a bollocking. Although he had changed after football – 4–2 to Gordy's team – his face was still mud-streaked and he smelled of sweat and beer. There had been two pints in the Plough and then most of them had adjourned to Bobby Welch's place in Camberwell for an after-hours session. Charlie, Bruce and Buster were still there. Tony, his head swimming with alcohol on an empty stomach, had headed back, no doubt to a ruined, cremated lunch.

'Marie,' he shouted as he came in, his nostrils twitching. Lamb. And it wasn't burned.

'In here, luv.'

His wife was in the lounge, watching television. 'Sooty?' he asked as he walked in, dumping his kit, just in time to see Harry Corbett get a squirt of water in his eye.

'Just waiting for *Oliver Twist* to come on.' She struggled to her feet, her belly weighing on her now.

'Sit down. Sorry I'm late.'

'Knew you would be. Didn't put dinner on till late. Be ready about six.'

'Lovely.'

'Shall I run you a bath?'

Even in his slightly befuddled state, Tony sensed something was up. A campaign was under way. 'What is it?'

'What's what?'

'Whatever it is that you have to tell me.'

She smiled at him, showing too much gum. 'Oh nothing, Tony. It'll wait. I'll run you a nice hot bath. There's a pale ale in the kitchen, if you fancy.'

He didn't really want the beer, but he dutifully sat in a soapy bath cradling it, going over what had happened that day. Although things had developed in fits and starts, some kind of shape was taking place to the tickle. Jimmy White was quartermaster, to source any gear needed for what Bruce was calling 'the mission'. Roy was, perhaps, to drive the train. Brian was to explore the possibility of establishing a base near the spot where the train was to be stopped, but not too near. Charlie and Gordy were to come up with ways to move more than a dozen men around without attracting attention. Roger was to go back and check the timings of the TPO mail trains and that the signals would present no unforeseen problems. And Bruce? Bruce was going to pull it all together.

'More hot water?'

His wife came in and turned on the Ascot, which ignited like one of the Americans' space rockets, spitting steam before a thin stream of scalding water came out.

She sat on the edge of the bath as it roared away. 'I have been thinking, Tony.'

Here we go.

'I've been thinking we should move. I know we were joking about the doctor saying we need a bigger place, for the baby. But it's true. A garden would be nice, wouldn't it?'

Well, he couldn't say he hadn't seen that one coming. She had been talking about a nursery for the boy or girl, been collecting colour cards from Woolworths. 'Y'know, when business picks up . . .' he began.

'Thing is, my sister Alice has heard about this place for sale.'

'For sale?' He sat up, sending water slopping over the rolltop, and switched off the Ascot. 'I can't afford to buy anywhere.'

'You could get a mortgage.'

'Not once they have seen the books. It's been a bad six months.'

Her voice hardened. 'Oh, I'll tell the baby that, shall I? "Sorry we are living in a shit-hole with a gas heater that might kill us all one day and one bedroom with a nasty patch of damp in the corner. Been a bad six months, see".' Her long-lost Irish accent always surfaced when she was angry. He saw her touch the bump and grimace slightly.

Tony blew out his cheeks and slumped back, sliding down until the water was up to his chin.

'I'm trying. Trying to make it right.'

She leaned forward, so her face was level with his. 'I know

you are. I'm not daft. I know you have something in the works, something I am not to know about. Since when did you play football? On a Sunday? And go drinking with the lads?'

'It's all right. I'll knock it on the head. There're dozens of blokes who would kill for a sniff of this.'

She swirled her hand in the water. 'Don't be too hasty.'

'What?'

'I said, don't be too hasty. About knocking it on the head.'

'What about all that "I don't want my baby growing up with his father in pokey" stuff.'

'Well I don't, it's true. But maybe he won't. Maybe it's something worth taking a chance on.' She flicked some suds at his face. 'Is it?'

Tony suspected a trap. She was waiting for an admission of guilt, and then she would bring the house down around his ears. He kept quiet.

'Come on, I'm your wife. Shouldn't this be a joint decision?'

All he offered was a shrug.

'Look, this place, it's nothing too grand. Off the Holloway Road, not far from Alice. But she'll be able to help with the baby, and the landlord is willing to rent it for six months till we have enough of a deposit saved . . .'

'You've seen it?' he asked.

'Yes. You know those nice roads, on the left as you go down towards the cinema?'

He did. They were expensive, for that area at least. Neat Victorian terraces with, as she said, gardens, albeit small ones. 'So who's keeping secrets now?'

'I was just waiting for the right time to bring it up, Tony. Just like you were waiting for the right time to tell me.' Her hands plunged into the water and he felt her grip his testicles and give a light squeeze. 'It's something big, isn't it?'

She was smiling, but even so, he slapped her arm away. 'Yes. Yes, it is.'

'Good.' She stood up and brushed the suds from herself. 'Dinner's almost ready. You can tell me all about it over a nice Sunday lunch.'

Fuck a very large duck, thought Tony. Wonders would never cease. 'Tell the wives nothing,' Bruce had advised. Easy for you to say, Tony thought. You don't have one like Marie.

Thirty-six

Cornwall, June 1963

The boy who had been first to spot the woman's torso was eleven years old, but looked younger. He had a head that was too large for his skin-and-bone body, saucer eyes and a scalp almost shaved clean but for a ridge of hair running along the apex of his skull, like a wayward privet hedge. Or someone from *The Last of the Mohicans* who had been left out in the rain, thought Billy.

He lived with his parents in a low granite-and-slate cottage on the edge of the village. The interview took place in the kitchen, where a blackened range heated a pot of what, from the smell, was fish stew and a kettle, boiling for tea. The sinewy parents sat either side of the boy, reassuring him he had done nothing wrong.

'Bull's-eye?' offered Hatherill. From his suit pocket he produced a crumpled bag of the boiled sweets and offered one to young Harry Bone.

'Go on, son,' said Harry Senior.

The boy reached out a grubby hand and took one. Hatherill offered them around the table and, when there were no takers, popped one into his own mouth. There was silence, apart from the sucking of the bull's-eyes and the building urgency of the kettle.

'So, Harry,' slurped Hatherill, 'do you remember when you first saw the body?'

'Didn't know it was no body,' the lad said truculently.

Harry Senior flicked the boy's shaved head with a bony finger. 'Sir.'

'It's all right. He can call me George. That OK, Harry? Good. Now, I appreciate it could have looked like any old bit of driftwood or flotsam. But when did you first see it?'

'Would have been a Saturday,' he said. 'I know 'cause I had helped Dad at the garage in the morning and then walked down to the beach. Saw it then.'

'Which Saturday would this have been, Harry?'

'It would have been the fifth,' said Mrs Bone as she got up to make the tea.

'So about two and a half weeks ago.'

'Suppose. Yeah.'

'And what did you think when you saw it?'

An exaggerated shrug. 'Nothing.'

Hatherill worked on his bull's-eye some more. 'Well, not nothing. You never think nothing. But did you think: "That's nothing important" or "Oh look, there's what looks like a body, but it can't be"?'

'Dunno.'

'You have to understand,' said the dad, in his thick accent, 'that we get lots washed up here on the Cornish coast. Used to it, y'see. Not worth making a fuss over.'

Even a dead body? thought Billy.

'Tell you what. How about we have a nice cup of tea, we grown-ups, and then you take me down to the beach and show me what you saw and when.' He looked at the parents. 'How would that be?'

Twenty minutes later the trio – Billy, Harry and George – were traipsing across the sand of the bay, with the boy four paces ahead. Gulls wheeled overhead, screeching as if complaining about being denied their human flesh to feed on. The tide was coming in, the sea docile, the sun trying to break through. It was a beautiful long stretch of beach, framed by black rocks, moulded into fascinating shapes. Nice holiday spot, thought Billy. Or, at least, he would have thought so if he didn't keep seeing that ruined torso, flopping about on the foreshore, being poked and pulled by the waves.

'You are wondering how you can ignore a body, aren't you?' the TM asked Billy.

'It crossed my mind.'

'Think of what this place was. Treacherous coast. Lots of shipwrecks. Not all of them natural. Wreckers, you know? Luring ships onto rocks . . .'

'I thought that was all, you know, stories.'

Hatherill simply raised an eyebrow. 'Put it this way. There is nothing remarkable about a body washing up on the beach hereabouts.'

Billy pointed at the boy. 'Not even for a nipper like him?'

'Especially not for a nipper like him.' He raised his voice. 'Where was it, Harry?'

'Over here.'

They swerved to their right, and Harry took them to the sea's edge, close to a cluster of three jagged, seaweed-encrusted rocks. The boy indicated a spot in front of them. Billy looked around. It was possible the outcrops had hidden the corpse from most people's view.

'And what was the tide doing?' asked Hatherill, lighting a cigarette. He looked slightly comical in his tweed suit and shiny black brogues, peering through his thick glasses at the lad, the sea edging closer to his feet with each lap of the waves.

'Tide were in. The thing was just here. It had seagulls on it. I didn't know it were a body right then, honest. Thought it was a seal.' Then the lad burst into tears.

Hatherill stepped forward and shot an arm round him, pulling him close. With his cigarette, he indicated that Billy should walk back up the beach and leave the two of them alone.

As Billy began the trudge back towards the low cliffs, he wondered what the hell he was doing out here. Why had Hatherill insisted on dragging him to Cornwall if he was going to exclude him? He had anticipated being Robin to the Top Man's Batman, Tonto to his Lone Ranger, but he was being treated more like Jimmy Olsen – the annoying kid – to his Superman. Or Boo-Boo to his Yogi Bear.

He reached a rock arch, expertly carved by the Cornish storms from the cliff-face, and sat at its base. He watched the two distant figures patrolling the shoreline, deep in conversation, devouring more bull's-eyes as they spoke, and pondered on what was going on back in London while they were messing about in the sticks.

'I fuckin' hate the countryside. It stinks. Phoar – cop a load of that. Worse than one of your farts, Gordy.'

'Shut up, Buster,' said Bruce. 'Wind your window up if you don't like fresh air.'

'Fresh? What's fresh about a cow's arse?'

They were heading west, past a string of dairy farms just outside Aylesbury, in the Jag they had borrowed off Brian Field. A 3.8. Roy wouldn't have approved, but Bruce was enjoying it. He clocked the milometer. More than twenty miles from Bridego Bridge so far.

'How much is this place?' asked Buster.

'Five thousand, five hundred pounds.'

299

Buster whistled.

'It's a whole farm, you cunt,' said Gordy.

'We got five grand left in the pot?' It was a good question, because the 'seed' money from the airport job was almost gone.

'I spoke to Brian. He'd do it through his boss, all above board. Make sure we only have to put ten per cent down for now. We can raise the rest, no problem. Go to the Frenchman if we have to, eh, Buster?'

Frenchie the Banker had put some money up for the airport, in return for a hefty percentage. 'If we have to.'

They had crossed over the A418, and were travelling on the B4011. The destination wasn't actually on the OS map, but Bruce had marked the spot with a Biro'd 'X', like a treasure map. 'The turning is at Oakley, on the Bicester Road.'

'Yeah, I remember,' said Bruce. He had already seen the farm, even met the owners, and knew exactly where it was. He wanted a second opinion about the place and location, that was all.

'And you've seen what is at Bicester?' Gordy asked.

'No.'

'The Army.'

'The Army,' repeated Bruce thoughtfully.

'And what do the Army do?' Gordy asked.

'Manoeuvres,' said Bruce.

'Sometimes at night,' added Buster, catching on.

300

'Brilliant.' Bruce's brain kicked into overdrive, as they all knew it would. 'That's bloody brilliant.'

They drove on in silence, each digesting what this new strategy might involve. In his mind, Bruce was already creating his uniform. Maybe he would get to be a real Colonel after all. A Major at least. Who was going to suspect the Army? Who was going to stand up to them? It was the perfect front.

'It's along here somewhere,' said Gordy eventually. 'Turning on the right.'

Bruce found the track leading to the farm, and bounced the Jag up the muddy lane, the cows to the right watching its progress with their blank stares.

'It's got a main house, ugly but big enough for the number of blokes we'll need, mains water, a generator for electricity, and plenty of outhouses, including sheds and a garage the size of an aircraft hanger. Means we can get everything under cover, in case of choppers.' Helicopters were a new threat; the police didn't have any of their own, but the RAF was only too willing to lend a hand.

'Twenty-seven miles,' said Gordy, looking at the clock. 'About a thirty- or forty-minute drive from the bridge. If you don't have a Jag.'

''Bout right, I reckon,' said Bruce, 'for somewhere to lie low till the worst of the scream blows over.'

'It's a bit of a shit-hole. What's it called again?' asked Buster, as the Jag took a right through an open gate and the first of the smallholding's down-at-heel buildings came into view.

'Leatherslade Farm,' replied Bruce.

They took the boy back home from the beach as the afternoon turned cold once more, with grey-tinged clouds lining up on the horizon and a shrill wind whipping low across the sand. Hatherill told the parents that he was a bright lad who had been most helpful. They offered the Commander and Billy a glass of wine. Hatherill readily accepted this unexpected bonus; Billy, suspecting any wine would have been made in the kitchen sink, opted for a small scotch instead.

After they said their goodbyes, they walked back to the digs at the pub. 'Not a bad drop of claret, that,' said Hatherill appreciatively, smacking his lips. 'I fancy another. Join me? Then we'll have dinner.'

They settled into the corner of the inn, Hatherill with his large glass of red, Billy with a pint of mild. After he had taken a sip of wine and slurped it around his mouth unattractively, Hatherill gave a sigh of contentment then said, 'I'm just going up to my room to fetch something.'

Billy sat back, looking at the pictures on the walls. Seascapes mostly, some terrible oils, plus old pictures of lifeboat crews. A few of the locals glanced his way now and then, one or two of them muttering afterwards. The Inn of the Seventh Happiness it wasn't, he thought. He'd have as warm a welcome if he was carrying the plague.

He moved to the bar and ordered a packet of crisps – a transaction carried out mostly in grunts on the part of the barman. The crisps still came with a little twist of blue paper for the salt, a touch that was disappearing rapidly in London. He was shaking the bag to distribute the salt evenly when Hatherill reappeared and placed a large padded envelope on the table. The TM then ignored it as he went back to his wine.

He slurped some more before he spoke again. 'Why did you want to become a copper, Billy?'

The younger man had to smile. 'If I had a penny...'

Hatherill laughed with him. 'Me too. But you have to examine it, don't you? Why am I doing this? Is it because I read *PC49* or watched *Dixon of Dock Green*? I suppose some of the kids watching *Z Cars* might be pulled in by that, eh? A whole generation of Barlows and Fancy Smiths. But that's not it with you, is it?'

'No.'

'It's to make a difference, isn't it? In a way an insurance clerk or a bank manager never can. We can influence society. We can find out who that poor dead girl is and we can affect people's lives. For good or bad.'

Billy wondered if the wine had gone to the Top Man's head. 'What did you get from the lad?'

'Not much. I got more from the parents.'

'The parents? They hardly said two words.'

Hatherill winked. 'Ah, but what they *didn't* say was important. And what they did.'

Billy racked his brains, but could think of nothing but polite chit-chat. 'Would you like a cup of tea? How about a nice glass of wine? A scotch then, how would that be?'

The pub's dog, a rough old collie, raised itself from the carpet, padded over and looked at Billy, its rheumy eyes on the crisps. He made to give it one but the dog bared its teeth. Talk about biting the hand that feeds you, he thought.

'The girl's head wasn't sawn off, Billy,' Hatherill said quietly. 'The pathologist is wrong.' He took more wine. 'The thing is, if she had been on the beach for a week, washed back and forward, those marks could have been caused by the sand. I've seen it before. Body washed ashore at Margate that had come all the way round from Lowestoft. Woman in a dinghy, caught in a storm. Bones sticking out of limbs when she was washed up, and what looked like wool covering her. She was left there for a few days because they thought it was a sheep. But it was kapok. The stuffing of her lifejacket looked like sheep's wool. But in those few days, the ends of the bones were abraded by the sand. Same here.'

'So . . .'

'So there was a big storm a few days before she was first

spotted by the boy. He said so. Here and in the Channel. I want you to check all the shipping companies, see if they have any missing passengers.'

'Missing passengers?'

'Woman overboard.'

'You think she came off a ship?'

Hatherill sipped his wine once more and looked at it admiringly, swirling it in the glass. 'This really is very, very good. You don't expect such good wine in Cornwall.' He glanced around the dark, scruffy room, which smelled mostly of shag tobacco and stale beer. 'Especially in a pub like this. Must compliment the landlord. Yes, I think she came off a ship. Either in the Atlantic or the Channel. The head could easily have been swiped off by a propeller, especially if she went over the stern. My only question is, was the bobby who found her in on it or not?'

Billy had lost the thread. 'You mean PC Trellick? In on what?'

'You know there are two kinds of bent policemen? Some bend the rules so they can get the villain. We call that bent for the job. There are others who are obviously in it only to feather their own nest. Bent for themselves.'

'You are wondering which Trellick is?'

Hatherill held the last inch of wine in his glass to the light, checking for sediment. 'No. He's a third type, I think, one we don't get so much in London. Bent for his family. That's a different kind of pressure. No, I'm not wondering about him.' He grabbed the padded envelope and slid the contents out onto the table. 'I'm wondering about *you*.'

Billy stared down at the red and silver object before him. There was a screaming in his ears, a hundred jumbled questions melded into a cacophony, and a rising feeling of panic clutched at his chest. There was no mistaking what it was. It was a common enough item, but he recognised each dent on the lid. It was the Oxo tin from under his bed, the one containing his three hundred and thirty-three pounds, ten shillings.

Thirty-seven

London, June 1963

Roy had cut a hole in the chain-link fence two weeks ago and it still hadn't been repaired. Careless. He pulled back the wire and stepped aside to let Bruce climb through. It was gone midnight and, although a few blue-ish lights shone in the shunting yard, there was no sign of another soul.

Nevertheless, Roy kept his voice down as he ducked through after Bruce.

'Thing is, lying low at this farm, aren't we sitting ducks? We could be down the M1 and back in London in, I dunno, thirty minutes. Forty tops.'

'And if they put up road-blocks?' said Bruce, bored with the argument. 'And I told you, imagine it on *Police Five*.

Did anyone see a convoy of high-speed cars entering London? Yes, they bloody well did.'

They slithered down an embankment onto gravel and paused, ears pricked, listening for any sign that they had drawn attention to themselves. An owl hooted, so clear and clichéd, Roy thought it must be fake and said so.

'What, you think we've stumbled into an Apache raiding party?' Bruce hissed.

They straightened their overalls and strode towards the dark, angular shapes of the parked rolling stock, as if they had every right to be there. Bruce had a torch with him, but he kept it off. It would do to blind anyone if they were confronted.

'Look, Roy,' he whispered as they walked. 'I know you don't think a tickle is complete without a fast motor, but this one is different. I still want you in charge of the transport, goes without saying. Happy if you bring Tony in. But no Jags or Daimlers, OK?'

'OK.'

'Fuck's sake, you might even get to drive a train. That should keep you happy. Where is it?'

'Follow me.'

They moved between dark, silent coaches and wagons, crossing over the tracks, Roy looking to left and right, hoping to find the engine he had picked out on his last venture into the yards.

'They've moved it,' he said.

Bruce sighed. 'It's a train, lad. That's what they do. Move.'

'Let's try over here.'

The coaches, trucks and tankers gave Bruce the creeps. They were slumbering behemoths, mechanical dinosaurs parked into dormitories and he felt as if the creatures could wake at any moment. Lights would come on, vacuum pumps throb, steam lines hiss, and one of them would demand to know what they were doing. Could be his gran had read him *The Little Engine That Could* one too many times as a kid, he reckoned.

'What about that one?' asked Bruce, pointing to a square block of metal on wheels.

'No. That's an 0-Eight. I want an 0-Three.'

As their eyes adjusted to the half-light and deep shadows, Roy tugged at his sleeve. 'Seen it.'

'That thing?' It was a squat little shunter, sitting alone on an empty section of track. 'It's a bloody great monster that pulls the mail. Not something you wind up.'

'They're like cars. If you can drive a Mini, you can drive a Roller.'

Bruce wasn't convinced, but followed Roy to the engine. He flashed the torch to locate the footholds and they both clambered up the side. Roy unzipped his leather jacket and produced a thick, well-thumbed book. On its cover were the words NOT FOR THE GENERAL PUBLIC.

'What's that?'

'The manual.'

'You nicked it?'

'Drivers leave them lying around all the time. They just get another one. Shine the torch on the controls, will you?'

Bruce did as he was told and Roy thumbed through the book.

'Thing is, Bruce, if I am to drive the train, which I am happy to do, what do we do with the other driver? The real one.'

Bruce didn't understand the question. 'We'll take care of him.'

'That's what I'm worried about. I don't . . . you know. I never like the heavy stuff.'

Bruce stifled a laugh. It was hard to imagine the diminutive driver ever getting tucked into anything physical that didn't involve nuts and bolts. That had been enough. 'Me neither, Roy. That's why we have double acts like Wisbey and Welch. Look, you see those ugly fuckers climbing into your cab, you'll likely shit yourself. There'll be no problem, I'm sure. But you stay out of the way until they need you. OK?'

'OK.' Roy located the page he wanted. 'Here we are. There'll be a key.'

'A key?'

'Like a car. But they always leave them lying around.' He began to run a hand over the metal shelves and surfaces. 'Here we are.' He fetched a bunch of keys from the top of the black metal control box, placed one in the ignition slot, then a second, until he had the right one and it turned freely. He pressed the starter button. The diesel coughed twice and rumbled into life.

Bruce felt the vibration through his feet. 'That it?'

'No, we got to wait for the air pressure to hit about sixty pounds.' Roy tapped a dial. 'Or none of the controls work. Release the handbrake, will you?'

Bruce looked around the cab. 'Where?'

'Behind you.'

Bruce turned to find a metal disc with projecting handles on its perimeter that looked like a shrunken steering-wheel from an old sailing ship. Stamped on the wall above it was an arrow with Off in one direction, On in the other. He heaved it towards Off.

'Right, we're at pressure. Track ahead clear?'

Bruce swung his head out of the open-sided cab. There seemed to be a decent length of shiny clear rail, but then darkness shrouded the far end, masking whatever lay further on. 'For a few hundred yards.'

'All I'll need to show you.' Roy gave a big grin, as if he really was a boy who got to become an engine driver.

Bruce shivered, the heat drained from him by the cold metal surrounding them. 'Get on with it, Stephenson.' Roy looked blank at the reference. 'Stephenson's Rocket? Oh, just fire her up.'

Roy began to fuss with the controls. 'The throttle's not working. Odd.' Then he remembered. 'There's a dead man's pedal somewhere. Here!'

He stomped down on a metal plate and the diesel gave a jerk forward. Roy hooted with pleasure. 'Easy, see?'

They crept down the track, gathering speed on the incline.

'OK, you can stop now.'

The dumpy shunter carried on accelerating, the power unit thumping with urgency. It was moving at faster than walking pace now.

'*Roy*. You can stop the train now.'

Roy began to look at his book, flicking through the pages with a rising sense of panic. 'This should be the fucking brake.' He waggled a lever back and forward. He remembered there were two brakes, one for the engine and one for the actual wheels, but nothing he pulled or pushed made much difference.

'Step off the dead man's thing.'

'I have,' shouted Roy. They were rolling down a slope, he realised. Gravity was in control now. He squinted ahead into the night, to see if he could spot any obstacle on the track. 'Bruce, put that handbrake on. Bruce?'

He turned. Bruce was nowhere to be seen.

'Oh, Jesus.'

Roy grabbed his manual, stepped out onto the side of the loco, feeling the wind tugging at his hair as the speed increased. Then he closed his eyes and launched himself off.

He hit the gravel awkwardly, felt his ankle go, and rolled down an incline. Behind him the rails were humming as the engine rolled on.

'Come on.' Bruce appeared out of the night, grabbed Roy under the arms and pulled him to his feet. 'You all right?'

Roy put weight on his left ankle. There was a twinge, but it would hold.

'The runaway train came down the track and she blew . . .' Bruce sang softly.

'Shut up,' Roy snapped, limping away.

As they moved back towards the fence there came the sudden screech of metal on metal, a loud bang, then more tortured groans, followed by silence. Roy could smell burning. A flicker of white flame flared, searing his retina, then died.

They increased their pace, Roy ignoring the pain in his leg. As they reached the fence, he turned to Bruce. 'You know what?'

'What?' Bruce asked.

There was a loud bang behind them as something detonated, and both ducked through the fence. There was smoke in the air, thick and oily. 'I think we'd better give Biggsy a call about that train driver. It's not as easy as it looks.'

'Her name was Eliza Dunwoody. Liz Dunwoody to her friends – of which there were very few, by all accounts. She was from Birmingham.'

'Birmingham?' Police Constable Simon Trellick repeated, as if the thought baffled him.

They were in a borrowed office at the police station at Newquay. Hatherill was seated behind the desk, Trellick was standing in front of him, while Billy was positioned near the door, out of the Constable's field of vision. It was a technique designed to disorientate. Whenever Hatherill asked a question of Billy, Trellick wanted to turn but, at attention, could not.

'People do come from Birmingham, you know, Constable. Quite a number, so I hear. Just because she came from a landlocked city doesn't mean she never went near the sea. What else do we know, DC Naughton?'

'That she was on board the *Empress of Canada*, out of Liverpool to Montreal. At Montreal, she was considered too "distressed" to enter the country and was returned on the ship. At Liverpool, it was discovered that her cabin was empty. However, there was a suspicion that she had simply wandered off the ship, down the gangplank and into the city.'

'Now we know different,' said Hatherill. 'It was a bad return crossing, by all accounts. Plenty of storms. A distracted person might easily have been swept over.'

'Or a disturbed one might have jumped,' added Billy.

'Indeed.'

The Police Constable's shoulders relaxed a little. 'Well, I'm glad that is cleared up. The family will claim the body, I suppose.'

Hatherill nodded. 'With some reluctance, I might add. Seems she was not the best-loved member of the Dunwoodys. There is some bickering over who will pay for the burial.'

Billy watched the PC's head shake back and forth in disbelief. 'Charming.'

'Well, yes, absolutely. Charming.' Hatherill lit one of his cigarettes. He didn't offer them around. He waited until he blew his first, satisfying cloud of blue smoke before continuing. 'Some might say it was charming that her body was left on the beach to be tossed around like a piece of driftwood. To be defaced by the seagulls and crabs, like carrion. Some might say that was very charming indeed.'

Billy could see that the copper's neck had coloured above his white shirt. 'Sir, you have to understand people around here . . .'

Hatherill banged the desk with his free hand. A photo frame fell onto the floor and its glass cracked, but he ignored it. 'You don't have to understand "people round here" to smell greed when it gets into your nostrils. Yes, *greed*. Not compassion or otherwise, but greed. How else do you explain the fact that the Bones family serve a claret that wouldn't disgrace White's or Simpson's?' He paused, as if he really expected an answer. 'Well?'

Trellick shuffled. 'I don't know, sir. Relatives—'

'The same relatives who supplied the pub with the identical claret? If we were to search your mother's house, would we find a bottle or two? Well – would we?'

'I don't know.'

'I think you do. I think you know that the storms dislodged cases and cases of the stuff, destined for the warehouses of Bristol. And they ended up here – on the same beach as that poor woman. And if you reported the body, then the beach would have been sealed off and any further bonanza confiscated by the authorities. It was like, what's that film?'

'*Whisky Galore*,' Billy offered, having been primed to do so.

Hatherill smoked on for a while, his face set into a mask of annoyance and disappointment. Trellick's neck was glowing crimson and glistening with sweat now. Billy almost felt sorry for the young PC.

'*Whisky Galore*,' Hatherill finally repeated. 'Although in the film, I don't believe there is a body to get in the way. So in *Claret Galore*, the body becomes invisible. A kind of collective blindness grips the whole village. "Body? What body?" Then, once the locals are certain that all the cases that are coming their way have been washed ashore, the scales fall from their eyes. "Oh look, it's not a shop-window dummy, after all. Or a seal. It's a person. Somebody's daughter. Perhaps somebody's wife." Marvellous. "Let's call the authorities." Is that what happened, son?' He didn't wait for a reply. 'I think it was.'

'Sir . . .'

'No, don't say anything. You'll just dig yourself in deeper. I suspect you are not a bad local copper. I think that in five years' time, if some landlord leans on you to turn a blind eye, you'll tell him to fuck .off. Even if he is your uncle. Oh, aye. A tight-knit community all right. Too tight-knit.

I tell you what I am going to do. I'm going to write my report about the woman, and I will not mention my suspicions about the wine.'

'Thank you, sir.' The young officer's voice shook with relief.

'At the same time, you are going to put in for a transfer. You are going to say you need wider experience and I am going to agree. Bristol, perhaps. See what big city coppering is about. How does that sound?'

The reply was flat. 'Very good, sir. Thank you, sir.'

'I think you could show a bit more enthusiasm, son. After all,' Hatherill stared at Billy, to emphasise that his words weren't only aimed at Trellick, 'I'm giving you a second chance.'

The Night Mail screamed by, its distinctive maroon livery a blur, the porthole-like lower lights above the bogeys one continuous streak of silver. The horn sounded its double-note warning and dopplered into the night. Five feet from the train, the slipstream tugging at his clothes and distorting his face, Bruce Reynolds checked his watch, the hour he had spent crouched in the damp chill of the dead hours of the early morning forgotten.

'Two minutes late,' he said, once silence had descended, broken only by the groan and click of the steel tracks.

'Terrible,' said Charlie, looking down the line at the intense green lights and, beyond them, the fuzzy glow of Cheddington station. 'What's the average?'

317

Bruce had sent someone up to Sears Crossing every night for the nine previous nights, making him sit in the bushes, waiting for the Up train to roar by. 'Never more than fifteen minutes either side of three-ten.'

'It's high, isn't it? Off the ground.'

'We'll need ladders, short ones. I'll get some measurements.'

Charlie pointed to the spidery gantry that straddled the tracks. 'And that's the light Roger will fix?'

'Yes.'

There was a beat. The overhead lines hummed with unheard conversations. 'You happy with the crew we have?'

'The new faces? Well, Bobby's all right.' They knew Bobby Welch as a man who dabbled in crime, although not usually anything on this scale. He was, as Bruce liked to say, small beer, but he wouldn't have anything too challenging to accomplish. 'Tiny Dave did well enough at the airport. Jim Hussey is solid enough. What about you?'

'Beggars can't be choosers.'

'Yeah, well,' said Bruce, zipping up his jacket and turning away from the tracks. 'Maybe we won't be beggars after this.'

Charlie gave a low, rueful laugh. 'I think we said that before Heathrow.'

'Yeah. Well, maybe this is our second bite at the cherry, eh?' But his words were drowned out by another fast-moving train, punching through the night.

'What?'

'Nothing. We move it along to the next stage.'

'What's that?' asked Charlie.

'Getting the grub in.'

Thirty-eight

Battersea, South-west London, June 1963

'I do not know why I am doing this, Tony. I *pay* people to do this for me.'

Janie Riley sat in the passenger seat of the Hillman Husky, arms folded, her lower lip jutting out in a display of serious petulance. She had her hair backcombed and it had been dyed blond. She looked like the singer out of the Springfields. Yet the voice coming out of her mouth was one he hadn't heard before. It was posh, refined, with all the vowels and consonants present and correct.

Tony turned off the engine. 'I don't know why I'm doing it either. As Bruce said, horses for courses.'

'Well, why can't he use that cheap whore Mary Manson?'

Mary Manson was not a cheap whore. She had, however,

begun to nudge out Janie as Bruce's 'companion', turning up in the pubs and clubs where Janie once held sway. Janie wasn't sure what she had done to rock the boat. Was it her fault that Colin had rubbed Bruce up the wrong way with some hare-brained scheme about old Greek marble?

'Janie, I don't like shopping any more than you do. But everyone has a job to do. Today, yours is to help us out here.'

'Like some fishwife.'

'Don't you mean housewife?'

She glared at him. 'Fuck off.' It was, he thought, strangely attractive to be sworn at in a cut-glass accent.

She climbed out of the car, slamming the door with hinge-threatening violence, and clattered off towards the cash and carry in high heels.

Tony pulled out the handwritten shopping list and the wad of cash Bruce had given him. He guessed it was best if he didn't mention that Mary Manson had drawn up the items to be bought. Fifteen or sixteen men staying for a week in a farmhouse were going to need food and essential supplies. He locked the Husky and scanned the list as he went. Twenty-four tins of luncheon meat, four packets of Oxo, four bottles of Bovril, Campbell's soups, various flavours, corned beef, Shippam's paste, ketchup – lots of ketchup – Fairy washing-up liquid – he could imagine the fuss over who would do the bloody dishes – Maxwell House coffee, catering size, Kellogg's cornflakes, Weetabix, Ready

Brek, Typhoo tea, lots of sugar, crackers (Ritz and Jacobs both specified), baked beans, tinned peas and potatoes, jam, sardines, Lifebuoy soap. The list went on, covering, it seemed, everything except booze, which Bobby Welch, the club owner, was taking care of. It looked as if Bruce was planning to feed and clean an army. Well, in a way, that was what it was. An army of villains.

Who would have thought that robbery, with or without violence, would be fuelled by two dozen cans of Spam?

He finished reading and looked back at the squat little van. It was the first time he had found a use for the Husky – none of his customers had expressed any interest in such a humdrum machine, and he was thinking of offloading it – but already he wondered if it was going to be big enough for the supplies.

Tony reached the entrance where Janie was leaning on a shopping trolley. The cash and carry was like a vast cathedral of consumerism. Instead of pews, there were rows of goods on pallets, piled high, most of them Brobdingnagian-sized 'extra-value' packets or smaller items in multiples of a dozen or a gross. You could shop for surviving a nuclear strike here, Tony thought. Maybe people did just that. Those bloody Civil Defence ads on TV would make anyone panic.

Janie snapped her fingers. 'Let me see that, will you?'

'Do you speak to all your staff like that?'

'Just the handsome, insolent ones.'

He passed it over. She glanced down it as she wheeled

the trolley, stopping in the first section. Then she gave a little whoop of satisfaction. She had noticed an omission. When she spoke, the Janie of the Soho bars, voice rasped by cigarette smoke, had returned.

'And what are you going to do? Wipe your arses with the *Sporting Life*? Here, give us a hand.' She reached up to pull down one of the twelve-packs of Bronco lavatory paper. 'You'll need a lot of this, all the shit you blokes talk.'

'Hold on,' Tony said, remembering something.

'What is it now?' Janie had reverted to the posh bitch.

'Gloves.' He held out a pair.

'Gloves? Oh, lord. Why on earth?'

'Bruce's orders.'

'Did he say they had to be brown gloves? Did he supply any black ones?'

He was losing patience now. 'Janie, it's not fuckin' Hardy Amies. It's a cash and carry. I don't know what it is with you and Bruce and Mary and, frankly, I don't care. Just put the fucking things on.'

She smiled. 'My, you really are quite attractive when you flush like that. Do you go that colour when you fuck?'

He put his hands up. 'Married. Baby on the way. Wife has carving knife and knows how to use it. What's more, I might be stupid, but I'm not stupid enough to get between you and Bruce. Clear?'

'You flatter yourself, mister.' Then she smiled. 'Is your wife all belly and big blue-veined tits?' She squeaked in a pantomime imitation of a woman's voice. "'*Oh Tony, don't spunk on the baby's head. Let's wait till the christening*".'

'Put the gloves on, Janie.'

With a display of huffing, puffing and tutting, she thrust her hands into the oversized gloves. They loaded a couple of packs of the toilet paper into the trolley. Then she consulted the list again.

'No salt? Tony, be a dear and get that drum of Saxo over there. And you could do with some fruit. A nice tinned fruit salad. Del Monte, perhaps.' She was being sarcastic now, he could tell, ridiculing them. 'And condensed milk. Carnation. Bruce has a sweet tooth, you know. And candles. In case the power goes. Who in blazes wrote this?' Tony kept mum, allowing himself a tiny shrug. 'I'm going to have to go through this carefully. You push, darling, I'll follow. Then maybe we can have a little celebration later, when we're done? Just the two of us.'

'No.' Tony had no desire for any part of his body to be used as an instrument of revenge against Bruce. 'Isn't going to happen.'

Janie scowled and muttered something obscene. Tony grabbed the handle of the trolley. It was going to be a long, long day.

Commander George Hatherill fell asleep soon after they settled into their seats on the train to Paddington, and seemed determined to snooze all the way to London. Billy

Naughton was left to gaze out of the window at an aston-ishingly verdant landscape. The cold winter had given way to a wet spring and now a damp summer. 1963: The Year of Crappy Weather. Farmers and holidaymakers grumbled, but fields and hedgerows seemed to glow a deep, happy green.

Billy tried to digest all that had gone on while he had been in Cornwall. Hatherill had refused to answer ques-tions about how he obtained the Oxo tin, whether Billy had been personally targeted, or if it was a general sweep. He simply said that the 'old way of doing things' was going to come to an end. He didn't want young coppers like Billy caught up in it.

The TM had admitted that his own record was not without blemishes. Apparently, he had been wrong about the Free French in London: he had reported that they had interrogated one of their own men, suspected of being a spy, who subsequently hanged himself. He now believed that the French had had a torture chamber in St James's and had behaved like Nazis. 'But it was war. And they were our allies. What good would the scandal have done? I wanted to believe them, so I didn't follow my instincts. I have regretted that ever since. They murdered some of their own. I am sure of it now.'

He also lamented some of his persecutions of the queers. 'You don't appreciate how angry Burgess and Maclean made us. Those, those . . . buggers. So we overstepped the mark sometimes, I think. Putting out agents provocateurs, fishing for homos. Not a decent use of police resources, in retrospect. They can't all be Commie spies, can they? The queers, I mean.'

But misjudgements in his own life, he went on, like the Duke Street torture chamber, meant he always gave coppers such as Trellick a second chance. Never a third, mind. But a good second.

Then he had settled down and fallen asleep, apparently content. Cornwall hadn't given him his Last Big Case, but it had given him the quiet satisfaction of solving a mystery and perhaps that of saving a young policeman's career, too.

Billy had assumed he would be severed from Duke, and said so, but Hatherill had said no. He had to confront temptation and deal with it. Running away was no answer. And Len's turn would come, the day when he had his hand in the wrong till.

Billy took himself off to the dining car for breakfast, treating himself to ham, egg and chips. He felt strangely calm, quietly elated almost. It was as if he, as well as the Cornish PC, had been given a fresh start. From now on, he would be a good copper. From now on, he would do the right thing.

As arranged, Tony dropped off the supplies with Jimmy White, who was acting as quartermaster, storing all the gear they needed in lock-ups across London. They would be taken up, along with some of the team, by lorry once the purchase of the farm was complete. Afterwards, Tony had given Janie a lift to Waterloo, where she would catch a train home, and he carried on north, glad to see the back of her.

When he got to the Holloway Road house, his brother-in-law Geoff was in the kitchen, a mug of tea in his fat hand. He was a big lad, with short ginger-ish hair, a round face and full lips. Tony often wondered if Geoff and his wife were actually biologically related. Because if someone was shuffling the genes, they were playing with a marked deck.

Tony wasn't best pleased to see Geoff. He had to have something to eat then go and meet Jimmy and Roy over in West London. They had uncoupling practice. Bruce wanted three people who could unhook the HVP from the rest of the train, just in case. As three who had professed a desire not to wield the coshes, they had nominated themselves.

'All right?' he nodded brusquely.

'Do you want some, love?' asked Marie, rising to her feet with a soft, involuntary groan. 'It's fresh in the pot.'

'Stay there, I'll do it.'

She slumped back down.

'I were just saying, Tony. She's looking well, my sister, isn't she?' said Geoff.

Tony nodded. In fact, she had progressed from being 'blooming' as they said, to the puffy, sweaty when-will-it-be-over stage. Moving was an effort, and her squashed lungs

327

weren't allowing her enough air. And she snored at night. 'Yeah.'

'Tony, I hope you don't mind, but I mentioned that thing to Geoff.'

'What thing to Geoff?' he asked as he checked the contents of the teapot and fetched a mug from the cupboard.

'That thing we talked about the other night.'

He turned and glared at her. Pregnant or not, she was out of order. 'You had no fuckin' right—'

Geoff half-rose from his chair. 'Hold on, mate.'

'Fuck off, Geoff. Stay out of it.'

'I didn't say much, luv. Just that . . . well, there was this thing.'

Tony put his hand around his forehead and squeezed his temples. 'Jesus.'

Geoff bleated his next words. 'I just haven't got much on, Tony. I said that to Marie, and she said you might have something you could put my way.'

'I don't. I don't have anything.' He looked at his wife, daring her to challenge him. 'It's not mine. Christ, I'm only there as a bloody tent-peg. Sorry, mate, no can do.'

'Tony . . .' Marie began.

'No can do,' he repeated forcefully, wagging a finger at each of them in turn. 'And if either of you mention this to anyone . . .' He thought of Charlie Wilson, and what he did to the Jag thieves. They got off lightly compared to anyone who threw a spanner in this works, especially at this stage.

'Look, it's not nursery stuff, all right? Big boys. Some nasty bastards. As I said, I would if I could, Geoff. If it goes off, I'll be able to bung you something, get you on your feet.'

'Yeah.' The big man stood, managing a smile that was a half-grimace. 'No harm done.'

Tony watched him grab his jacket, slip it on and leave, those three final words bouncing round the inside of his head like sub-atomic particles in a cloud chamber, as if there was nothing in there to impede their passage. *No harm done.*

Bruce clapped his hands to get the meeting started. 'First off, apologies for absence,' he announced. 'Brian Field can't be here. And Stan, the train driver, he isn't here because we didn't ask him. I would like to welcome Bobby again – thanks for the use of this room, Bobby, and we can all get a drink downstairs later – and Jim and Tommy. Some of you won't know Tiny Dave Thompson yet. He was at the airport with us. 'Nuff said.'

Bruce cleared his throat. 'Now the purpose of this meeting is logistics. To make sure we have everything we need to carry this job out and to do it in some comfort.' Roger gave a feeble cheer. 'Tony, here, has been the housewives' choice and done some shopping. He has the canned gear, the tea, the sugar and so on. Bobby has said he'll bring some beers and spirits from the club. And he'll only charge us whole-sale. Always have a publican on any job, I say. Nearer the time we'll need perishables. For those of you who don't know, that means things that go off. Like Buster's insides when he's had six pints.' Someone groaned at the thought.

'Jimmy – we don't know how much cutlery and so on is at the farm yet. We need eighteen sets, just to be on the safe side. And light bulbs. You got some ideas about mattresses? And we'll need sleeping bags. Maybe Jimmy and Tommy can help on that score? Lovely. Charlie, being well-connected on The Fruit, can get us some fruit and veg from the market, can't you? I am partial to Cox's Orange Pippins m'self, but whatever. Thing is, we don't know how long the scream will last. Could be a day, could be a week. But if we keep our heads down, that'll be fine.' Bruce looked from face to face to be certain they understood. 'Roger and I have both got Hitachi shortwaves, so we'll keep an ear for what the bastards are up to.'

Bruce consulted his list. 'We need uniforms for the Army disguise – Gordy, Charlie and Roy are on that. Red berets if you can. Parachute Regiment. *Who Dares Wins* – remember that. Buster is sourcing walkie-talkies so we can communicate up and down the track. Whitey is going to buy one Land Rover and I have found an ex-Army Austin truck for three hundred quid in Edgware. We need another Land Rover. Tony, you got one lying around? Well, can you get me one? Doesn't have to be bought, you can put new plates on it. Ronnie, if you could take charge of making them look like kosher Army trucks. Which doesn't mean like the Israeli army. Like the real thing, serial numbers, badges and all.

Stan still OK?' he asked Ronnie. 'Good. I'll meet him later this week. He knows he's on a drink for this, not a whack? Keep reminding him, will you? Roy, you will let Jimmy know anything you need for cutting wires and uncoupling coaches.' Roy said he would. 'And get two of everything. You drop one in the dark, I don't want the whole thing to go tits up because of a pair of missing pliers, understand?

'Big Bad Bobby Welch here has requested handcuffs, which is a good idea. Might have to restrain the driver or the sorters. Gordy, can you get some? Six pairs. Say it's for magic tricks. Or fancy dress. Bobby also requested a shooter to scare the driver. Not a good idea. I said it before, I'll say it again: no shooters, real or otherwise. Is that clear?' Bruce paused, just to ensure the point was taken. 'Roger, you have all you need for the light change? Again, double it. Back-up everything. We don't want to be there watching the Six-Five Special rolling down that line through a green light, do we? And gloves. I want everyone to bring two pairs. And you wear them at all times. There must be no prints anywhere. Brian is going to arrange cleaners to sanitise the whole place after we have gone. If the coppers do locate the farm, they won't find so much as a skid-mark on a toilet bowl.'

Bruce took a long breath, and consulted his list again. 'OK, now we come to alibis. You will need alibis, too, for the time we are away. And not "I was alone watching Michael Miles on the box for a week". A good one with lots of witnesses, preferably a vicar or a nun. Similarly, you will need some idea of what you are going to do when you get back to London and where to put your money. At the very least you are going to have a good few grand. I don't have to tell you that there are plenty of snot-rags out there who will offer to take it off your hands. Be very, very careful. Wives and girlfriends will sniff out you're flush the moment you walk through the door. They like a spending spree, and women have very different ideas to us. To them, a diamond ring from Bond Street isn't a spending spree. That's just what they deserve.' Buster gave a rueful chuckle. 'Talking of money, Charlie, what about the horsebox? Charlie is bringing up a horsebox because it won't look suspicious and you can transport a lot of bags in it. Buster, you can always sit in it and neigh, just for authenticity.'

Bruce gave a wry grin and put his list down, saying, 'Now we need to talk about where we'll each be on the tracks and what our job will be. Any questions so far?' He looked around the room. 'Good, because I have my blackboard here to go over what will happen on the night. All right, all right, settle down. Fuck me, I feel like Mr Chips some-times. Oh, one thing I forgot. As I said, we might be holed up for some time. So I've got us a Monopoly set.'

'A fuckin' Monopoly set?' Jim Hussey turned to Tommy Wisbey, who was sitting in the back seat. Roger was driving them back towards Brighton, where they were to pick up the last of the cash from their previous train jobs that was being 'minded' by one of the operators on the West Pier. It was time, as Bruce said, to concentrate on the Big One. For the moment, the South Coast Gang was being wound up.

It was the early hours, little traffic. Roger was sober, careful as they hit the A23 south of Croydon; he didn't want to be walking any white lines for a policeman. The car stank of the other two men's beer and fags.

'Who Dares Wins?' added Wisbey.

'Oh, you can't have a shooter because it might go off and hurt somebody,' lisped Hussey in a high-pitched feminine voice.

'Hey, lads,' said Roger meekly. 'Have some respect. It's Bruce's tickle. He calls the shots.'

'Or not havin' the shots.' The other two giggled like very overgrown schoolboys. 'He treats us like we got muscle between our ears sometimes.'

'Yeah, well sometimes you have,' said Roger, suddenly angry. 'Look, he wants you for what you are good at. Puttin' the shits up people. Now if you want to join the cooking and dishwashing rota—'

'Fuck off. Can't we get some bird in for that?'

'And a bit of the other while she's at it.'

Roger shook his head. They were nice enough boys, but something on this scale was beyond their experience. Hussey was a car thief who readily used his fists whenever he deemed the occasion demanded it. Which, when he was in his late teens, had been surprisingly often. Now he had calmed down, and tried his hand at pickpocketing. If caught, though, he was still liable to try and punch his way out of trouble.

Tommy Wisbey was a bookmaker and thief who intimidated by his size and rarely needed to thump anyone. If he did, Roger was under no illusion that those ham-hocks of arms – he looked like Popeye when he stripped down – would cause some damage.

'Just do what Bruce wants and you'll get your whack. Equal shares, he said, once the expenses are deducted. How fair is that?' Bruce could easily have upped his own stake, or insisted that the originating gang – the Heathrow boys, essentially – deserved a higher cut. But Roger knew Bruce thought an unequal division of the spoils led to resentment, which might cause someone to grass when his perceived 'tiny' whack ran out. There would, after all, be a hefty reward on offer.

'You know he said we might need a few more bodies?' asked Wisbey. 'Not for the washing-up, but at the train. What about Freddie Foreman? Or Frankie Fraser?'

Hussey shook his head. 'You'd have to keep those two on leashes.'

'Nah, they're all right. Good boys,' insisted Wisbey.

Roger knew the names. They were a couple of enforcers for the likes of the Richardsons and the Krays. They had reputations for violence that left Bobby Welch, Tommy and Jimmy looking as threatening as Rag, Tag and Bobtail. Bruce wouldn't like that. There was something else Bruce wouldn't like. 'Fraser is red-hot, isn't he?'

'I suppose,' said Wisbey.

'He was on *Police Five*,' said Hussey. 'Wanted for doing some bloke.'

'So don't approach anyone till you've cleared it with Bruce or Charlie or Gordy. They only want people they know, remember?'

The other two grunted. The euphoria caused by alcohol fading, they lapsed into silence, their arms folded. Jim's head began to nod as he fell into a fitful snooze.

After fifteen minutes, Tommy Wisbey spoke.

'There's one thing I'm really pissed off about, Roger.'

'What's that?' asked Roger, annoyed that they should be so ungrateful. Plenty would take their places.

'Meself, I prefer Cluedo.'

Thirty-nine

Bridego Bridge, July 1963

'Here we go. Now!'

Roy let the clutch in and Tony felt the brand new Mini Cooper S judder as the power hit the front wheels. Next to them came the deeper roar of an Austin Healey 3000 Mk II roadster, with Bruce behind the wheel.

The two cars shot out of the car park next to the fishing pond and turned right, Bridego Bridge receding rapidly in the Mini's mirror. Unlike the Healey, which filled it.

'He's got more power than us,' shouted Roy as he worked the Mini's gearbox.

The Austin pulled out behind them. Tony could see it in his wing mirror, Bruce behind the wheel, Gordy somehow folded into the passenger seat. It was a race and the last one to Leatherslade would buy lunch at the Red Lion pub in Brill. Bruce had taken the Austin Healey on 'a test drive', as he was considering buying one when he got his hands on the cash. This probably wasn't the kind of test drive the garage had in mind.

'Read the map,' Roy instructed. 'Check the sharpness of the bends, and whether they are right- or left-handers.'

The Mini was shifting, the little tuned-up engine doing its best to roar, although as the Healey drew close they could hear the deeper note of its larger lump.

'Right at the end,' said Tony. 'T-junction.'

Tony's mouth went dry as he watched the turning approach. Roy appeared not to know where the brake was. At the last moment, he stamped on the middle pedal once, changed down, then went back on the gas. Tony hoped nothing was coming. Roy leaned on the Healey slightly and flung the little Mini to the right.

'Disc brakes,' Roy grinned. 'Fuckin' brilliant. Much better than the standard Mini.'

The Healey fell back as it took the bend in a more refined manner. Then Tony watched it grow larger in the mirror once more as Bruce got the power back down.

'Sharp right at Ledburn. You have to go into the village. Watch—'

Roy jerked the Mini out and zipped by a dawdling Triumph Herald, then tucked back in.

'Did I say right?' Tony corrected. 'I meant left.'

'Keep it together, Tone. There're only two choices, after all,' Roy laughed. 'Right or left?'

'Left. My side,' he clarified.

A pair of decent-looking pubs went by in a blur and Roy took the turning. Tony caught sight of startled residents, stepping back from the kerb as the two cars powered recklessly through their hamlet.

'Long straight section to a crossroads.'

'How long?'

'Half a mile.'

'Not enough for him to have us.'

Tony looked up from the map. It was beautiful rolling countryside, the roads lined with hedgerows, guarded with stands of extravagant horse chestnuts.

'How far? This it?'

'No. Be signposted Wing.'

'Hang on.'

A throbbing filled the Mini's cabin. 'Christ, he's right behind us.'

At a particularly splendid horse chestnut, Roy put the Cooper S into a power slide, the snub rear-end poking out, almost touching the Healey's gleaming chrome bumper. Bruce backed off, giving Roy enough space to complete the turn, catch the drift and get the full bhp of the 1071cc engine onto the asphalt.

Tony, his heart thumping away, checked the OS map once more. 'Through Wing, left towards Cublington.'

Another couple of pubs, more outraged country folk and a left turn. The ominous black Healey was behind them again.

'Crap,' said Tony. 'You should have gone left there at the fork.'

He turned and watched the roadster take the correct route and disappear from view.

'No problem.' Roy braked, and Tony shot out an arm to steady himself on the windscreen as the front end of the Cooper dipped viciously. The driver found reverse first time and the gearbox whined as he took the Cooper back and resumed the chase.

'I though the left was the main drag—'

'Doesn't matter now,' Roy said evenly. 'Next?'

'Cublington. Some sharp bends.'

'Good.'

There was no sign of the roadster until they took a narrow bridge – Tony with his eyes closed in case there was anything coming their way on the other side – and landed with a spine-jarring crack.

'What the fuck was that?' he asked.

'Suspension bottoming,' said Roy. 'Needs better shocks.'

They watched the handsome rear of the Healey diminish in size as it pulled away. Roy darted the Mini forward, sweeping into the bend. Tony felt the body roll and, he swore, two wheels lift.

'Long left curve,' said Tony, 'then a bloody sharp right.'

'Brilliant. He can't do the bends. He'll have us on the

straight, but that thing doesn't handle.' He flashed a knowing smile. 'Not for Bruce anyway.'

Tony knew he was a good driver, a very competent road-man. But Roy was something else. His gear changes were sharp, precise. The rev counter never made wild swings, the engine note remained constant, and the speedo stayed well over to the right. He was what they called a 'natural', the kind of driver who had a feel for both the car and the road.

'That right-hander's coming up.'

'Hold on, 'cause I'm not slowing.'

They emerged almost on top of the Healey. Roy let out a whoop. 'He missed a gear, I'll bet.'

With the precision of a slot-car, the Mini pulled out and zipped past the Austin. Tony looked up and caught a glimpse of Bruce's mouth working overtime. He didn't have to be a lip-reader to guess what words were coming out. The next section, between Oving and Pitchcott, was twisty enough to thwart Bruce and the Austin Healey. It would come burbling behind, threatening to shoulder the Cooper aside, but Roy brilliantly used the bends and curves to his advantage.

'Railway bridge. Not our railway line, though. Long hill down to Chearsley. It's straight.'

Roy nodded and pushed the engine to the red line. The Healey fought back again, edging closer. 'He's got us. Shit.'

Tony looked over his shoulder. Gordy was jumping up

and down in his seat, willing Bruce on. The bigger sports car reeled them in until, like a stately liner, it glided past. Gordy flashed a V-sign.

'Nice,' said Tony.

'Don't panic. Just enjoy the scenery on this stretch. We'll come back at them.'

Tony had to admit that the Chilterns did look lovely, streaked with sunlight, interrupted by the shadows of low cloud. On a nearby hillside to his left, Tony saw a strange observatory, a domed housing for a large telescope, but didn't feel he could distract Roy from his focus on the road.

'He's pulling away. Any bends?'

'Sharp right to Chearsley, coming up. Really sharp.'

'How sharp?'

'Ninety degrees. Then through Chilton, on the B4011 and we're there.'

Roy didn't reply, just grunted as they recovered ground on the right-hander, driving through the narrow lanes as if they were tied to the Healey's rear bumper. Nice big houses, thought Roy. Gardens, horses, conservatories, but such was their speed he had little time to process much more than flash images. Roy suddenly dived into a gap between the Austin and a brick wall that didn't seem to be there. Tony's eyes flicked shut again. When he opened them they were through and in front, into the final twisting lanes that would take them to Leatherslade Farm.

'Fuckin' Land Rovers and lorries my arse,' Roy said. 'You can't beat a quick motor.'

They turned right up the unmarked track that led to Leatherslade, Roy finally allowing the Mini to breathe, dropping to second as he manoeuvred between the ruts and potholes.

'What time?' he asked.

'Eighteen minutes,' said Tony.

They pulled over in front of the house and Bruce drove alongside. He climbed out and leaned on the hardtop of the Healey. 'You were lucky there're so many bends,' he said to Roy. 'It'd eat that little toy otherwise.'

'Tell you what, after you've bought lunch, let's swap cars and do it in reverse. See how you get on then.'

Bruce considered this as he watched Gordy unfold himself from the passenger side. 'What, and ruin my excuse?'

'You change your mind about the Jags?' Roy asked.

Bruce frowned. To him, the race had been a bit of a laugh, not to prove a point.

'No, Roy. I told you, the money will weigh over a ton. We need a lorry. We stick with the plan.'

Gordy looked a little pale after being thrown around by Bruce. 'Yeah. Fuck that. We stick with the lorry and Land Rovers.'

Roy did his best to hide his disappointment, and indicated his acceptance. He just hoped Bruce didn't live to regret it.

Forty

Headley, Surrey, May 1992

Bruce took off his overcoat and sat down at the kitchen table while I put the kettle on. Roy, apparently dazed by his old boss's arrival, stared at him, open-mouthed.

'Nice whistle,' he finally said.

'Thanks.' Bruce looked down at the jacket. 'Mark Powell. He said I should sue Michael Caine for stealing my look.'

There was something in that. Bruce had looked a little like Harry Palmer-period Caine in his youth, and the two had run across each other in the early days at the Establishment, when the actor was out and about with Terry Stamp. But I wasn't worried about where Bruce got his suits made or whether his style had been purloined for *The Ipcress File*. 'What are you doing here, Bruce?' I asked.

'Naughton called me.'

I didn't mention that Bill Naughton had said Bruce was too busy to help out. He was entitled to change his mind.

'Good of you to come, mate,' said Roy.

'Well, I didn't want to leave you hangin' in the wind, did I? I don't think we've got very long, judging by the activity out there. The heavy mob has heaved up close to the gate. With machine guns.' Bruce nodded towards the pistol, still held slackly in Roy's hand. 'That'll be as much use as a fuckin' ice-cream dildo.'

From his jacket pocket, Bruce produced cigarette papers and tobacco and began building a fag. He looked up at me.

'How you been, Tony?'

'Can't complain,' I said, rinsing out the teapot. 'You?'

'I do OK.'

'What you driving now?' It was Roy.

'Don't ask,' shuddered Bruce. 'Ashamed to say. You know those fuckers sold my Austin Healey? The Mark Two Three Thousand? Lovely motor. Christ, I'd like that again. In order to claw back some of the proceeds, they said. Fetched double what it should've.'

'The power of celebrity,' I said as I poured the boiling water into the pot.

'Notoriety,' he corrected.

'Should've used fast cars,' said Roy.

'Leave it out, Roy,' Bruce said, not without kindness. 'Water under Bridego Bridge.' He shot me a glance that was loaded with meaning. 'We should have done lots of things. Can't change the past. Not unless you're bleedin' Doctor Who.'

After I had made the tea, I fetched the bottle of Johnnie Walker and placed it on the table, along with some glasses from the drainer. To my surprise, Bruce pulled out a block of dope, unwrapped the foil and scorched one corner with a lighter.

'Don't look so shocked. I picked up the habit at Maidstone. A good prison. You ever do Maidstone, Roy? Towards the end of my stretch, I had a year in the library there and a year as a gym orderly when I used to run ten miles a day, play badminton and then swim. Fucking marvellous life. No women, apart from those in Razzle and Club International. At least you didn't get any aggro from those girls. And Gordy, bless him, would send the odd beauty in for a quick fondle, just to let me know I was still alive down below. I got into smoking dope there.' He chuckled. 'Montecristo Number Twos being hard to come by. Stuff was a fuckin' revelation. Two happy years.'

I thought he was joking. And my expression must have given that away, since he went on, 'Straight up. When I came out I felt like doing something so I could go right back in for a joint with my pals. Now that is what you call institutionalised, eh?'

'Tell me about it,' muttered Roy. 'I was saying the same thing to Tony earlier. It's easier inside, somehow.'

345

Bruce gave a grin then lit the roll-up, taking a lungful and holding his breath while he passed the joint to Roy. The little man took a hefty toke.

Very clever, Bruce, I thought. He wasn't going to talk him down, he was going to dope him out.

The sweet aroma filled the air and I poured myself a finger of scotch, shaking my head when the joint was offered to me.

'Governor in Maidstone used to come in and say: "Bit smoky in here, isn't it, lads?"' Bruce told us, 'but while it was just dope, he was happy enough. The first two weeks after coming home, I'm walking on air. Life is sweet. I'm famous, I have friends, family. Then it hits me – bang! Like a train.' He winked. 'Or a cosh. That's it. Washed-up. Depression, it's a terrible thing. Eh, Roy?'

The driver simply nodded thoughtfully.

Bruce took the spliff back and sucked on it a while longer, indicating I should pour the tea. As I did so, he let out a long thin stream of smoke from pursed lips. 'Well, I'd like to say the gang's all here, but it's not, is it? But while we are gathered together in this cosy place, Tony, maybe you can answer me a question.' His eyes shone brightly and his mouth was drawn tight.

'What's that, Bruce?' I asked, my hand shaking slightly as I lifted the teapot.

'Why the fuck you grassed us up.'

Forty-one

6 August 1963

As arranged, the men came to the farm in dribs and drabs, their arrival staggered so as not to arouse suspicion from any nosy neighbours. Brian Field met several of them at the railway station during the course of the day, ferrying them backwards and forwards.

Tony drove up with Roy the morning after they had practised yet another decoupling in the shunting yards. Roy had mastered both types: the flexible screw kind, which required turning a tensioner before you could unhook them, and the buckeye – the commonest kind on HVPs – which had a simple release chain that you tugged to break the connection.

'The important thing,' he impressed on Tony, 'is that

when you take off the vacuum pipe for the brakes, you have to reattach it to a dummy on the HVP. Otherwise the vacuum won't build because it'll leak out the open end.'

Confident now that he knew all there was to know about coach connections, nevertheless Roy was on edge, Tony could tell. They were driving north in a drab-coloured Land Rover, stolen from near Leicester Square by Bruce and Tony and painted by Ronnie Biggs, who had also sketched out the Army numbers he would fill in at the farm. If nothing else he was a good signwriter, that Ronnie Biggs.

'You all right, Roy?' Tony asked.

'Yeah, just thinking. Got a couple of Goodwoods coming up.'

'That all you thinkin' about?'

'It seems to me, Bruce isn't listening. I mean, I know it's his job and all, but . . .'

'But?'

'I think the farm is a mistake. I think we should have a decoy lorry we leave halfway to London. And there's too many of us. Fuck, it's like a real bleeding army, isn't it? You know, Bruce, Charlie, Buster, Gordy – even though he's a flash bastard sometimes – I know they are up to it.'

Tony thought this must just be the nerves talking. He had them as well, although Marie's change of heart had steadied them somewhat. Now there was no subterfuge at home, he found he was able to relax more. 'Is that all that's up?'

Roy smiled. 'I got offers of sponsorship. Esso and Shell, both bidding me up.'

'Great,' said Tony, with genuine enthusiasm. 'So you are thinking you don't need this?'

Roy shook his head. 'No, not at all. Hundred per cent, me.'

There was an undercurrent of irritation there. 'Timing's crap though, eh?'

'You said it.'

'Look on the bright side, Roy.'

'What's that?'

'It comes off, you can always put "Sponsored by Royal Mail" down the side.'

Roy laughed at the thought, then glanced at the fuel gauge. 'I'd better get some squirt.'

They pulled into a garage on the A40 and Roy got out to fill up the tank. It was then Tony noticed the kid.

'Fuck.'

He stepped out of the Land Rover and walked over to the boy. He was around ten, school blazer, short pants. 'Hi there,' Tony said, looking round for his parents. There was a Vauxhall Cresta at another pump, the attendant filling her up. No driver. 'Collect car numbers, do you?'

The boy nodded sheepishly. He turned around the note-book, which was filled with places, time and dates and licence numbers.

'Like trainspotting, is it?'

Another nod.

Tony glanced over at Roy, who was paying off the lanky lad who had pumped the three star. Roy shot him a quizzical look. Both of their Land Rovers had the same number-plates – the legit one from the vehicle that had been purchased as well as this nicked one – so if cops checked the reg against the make, it wouldn't throw up an anomaly. If, however, by some coincidence someone clocked the registration of the other, being driven by Jimmy, and the police realised they had two vehicles in one place on the day with the same number, then alarm bells could ring. It was all 'what if' and 'possibly', but Tony had to think what Bruce would say. And didn't they get caught by number-plates in that movie *The League of* fucking *Gentlemen* Bruce was always banging on about?

'Can I see?' Tony asked, taking a step closer.

Reluctantly, the lad handed over the red exercise book.

'Just Land Rovers, is it?'

'Army.' It was a whisper.

'Army vehicles. Got any tank transporters?'

The kid pointed enthusiastically to an earlier entry.

'They're the best, aren't they? Sad to say, you've got the wrong one here, mate. Ex-Army, you see. Just bought it. Haven't had time to respray it. Just took the badges off. Sorry. I'll rip—'

He went to tear the page out when he heard a gruff voice behind him.

'Jeffrey. Are you bothering this man?'

350

It was the father, forty-ish, ex-military himself by the look of him and the dazzling polish on his brogues.

Tony turned. 'No, not at all, we was just talking car numbers. Telling him it was ex-Army.'

'Sorry. Boy's obsessed. War films, soldiers, model kits.'

'I was the same. Anything with John Wayne or William Bendix.'

The man sniffed at the mention of Hollywood's war. 'Yes, well. Look at the travesty of *The Longest Day*. Did you see that? We were hardly in it, according to the Yanks. You hear what one of the producers said on the radio? "There'll always be an England . . . just as long as America is around to save its backside". Bloody cheek.'

'Well, nice chatting to you.' Tony, sensing a sore point about to be scratched until it bled, offered the book back. The sulky boy snatched it.

'Jeffrey, manners.'

Roy was back in the car and sounded the horn to help extricate Tony. 'Right, got to go.'

As he turned, he caught a movement from the corner of his eye. The lad was scratching out the Land Rover's reg, even as the dad turned him away back towards the Vauxhall. Now he had to hope the father erased the incident from his mind as well.

When they arrived at the tatty farm, Bruce, Buster, Jimmy White, Ronnie Biggs and Stan, the train driver, were all there in the house. Stan, who had been kept tucked away till now, was in his fifties, thin and cadaverous-looking, and was mostly occupied in using his nicotine-stained fingers to make roll-ups. The others were unpacking the supplies and laying out the uniforms and balaclavas. Roy and Tony set about emptying their Land Rover so Biggsy could make the final adjustments to the paint job.

'Gloves!' Bruce kept reminding them. 'At all times. Even when you eat or wipe your hairy arses, OK?'

While they were unloading, a Jaguar appeared on the track, driving up towards the house. Tony relaxed when he saw Brian behind the wheel. As it swept to a halt, flicking gravel everywhere, Roger Cordrey, Ralph, his new assistant, and Jim Hussey climbed out. The latter looked even bigger than he remembered.

'Morning,' said Roger nervously, hefting a series of empty suitcases out of the boot. Clearly, he was expecting plenty of loot. 'Lovely day for it.'

Lovely might be going too far, but at least it wasn't raining and the sun beamed out from behind the clouds once in a while. What a summer. Still, he would be able to afford to take Marie and the baby somewhere warm after that night. He hefted the last crate from the rear of the Land Rover and said, 'OK, Ronnie, all yours.'

'Do me a favour,' said Biggsy from the side of his mouth. 'Keep Stan company, will you? Feels a bit left out with this lot.'

'I'll get Roy to talk trains with him. I swear he likes them more than racing cars now.'

'Good one.'

'Oi, everyone!' It was Buster at the door. 'Bruce wants the vehicles away and everyone inside, curtains drawn. And tea's up for those that want it.'

Tony looked at his watch. It was early afternoon. At least twelve hours before they would pull out and head for Bridego Bridge and Sears Crossing. Time enough for a few rounds of Monopoly.

'There's someone coming!' shouted Buster from the kitchen.

Bruce leaped to his feet. 'Who is it?'

'Not one of ours. Someone walking up the drive. Jacket, gumboots. I think it's a farmer.'

'Everyone shut up!' said Bruce. 'Tony, you come with me.'

The pair of them stepped outside, blinking into the afternoon sunshine after the gloom inside. The man walking towards them was dressed in rough cords and an old waxed jacket, with a flat cap on his head. He certainly looked like everybody's idea of a Farmer Giles. 'Afternoon,' he said brightly.

'Afternoon,' said Bruce. Tony could see he was looking around for anything suspicious that they might have left out in the open. But the Army truck and Land Rovers were well hidden. Only the number of tyre tracks gave all the activity away.

353

'Wyatt's the name. Thought I saw some movement over here. You the new owners?'

'No,' said Bruce. Then he dried up.

Sensing the hesitation, Tony jumped in. 'We're the decorators. They've just asked us to come over and spruce the place up. Lick of paint inside.'

The man grunted. 'Well, it could do with it. Who is the owner then?'

'A Mr Field,' said Bruce. 'Leonard Field. From Aylesbury.' This was true; Brian had put the farm in the name of another Field – but not a relative – who would be paid a drink as a front man.

'Thing is, I rent the field over yonder – for my sheep. And I was wondering if Mr Field would allow me to continue.'

'Can't say,' said Bruce.

'But unless you hear otherwise,' Tony said, 'you just carry on as before. We'll mention it to him.'

'That's very kind.' He hesitated, as if expecting to be asked in for a cup of tea.

Bruce, however, just glanced over his shoulder, saying, 'Well, best get back to it.'

'Yes. Right. Thank you.'

They watched the man walk back down towards the farm's gate. He turned once and raised a hand and they returned the gesture.

'Fuck,' said Bruce.

'Be all right,' said Tony, echoing the words of Geoff, his brother-in-law. 'No harm done.'

'He's seen my face.'

'You know what people are like. He'll have forgotten it by the morning.'

'Yeah.' But Bruce didn't sound convinced.

They turned and headed back in. 'Still,' suggested Tony, 'we can always go round to his place and kill them all, just to be on the safe side.'

Bruce's eye darted to him, thinking he was serious. Tony cracked a grin. The sight of Bruce laughing as they stepped into the half-light of the house reassured the others that all was well.

By early evening most of the team had gathered together. Charlie Wilson and Bobby Welch had swelled the numbers at around three in the afternoon. Tiny Dave Thompson, the London Airport man, had come by Morris Oxford. He would supply extra clenched fists just in case anything went wrong with the sorters.

Tony knew there had been some heated arguments amongst the principals over the final numbers. Extra bodies diluted the whacks. Charlie was also worried about security, that if outsiders were brought in, word would leak out about something big going down. It only needed a rumour for the Heavy Mob at the Yard to start sniffing around the usual suspects. Which certainly included Charlie and Gordy after the airport job.

355

But as Bruce had insisted, with only limited time on the track, the more hands, the greater the number of sacks they could load, therefore the larger the pot to be divided between them. Everyone knew that Bruce, Charlie, Gordy and Buster would take a slightly larger cut to compensate for their longer prep and expenses. Roy too, perhaps – that was down to Bruce. The rest would be divided equally, once the 'drink' for Stan and a few others had been deducted, including a whack to Brian and one for the mysterious 'fixer' in Glasgow. That meant, with Tiny Dave a late addition, thirteen into whatever the dividend was. So, eighteen slices of the pie in all. It was one of the biggest firms Tony had ever heard of and, as he looked around the room, he felt fresh admiration for Bruce, Charlie and Gordy. Not many men could pull all this together and keep it quiet.

As the hours passed and the atmosphere in the darkened rooms grew oppressive, the firm split into smaller groups. Jim Hussey, Jimmy White and Ronnie played cards. Stan sat quietly in the corner, rolling one fag after another, sometimes smoking a pipe for light relief. Roger Cordrey lay on a mattress and dozed.

Most of the rest played Monopoly, although Bruce took up his role as the commander, moving among his troops, keeping morale up. Buster organised the kitchen, announcing it was Fray Bentos pies for tea, along with a rabbit stew, using an animal Jimmy White had sideswiped on the road. The former

Para was adept at living off the land. But one rabbit didn't go far among so many big chaps.

'Where's Gordy?' asked Roy.

'Ireland,' replied Bruce.

'Ireland?' asked a jittery Ralph, alarmed at the news of being a man down. 'Shouldn't he be here?'

'He will be. Brian is picking him up from the airport and driving him here. It's his alibi – that he was in Ireland.'

Bruce knew that Gordy was a little nervous, although he would never tell the others. After narrowly missing going down for the airport job, he felt exposed. No matter what the evidence, the Squad might lay the train at his door. Hence the alibi and his preference for arriving after dark. Gordy was taking no chances.

'Missus thinks I'm chopping wood in Wiltshire,' chipped in Ronnie. 'Lumberjackin', like.'

'She's gonna think choppin' down trees pays bloody well,' offered Buster. 'Will someone give me a hand in here? It's like feedin' the bleedin' five thousand. Anyone got any loaves and fishes?'

'Anyone fed the cat yet?' asked Roy.

There were a few howls of derision. The farm had come with a rather bedraggled tom, prone to pissing in corners and on beds. It wasn't universally popular, but Roy seemed attached to it.

'I'd best do it then.' Roy got up and went into the kitchen area, looking for something suitable for the cat. A bleary

Roger levered himself up from his mattress and followed. He began breaking open the packs of cutlery that Jimmy had provided. The first beers were cracked, although Bruce told everyone to take it easy. He didn't want anyone drunk on duty or busting for a piss at the wrong time. On the other hand, he knew some of them needed a little drink to steady their nerves. He himself would abstain, apart from a little nip of brandy from his silver Mappin & Webb hip flask, a present from Roy. The fact that Roy hadn't paid for it didn't detract from its value as a gift: it was an important memento of Le Furet's days as a Third-Floor Man. He would, however, smoke a cigar just before the job; a good Havana always calmed him down.

'After dinner, we'll check the uniforms and go over it one last time,' Bruce announced. 'Just to be sure we all know what we are doing.'

'I could rob that train in my sleep,' Tommy Wisbey said.

'I already have. And spent the bleedin' money,' Jim Hussey replied.

'Not on that shirt, did ya? Fuck me, it looks like the test card.'

Jim looked down at his black-and-white patterned top. Then he pointed at Tommy's slacks and cardigan ensemble. 'Hark at Beau Brummell there.'

'What about you, Bruce?' Bob Welch asked. 'What will you do with your whack?'

Bruce scratched his ear. He knew what he wanted: a trip

to America. That Austin Healey. Something nice for Franny. But after that, some land in the country. Bit of shooting, perhaps. Holland & Holland guns, tweeds – he'd always wanted a jacket with the leather elbow pads and 'action' pleats in the back – breeks, garters, shooting brakes, the lot. But all he said was, 'Mustn't count our chickens, Bobby.'

'I am going to buy Bond Street,' Tony announced, reaching for the relevant card and sorting out his £320 purchase price.

There was a pause before Jimmy White said, 'Bugger me, Tony. I don't think there's going to be that much on the train.'

'OK, you gannets, grub's up,' announced Buster. 'You grab a plate, a knife and fork and we'll serve you. And first one to make a crack about dinner ladies gets a fork in the eye. Clear?'

Bruce looked at his watch. 'And gentlemen, the Travelling Post Office Up train to Euston will have just left Glasgow.'

A ragged cheer of relief went up. At least it had begun now, the countdown to what should be a mighty tickle. In six hours, the convoy of thieves and heavies would be ready to roll.

There was another collective sigh of relief when Gordon Goody and Brian Field arrived, completing the firm. Gordy, who wore posh silk gloves, incongruous on a man of his bulk, had brought two bottles of Bushmills from his Irish jaunt. Brian, although nobody noticed at first, brought a long face.

The group was all sitting around the battered kitchen table, having tea or instant coffee, a low cloud of cigarette smoke coalescing above their heads. The conversation was bright and breezy, sometimes bordering on the hysterical, heavy with tongue-in-cheek insults. The only sour note of the evening had been when Bobby Welch had discovered that nobody had thought to bring brown sauce. 'You can't have ketchup with a Fray Bentos steak and kidney,' he had said. 'It's a fuckin' crime.' He failed to see the funny side of this outburst.

'We saved you some food, boys,' said Buster to the new arrivals as they walked in. 'Although I had to stab Jim to stop him scoffing it.'

Charlie, though, had noticed the two men's glum demeanour. 'What is it, Gordy? You called Glasgow?'

The big man nodded. 'Train left OK, but with hardly any bags. Our man estimates it can't be more than a hundred grand.'

There was a low groan. The entire firm had been building themselves up over the past hours to seeing serious cash, and the deflating of the atmosphere was palpable and rapid. Ronnie ripped his gloves off and threw them down on the table. Roger looked as if he might cry. Charlie gazed at Bruce, deep in thought, and said, 'Hold on, boys. It's not over yet.'

He knew that some of the crew weren't convinced they could pull this off, and some had not warmed to Bruce's methods and leadership. Charlie wasn't one of them. Bruce dressed things up in a load of old wank sometimes – the movies, the clothes, the bloody jazz music – but beneath it all was rock-solid planning. Pockets of urgent conversation had broken out. 'Just listen up, will you?' rumbled Charlie, in the kind of voice that made people pay attention. The murmuring stopped abruptly. 'Bruce? What do you think?'

'Is it worth it for a reduced take?' Bruce looked around the room and did the mental arithmetic. To a firm of this calibre that kind of money was hardly worth getting out of bed for, what with the amount of cash already laid down. None of these lads were doing this to be left with seven or eight grand. It would be the airport all over again – big risks, meagre takings. 'No, I think it is worth waiting at least two more nights, maybe three.' He saw some faces pulled. 'Come on, we've come this far. Fuck me, even D-Day was postponed once, you cunts.'

That got some laughs and the tension eased.

'There's something else,' said Gordy. 'They've put the three new HVP coaches on.'

'Shit,' hissed Bruce to himself. 'That's earlier than expected. Couldn't the bastards making them have gone on strike or something?'

'Can't we get into them, then?' asked Tiny Dave Thompson,

who hadn't heard that there was a new, more heavily armoured type of coach due into service

Bruce waved a hand. 'Yeah, yeah, but it adds twenty minutes or more. That's a lot. And there is the chance there will be more sorters in there, because the new ones connect to the rest of the train by a corridor. Bollocks.'

Brian spoke up, his voice even and calm. 'Bruce. Our man in Glasgow says he can take one HVP out, and that we should do the same to the one down here. There's only three been delivered. But it has to look like a fault, not sabotage, he says. Otherwise little alarm bells might ring.'

'Why the fuck didn't your bloke know these were coming on line?' asked Roger.

'I dunno,' said Gordy. 'Said he'd had to take a few days off. Personal problems.'

'Well, now we got personal problems of our own,' grumbled Jim Hussey.

'Be quiet, Jim, you great nancy,' said Roy to the big man, stinging him into silence. Bruce hid a grin. David and Goliath. The diminutive driver turned to Gordy. 'Did he say how? How to put the coach out of action?'

Gordy shook his head. 'No. Just said he had a couple of blokes he could bung a drink up there to make sure the new ones weren't available for a few days.'

'The brakes.' The two words were followed by a rattling cough.

All eyes turned to the new voice. It was Stan, spitting

stray strands of tobacco from his lower lip as he placed a fresh roll-up between them.

'What about them?' asked Bruce.

'You need to fuck with the brakes. There's always teething troubles with these new models. So it won't seem suspicious if both go out of action. Always happens. You block one of the pipes with what looks like debris. Not the main one, but the feeders to the wheels. Iron filings work, and carborundum paste. Just looks like someone connected the pipes without cleaning them properly and the rubbish built up.'

'How do you know that?' asked Jim.

'Used to teach it during the war. At Beaulieu. To the saboteurs being parachuted in to France.' Everyone looked at the skeletal old man with a fresh set of eyes. 'You know where they lay up the coaches between runs, don't you?'

'Wembley,' confirmed Roy. 'I could go and do it in the afternoon. They sit there for three hours or more then. Be back here by the evening.'

'No,' said Bruce firmly. 'Not you. You need to be here to uncouple the coach.'

'Jimmy can do that,' objected Roy, pointing to Jim White, who nodded his agreement.

'Which is why he stays, too. Back-up on everything.'

'And Tony knows how.'

'Apart from that,' Charlie Wilson, who had been brooding on the change of plans, spoke up, 'did he say why there are so few bags? Have we been rumbled? Someone talked out of turn?' He scanned the room accusingly.

'No, Charlie, calm down. He says the banks obviously haven't collected all the cash yet,' said Brian. 'Tomorrow might be better, or the next day. But not tonight.'

Bruce reached a decision. 'Tony?'

'Yeah?'

'You think you could mess with the brakes? You've been doing this uncoupling lark with Roy.'

'Sure I can. If Stan and Roy give us a few clues.'

'Piece of cake,' said Stan.

'Take Tiny Dave with you. Just in case there's trouble.'

Tiny Dave shrugged. It was all the same to him. Better a day off the farm than sitting cooped up for another twenty-four hours solid with a load of sweaty blaggers.

'OK,' said Bruce with fresh enthusiasm. 'So it's still on. Full steam ahead. Or full diesel in our case. We might get to be rich bastards, after all.' He picked up one of the bottles of Bushmills and unscrewed the top. 'But I suppose there's no harm in a little drink now. Get the uniforms off, I don't want you sleepin' in them, and grab a glass. And keep the bleedin' gloves on. Ronnie, that means you.'

'Oi, and boys,' said Bobby to Tony and Tiny Dave, 'if you are going back in town, pick us up a bottle or two of HP sauce, will you?'

'And some Kit-e-Kat.' It was Roy.

Bruce ignored him and concentrated on Tony and Tiny Dave. 'Apart from all that, keep your noses clean. You go in, bugger up the HVP coach, get back here. OK? Good. That's settled, then. Gordy, there's inflatable mattresses pumped up upstairs. Grab yourself a corner. We might as well get some sleep.'

Bruce waited until everyone else was busy, then signalled to Gordy and Brian to follow him outside. He stood looking up at the stars and a blurred, hazy moon, his mind racing. When he was aware they were behind him, he said, 'How much, Brian?'

'For what?'

'This drink. To take out the HVPs.'

'Ten.'

Bruce spun on his heel. 'Ten grand?'

'Per carriage. They've got a spare up there, remember.'

Bruce was speechless. The Glasgow link was already being well remunerated. He examined Brian's face, masked though most of it was by shadows, for signs of deviousness or naked avarice. He wouldn't be the first thief to pad his expenses.

Brian could read Bruce's expression. 'That's what they said, Bruce. They said if they were caught they'd be sacked. Had to be enough to make losing their job worthwhile.'

'How much do BR pay these days then?' Bruce snapped. 'Maybe we should just get a job on the rails.'

Brian spread his hands out, palms up. 'They'll have money

365

to lay out too. Watchmen to be paid off for turning a blind eye.'

'So it begins,' said Gordy. 'The shape of things to come.'

Gordy was right. Once they got a sniff of a big payday, the jackals all appeared. The price of everything went through the roof. Especially Blind Eyes. It would be even worse when they had the actual cash in their hands. 'We haven't got much choice, have we? Tell them to go ahead.'

Brian showed a nervous flicker of teeth in the moonlight. 'I already have.'

'Hello, is that the police? Yes, my name is Charmian Biggs. Look, I'm sorry to bother you, but I don't quite know what else to do. I'm at my wit's end. Sorry, I'm a bit tearful. Just a second. I'll have to blow my nose. This is a call concerning my husband, Ronnie Biggs. Ronald Biggs, yes. The thing is, he has gone off chopping wood in Wiltshire for some firm. No, it's just an odd job; he normally does painting and decorating. This is just a few days' casual work – well paid, he said. But I've just heard that his brother has died. So we are really keen to get hold of him, as you can imagine. No, Ronnie didn't even know he was ill, otherwise he wouldn't have gone. He is – was – very close to his brother. So I wondered, is there any way you can check on any woodcutting firms in Wiltshire? I'm sure that's where he said it was. Thank you, that's very kind. No, I'm sure you'll find him, and when you do I'm certain he'll be very grateful.'

Forty-two

London, 6 August 1963

'Charlie Delta Three to Foxtrot Delta Control. Have contact with silver Jaguar from the all-car message regarding a smash and grab. Proceeding along Langton Terrace. Over.'

'Roger that, Charlie Delta Three.'

'Control, I have with me DC William Naughton and DS Leonard Haslam. We are now turning into Keating Close. It's them, all right; he's seen us and he's put his foot down. Turning left into Baker Rise.'

'Charlie Delta Three, you're now car-to-car. All cars in Number One division switch to Channel Five. Repeat, Channel Five.'

'Control, this is DC Naughton. George, our driver, has

his hands . . . Jesus! . . . his hands full at the moment. I shall transmit the details.'

'Very well, Charlie Delta Three.'

'The car vehicle identification on the Jaguar is Bravo Yankee Romeo five zero two Alpha. He's taking a hard right into Yates Street. He's really throwing it around now. Ugh – sorry, dropped the handset. He's going mad . . . so are we.'

'Anyone able to lend assistance to Charlie Delta Three, now pursuing suspect Jaguar from all-car message one-one-nine-six towards Kilburn against the traffic?'

'This is Tango Bravo Two, am heading down Abercorn Place to try and intercept.'

'He's kerbed it. Lost a hubcap. He's back on track. Trying to lose us on these corners. Just into Foster Place. Repeat, Foster Place. Fifty yards behind now. There's a bloody woodentop standing in the road trying to wave him down. They'll have him. *Jump, you idiot!* Bloody hell. Hello, Control? Unknown PC managed to get a truncheon into their screen. Repeat, Jaguar now has no windscreen. They've punched it out. You should find that silly bugger and give him a commendation.'

'Roger that, Charlie Delta Three.'

'Into the tunnel at Finlay Street, touching seventy now. Going to lose radio cont— Hang on, one of the bastards has jumped out.'

'Please observe on-air protocol, Charlie Delta Three.'

'Charlie Delta Three to Control. One of the bastards

exited the vehicle at the eastern end of the Finlay Street Tunnel. Suggest you send unit to search the area. He's probably hurt himself after coming out at that speed. Oh Lord, there's a school crossing. Lollipop man. *Get out the way, you old fool!* Jesus, he's going to hit him. Watch out, George . . . Watch out for the kids.'

'Charlie Delta Three? This is Control. Come in, Charlie Delta Three.'

'Clear though school, Control. Charlie Delta Three left onto Stanley Lane, by the gasworks. He's on the wrong side of the road! He's swerving back over. That was close. No, he's clipped a lorry. All over the shop now. Steam. No, smoke. Smoke. He's got a puncture! He's slowing!'

'Control again. Reminder that suspects may be armed and dangerous, Charlie Delta Three.'

'Roger that. We are pulling over outside Marlowe House. They're getting out!'

'This is Tango Bravo Two. I have suspect Jaguar in sight, ready to assist Charlie Delta Three. Have DS Edward Boyle, an authorised firearms officer, on board.'

'Right. Charlie Delta Tango leaving vehicle to continue pursuit on foot. Fuckin' move it!'

'Charlie Delta Three. Please observe on-air protocol. Over.'

Forty-three

London, 7 August 1963

The sabotaging of the Mk 2 HVP armoured carriages presented little difficulty. Tiny Dave and Tony both wore overalls and carried toolkits, and nobody questioned their right to be moving among the coaches in the middle of the day. In fact, it would have been a brave man who questioned Tiny about anything, given his size and the scowl on his face, which suggested he had been sent to perform some horrible task and was not happy about it. Tony had slid under the gleaming HVP while Tiny Dave kept a lookout.

With new, clean fittings still uncontaminated by dirt and grit, it was a simple matter to undo the nuts, free the pipes and stuff a mixture of Swarfega and iron filings into each pipe. Stan assured them it would play havoc with the vacuum, and the Post Office would switch to an older coach. Engineers would then take a day or so to come from BR or the GPO to see what was up with their new babies.

Still, by the time he climbed from under the carriage and headed back to the Morris Oxford with Tiny Dave, Tony's face was streaked with grease and his hair felt like wire wool. He needed a shower.

As they drove away, he let out a sigh. 'Dave, do you mind if we swing by my place? We got plenty of time.'

'Where's that then?'

He gave him the address and Dave frowned. 'Holloway Road? Bit out of the way.'

'Nothing happens at the farm for another eight hours. Come on, Dave. The wife's about to drop one.'

'Yeah?' Dave looked sideways at him, to see if he was having him on. 'What's this job then? A christening present?'

'Something like that.'

'All right.'

'And I've got some brown sauce. The missus developed a bit of a thing for it for a few weeks. Bought loads of bottles. Now she can't even stand the smell of it.'

'My Jackie was the same with the boy. Marmite it was with her. Makes her gag now.'

They slid into the traffic, heading for his new house. It was a warm day, London finally bathed in full August sunshine, and Tony wound his window down. 'What will you do after this, Dave?'

'Bangkok.'

'Bangkok?' Tony asked, not sure where it was.

'I was in the Army in Malaya for a bit. Shootin' Commies. Went to Bangkok. Man, what a place.'

'You'll take Jackie?'

Dave looked at him as if he had just let one rip. 'Fuck off. Few months in Bangkok, on me tod, then I'll move to Hong Kong and send for her and the kids.'

'You kill any?'

'What?'

'Commies.'

'Fuck, yes. Shed-loads. That's one thing I don't understand about Bruce. Why we can't have guns. He's a funny fucker.'

'I don't think the GPO will agree after tonight.'

Reminded of what was at stake, Dave lapsed into silence, his meaty hands on the wheel, the car threading through London towards Tony's new place.

It was close to five by the time they arrived at the house. Tony slid out of the car, closed the door and put his head through the open window. 'Want to come in? Cup of tea?'

'Don't want to break up a nice domestic scene,' he said. 'I'll have a fag.'

'Won't be long. Get out of these overalls, grab the sauce, kiss the missus and be out.'

'Take your time.' Dave pointed down the road to the corner shop on Holloway Road. 'I'll get a paper.'

Tony took the five steps up to his house in one jump,

wondering how it was going to be carrying a pram up and down. Maybe they should have gone for something without a raised porch. Like he'd had much say in it.

He put his key in the lock, stepped in and at once smelled strangers. Cigarette smoke, whisky and something stale wafted down the hallway.

'Marie?'

'Tony? That you?' The voice from the lounge was querulous.

Tony walked in. Marie was on the settee. Two men were sat in the armchairs. On the coffee table in between them were teacups and biscuits. He recognised the man on the left. It was the detective who had come with the Stolen Car Squad to the garage.

Marie pushed herself up to her feet, the strain making her face flush. 'Oh, Tony.'

'What is it?' he demanded of the two policemen.

But it was Marie who answered. 'It's Geoff. The silly bugger went and did a smash and grab.'

'Geoff?' Tony asked, not sure he was hearing correctly. 'Your brother?'

There was a strange noise and for a moment Tony thought a tap had been left running. Then Marie groaned with a mixture of shock and embarrassment as the carpet beneath her feet darkened. Her waters had broken.

Assistant GPO Inspector Thomas Kett walked along the

platform at Glasgow station, watching the final prepara-
tions for the TPO's departure. It was his job to make sure
the sorting ran smoothly during the journey, that each of
the sixty-seven sorters in the ten regular coaches knew what
had to be done. Each coach had its own supervisor, the
majority old hands, so he had no concerns. The mail would
get through to London and the south-east, as it did almost
every night of the year, barring snowstorms and Christmas.

He reached the HVP, where British Transport Police and
the GPO Inspectors were overseeing the loading of the last
of the bright-red High Value mailbags containing cash.
'How many, Frank?' he asked.

Frank Dewhurst, Postman (Higher Grade) and in charge
of the HVP carriage, consulted his clipboard. 'Ninety-two
here. Another twenty or thirty to be picked up on the way
down south. Bloody cage is going to be bursting. When do
we get the new buggers back?'

The new coaches were fitted with much larger secure
lockable areas, so the HVPs weren't crammed in like passengers on a rush-hour Tube. 'I dunno, few days at least, so
they reckon.'

Thomas grumbled. The older HVP was draughty and
noisy, as well as scuffed and threadbare after years of continuous service. Some of the pigeonholes were disintegrating,
too, so if you weren't careful you ended the shift with a
handful of splinters. The new ones had high-density plastic
sorting trays. They had been given a teaser of what a modern

374

coach could be like – decent kitchen, comfy seats – and a couple had run with a different crew the previous night and now they were told they were withdrawn. 'Who's with you in there?' Thomas asked.

'Just Les.'

Leslie Penn, a good lad, but still learning the ropes. 'What, just the two of you? To do all the sorting?'

'We'll pick up Joe Ware and Johnny O'Connor down the way.'

'Where?'

'Tamworth.'

'Bloody hell, Tom, that's almost the end of the line.'

Frank Dewhurst made a show of pushing up his sleeves, secretly pleased at having something to do other than walking up and down between the other coaches during the journey. He reached for the grab rail and hauled himself aboard the HVP. It smelled of old wood, leather, glue, string and brown paper. It was a kind of homely mix, Frank thought. 'If you don't mind, I'll lend a hand. Put the kettle on, Les.'

Frank looked at his watch and leaned back out the door, shouting up the platform to the driver climbing into the cab of the beefy English Electric diesel loco. 'Let's get this bloody thing moving. There's our mail to deliver!'

The driver, Jack Mills, a veteran of these night runs, smiled, let go with his left hand and flashed a not unfriendly V-sign. There was always banter between BR and the GPO.

'Hold your horses. It might be your train, mate,' he yelled, 'but it's my effin' engine that has to pull it.'

'I counted ninety-two sacks into the HVP, although that is likely to be added to. Second carriage as always. And one of the older types. How much? I don't like to speculate. Over one million, clear. Maybe one and a half. Will that do you? I thought so. Right, that's me out of here. I'll tell Brian where he can leave my whack and Mark's as well. Plus drinks for the lads up here. The ones who fixed the coaches. No, I'll stay away from Glasgow. Mark will collect his down there. I'm coming south, too. Just in case Glasgow gets too hot for me. They are bound to know someone tipped you the wink. Right, there she goes, out of the station. A minute early, too. Over to you boys. And by the way, good luck. It's your train, now.'

Forty-four

**Leatherslade Farm, near Oakley, Bucks,
7 August 1963**

Bruce couldn't make sense of what he was hearing. While he thought, he scratched the skin beneath his gloves. It had been an oppressively warm day in the farmhouse. With the curtains drawn and no open windows, the temperature had climbed. It was early evening and most of the men had stripped down to vests or singlets. Gloves were still on, but they were becoming increasingly irritating. Still, Bruce didn't relent, bawling at anyone who so much as took them off to get some air to hot, sweaty palms.

Slowly, Bruce repeated what he had been told. 'So Tony went in for a cup of tea. You went back to his house? For a fuckin' cup of tea?'

The disapproval hit Tiny Dave like a slap across the face. Bruce made it clear he thought they should have driven straight back. 'And to get the sauce for Bobby.'

'Oh well, yes, the sauce. What's more important than brown sauce? So you stop outside and then Tony comes with two coppers?'

'And his missus. Holding her belly.'

'They got into squad cars?'

'Yup. But I reckon they was going to the hospital.'

'The Flying Squad do a lot of things,' said Charlie quietly, 'but they don't deliver babies. That's a different 999.'

'Could be they were after Tony for something else. This, maybe,' offered Roger.

'Not likely,' said Bruce, sensing a flash of the jitters from the signalman. 'Or we'd all be in it.'

'Tony's solid,' said Roy. 'You know that.'

'He'd better be,' muttered Gordy, expertly shuffling a deck of cards, despite his gloves.

'Forget Tony for a minute, can we?' Roy said. 'What about the train, Bruce?'

'Oh, yeah.' Bruce had neglected to tell them about his call to Glasgow. He had arrived back at the same time as Tiny Dave, discovering they were a man down. 'It's left on time. Close to a hundred HVP sacks. One point five million.'

Ralph, normally the quiet one, gave a low, appreciative whistle and laughed. 'Fuck me.'

'But what about this business with Tony?' asked Roger,

refusing to be swept along by the ripples of avarice spreading throughout the room. 'Should we wait for another night? Or forget it altogether?' The initial euphoria the signalman had shown for the enterprise had dissipated. He was nervous and sweaty now, complaining about missing his wife, outraged that he was expected to lie low at the farm with the others. Charlie had been designated to make sure he didn't fold on them. He only had to give Roger one of his looks and the whingeing died on his lips.

Bruce glanced around the room, at faces made yellow by cheap, low-watt bulbs and a half-dozen candles. He knew that some were thinking that, even now, police cars could be moving into position around the farm. 'We'll take a vote. All in favour of going ahead, raise their hands.' He waited until each man had made their decision. Charlie glared at Roger until the latter half-raised his arm.

'Right, then. It's unanimous. We go tonight.'

'The thing is, Tony,' drawled Len Haslam, 'it was your van waiting for the transfer.'

Tony was sitting in the interview room at Paddington Green, opposite Duke Haslam and Billy Naughton. He was both relieved and annoyed. Relieved because this was nothing to do with the farm or Bruce and the lads. Furious because his piece-of-shit brother-in-law had dragged him into this mess. Now he would miss out on his whack. The robbery would go ahead without him.

'What van?'

'Your Hillman Husky. There it was, parked up, just waiting for the loot to arrive. Classic switcher-oo. Oh, and Geoff had the keys in his pocket.'

'I told you, I bought the Husky off Geoff. He begged me to. Then while I was away . . .'

'Away where, Tony?' Billy Naughton asked.

'Southampton. Buying cars. Looking under them, examining engines. That's why I'm so dirty. You can check—'

'We will,' said Len Haslam.

Tony wasn't worried about that. As Bruce had suggested, he had set up a good alibi, well rehearsed, with his old pals in Falmer. He would have to kick it into play as soon as he got out.

'But about the Hillman Husky,' prompted Billy.

'It's mine, yes. But as I am sure my wife will have told you, Geoff came and borrowed it back. Or at least, I assume that is what he did.'

'And the Jag used in the robbery? Nice one, brand new.'

Tony shrugged. 'Not down to me. Look, have a heart, gents. My wife is about to give birth.'

'And you want to be there with the big cigar.'

'Yeah. Is that a crime now?'

The two policemen said nothing.

'I know you'd like to haul me in while you're at it, but I had nothing to do with it. Smash and grab? Is that my game? I might clock the odd motor now and then, but really.

Talk about barking up the wrong tree. Now, can I get cleaned up and go and see my wife?'

'Go on, fuck off,' sighed Haslam. 'But don't go off on any more expeditions, all right? Stay close to home, son.'

'I'm about to become a father. Where else would I be?'

'In the Scrubs if we find out you're lying,' said Billy. He looked up at the ceiling, as if a thought had just occurred to him. 'You know anything about a big job going off, Tony?'

'Yeah.'

'What's that?'

'My wife squeezing a kid out. Biggest job of all.'

Len managed a thin smile. 'Nothing about a Bank Holiday tickle? That was the whisper.'

Tony scratched his ear as nonchalantly as he could. 'Nobody's whispered to me.'

'Right. Piss off then.'

After he had gone, the two men lit cigarettes. 'What do you think?' Len asked.

'The Bank Holiday is a bit thin.'

Billy shrugged. It was a small nugget, but a nugget just the same, picked up in a pub. 'That's all I heard. Heavies wanted for a Bank Holiday job.'

'I hope you didn't dip into the fund for that. Still, Bank Holiday isn't till the end of the month.' Len took out his pocket diary and flicked through it. 'Twenty-sixth.'

'It's likely to be a bank vault, eh, Len? They might be after sledgehammer men. Which is why they need muscle.'

Haslam nodded, impressed by the boy's thinking despite himself. 'A three-day weekend. Gives them an extra day to break through walls and what have you. A bank, yeah.'

'But we've got time on our side. Whatever it is should leak between now and then, Len.'

'True.' He inclined his head to indicate the departed suspect. 'You fancy Fortune for the jeweller's?'

'Not really. His brother-in-law confirms he had nothing to do with it.'

'Yeah, right,' he said. 'Probably as thick as Pinky and Perky, those two.'

'I don't get that impression.'

Duke Haslam dropped his cigarette into the tin mug in front of him. It hissed as it hit the half-inch of cold tea in the bottom. 'You don't get that impression?' he repeated. 'Mr Hatherill teach you impressions, did he? Go on, do Max Bygraves.'

Billy's time spent with the Commander was a sore point. Len felt his protégé had been purloined and he had sensed a sea change in the younger man after his jaunt to Devon. After the West Country, Billy had been sent on a doping stakeout at Sir Gordon Richards's stables, at the request of the trainer, who was worried about some of his thoroughbreds' performances. Billy had not only caught a jockey administering powder to a favourite, but had picked himself up a strapping stable lass too. Billy was growing up.

'I can do Henry Cooper,' said Billy with mock severity, clenching a fist and waving it.

'What – bleed a lot?' Len sneered. He had been there at Wembley when Cooper had floored Cassius Clay, only for the latter to be saved when Clay's cornerman had protested that his fighter's glove had split. The delay enabled Clay to come back at Cooper and open up a cut on his eye, which led to the fight being stopped. All England was outraged for Our 'Enery, but Len felt the best fighter had won, even if he was an arrogant black bastard.

'I'm not saying Fortune is clean,' continued Billy. 'He doesn't smell right, I'll grant you that.'

Haslam bit his tongue. 'Doesn't smell right' was a prime piece of Hatherill Ham, fresh off the bone.

'But not for this. Geoff Barrow is an idiot. Not sure you can say the same about Tony Fortune. Still.'

'Still?' echoed Haslam. 'Still what?'

Billy Naughton raised his eyebrows and smirked. 'Still, let's put a tail on young Tony, eh?'

By midnight the tension in the farmhouse was building towards unbearable. All had changed into their outfits, the drivers and Bruce dressed as soldiers, most of those who would be on the track in boilersuits and balaclavas, although Roger had opted to dress like a vagrant, in case he was surprised on the gantry, and then he could pretend to be sleeping rough.

Bruce, outwardly calm and controlled, had to admit to some nerves. He checked and rechecked that he had everything he needed, that his walkie-talkie was functioning and that he had his balaclava, that the uniform – genuine ex-Army but altered by Franny to fit better – would pass muster. Yes, he had to admit as he looked in the full-length mirror in the bedroom, he did have something of the officer class about him.

It was hard to believe, after the months of speculation, planning and scouting, that it was about to go down. Even more incredible was the thought of the amount of money that could be his – theirs – by the end of the evening. He'd be rich. Properly rich, not just enough for a flash motor and a few good dinners. But seriously, stonkingly rich. Maybe for life. That would be good. Bugger the Aston; if there was more than one million, he'd go for a Ferrari GTO. True, they cost a fortune to run. But he intended to have a bloody fortune, didn't he?

Bruce consulted his watch again, marvelling at how the hands were crawling round. As the second hand swept past the six he cleared his throat. 'OK, lads.'

They all stopped what they were doing.

'Head 'em up, move 'em out.'

There was the clatter of mugs being put aside, the rough scrape of chairs being pushed back, the sudden burble of excitement. Cigarettes were stubbed out, board games abandoned, dregs of coffee swallowed. 'Candles, gents. Don't want to come back to see a smouldering wreck.'

Roy, in charge of transport, shouted out a reminder of who was in what vehicle. 'And keep your speed down,' he said. 'There's only one racing driver here and even he's on a go-slow.'

The men tumbled out past Roy into a lovely warm summer's evening, silvered by a big, friendly moon. The air hardly moved, wrapped round them like a light soft blanket. It was the kind of night, thought Bruce as he headed for one of the Land Rovers, where you could believe in fairies and elves. The kind of night where something magical might happen. A miracle, even.

He felt a hand heavy on his shoulder as he opened the Land Rover's door. It was Charlie. 'Just want to say, Bruce, no matter what happens. Nice one.'

It meant a lot coming from Chas. Almost twenty years they had known each other; from bombsites to train jobs, it had been quite a journey. Bruce watched his old friend slide into what they called the 'heavy' vehicle – Charlie plus Buster, Tiny Dave, Tommy Wisbey and Gordy. Bruce climbed into the second Land Rover, into the passenger seat next to his second cousin. 'Quiet' Ralph had volunteered to take Tony's role as driver; Bruce was happy with that. As Roy had said, it wasn't a race. He switched on the VHF radio that was tuned to Buckinghamshire Constabulary.

Bruce turned around, elbow on the seat. He had Roger, Ronnie and Stan in the back, the technical team. 'Everyone all right?'

'Fine.' Roger was licking his lips as if he hadn't had a drink for months. He looked strained. Stan was rolling another fag, a slight tremor evident in his fingers. Ronnie was Ronnie, relaxed, ready for what the night would throw at him.

Roy gunned the engine of the Land Rover and pulled away first, taking his fearsome crew with him. God help anyone who got in their way, thought Bruce. The lorry that would carry the cash came out second, a tired-looking Jimmy White at the wheel, Bobby Welch next to him, Jim Hussey in the rear.

Ralph let in the clutch and they bounced towards the track that led to the B4011 and the back roads to Bridego. Bruce checked the time. Twelve-forty. In three hours he would either be a hero to these men or a dismal failure.

Nobody spoke for the first few miles, lost in their own version of what the coming twenty-four hours might hold.

'Eh,' said Stan eventually. 'I just had a thought.'

Fuck me, thought Bruce, that must be lonely in there. 'What is it, Stan?'

'It's coming from Glasgow, right, the train?'

'Yes.'

'And the money is from banks up there?'

'That's correct.'

'What if they're all Scottish notes?'

Bruce laughed. They would be a bugger to shift; even trying to get a single Scottish pound note accepted in London was hard enough. 'Tell you what, Stan.'

'What, Bruce?'

'If they are, you can keep the lot.'

'Someone on the road ahead,' said Ralph.

A figure was caught in the headlights, a solitary man on a lonely road at some godforsaken hour. His hand was stretched out, thumb pointing east.

'Hitchhiker,' said Bruce. 'Keep going.'

This was no time for Good Samaritans.

Tony Fortune lay staring at the ceiling in the flat, unable to sleep, his mind churning and restless. It flitted from images of Marie and the lovely, crumpled baby that had reduced him to tears, and the sixteen men in the farmhouse – seventeen if you counted Brian Field – waiting to pull off a ridiculously audacious crime.

And his poxy brother-in-law. Banged up for armed robbery, having tried to prove that he, too, could be a getaway driver.

He was disappointed about missing out on the payday from the train, mainly for Marie's sake. Maybe the others would bung him a drink. He deserved at least that. Perhaps enough to pay for a nursery for the baby. And a nice pram. Marie would be home in a few days. He should get to work on doing some painting.

He leaned up onto one elbow and looked at his watch. Twelve forty-five. For a moment he imagined he could hear the grind of Army gears, smell the excitement and anxiety of the men in unfamiliar uniforms, see the gleam in Bruce Reynolds's eyes. Then he slumped back down and let his lids droop, willing sleep to come. Good luck, lads, he thought. Good luck.

Forty-five

Sears Crossing, 8 August 1963

Roy James's walkie-talkie crackled as he walked alongside the rails, heading for the gantry of the 'home' signal.

'Roy?'

'Yes, Bruce?'

'How you doing?'

'I've cut the telephone to most of the farmhouses. Had to leave one, because it would come down on some cowsheds. Make a hell of a racket.'

'OK. Trackside phone?'

'That's already out. How about you?'

Bruce was ahead of them all as point man, ready to send the alert when the TPO Up train left Linslade. 'Smoking a damn fine cigar.'

That's Bruce, Roy thought. Always doing it in style. Roy heard the steel rail beside him buzz and looked over his shoulder, beyond Bridego Bridge. 'Train coming,' he said.

'What?'

'From the south. Train coming. I'm getting down.'

Roy slipped behind one of the concrete huts at the trackside. A growling 08-type diesel shunter came by, its line of empty trucks rattling and groaning.

He waited until it would have passed Bruce before resuming the conversation. 'I'm going to the gantry now. What about Roger?'

Roger would have opened the control box for the 'distant' or 'dwarf' signal, then used a battery and crocodile clips to light up the amber warning light. Ralph's job was to connect up the last clip and to cover the bulb in the green light module, so only the amber would be showing to the driver. It was so simple, no wonder Roger wanted to keep it secret.

'He's just set up Ralph at the dwarf. Should be with you *toot sweet*. You still there, Ralph?'

Roy heard the reply. 'Check.'

'Good.'

'I need a piss.'

'You should have gone before we left,' said Roy.

Bruce chortled. 'Bottle it, Ralph. Where are you, Roy?'

'Coming up to the gantry now,' said Roy. He could see two figures at the base of the steel framework, Roger and Buster. Buster had his spring-loaded cosh in his hand.

Peering into the gloom, Roy could just make out Jimmy and Tiny Dave at the edge of the track and, on the western side, the shapes of Charlie, Gordy and Tommy pressed against the embankment. All were armed with pickaxes or crowbars, many of them stolen from the nearby BR tool-sheds. They were mainly for smashing into the coach, not maiming people. Buster's cosh, however, was different, specifically designed for the train crew. He had made it clear that he thought a quick, sharp dose of pain was the best way to cower the staff on board. 'Concentrates the mind,' he liked to say. Roy reminded himself to give Buster a wide berth.

'OK?' asked Roger, the tension making his voice tremulous. 'You coming up?'

Roy put the walkie-talkie over his shoulder and Roger did the same with his bag of tricks. They quickly ascended the ladder and stepped onto the walkway. Another train came by and the pair squeezed themselves into the metal. A horribly clammy cloud of steam and grit enveloped them briefly and was gone, as the loco puffed off towards London.

Roy spat some dirt from his mouth. 'No wonder they switched to diesels.'

It was cramped on the walkway but it afforded them a fine view up and down the track. Behind was Bridego Bridge, where the train would be unloaded. Ahead was Sears Crossing itself, actually the elevated track to nearby Rowden Farm, and beyond that the dwarf or distant signal which warned drivers to proceed with caution. Further on still was Colonel Bruce Reynolds, ready to leap in his Land Rover and drive back to Bridego, once he had spotted the Travelling Post Office and alerted them.

Roy shone the torch while Roger fiddled with his battery and wires. The Flowerpot Man put the clips onto the red signal's bulb, which glowed into life. He disconnected it.

'Now,' Roger said, 'for Katie's secret ingredient.' He mimed crumbling an Oxo cube before he pulled a glove from his pocket and slid it over the bulb in the green signal. He then craned his neck to ensure it masked the 'proceed' light completely.

'A glove?' Roy asked, unable to keep the incredulity from his voice.

'Can't be any old glove. Nice bit of leather, this.'

'We're going to rob a train with a glove?' Roy felt as if he had just discovered that David Nixon couldn't really pull a rabbit from a hat.

'It works, Roy. What's the time?'

'Five to three.'

Roger squirmed to make himself comfortable. 'Worst part, waiting. Hate it, don't you? Must be like the start of a race. Waiting for the flag.'

He was beginning to burble. 'Shut up, Rog.'

'Yeah. Sorry.'

Roy suddenly felt a pang of sympathy for the bag of nerves

sharing a walkway with him. 'How did you ever get involved in this, anyway?'

The answer was short, yet rueful. 'Ask my bookie.'

Well, he wasn't alone, there were several in the group who described themselves as 'bookmakers' but who were, in reality, more punter than bookie. If they did get the haul, Roy daren't think how much would eventually go on gee-gees or at the Sportsman or similar establishments. He spoke into the walkie-talkie. 'Bruce? We're in place. Over.'

'Good. Nothing yet. I'm going to flash my torch, three long signals. See it?'

'Yes.'

'That's the back-up in case the walkie-talkies fail, so keep your eyes open. How's Roger?'

Roger was now rubbing his hands together nervously. A twitch had appeared at the corner of his mouth. When he smiled, he looked slightly demented.

'A-One,' said Roy. Roger flashed him a thumbs-up.

'OK, over and out.'

Another train came from the south, a diesel this time, its engine thumping lazily. It passed over Bridego, its blazing lights raking the track ahead. Roy hoped everyone was well tucked away.

Then he heard the grinding of brakes and the falling note of an engine losing power. The train was stopping.

'Shit,' he said.

Roger stirred himself. 'Signals are on green. Silly buggers shouldn't stop.'

The locomotive came to a halt beneath them. Even above the rumble of the idling engine, they could hear muffled voices from the cab. The walkie-talkie gave a squawk and Roy switched it off.

He saw movement in the darkness to his left, where some of the heavies were. He could imagine what they were thinking. *We'd best take this train out, too.*

There was the sound of hearty laughter at a shared joke from the cab. They wouldn't be chortling if they knew the kind of blokes who were concealed a few yards away from them, thought Roy.

Then, the sound of running water – a heavy stream, slowly weakening. One of them was taking a piss.

As soon as it had finished the diesel note changed to something more urgent; there was a jerk, a clank and the train moved off.

'I should report them for that,' said Roger with genuine exasperation.

Roy switched the walkie-talkie back on.

Silence descended once more over the silver-washed scene. The moon appeared to have grown brighter, the night warmer. Roy was sure the latter was from the burst of adrenaline when the loco had stopped. He was well aware now how easily it could all go wrong. There must be simpler ways to earn a Formula One car, he thought to himself.

'It's coming. This is it.' For a second the words seemed to make no sense. What did he say? Was that Bruce? Roy looked at the walkie-talkie in disbelief. 'Repeat, this is it, chaps,' the voice said again. 'The real thing.'

Fuck.

Roy poked Roger into action and switched on the torch. The beam wavered slightly, but he had to admire Roger's steady hand as he slipped the glove into place, positioned the battery and connected the clips. No sign of nerves or twitches this time. 'Done!' he exclaimed.

There was now a red light at Sears Crossing.

Forty-six

Sears Crossing, 8 August 1963

Driver Jack Mills swore when he saw the dwarf signal glowing amber. They were on the final run into Euston. No more mail to pick up or coaches to be added – his engine was pulling twelve carriages now – no more swapping of GPO personnel as shifts changed. Once the train was into Euston, then he could sign off. There would be the rigmarole of transferring the HVP sacks to the East Central District Post Office and distributing it to various banks, including the Bank of England, but that was no concern of his. He would be well into his second mug of tea, having polished off a decent breakfast, by the time the train was emptied.

Odd, Mills thought. The dwarf signal's rail magnets

normally triggered an AWS, an Automatic Warning Signal, in the cab and a horn sounded when the light was at 'caution'. But neither had kicked in. He would have to report a malfunction.

'Red,' said David Whitby, his young fireman.

'I can see that, son,' he said, although Whitby was only showing his driver that he was paying attention, that he could see the main signal was on red, demanding that they halt. Mills applied more braking and the massive engine shuddered as its power was curtailed, like a great stallion pulled up too soon.

Whitby moved to the door of the loco, ready to jump down and make the call to determine how long they would be stuck at Sears Crossing.

Inside the HVP carriage, Assistant GPO Inspector Thomas Kett was only vaguely aware of the train slowing. He, Frank Dewhurst and Leslie Penn were busy sorting the last of the letters, the ones with such appalling writing that they had been set aside so that all three men could work on interpreting the scrawl. They had also picked up two junior sorters, John O'Connor and Joe Ware along the route.

'Is that Cheltenham or Chelmsford?' he asked Frank. 'There's no bloody county.'

'Chester-le-Street.'

'You sure? Les, what does that say?'

'Stopping again,' said Les absentmindedly. He glanced out of the grimy, barred windows, but that told him very little. He looked at his watch. Almost a quarter after three.

'Never mind that. What do you reckon it says?'

'Chesterfield.'

'Oh, for cryin' out loud.' They had stopped completely now. Thomas placed the troublesome letter aside for a fourth opinion. 'Put the kettle on, will you, Joe? Be in here another hour at least at this rate.'

'For fuck's sake,' said David Whitby loudly as he put the phone to his ear. The line was dead – which meant a walk to a signal box or to another phone. And that would be down to him.

He looked back up the train at the cab, wondering if he should tell Millsy that the phone was useless before wandering off. The light was still red, but he should go and consult with his driver. He gave the phone one last go, but there was still not so much as a crackle on the line. He replaced the receiver and began the walk back to the front of the train, when he saw someone ahead. No doubt an engineer come to fix the phone.

'What's up, mate?' he asked the dark figure. He could see others behind the worker, although they appeared to be ducking under one of the coaches. 'Something wrong?'

The man stepped forward and Whitby could see he was wearing a woollen balaclava. Just his eyes and mouth were visible. He looked like a Black and White Minstrel. Why would he have that on? It was summer now. Those nights were past.

There was, however, no mistaking the purpose of the implement waved in front of his face as the man – shorter than Whitby, but a lot bulkier – grabbed his arm. It was a powerful grip.

Then he felt other hands on him, pinning his arms, and sour breath washed over his face.

'Say a word and you are fucking dead,' hissed the little man with the evil-looking cosh.

Whitby's mouth went dry and his brain tried to make sense of the fragmented thoughts crowding into it. 'Yeah, all right mate,' he managed to say. 'I'm with you.'

'Go with him, then, and keep quiet.'

Buster watched Bobby Welch lead the cowering boy away and headed for the cab. Let's hope the driver rolls over that easily, he thought.

Thomas Kett accepted the mug of steaming tea from Les, grateful at that moment that they had halted. It would make a change to have a drink without all that rolling about. Although you got used to it – old GPO hands rarely spilled a drop – it was nice to sit down and not have to make all those compensatory muscle movements.

Just then, he heard the hiss of escaping air from the rear of the HVP and cocked an ear. The coach was connected to the rest of the train by a fat umbilical that carried the vacuum. 'What's that?'

Leslie listened as he drank his own tea. There was the faintest of metallic sounds.

'It's Chelveston.'

The other two looked at Frank who was leaning against the cage that held the red High Value sacks. He was holding up the envelope with the disputed destination.

'Chelveston?' Thomas asked. 'You sure?'

'Chelveston, Northamptonshire,' Frank said with certainty in his voice. He scribbled the county onto the envelope with a chinagraph pencil and tossed it into the appropriate bin.

Thomas listened once more but the hissing, whatever it was, had stopped. He drained his tea. 'Come on, Millsy, let's get a move on.'

The uncoupling of the buckeye link and vacuum tube complete, Roy straightened and stepped back from the train. As he did so, an unexpected roar suddenly engulfed him and the punch of compressed air threw him back against one of the coaches. The train on the other track blasted by like a roaring fireball, all wild noise and lights. Winded, he looked up at the locomotive. He could see someone hanging from the cab's grab rails, pulling himself in. Jesus, it must nearly have snatched him off, the way the GPO trains plucked mailbags from waiting arms. The lucky bastard disappeared inside.

Roy ducked under the train and ran back to the embankment at a crouch. From the road that ran parallel to the track came the urgent, rising note of the Land Rover's engine, racing to get Bruce back to Bridego Bridge. He just hoped the Colonel had remembered to lay out the explosive charges as Roger had instructed him, to make sure no train, coming through the genuine green signal outside Lechslade, rammed into the back of their one. That would put the cat among the pigeons.

He found the young fireman huddled on the grass, shaking, Bobby standing over him. Roger was sitting next to them, rolling up his trouser leg. He uncovered a bad gash, visible in the light bleeding from the HVP coach. 'Caught it on the gantry,' he whispered.

'Be fine,' said Roy. He grabbed the fireman and hauled him to his feet. Bobby gave him a last shove. 'Where you from?' Roy asked him.

'Crewe.'

'Name?'

'Dave.'

'Stay calm, Dave, and there's a drink in it for you,' said Bobby.

'Stay calm,' repeated Roy, as he looked at Bobby, 'and do as you are told, because there are some right hard bastards here.'

Then he took the fireman's arm and led him towards the front of the train, towards the worst of the right hard bastards.

*　　*　　*

Jack Mills thought it was David Whitby climbing up onto the footplate.

'What did they say, lad?'

He looked down onto a black, wool-clad face.

'Who the fuck are you?' He wasn't frightened by the sight, more angry at the intrusion.

He didn't catch the muffled reply, but it certainly wasn't friendly. As the man began to haul himself up, Mills could see the cosh in his hand. Now he felt a tremor of fear pass through his body.

He aimed a kick and felt the satisfaction of it landing home. Someone was pushing the man from behind, though, and he carried on coming. Mills swung at his face, turned round and flicked the exhauster off, killing the train's vacuum. Let them try and take his train *now*.

'Hit him!' the intruder yelled. Only then was he aware of other men, climbing from the opposite side. Too many coming in for him to take on. He kicked again at the first one, but the man was inside the cab now, and rising to his feet.

'Bloody hit him!' someone yelled again. 'What you waiting for?'

'Get off my train—'

A spark of white light exploded in front of Jack Mills's eyes. He felt something warm trickling over his left eye. There was another blow, this time to the back of his head and his legs buckled.

'Out the way, he's going down!' were the last words he heard as the rough steel of the footplate rushed towards him.

Charlie, still spooked by nearly being sucked into oblivion by a passing express, helped pull Stan up onto the footplate. He saw he still had his pipe in his mouth, albeit unlit, and he snatched it away, jamming it in the top pocket of his boilersuit. The footplate was getting crowded now, and Buster and Tiny Dave struggled to get the comatose Jack Mills out of the way. Eventually, they dragged him into the corridor that connected the twin cabs of the loco.

'What happened to him?' asked Stan, looking down at the blood on the floor, his voice high and tremulous.

'Must have slipped,' said Charlie, not sure himself what had occurred while he had been clinging onto the grab handles for dear life.

'Hit his head on the floor,' said Buster unconvincingly.

'Come on, Stan, time to earn that drink,' said Ronnie Biggs, whispering gently into his ear.

The solid wall of men parted, and Stan took his place at the controls.

'Take your time,' said Ronnie to the visibly shaking replacement driver.

'But not too much of it.' The unmistakable form of Gordon Goody loomed over him.

Yet more people pressed into the cab.

'All aboard,' someone said.

'Shut up,' snapped Charlie.

'He means everyone is here,' said Buster grimly. 'We can go.'

Stan's hand hovered uncertainly over the dials and switches. The diesel was still running at idle, but the controls were unresponsive. He pressed on the dead-man's plate at his feet. Still nothing. He tapped one of the dials, its needle way to the left. 'I can't get a vacuum.'

Roy groaned.

'What?' Charlie asked. 'You can't get a what?'

'You said you'd driven one before,' said Gordy, his voice like pressed steel.

'I have. Well, sort of.' Ronnie thought Stan was going to cry. 'Not this big, but similar. I think they've changed something, though. I just have to get the brake vacuum before the controls respond, but it's not—'

Gordy growled, low and threatening. 'Can you drive this fucking thing or not?'

'Give me a minute.'

Charlie put a hand on Stan's shoulder. It wasn't a friendly gesture. 'We haven't got a fuckin' minute.'

Ronnie, too, was beginning to brim with anger and not a little shame. Stan was his man, his entrée to the firm, his bargaining chip, his guarantee of a whack. And he was fucking up. 'Stan, come on, mate. Release the brakes and let's get out of here.'

There followed thirty seconds of tense silence, broken by the passage of another train. Charlie realised how exposed they were, crowded onto the footplate. Any passing driver or fireman might wonder why there appeared to be a fancy-dress party going on in the cab of an English Electric D class. 'Come on, Stan. We are sitting here with our dicks hanging out.'

'Still no vacuum.' The number of men behind him and the threats had shot his nerves. Every control looked unfamiliar to Stan now as the panic overwhelmed him.

Roy prayed he had connected the pipe to the dummy properly, otherwise this was all his fault. If that leaked, the vacuum could not form.

Gordy shouted over his shoulder, 'Get the other driver. Now.'

Stan began to protest, but shovel-like hands slid under his arms and he was lifted from the seat like a baby from its cot.

A cacophony of urgent voices filled the cab.

'Get him here.'

'What's wrong with him?'

'He'll be OK. You'll be OK, Pops. It's worse than it looks.'

'Someone give him a handkerchief.'

'What dopey cunt hit him?'

'He fell.'

'Yeah. Like fuck. There you go.' A crude bandage was

tied around the driver's head. He was manhandled into his newly-vacant seat.

'Let's go. Now!'

'Bruce'll be having kittens.'

'I can't see.' Mills managed to get himself heard over the racket. 'I can't see.'

'Wipe his eyes.'

'No, I think I've gone blind.'

Charlie leaned in close, so that the rough balaclava touched the driver's cheek. 'Nice try, old man.'

Then Gordy spoke: 'If you don't want some more then you'll drive this fuckin' train.' He showed him the pickaxe handle he was carrying. 'Do you understand?'

Mills looked around at all the masked faces and the eyes, some pleading, many threatening, staring down at him. 'All right, I'll do it. Throw that switch there,' he said.

'Where?'

'On the bulkhead. The exhauster.'

It was Roy who found the device and depressed the lever. Immediately a whining began as a compressor kicked in. 'Be a second,' said Mills. 'We just got to get the vacuum.'

'Fuck!'

'Told you.' It was Stan, bleating. 'I told you it was the air.'

'Shut him up, Ronnie,' said Buster. 'Or I will.'

The train gave one small, tentative movement, more spasm than forward progress. Then it began to move, slowly but smoothly, the huge engine merely purring at a tenth of its power. Roy, pressed against one of the steel walls, held his breath, hoping once more he had disconnected everything correctly. He leaned out of the open door as Mills accelerated slightly and saw the gap opening up between the HVP and the rest of the GPO carriages. 'We're clear,' he said with relief.

'Where we going?' asked Mills.

'Cuba!' someone shouted.

'There'll be a white marker head. About half a mile, give or take. Keep your speed down,' said Charlie.

Gordy took Roy's place at the door, looking ahead now, although glancing back to see if there was any sign of an alarm being raised. All was quiet.

Mills wiped a hand over his face, trying to clear the mix of blood and sweat still trickling into his eyes. He stretched forward and wiped the cab windows. They were steaming up from all the hot bodies and warm breath. 'What kind of marker?'

'White sheet,' Charlie said.

'I see it,' announced Gordy. 'Get ready.'

Mills began to slow.

'Keep going. Keep going. Here.' The train pulled up sharp. 'Bit further.'

'Make your mind up,' Mills said, a flash of his old anger surfacing.

'Shut it, Pops.' Charlie poked him with the pickaxe

407

handle and the driver shunted the loco forward a few more yards.

'Perfect!' yelled Gordy.

The cab quickly emptied of the men. The difficult technical part had been completed successfully. Now it was time for brute strength.

The five sorters in the HVP groaned and cursed as the train stopped again with a succession of fits and starts and one final jerk. Thomas suspected Jack Mills was messing about, trying to make them spill their tea.

'I'll have his bloody guts—' he swore.

The clang of metal on metal was so loud that Thomas thought they had crashed. But there was no feeling of any impact. Then came the sound of glass breaking, and shards of it shot across the interior of the carriage.

Joe Ware dropped the bundle of letters he had been holding. His voice was high-pitched, loaded with terror. 'Someone is trying to get in.'

A tortured creaking came from one of the doors as a crowbar found a gap.

John O'Connor, the second junior sorter, strode over and began heaving the mail sacks in front of the entrance. Joe immediately came to his aid. 'They're barricading the doors!' came a muffled voice from the outside. 'Get the guns.'

John stepped back in shock and looked at Thomas Kett. 'Did he say guns?'

Thomas had heard 'get the cunts' but either way it wasn't good. He looked around for something to defend himself with. Frank had picked up one of the tin mugs and weighed it in his hand. Thomas found himself gripping the carriage broom like a short-staff.

Part of the structure splintered with a loud crack, almost like a gunshot. More glass shattered, the noise inside the carriage deafening. One of the doors popped back with a defeated screech, and hooded figures crowded in through it. A second swung back, and more masked men piled in. There seemed to be dozens, and as they entered they emitted a collective roar, like a pride of lions closing in for the kill.

Thomas dropped the broom he had been holding. Frank stepped in front of him.

'Look here—' he began, but a pickaxe on his arm silenced him. The tin mug fell from numb fingers. Then there was a masked face in his, spittle spraying him. 'Get over there. Now. Fuckin' move it or you're dead.'

He was shoved and found himself at one end of the carriage, heaped on the floor with his colleagues. Another of the masked men came over, his voice low and full of menace. 'We don't want to hurt you. Let us get what we came for and we'll be gone. All we want is the money. Mess us about and it'll be a fuckin' nightmare. Understand?' This was backed up with a wave of an iron bar. 'Do you understand? Right. Stay there and don't move a fucking muscle.'

'This is it!' someone cried.

An axe swung through the air, there was a sharp snap, and the lock on the HV cage careered across the floor. Frank heard the rip of a sack being cut and pulled open, then a collective silence.

'Fucking hell.' It was a sound of relief and amazement.

'The Colonel says form a human chain. Move it!'

Colonel? Was it the Army? thought Frank. Some deserters, a rogue unit perhaps? He raised his head to get a look at them. There was indeed, a man in a military uniform.

'Frank. Don't be bloody stupid,' whispered Thomas. 'They're out of our league.'

'Shut the fuck up or we'll gag you!'

Frank let his head drop and risked putting a hand on Les, who was shaking. Like the man said, all they wanted was the money, he reassured himself.

Bruce Reynolds peered at his watch as the men formed up into a line. There were more than a hundred bags and, as the first came down the slope towards the waiting Land Rovers and the Austin lorry, he could see that they were not lightweight sacks, either. As one dropped from the open door of the carriage into Roy's arms, the little man grunted as he took the strain – and Roy was fit. Within five minutes men were panting and wiping sweaty brows. Several pulled off their balaclavas. Bruce didn't mind. There were few people to see their faces. Gordy, Jimmy and Bobby were the ones still actually inside the HVP. They knew enough to keep their faces covered.

As Bruce checked the human chain doing the unloading, Roger dropped one bag and struggled to retrieve it. Bruce took his place in line. 'Get in the lorry, and stack them,' he said.

'Right-oh, Bruce.'

'Where's Ronnie?'

'In the Land Rover with Stan.'

Bruce, not yet aware of the full story of what had gone on in the cab, said: 'Tell Ronnie to get out and help. Stan's done his bit.'

'Like fuck,' someone said, but Bruce ignored him. Whatever happened, the train was in place, the moneybags being unloaded, and there were no casualties on his side.

He carried on with the rhythm of grabbing the sack from Buster, turning and passing it to Tiny Dave Thompson. One-two-three-four, hup, one-two-three-four. Mindless repetition. It was just like being in the real Army. Except, judging by the number of sacks that kept coming in an apparently endless stream, he was going to walk away from this richer than he ever dreamed possible.

Guard Thomas Millner sat at the rear of the train, bored. He had read his copy of the *Daily Express* from cover to cover and had flicked through *Tit-Bits*. He had enjoyed the article on Diana Dors and UFOs. He had seen a few strange

411

things himself during his years going up and down the line, although nothing as spectacular as Miss Dors's cleavage. Now, though, all reading matter exhausted, he was keen to get home. There had been more stopping and starting than usual on the trip. There must be trouble, too, because the dials told him the vacuum had bled out of the system.

He waited a few more minutes, then climbed down and began to walk towards the front of the carriages. It wasn't until he was halfway along that he realised something was wrong and broke into a trot. There were only ten carriages. Somehow, the engine and the front two had gone on without them. He sprinted back, suddenly aware that he would have to put explosive warning charges on the line, as they were likely to be stuck for some time and he didn't want to be tail-ended.

As he ran, banging on the carriages to alert the sorters, he tried to think how it could have happened. He had never heard of a loco breaking free from its load before, not without the driver sensing something wrong. There was only one other explanation and that was just as ridiculous: someone had stolen the front of his train.

Frank heard a voice barking orders from the doorway.

'Pack it in! Time to go!'

'There's only a few left,' one of the breathless robbers inside the carriage protested.

'Leave them! We're pulling out.'

Frank sneaked a glance at his watch. Forty minutes they had been lying there, at least. It must be almost dawn. Probably why they were pulling out.

A few more minutes passed and two new bodies joined them. Jack Mills and his fireman. Whitby looked scared but unharmed; Jack was clearly in a bad way.

'Bastards.' It was Thomas.

One of the robbers strode over purposefully and Frank braced himself for blows. 'We're going to close the doors. Don't move for at least thirty minutes.'

They heard the man leave with one last shouted instruction. 'Anyone comes out, shoot them! Got that? OK.'

There came the stutter of vehicle engines starting, the high whine of reverse gear and the deeper note of the vehicles pulling out. There was no sense of urgency; they drove slow and steady and he could hear the rise and fall of the engines as the gears changed for quite a while before silence fell.

'You OK, Jack?' asked Thomas.

'Not too bad. Bit of a headache. They gave me a cigarette.'

'Everyone else all right?'

'Shush,' hissed Joe Ware. 'There's a bloke with a gun out there.'

'Bollocks,' said Frank. 'How's he going to get away?'

'Maybe he's got a motorbike,' Leslie Penn suggested.

'Could have,' agreed Thomas.

'But would you want to play British Bulldog out there?'

'Old Tom Millner must have raised the alarm by now,' said David. 'Even he must have noticed half his train's gone.'

'I'm going outside,' said Frank.

'Just wait a few more minutes,' counselled Thomas Kett.

Frank, furious that his carriage had been violated, struggled to his feet. 'They're going to get clean away.'

'Good luck to them,' said Whitby.

'What?' Frank asked.

'I mean . . . you know. I hope we don't see them again.'

Jack groaned.

'I'll get him some water,' said John O'Connor.

Frank crossed to the battered, twisted door and yanked it open. The remnants of the glass fell out of the frame and cascaded around his boots. 'Hello?'

He poked his head out and pulled it back in quickly. No bullets whizzed by. Then he did it again, letting it linger a little longer. The third time, he leaned right out, scanning up and down the track. In the strengthening light, he could see figures approaching from the abandoned part of the train.

'It's OK,' he said. 'They've gone.' He jumped down, then shouted back at the men inside. 'Come and give us a hand.'

'What are you going to do?'

'I bet they've cut the phones. We'll stop a train.'

Thomas Kett appeared in the doorway. 'What then?'

'Hitch a lift to the next station and phone the police.

Sixteen, seventeen minutes they have been gone. They can't have got far.'

Bruce Reynolds had the VHF radio tuned to the police as they rumbled through slumbering villages and hamlets, taking their tortuous route back to the farm. There had been nothing on the airwaves, no mention of the robbery, and as they got closer to their hideout, Bruce's sense of euphoria grew. It wasn't over yet, so he forced himself to keep a cap on it. They had to unload the lorry, get the vehicles undercover, count the money, and divide it into whacks and drinks. Hours of work.

Good work, though. The very best kind of work.

It was the type of job that would be spoken of with admiration for years to come, growing in the telling, knocked around in seedy pubs, clubs and spielers across London. It would be like Olivier in *Henry V*: '*And gentlemen in England now abed, Shall think themselves accursed they were not here, And hold their manhoods cheap whiles any speaks that fought with us upon St Crispin's Day.*' Although no doubt someone would come up with a better name for this day than that. The Big Train Job or some such. But one thing was certain about those stories: he wouldn't be around to hear any of them. He would be long gone.

Bruce turned to the rear of the Land Rover, to where a group of tired but happy men had shed their masks and unzipped their coveralls. He grinned at them and began to whistle one of his favourite songs. Tony Bennett. Second only to Sinatra in his estimation.

It was a moment before they recognised it, and collapsed into laughter: 'The Good Life'.

Commander George Hatherill's first job of that day was to stay calm and try to make sense of the rumours and counter-rumours flying around Scotland Yard. He stayed in his office with the radio on and asked for the wilder speculations – the train was full of diamonds! – to be filtered out before they reached his desk. He had got into the Yard at seven-thirty. Three hours later he was given a copy of an exceptionally early edition of the *Evening Standard* that would go out that morning. The robbery had come too late for Fleet Street dailies; the *Standard* and the *News* had sensed a way to make a killing by jumping into the breech. *ROBBERY SPECIAL!* it screamed.

£1,000,000! the headline thundered. *BIGGEST EVER MAIL ROBBERY*.

'Get Tommy Butler in here,' he instructed his secretary over the intercom.

'Sir.'

'And get me the Chief Constable of Buckinghamshire on the line.'

'Of course.'

He went back to the newspaper. The reporters had done a fine job, he thought begrudgingly. Midland, Lloyds and

National & Provincial had all admitted to having money – 'many thousands' – on the train. The hacks had also contacted the Postmaster General, Reginald Bevins, who was on holiday in Liverpool – who on earth went on holiday to Liverpool? Hatherill wondered – and badgered the man into declaring a ten-thousand-pound reward. Well, it was a decent sum, enough to bring some rats out of the gutters.

There was a side-panel interview with David Whitby, twenty-six, the fireman, with another headline: *'IF YOU SHOUT I WILL KILL YOU,' I WAS TOLD.*

Hmmm. Perhaps he was. But someone ought to stop witnesses talking to the press before they had been properly interviewed. Otherwise the public might start believing whatever the scribblers made up in preference to the truth.

The phone rang and he was told it was Brigadier Cheney, Chief Constable of Buckinghamshire, on the line.

'Hello, John. How are you coping?'

'Us country bumpkins, you mean?'

Ouch. Sensitive. 'No, John. Just wondered if you needed any help. Takes a lot of manpower, this sort of thing.'

Cheney sighed. 'I don't think we need many more at the scene just now. There's our lads, the British Transport Police and GPO Investigation Branch. Quite a bunfight.'

Hatherill hesitated. 'You know they'll be London chaps, don't you, John?'

'That's yet to be established, George.'

Oh come on, he wanted to say. How many hardcore

417

robbers come out of Leighton Buzzard? 'Well organised, though. Suggests London.'

'I've already had Glasgow on the line, claiming it must be someone from their patch.'

'Could be, John, could be. But my waters tell me London.'

'I'm not moving things down to you.' The man sounded uncommonly tetchy. The political manoeuvrings had started already.

'Of course not. I'm not trying to take over, John.'

'I've also had the government on.'

'The government? The funny hats?'

'No, not those buggers. The PM's office.'

'The PM? Why?'

'Oh, not him personally. Some lackey. Just very keen to stress that Mac is concerned that this reflects badly on the whole Establishment. That not even our money is safe now.'

Macmillan's government had been reeling under a variety of scandals, from Profumo to continued fallout from Burgess, Maclean and Philby. There was also, Hatherill knew, anxiety about Mac's wife's own affair with Bob Boothby coming to light, perhaps through some juvenile, muck-raking magazine like *Private Eye* or even the scurrilous TV series *That Was The Week That Was*, which lampooned Mac mercilessly. And now, after all the attacks on the political establishment, the fiscal system had been whacked with a crowbar by opportunist footpads.

'What did our young man from the PM's office suggest?'

'The slimy little sod suggested that perhaps this was too big for a provincial police force. Matter of national importance, he said.'

That explained the prickliness. Cheney had been ordered to bring in the Yard and had resented the phone call from Hatherill, thinking it was a two-pronged attack. 'They haven't been on to me, you know,' Hatherill said. 'Mine was a genuine call. There's no civil servant poking me up the arse with a sharpened brolly.'

Finally, the Brigadier laughed and Hatherill could feel the irritation leaving him. 'Pleased to hear it.'

'Who have you got on this, John?'

'Detective Superintendent Fewtrell is in charge. Good, solid copper, you'll like him. But he's on his way to London. There will be an all-party conference at the GPO this afternoon. I'm sure you would like to attend.'

'Absolutely. But, John, this happened in your backyard, not mine. We'll bring it all to you.'

'I appreciate that, George.'

There was a knock at the door and Tommy Butler put his head around it. Hatherill beckoned him in. 'Anything you need for the minute?'

'Talcs.' He meant fingerprint officers with their dusting powders.

'I'll get some over,' Hatherill said.

'Thanks. The briefing is at two p.m. – I'll send details across.'

'Thanks, John.'

Hatherill cradled the receiver and looked up. Butler was standing, as impassive as ever, hands crossed in front of him. The Commander explained the gist of his conversation.

'He'll need more than some dusters,' Butler grunted.

'I know, Tommy, but let's give our country cousins their day in the sun. Although if this job wasn't put together from down here I'll eat my gold watch.'

'What about Glasgow?'

'Doubt it,' Hatherill said. 'If that was a Glasgow firm they'd still be mopping the blood off the rails.'

Butler thought this over and nodded. The Scottish lads prided themselves on sudden, explosive violence, often of the most vicious kind. Razors and chains and coshes filled with wet sand for starters. And lately, guns. 'They won't be able to keep a million quid quiet, will they?'

'Unlikely. Look, no matter what happens at the conference, I want you to set up a team for this. Can you do that today?'

'Me?' Toes would be trodden on: Millen, Williams. 'Not Ernie or Frank?'

'I think this is your kind of dance, Tommy.'

Butler allowed himself a small, satisfied grin.

'Let me deal with how the hierarchy will work out. Tap every snout and snitch. Now it's all over the papers, you bet there'll be people saying, "Well, I could have been in on that, they asked me but . . .", and who knows, one or two of them might even be telling the truth. I'm also going to prepare a press release saying that there is a newly formed London Train Robbery Squad and that Tommy Butler is to head it.'

'Why release that?' Hatherill didn't normally shout about internal reorganisations or promote individual personalities. Apart from his own.

'Let's not beat about the bush, Tommy. When they hear Fewtrell is heading the team against them, they'll shrug. When they hear it's you who's after them, they'll shit themselves.'

Bruce had gone to bed before the count was finished. The room was crowded and airless and, coupled with the release of the tension that had gripped him for so long, his body felt like rubber. He had stayed long enough to see about half the 120 bags ripped open, to know that most of it was good gear, with non-sequential numbers, and that only a small proportion were clearly damaged notes destined for destruction. And there were relatively few Scottish ones.

He wriggled into the sleeping bag and lay down, his head swimming with fatigue for a moment, but he plunged over the edge into a dark chasm almost immediately.

Ronnie woke him in the early afternoon with a cup of tea. He looked done in, too, his hair plastered to his forehead by sweat. Ronnie had worked like a demon, mainly because he felt bad about Stan. He wanted to make sure he had properly earned his whack by the day's end.

421

Bruce took the tea in his hands, still encased in leather gloves. 'Thanks, mate. All done?'

'Yeah, just about. Lot of ten-bob notes nobody seems to want.'

Bruce shuffled upright, the lower half of his body still in the bag. 'Too grand for ten-bob notes, are they now? Fuckin' idiots. It's all money. I'll have them.'

He heard a burst of laughter and whooping from downstairs, and asked, 'What's that?'

'Buster's organised a Monopoly tournament.' Ronnie smirked. 'They're playing with real money.'

'Cunts,' Bruce laughed. 'They still got gloves on?'

'Few of them took them off to count. It's not easy, you know. Don't worry, they put Elastoplasts over their fingertips.'

'I hope so. So what's left to do?'

'We have to divide it into the whacks. Decide what to ditch. You know, which notes are too damaged or too Scottish. Thought you ought to be there for that.'

Bruce took a sip of his sweet tea, feeling his teeth tingle. Too much sugar.

'Bruce?'

'What?'

'Sorry about Stan. He was down to me, and—'

Bruce waved a gloved hand at him, dismissing the words. 'I wasn't there. I don't know what went on in the cab. The train arrived at the bridge. We got the money. That's all that matters. What are they saying on the radio?'

'"Vicious cosh gang robs train of one million and gets clean away".'

Bruce balked at the description. That was wrong. They weren't thugs, they were thieves. Having to hit the driver was a pity, but perhaps he had been playing the hero. Bruce would wager he would be now, milking it for all he was worth. It wasn't as if it was his bloody money. It was theirs. 'How much is the count?'

'I thought you'd never ask. Give or take . . .'

Bruce could tell from the tone it was going to be a surprise. 'Go on, spit it out.'

'Two point six million.'

The size of the figure hit him like the diesel loco they had just hijacked, driving the wind from his body. A pain started in his chest, as if the ton and a half of money was pressing down on it. Two point six mil? Bruce struggled to his feet and put his glasses on. 'Well, that'll do us, I suppose.'

A thought rattled through his brain and was gone, like a passing express. He registered it and tucked it away, but not before he allowed himself a little shiver. Two point six million. *It's too much money.*

Forty-seven

Headley, Surrey, May 1992

The sweet, pungent aroma of dope filled Roy's kitchen. I wondered if the fumes were affecting my higher centres, if my hearing was hallucinating. I realised my jaw was almost touching the floor.

'*What?*' I asked. 'Bruce, you can't be serious. I know I let you down . . .'

He took another hefty toke and passed the joint back to Roy. 'I know you did, too, Tony.'

'But I didn't grass you up, mate.'

'So you say.'

I found I didn't feel frightened, despite the ominous turn events had taken. If it had been Charlie, Gordy or Buster with the gun, then I might have thought there was a chance of being shot. But I was fairly certain Roy wasn't going to blast me. And it certainly wasn't Bruce's style. If he had asked Charlie to top me – and I only had Roy's word for that – it might have been a figure of speech.

'I wish I'd been on the track that night.'

'Do you?' asked Roy.

'I don't think there're many people would swap places with any of us,' said Bruce. 'Oh, to begin with maybe. That morning, when we got back to Leatherslade, fuck, I'll never forget that feeling when we realised how much we had.'

'The news came over the radio,' said Roy. 'At . . . what time was it the police first mentioned it?'

'About four-thirty, quarter to five.'

'"They've stolen a train", they said. "Got a million quid".'

Bruce laughed. 'It was Ronnie's birthday. He started singing "Happy Birthday to me . . ."' His face dropped. 'That was the high point, I'd say. Then look what happened to us. Roy? Promising career pissed away.'

Roy flinched, but there was no arguing with the assessment. When Roy had come out he had tried to pick up where he had left off out on the track. But a dozen or more years had gone and so had his reactions, although his nerve was still intact. But three drives, three crashes, the third breaking his leg, demonstrated what prison had robbed him of.

'And Ronnie? Fuckin' clown in Rio. The town joke. And bloody homesick, so I hear. Charlie? Shot by some pikey on a fuckin' bicycle. What's the world coming to, eh? Shot in front of his wife, too. I mean, we kept the wives out of it. There's no respect any longer.'

I felt a flash of irritation. I knew it was the drugs making him loquacious, but still. Old gangsters telling you that the world has gone to shit, about when you could leave your back door open, coppers gave you a clip round the ear and the Krays were nice to kids and old ladies. I was surprised at Bruce – such rose-tinted sentimentality wasn't his style. It must be the dope, I reckoned.

'Leave it out, Bruce, he was messin' with the bloody Colombians. They don't know the old rules, do they? They kill you, your wife, your kids. Charlie was out of his depth.'

Bruce raised his eyebrows, but I could tell he agreed. Nasty in South London was not the same as nasty in Medellin.

'Buster selling flowers.'

I laughed. 'At least he got a movie made about him.'

Bruce sighed. 'Didn't even recognise myself in that.'

I knew he had been a paid adviser on the movie, *Buster*, but said nothing. I thought Larry Lamb had done a half-decent job of capturing him, given the quality of the script. But it made Buster out to be like Charlie Drake the comedian, whereas I remembered him as a scary little fucker.

There was always some confusion over who coshed that driver. They claimed there was too much going on to be certain. My money, though, would be on the flower-seller and his spring-loaded cosh. Not that the movie had had the guts to show that.

And even if he didn't land the blow, I heard it said that Buster had a 'Let Him Have It' moment in the cab, yelling for someone to clout the poor bloke. It was just one of those things where the truth had become very blurred over the past thirty years. Just like the role of a snitch.

'You know, Bruce, maybe *nobody* grassed you up.'

'Bollocks.' It was Roy. 'Why would you say that? They was on us like a ton of bricks from day one.'

'Because of the driver,' I said. 'Because someone hit the driver.'

Bruce laughed. 'You're kidding. If we'd coshed that driver and got a hundred grand, you think there would have been that hunt? Don't get me wrong, it was fuckin' stupid. But when they found out how much money there was – two and a half bloody million – then it was all hands to the pumps. And they leaned on every source they could.'

He sucked the last of the life from the roach and put it out in a saucer, adding, 'Well, I suppose it doesn't matter now.'

I realised he still had his suspicions about me. 'Fuck this.' I stood up, walked over and made to snatch the gun from Roy's hand, but he was too quick for me. He placed it on the table out of my reach, with his hand spreadeagled over it.

There was a pause while they wondered what I might

ROBERT RYAN

do, and I let them ponder for a couple of heartbeats. Then I slammed my fist on the table and headed for the door.

'Oi,' said Roy, getting to his feet and raising the pistol. 'Where d'you think *you're* goin'?'

'Leave it out.' Bruce pulled him back down into a chair. 'Build us another one, Roy,' he said, passing the tin over to him.

Roy did as he was told. I backed towards the hallway.

'Where *are* you going, Tony?' asked Bruce.

'You want to know who snitched on you? I'll get you the man who knows.'

'Who's that?'

'Billy Naughton.'

Forty-eight

GPO Headquarters, London, 9 August 1963

DS Malcolm Fewtrell's train robbery conference took place in a stuffy, first-floor room that was too small to contain all the interested parties. Only the press was excluded; that still left the CID, the Robbery Squad, the Flying Squad, the London & Provincial Crime Squad, the Intelligence Squad, the Bucks CID, the GPO, British Rail and six banks, as well as the government in the shape of two junior ministers.

George Hatherill had positioned himself in the second row of metal-and-canvas chairs. Tommy Butler was at the back of the room, with Jack Slipper. He had to admire the elegant Fewtrell's composure. He was dressed in a three-piece suit with a crisp white shirt and a red-and-blue striped tie, and displayed no signs of nerves as he stepped up to the dais.

'Good afternoon, ladies and gentlemen.'

Hatherill looked around. He could see plenty of gentlemen, but he couldn't spot a single lady. But then, Fewtrell had a better view of the room.

'Before we start, I would just like to remind you that this is a briefing for concerned parties. I shall explain what we know so far at this very early stage, and then invite questions. But what is discussed in this room should go no further. The press are not necessarily our allies on this one.' Fewtrell took a sip of water. 'Do you think we could open a window? Thank you.'

He held up a newspaper. 'My local, page one. For those at the back, the headline is: "The Great Train Robbery".' There were some sniggers. 'Just in case you are not familiar with silent flicks, that was the title of a very old film. A Western. One of the first, I believe, if not *the* first. So, straight away this sounds like something romantic, daring, dashing. It isn't. I am certain we all recognise this for what it is. A sordid crime, committed purely for gain. We are fortunate that only one man was injured, the driver. I am sure the gang would not have hesitated to use force on anyone else who put up too much of a fight. The driver, Jack Mills, has been seen by a doctor and is doing reasonably well. As to the estimate of the amount taken, it has now passed two million.' There were some low whistles. 'And the bad news is, we have recorded serial numbers for a tiny proportion of that.'

A significant amount of the notes had been designated as too worn to remain in circulation and been scheduled for destruction. Nobody recorded the numbers of those sacks. And the scruffy oncers and fivers would be a lot easier for the thieves to spend without attracting suspicion than crisp new notes.

'What proportion, Chief Superintendent?' someone asked.

Fewtrell looked irritated. 'Could we save the questions until the end, please? Otherwise we'll never get through. We do have a press conference to give later. But to answer that one question – less than two thousand pounds.'

There were audible gasps and Fewtrell nodded to signal his agreement. It seemed inconceivable that the gang could have got away with so much untraceable cash.

Fewtrell then went through the mechanics of how the train was stopped and the timetable of activities. He read partial statements from each of the witnesses. Then he said something that was music to Hatherill's ears.

'We will, of course, need the assistance of Scotland Yard in this matter. I find it hard to imagine that these are first-time criminals. It is likely we have come across them before, which is why the coaches and signals are still being worked on by the fingerprint boys. I don't need to tell my colleagues in the police force of the criminals' common modus operandi in these cases. The haul would have weighed between one-and-a-half and two tons. Tyre-tracks at the scene suggest at least one lorry. Such vehicles are normally dumped within a few miles and transferred to smaller, faster cars. But one of the robbers said something curious. "Don't leave for thirty minutes." Now, I think that is a psychological slip-up. Don't worry, I am not going all Herbert Lom on you. But let us say it would take them half an hour to get to their hideout and under cover. Might that not dictate what he says to the poor GPO men. "Lie down, don't move for thirty minutes, by which time we will be underground." Which means that we are looking for a changeover site at a distance of not more than thirty miles. We also have unconfirmed reports of a hitchhiker passed by an Army convoy in the early hours. Exact location not known, but to the west of where the robbery took place. At the moment, we are checking with the Army as to whether any official convoys were on the road at that time. As you can appreciate, it is a large undertaking. However, at least some of the robbers wore Army uniforms, so it is looking as if the two may be connected.' He took a deep breath. 'Now, any questions?'

Hatherill's hand shot up. Fewtrell pointed to him and he gave his rank and name to the audience. 'Were there any clues to identities? Names used in the heat of the moment?'

'No. As I said, they were careful not to mention any names, but one of the thieves called another "Colonel", although Frank Dewhurst is fairly sure the man was a Major.

A rag-bag of ranks. Mind you, we can be sure that these layabouts wouldn't know much about Army ranks anyway – probably spent their whole National Service in the glasshouse. Colonel could be a nickname.'

Hatherill thanked Fewtrell and the questions continued. Hatherill meanwhile wrote a single line on his pad.

Any criminals nicknamed the Colonel??

Forty-nine

Leatherslade Farm, 10 August 1963

It seemed as if there was no other subject on the radio. Every news bulletin was about the 'Crime of the Century' or 'The Great Train Robbery' and each time, the amount stolen crept upwards. It was as if the GPO thought the public couldn't take the shock of the revelation of the final sum all in one go and had to be fed it incrementally.

The VHF, too, hummed with information about what the police were up to: fingerprints, helicopters, motorbike patrols. It was odd, thought Bruce. He had imagined them lying low, relaxing, till the scream blew over. But this wasn't a scream, it was the howl of a wounded animal, thrashing around, looking for revenge.

The atmosphere in the farm was tense. The money had been stacked, pending the final division of the spoils. Although the conversations still revolved around what they would do with such a windfall, the topic was kicked around in a desultory fashion. Each man knew they had to get the money somewhere safe and then hang onto it before they could do anything as mundane as spend it.

That evening, Brian turned up to collect his own whack, the Jock's and various other 'drinks' he had laid out. The new arrival stood in the kitchen with Charlie, Bruce, Ronnie and Roy.

'I got a call from Tony Fortune,' said Brian.

'Yeah?' said Bruce. 'Where was he?'

'In a call box. He says well done. Turns out his brother-in-law pulled some stunt. They came to question Tony about the motors and his wife started to drop the kid. He couldn't get back up here.'

'I suppose he still wants a whack?' asked Charlie, who had taken a keen interest in the division of the money.

'Bollocks to that,' said Ronnie.

'He deserves something,' Roy retorted. 'As much as your bloody driver. And you'd have been more pissed off if he had come back with the Old Bill on his tail.'

Brian nodded his agreement. 'I told him he could earn the rest by acting as dustman.'

Bruce watched Charlie make a salt-beef sandwich, adding

more salt from the cylinder of Saxo. The gloves were still being worn, but after all the manhandling of sacks and money, they were falling apart.

'Fair enough. Long as the coppers have lost interest in him.'

Brian Field waved his arms to indicate the farm around them. 'The police have lost interest in everything else but this. They want to know where you are holed up. We're top of the bill at the London Palladium. The star turn. *Numero uno* attraction now.'

Bruce's stomach contracted at that. He didn't want to be a star. Not in that sense. Not Public Enemy Number One. It was hard to face up to, but as he had feared when he heard the total, it was possible there was just too much money. The authorities couldn't turn a blind eye to £2.6 million. It was like having a target painted on your back.

Buster entered the kitchen, frowning.

'What is it?'

'On the VHF. The order has just gone out to search all isolated buildings for Army-type vehicles.'

'Where?' asked Brian Field.

'Within a thirty-mile radius of the robbery. They have also appealed to the public to check any suspicious properties. There are roadblocks to stop and search any large vehicles.'

'Shit,' said Charlie through a mouthful of sandwich. 'There goes using the horsebox. Not unless we can get a horse to put in it.'

'No bloody room for the cash then,' said Buster. 'Use your loaf, Charlie. Have to take it out in dribs and drabs.'

'Riskier, in some ways,' said Bruce.

He scanned Brian's face for signs of alarm. The rest of the people at the farm – Stan and perhaps Ralph excepted – were pro villains. No matter what the police had on them, they'd stay calm and dumb. Bruce would make sure Ralph played it right, but Brian Field was a mere solicitor. However, there was no sign of panic in his eyes, which was good.

Ralph spoke up. 'How far are we from the train?'

'We're about twenty-seven miles away,' said Bruce. 'Give or take.'

They all understood at once. The idea of lying low for a week was shot. They would have to start pulling out. Charlie was thinking the same as Bruce. 'We'll have to have it on our toes. And any of us with form, we'd better have a fuckin' good story to tell.'

'And if we aren't at home when they come looking . . .' said Roy, letting it tail off. Like the others, he was well aware that the London Airport robbery was similar enough in planning and execution for the Yard to make connections.

'Brian, remind me, what do you need?'

'A whack for the man in Glasgow. The cash for the HVP coach boys. The finder's fee for Mark who introduced me to Jock. We can put the last two together. Mark says he will see the railwayman all right. And my share, of course.'

A lot of money, thought Bruce, then stopped himself. There was enough to go round. Even for this Mark, who had done fuck-all apart from make the intros.

'And some drinks for the boys in the estate agent's office maybe,' Brian continued. 'Few grand. Just in case they tumble this place. We want to make sure our stories tally and that nobody can remember what you look like, Bruce.'

It occurred to Bruce that perhaps Brian was padding his total. It didn't matter: he had brought in Mark and the Jock in the first place.

'Charlie will help you count it out. Won't you, Charlie?'

'With pleasure.'

'You've got cases with you?' Bruce asked. 'We're running short.'

'In the car,' said Brian.

'Start counting it out then. Charlie will show you which piles you can use. We'll leave in the morning. Staggered. We do this co-ordinated, we stick together, and we stay in contact. It's all for one and that crap. We are a unit, a good one, let's stay that way.'

'What about the farm?' asked Charlie.

'We clean it till it sparkles. Then we clean it again. Then we get Tony to come up and do it again. And anything we can't clean, we burn.'

Charlie Wilson was just parking up his Rover outside the Ten Bells, opposite Spitalfields Market, early on Friday morning, when he heard. He had dropped off Gordy at the Tube, so he could go back to Putney, then Charlie had driven to East London to kick-start his alibi: that he had been 'on The Fruit' every morning that week from 5.30 a.m. There were a dozen porters and a couple of traders who would swear to it, no problem.

It had been dark when he had left the farm, now his eyes felt tired and gritty in the grey light of an East London dawn. The others would be scattering, too. Bruce had announced he was going off to buy a couple of Austin Healeys, Roger that he would buy a car in Oxford, and most of the others would be ferried by Brian to hole up at his place for a night or two.

Roy, sensibly in Charlie's mind, had opted to travel back to London by train rather than join Brian's party. Tiny Dave Thompson, too. It was a mistake to have too many people in one place. Too much cash to be able to explain away.

In the boot of Charlie's Rover was his share of the haul, £150,000, plus Roy and Tiny Dave's whacks and a big drink for Frenchie who had stumped up some of the investment cash when the funds ran low. It was a lot to get rid of. He felt as if he could sense the heat from the bundles of notes bleeding from the boot. What was that song? 'Too Hot to Handle'. Bloody right.

He was about to turn off the ignition when the news came on the radio. The robbery was, of course, the first item. A special unit had been put together at Scotland Yard to run down the Great Train Robbers. It was to be headed by – he knew what was coming even before the announcer said the name – Tommy Butler.

Tommy Butler. A right attention-seeking humourless weirdo, who lived with his dear old mum and, therefore, only had the job to occupy his time. The Grey Fox. The Sad Bastard, more like. If he was bent, he was Bent for the Job, but although Charlie had heard rumours about bungs and backhanders, they needed to be taken with a large pinch of Saxo. Still, a special unit at the Yard – that sounded serious.

The bulletin continued with news about the train driver. He was out of danger and out of hospital, but still very poorly. The driver, the driver, the driver. They pushed it forward every time, just in case people should get the wrong idea about the job. Just in case someone felt like saying, 'Good on ya, son.' There it was, the shadow of – what was the old cunt's name? – Jack Mills. He would be on TV soon: bandaged head, black eye, hangdog look, blinking into press flashbulbs. Fifty-eight years old. Coshed mercilessly. What sort of men are these? Hunt them down, now.

The firm was caught between Butler and Mills and a ten-grand reward. They were fucked. No matter what Bruce had said, this was no time for musketeering. It was every man for himself.

Fifty

There was only one show in town now for any self-respecting copper. If you weren't in it, you weren't just second division, you weren't even in the league. You were a kick-around Sunday side. The Train Squad, on the other hand, was Liverpool, Man U and Spurs combined.

An uncharacteristic gloom had settled over the Flying Squad room. They weren't used to thinking of themselves as second-best. Yet every other case paled beside THE GREAT TRAIN ROBBERY as everyone called it. Always said in CAPITALS. Len Haslam took his exclusion from the inner core particularly poorly, although Billy Naughton had half-expected Hatherill to bring him along and couldn't help feeling a little snubbed too.

441

But the top guys wanted this for themselves. Glory and headlines beckoned for whoever nailed these blokes, and the big boys wanted their share of it, that much was certain. As someone said, such Big Guns hadn't been wheeled out together since the Somme. Sequestered in their room, festooned with the brown cables of extra phones hanging from the ceiling, were George Hatherill, Ernie Millen, Tommy Butler, Frank Williams, Peter Vibart, Gerald McArthur, Jack Slipper and Jim Nevill. They were sifting through what little evidence they had so far.

The rest of the Squad was on donkey work, tapping snouts and sifting records of those most likely to have a finger in the GTR pie. Billy and Len had done both those things and presented their findings. Len had put Gordon Goody at the top of his list of those worth a tug, because of the London Central Airport job, but no snitches had mentioned his name, nor any of the known blaggers they had pulled in for it. But the airport job was not the only possibility: those behind the Finsbury Park wages snatch, the Hatton Garden ram-raid or the Bishopsgate vault would have the right kind of pedigree, too. Old case files were dusted off and reexamined to see what names had cropped up in the frame back then.

But unless they could bring something concrete to the table, both Len and Billy knew they were out in the cold, shut out of the biggest investigation for years. *What did you do during The Great Train Robbery, Daddy?* their children would ask. *'Fuck-all,'* would be the sullen reply.

Still, they had been told that the information fund was temporarily bottomless and that they should start casting cash around, like chum bait on the surface of the sea. Sooner or later, they would get a nibble.

'DC Naughton, line five!' the operator shouted.

Billy closed the file on his desk and dragged himself over to take the call. He was barely gone two minutes and when he returned Len noticed there was a fresh spring in his step and a glint in his bloodshot eyes.

'Who was that?'

'Come on.' Billy scribbled a request chit for a driver and car and passed it to the Duty Sergeant.

'What? Who was it?'

'Just some old dear reporting suspicious activity behind a Post Office. We've got to check it out, though.'

Len just about caught the fast wink that punctuated the sentence.

'You coming?'

Duke stood and stretched as if being dragged away from a session with Sophia Loren. 'Oh, OK.'

As they hit the corridor, heading for the garage, Len stopped Billy. 'Well? I know that was for the benefit of the big ears in there. Some old dear? Some old L.O.B., more like. What's really going on, Billy?'

He was right; it had been a Load of Bollocks. 'It was Marie – Tony Fortune's wife.'

'She out already?'

443

'No, she's still in hospital. Wants to see us. You got some money for flowers?'

'A few bob. What does she want to see us about? She's not putting the kid down for Hendon already? What's so urgent?'

Billy let rip with a 200-watt grin. 'She wants to give us the Train Robbers.'

Tony Fortune met Brian Field in a transport café off the A1. Brian looked bloody awful and his hands shook. At first Tony thought the stress had got to him, that he had cracked under the strain.

'You OK?' he asked as Brian's spoon rattled in the mug.

The other man gave a wry smile. 'Nothing a bacon sandwich won't cure. Me, Tommy Wisbey and Bobby Welch tied one on last night.'

He didn't mention that they had tied one on the night before, too. He did explain how the gang had split up: Bruce and Ronnie Biggs had left in one of the Austin Healeys, Jimmy White and Ralph in the other. Charlie and Gordy had gone together, while Roger had a Wolseley he had paid £375 cash for in Oxford and had left in that. Roy and Tiny Dave had been dropped off at Thame. Brian had done the same for Stan the driver an hour later.

Then the remaining crew had been ferried to the Fields' place and there had been a two-day celebration. It was quite raucous; at one point one of the neighbours had complained. But the robbers had gone now.

'What did Bruce say?'

'I've forty-eight grand in the van outside. He says you are owed that much.'

Tony's throat went dry. 'Cheers.'

'There's the same again if you take care of the farm.'

That sounded unpromising work. 'It must be crawling with police up there.'

'They haven't got that far out yet. You'd be OK if you take the A40 and approach it from the west. I'd come with you, but there's a lot to do my end. A fuck of a lot.'

Tony thought for a moment. It might just assuage the guilt and frustration he felt at missing out on the job. And the cash would certainly help placate Marie. She had left a deposit on a Silver Cross, just like the Queen used. He could be in and out before anyone saw him. 'What do you want me to do at the farm?'

Brian signalled for his bacon sandwich. 'At this stage of the game? Don't fuck about, Tony. Torch the lot.'

'Hello, is that Aylesbury police? Yes. My name is John Marris. Like the potato, yes, but with two "r"s. I'm a farm labourer, a herdsman. I live on Oakley Road, and I thought you might be interested in what I have just seen. I was woken last night, in the early hours, by lots of comings and goings. Cars and the like. I knew they must be coming from this farm, you see. So today I just had a peek, a bit of a nosey, wondering what the new owners were up to. It looked deserted, but all the curtains were drawn,

445

like. In the middle of the morning. Thought that was odd. Except that each one had a corner turned up. As if someone wanted to spy on anyone coming up the lane. I nearly left then, because it was a little creepy, but I went to one of the outbuildings. There was a lorry in there. A yellow one. Yes, yellow. Just been painted, though. Still wet. Then next door there was a locked garage. And round the back, a pit where things had been burned. Clothes, mostly, I think. Well, I haven't got a phone so I am calling from my employer's house. The number? OAK five seven four nine. I heard on the radio there was a reward? All right, I'll wait until someone gets back in touch. Oh, you'll want the name of the place. It's called Leatherslade Farm. Righty-o, thank you.'

Even the Veuve Cliquot tasted sour to Bruce. He and Fran were holed up in a flat in Queensway. Mary Manson was looking after their son, Nick, just in case they had to move quickly. The place was in someone else's name, so he was quite happy to have champagne and smoked salmon sent over from Fortnum's. And they weren't the kind of company surprised by payment in cash.

So they drank champagne and decent claret and ate well, but Bruce found he could hardly move from the chair in front of the TV, the news bulletins came so thick and fast. On each one he expected to see a shot of the farm, those outhouses, the kitchen with its supplies, and grinning among them Fewtrell and Butler, the two coppers vying for the limelight. They were like Arthur Lucan and Kitty McShane, or Jewell and Warris, those two – a double act you suspected hated each other away from the public gaze.

Bruce went over and over what could tie him into the robbery. The farm; the purchase had been handled by Brian Field's firm, mainly his associate Leonard Field and his boss John Wheater. They had met Bruce and Gordy. Weak link. So had the previous owners of Leatherslade. Stupid. He had also stashed his whack in a garage rented in his own name. Careless. It was time to put those things right.

Late afternoon, fifteen minutes before the 5.55 news, he grabbed his coat.

'Where you going?' Fran asked.

'Make a call.'

She didn't ask any more, simply refilled her glass and carried on watching *Billy Bunter of Greyfriars School.* Bruce was worried, but then that was his job. They would be all right.

He went to the call box and dialled Brian's number. He let it ring, put the receiver down and called again. He did this four times in total. No pick-up.

Bruce put the phone down for the last time, his anxiety heightened by the worms in his stomach.

A new plan was needed. Step one, move the money somewhere safe, perhaps away from London. Step two, start planning for a proper safe house. Oh, and step three, make sure the farm was sterilised.

*   *   *

Janie Riley had waited patiently for the phone call from Bruce. Just to let her know he was all right. That they could meet sometime. To thank her for her help. To give her a night out. Just like the old days. Smoking, drinking, jazz and sex. Four things she rarely got at home.

Nothing.

But the papers were full of his exploits, even if his name hadn't been put to them. Clearly, he had taken the cash and gone without so much as a by-your-leave. Off with Franny or Mary or even some other woman. Not a thought for Janie. Sent her to buy the grub, that's all she was good for. She should have been there to see it, to revel in the whole caper. She deserved that.

'Bastard,' she said to herself as she left the house and walked down the pathway towards the elaborate gates depicting rampant peacocks. Hideous. But her husband liked them. And it was his money. Besides, they didn't look out of place in this part of Surrey.

She turned left and walked into the village, past the green where the cricket club was setting up. A few looked over at her, in her bright floral summer dress and oversized sunglasses, and she let her hips sway a little more than usual. They'll be polishing their balls on their whites a little more vigorously than usual now, she thought.

She slipped into the red phone box outside the Post Office. Best not use the line at home, just in case. Afterwards she would go into the Cricketers and have a quick gin and tonic, even if it was only lunchtime.

She dialled the number written on a scrap of paper. She wouldn't tell them everything. She would just give them one or two. Bruce. Oh, and that smug git Tony Fortune. He had pissed her off that day when they were shopping. She could tell what he thought of her. He deserved to go down, too.

'Hello,' she said in her roughest voice. 'Is that Scotland Yard?'

The police Rover pulled Tony before he had even left London en route to the farm. He watched the light in the rearview mirror of his two-tone powder-blue Ford Capri coupé that he had taken from his showroom. The Capri was nifty, but there was no way he could outrun the Rover.

He slowed, changed down using the column gearshift, and pulled over, then studied the rearview mirror, watching the two uniforms approach.

A knuckle on the window. 'Step out of the car, sir.'

He wound the window down. 'Why, Officer? Was I committing an offence?'

The man crouched down. He had a bruiser's face, square and solid-looking with a five-o'clock shadow you could tell no razor could banish completely. 'Mr Anthony Fortune?'

Fuck, fuck, fuck. 'Yes.'

'Can you step out of the vehicle?'

Tony opened the door and did as he was told.

'Thank you, sir. Could you tell me what is in the boot, sir?'

'Jack. Spare wheel.'

'Mind if we take a look?' The policeman smiled. They were going to take a look come what may.

Tony reached in, pulled the keys from the ignition and handed them to him. 'Be my guest.'

The copper tossed them to his colleague.

'How did you know it was me?' asked Tony.

'Oh, an all-car message, sir. Quite distinctive, this vehicle. Bit of a lady's colour though, blue and white.'

'Bloody hell!' the other policeman yelled.

Tony sighed.

'Derek. Look at this.'

He followed Derek around to the rear and the three of them stared into the gaping boot and its eight cans of petrol and rags. Thank God he'd parked the cash Field had given him with old Paddy his mechanic before picking up the Capri.

'What's this?' Derek asked, as he picked up a can and shook it.

'Petrol.'

He unscrewed the cap and sniffed. 'I can see that. You going somewhere?'

Tony sighed again. 'On a very long trip, I should imagine.'

*　　*　　*

450

'Hello, is that Brill police station? Who am I speaking to? Sergeant Blackman. Look, Sergeant, it's John Marris here. I called Aylesbury the other day and they never got back to me. I know they are busy, that's what I am talking about. The robbery. There is a farm here with a suspicious vehicle in it. And nobody has been around for days. I checked. Leatherslade. You know it? Yes, sold a few months ago. Never seen the owners. You'll send a man down, will you? Good. Because something funny has gone on there. Will you come yourself? Right. Constable Woolley. Tell him I'll meet him at the end of the lane in an hour. How's that?'

Fifty-one

New Scotland Yard, 11 August 1963

George Hatherill lit a cigarette and offered them around to Len Haslam and Billy Naughton. They were looking very pleased with themselves as they took one each. He wasn't so sure they had any right to be smug, not yet.

'So what have you got on this Tony Fortune?'

'Nothing yet,' said Duke. 'We're still questioning him.'

'But you are sure he is in the frame?'

'Tangentially.'

'Tangentially? Big word for you, Len. Did Billy here teach you that?' Hatherill wagged his cigarette at Duke. 'Expand on that.'

'We have two reasons to believe he was involved. One

we'll explain in a moment, another from an anonymous tip-off. A woman.'

Hatherill snorted. Anonymous tip-offs didn't count for much, as far as he was concerned. They were often more about settling scores than the truth. There had been lots of them so far, many no doubt naming the actual villains, but with no proof offered.

'ABC, lads. ABC.' It stood for Assume nothing, Believe nobody, Check everything. 'She give you anyone else?'

'Bruce Reynolds. But we already have him down as a person of interest.'

'And you can't pull him just on some mad bint's word. Got to be better than that. And if Fortune does put his hands up for it, before you charge him in connection with the train you'll have to take him to Aylesbury.'

'We appreciate that, sir,' Billy said.

'And why aren't you taking this to Mr Butler or Mr Millen?'

Because you are the kingmaker in this, Len thought. The Big Cheese.

'Well, as Len says, apart from the tip-off, it's tangential at the moment. Thought we'd run it by you first. You might make connections we can't.'

Hatherill shook his head, well aware he was being flattered. 'I'm not sure why you are wasting my time with this, lads. We've pulled in almost every lowlife. What makes Tony Fortune so special?'

'His wife.'

'I thought you said she had just given birth? I don't recall a pregnant woman being involved at Sears Crossing.'

Len and Billy exchanged glances, confirming to each other that it was time to come clean. Knowing he had Hatherill's ear, Len let Billy do the talking.

'The wife is speaking partly in riddles and nods and winks.'

'That's women for you,' smiled Hatherill. 'Especially after they've had a baby.'

'We think Tony Fortune was offered the job but for some reason turned it down. Yes, I know half the villains in London are claiming that. We also think that the wife's brother knew about it.'

'Where is the brother?'

'Norwich.'

'The prison?'

Billy nodded vigorously. 'Sir. He was the driver on an armed robbery last week. Grafton Street?'

Hatherill waved him on with an impatient gesture of his hand. 'I know about it, yes.'

'Geoff, the brother, is up to his eyes in debt. When the train didn't come off for him, he went with the Clarence Brothers. Big mistake. Now he is looking at ten years.'

'But?'

'Marie Fortune reckons that if Geoff's charge were dropped to being an accessory – just driving, in other words – he might give us some names.'

'But Tony Fortune won't?'

They both shook their heads.

'Tony Fortune isn't stupid.'

'But this Geoff is?'

Len gave a grunt that might have been a laugh. 'He'd have to be, to drive for the Clarences. They make the Richardsons look like *The Brains Trust*.'

'Does Fortune know you have spoken to the wife?'

Again, they shook their heads in unison. 'He hasn't put anything together yet,' said Billy. 'He's not even sure why he was pulled. We're certain of it.'

'Good. Keep it like that. Wife might come in handy later as a bit of leverage.' Hatherill smoked on, thinking for a moment. 'I am assuming you lads would like to be attached to the Train Squad for this. Should it pan out, I mean.'

Neither of them denied it.

'In which case, I think you can leave this matter to Ernie Millen and me.'

'Sir?' Len asked incredulously. 'What do you mean?'

'Mr Millen and I will travel to Norwich. I'm sorry, but if you are right, this is too important to . . .' His words tailed off.

'Leave to junior officers?' Billy suggested.

'In a word, yes. You keep quiet about this. It has to be approached carefully. We also have to make sure no word of this gets out, certainly not into the prison population.'

He could see disappointment in both their faces. 'In the meantime, drop everything else, report to Jack Slipper, see if he has anything needs chasing up.'

It took a moment for the last sentence to sink in. Slipper was one of the Train Squad. And if they were working for him, they were too.

'Sir.'

'Thank you, sir.'

'Go on, piss off. Go and catch some train robbers, make me happy.' As they were almost out the door, he spoke again, softly. 'And boys, this better be right. I have many ambitions for what little time I have left in the Force. Going to Norwich isn't one of them.'

Ten minutes later the phone rang. It was Brigadier John Cheney, Chief Constable of Buckinghamshire, and what he told him put a big smile on Hatherill's face. He put down the receiver and then called the operator. 'Get me the Forensic Science laboratory. We've found the hideout.'

'Mrs Clark, is it?'

The fifty-year-old woman who had opened the door looked Roger Cordrey up and down and seemed relieved, probably because he wasn't Irish, black or a dog. 'You've come about the garage?'

'I have.' Sitting in the little Austin van behind him was his old pal Bill Boal, who had come along to help with the next stage of the job, stashing the money and starting a legitimate enterprise to account for it. For which they needed a garage. 'Yes. I telephoned.'

'Just that I've had some very strange people ringing. It's only around the corner. Would you like to see it?'

'Yes, please,' Roger said politely. 'But I am sure it will be fine. Just as long as it's dry.'

'Oh, very dry. My husband was a stickler for keeping it clean and dry. There are no oil stains and you could eat your dinner off that floor. Come in, I'll get you the keys and the rental agreement. Would your friend like to come in?'

Roger looked back over his shoulder. 'No, he'll be fine. We are going into business together.'

'Locally?'

'Wimborne. But we'll base ourselves in Bournemouth.'

'Well, come in, come in.'

Roger stepped inside a house crammed full of china ornaments. He kept his hands pressed to his sides in case he inadvertently sent a windmill or a doe-eyed flower-seller crashing to the floor. 'What line of work are you in?'

'Flowers.'

'Lovely. Come through to the kitchen.'

Roger walked down the hallway. The kitchen wasn't any less hazardous, as every inch of the wall seemed to have decorative plates hanging on it.

'If you'll just put your name, address and telephone number down here. And I'll need a month's refundable deposit and a month in advance. There are two keys. I'll keep one. Don't worry, I won't go in. It's just in case you lose yours.'

Roger hesitated. 'Two of us will be using the garage, so we'll need both keys. My friend outside in the car, Bill – we share the car.'

Mrs Clark's face seemed to fold in on itself. She wasn't happy.

'It's unlikely we would both lose them, but we'll copy the serial numbers just in case. And pay for any replacement.'

She looked partially mollified. 'Very well.'

'And I can give you the deposit plus three months' rent now. In cash.'

Her face unfurled. 'Oh, well. How rude of me – would you like a cup of tea while you count the money out?'

'Yes, that would be very nice.'

'Then I'll walk you round and show you which one it is. Nice blue door, only just painted before . . .' She put a hand to her throat. 'Sorry, before my husband passed away.'

'I'm sorry to hear that.'

'It's why I don't need the garage, you see.'

'We'll take good care of it.'

'I'm sure you will.'

She watched while he counted out the rent in one-pound notes. She looked at the tower of cash sitting on her kitchen table, and at the impressive roll he had peeled them from. Cash. Bundles of it.

As her husband used to say after a few pints, 'If it looks

like shit, smells like shit and feels like shit . . . it's probably shit.' She hated the crudity, but William hadn't risen to Sergeant in the police force without a good nose for a wrong 'un. And he would say this one stank to high heaven.

'Here are the keys. Why don't you walk round, take a look and we'll have the tea when you get back and sign if you are happy?'

'Very well.'

'Fourth one in. Blue door.'

As soon as he had gone, Mrs Clark went to the telephone in her hall. She didn't pick it up until she heard the engine of the van they had arrived in start up. She watched its blurred image through the glass of the front door as it pulled away and executed a U-turn.

Picking up the receiver, she was about to dial, then she hesitated. She was probably imagining things. Bucks was a long way from Bournemouth, after all. Still, 'report anything suspicious' they had said. She dialled.

'Hello, operator? Can you get me the Desk Sergeant at Poole police station?' This was her husband's old station. She would get a sympathetic hearing there. And wouldn't it raise a smile in his former canteen if William Clark's widow were responsible for capturing the Great Train Robbers?

Bruce was the first to arrive. He parked his Austin Healey in the gravel car park of the café, just off the North

Circular Road. It was five days since the robbery, and the news was still full of bluster and exaggeration.

Roy pulled in next in his Mini Cooper, with a scowling Charlie in the seat beside him. Just Buster now and they had the quartet who would travel back to the farm. Charlie hoped Buster would bring a larger motor so they could all fit inside in comfort. He wished he'd used the big Rover.

Bruce stepped out, careful not to scuff his new elastic-sided boots. When he saw the other two he had to laugh. 'Christ, we look like a bloody Freeman's catalogue.'

Roy looked down at his new clothes, the roll-neck and cardigan combo and dark blue slacks. 'Speak for yourself. This lot cost some serious dough.'

Charlie had on a dark but well-cut suit that wasn't Burtons either.

'You lads been putting it about?' Bruce asked, only half-joking.

'Is that a Huntsman?' Charlie asked by way of reply, pointing to Bruce's suit.

'Davis. And I had it on order months ago. It's not off the fuckin' peg.'

They walked towards the café, one eye open for Buster. 'Speak to Field?' Charlie asked.

'No, his missus. He was out.'

'He's always out.'

'Has it been done?' Roy asked.

Bruce shrugged. 'That's why we have to go and check.

460

I can't get hold of Tony Fortune, either. What's in the farm that might cause us grief?'

'Buster left some clothes behind,' Roy said. 'We couldn't burn them all because of the smoke.'

'And there are the mailbags in the basement,' said Charlie.

'They can't get prints off mailbags. And we always wore our gloves,' Bruce reminded them.

Both looked down at the floor. Not always, the guilty glances said.

'OK, there were a few lapses. But I scrubbed that place till my fingers bled. Remember?'

Charlie did recall. He had had a go about the scrubbing and Bruce whistling that stupid Flash 'Spring Clean' jingle.

'I said you should open a cleaning agency.'

'So it's got to be pretty clear of dabs. But when Buster gets here, we'll go there, burn the lot. After all, we own it. We can burn the fuckin' thing to the ground if we want.'

'Should've been done by now,' said Charlie. 'There's something else worrying me.'

'What's that?'

'Stan.'

'What about him?' asked Bruce.

'You know.'

Bruce knew. He could tell by Charlie's expression. He was a frightening cunt when he had it on. Charlie might have his doubts about Brian Field's robustness but he was absolutely 100 per cent sure old Stan would fold if questioned.

'No,' Bruce said.

'No what?'

'No topping people, Charlie.'

'I wasn't—'

'Yes, you was. Nobody gets killed.' Bruce used all the firmness he could muster. He couldn't back it up with violence, but he hoped he still had some authority left.

'All right, mate. Just thinkin' out loud.'

They entered the café, which was empty at that time of day, ordered three teas and sat at a red Formica table near the door. Roy played nervously with the tomato ketchup container.

'You fixed OK, Roy?' Bruce asked. 'Still in the flat?'

'No, thought I'd stay clear of that, just in case.' He had only gone there to dispose of his railway books and the Triang train set. 'I'm staying with me mum,' he said. 'I can't go far. I got races.'

'Charlie?'

'At home with Pat and the kids. What else? Got nothing to hide. You?'

'Thinking of moving out a bit. Look, lads, it's only a matter of time before we get tugged. They'll take in anyone who could do this. I reckon there're only about thirty blokes, maybe fifty, tops, in the whole country who would be capable of what we did. We know who they are and therefore so do Butler and his chummies. So they'll get to us eventually.'

The teas arrived and they spooned sugars in. All looked up as Buster burst into the café, his podgy face pulsing red. He looked like a traffic light, thought Bruce. Or a railway signal. Buster glanced at the girl behind the counter, took a deep breath and composed himself. 'Another tea, love.'

Then he put the folded newspaper on the table, spinning it slowly so all could read. It was the *Evening Standard*. There was a big splash headline.

YARD CHIEF HATHERILL ANNOUNCES . . .
We've found the gang's hideout!

Bruce picked up the newspaper and scanned down the article, picking out relevant phrases. *Mailbags found . . . food stocks for many men . . . money wrappers in basement . . . attempt to burn clothes . . . Yard has called in Detective Superintendent Maurice Ray, the 'Bernard Quatermass' of fingerprints.* He had drunk with Maurice at the Marlborough. Nice bloke. For a copper. Then he stopped at one sentence and felt his throat constrict.

Malcolm Fewtrell of Buckinghamshire CID described the Leatherslade farmhouse scene as 'One big clue'.

One big clue? What did that mean? He threw the rag back onto the table and Roy pulled it towards him.

'Oh Christ,' said Roy. 'Oh Jesus fuckin' Christ.'

Charlie leaned over and his face grew darker. Those steely eyes narrowed once more, leopard-like.

Bruce pulled at his earlobe, a sure sign of agitation. 'I tell you what, Charlie,' he said softly. 'Next time you see Brian Field or Tony Fortune, do me a favour.'

'What's that?'

'Have a word with them.'

Charlie nodded almost imperceptibly. 'Strong words, Bruce. Very strong words.'

Fifty-two

Dorking, 15 August 1963

It was Jenny's thighs that did it. Colin normally gave his neighbour a lift to work and so far they hadn't had much more than a kiss, a cuddle and quick play around the stocking-tops. But the Morris Minor was in for a service and Colin had suggested he could manage to give her a lift to the factory where they worked – he on the shop floor, she in accounts – if she didn't mind riding pillion on his Triumph.

So Jenny had worn tight black slacks that had drawn a disapproving tut from Colin's wife as she had thrown her leg over the machine in the driveway. Colin felt her thighs hot against the top of his buttocks and an idea began to form in his fevered mind.

Jenny noticed the filthy look she was getting, even more intense than usual. 'I'll be changing at work, Mrs Rogers,' Jenny said with a smile as the wife glared at her from the doorway. 'Can't wear a skirt on this, can you?'

Colin didn't have a spare crash helmet for her, so he forewent his own, but still put on the goggles. He waved to his wife, kick-started the bike, and set off.

'I'm taking a different route!' he yelled over his shoulder as they burbled to the end of the road.

'What?'

'Different route.'

'OK.'

'Stay off main roads. Avoid the A25. Safer.'

'As long as I'm not late.'

'Hold tight!'

She did so and he felt her breasts press into his shoulder-blades. She squealed when he took the first bend, her legs pinching together.

Colin felt the stirrings of an erection as he twisted the throttle. Her hair was whipping across his neck and, as she leaned closer, he could feel her breath, smell the Yardley.

A car overtook them, forcing him towards the kerb. He was a little rusty so he slowed his speed. 'All right, Jenny?'

'This is fun!'

He took a left, leaning the bike over steeply, feeling the grip of her thighs tighten. There was little traffic now so he let the speed creep up and they roller-coasted over the gentle undulations, Jenny laughing every time her stomach dropped. Ahead was a patch of woodland known locally as The Bluebells, although it was the wrong time of year for the flowers.

He backed the throttle off and changed down, letting the engine idle as they coasted to a halt.

'What's the matter, Colin?'

'Overheated.'

'What, the engine or you?' asked Jenny with a grin.

'A bit of both. Hop off.'

'I can't be late.'

He watched her slide off the seat and made a pretence of sniffing it. She slapped him, giggling. 'Oi, don't be a perve.'

He heaved the bike onto the stand and said, 'Five minutes.'

'Yes, I'd heard that about you.'

Taking her by the hand, he led her over the grass verge towards the trees. There was very little traffic on this B road, so he wasn't worried about the bike. He was more concerned about doing something about the bulge in his trousers.

He stopped at the first tree, leaned Jenny against it and kissed her. She snaked her hands around his neck to pull him close. He squirmed against her and worked a hand onto the sweet, warm flesh beneath her sweater. A horn hooted and they turned to see a Cortina, the driver shouting something unintelligible and flashing a thumbs-up.

'Not here, Colin,' she whispered.

She led him deeper into the stand of trees, where sunlight streaking through the random grid of the canopy made glowing jigsaw patterns on the forest floor.

'Here,' he suggested.

'No, just a bit further.'

'So I'm hoping.'

She slapped him again. 'We should have brought a blanket. I don't want to turn up all mucky.'

'We can use my jacket.'

The ground sloped down to a small fern-filled hollow. As they stepped into it, Jenny's foot snagged and she stumbled forward.

'Ow. What was that?'

Colin bent down and extracted a smart pigskin holdall from the undergrowth. 'Someone's bag.'

He stood and looked around. The bag was new and, judging by its condition, it hadn't spent more than a night out in the open, if that.

'Let's go,' said Jenny, suddenly spooked. 'Your engine must be cool by now.'

'Hell-o,' shouted Colin tentatively, aware his opportunity was slipping away from him. His own engine hadn't cooled at all. 'Anyone there?'

'There's another bag, look. A briefcase.'

'Don't touch it. I'll open this one,' he said.

'No.'

'Why not?'

Jenny put her arms around herself, suddenly cold. 'Doesn't seem right.'

'There might be a name and address.'

'Go on, then.'

He tugged at the zip, which was stiff from the pressure of the bag's contents. He had only got it a third back when the first bundle of notes sprang out. He lifted it up with thumb and forefinger. Then flicked it. Fivers. It was all fivers.

Jenny popped the lock on the briefcase. She gave a little gasp and held its gaping top for Colin to peer inside. That, too, was full of fivers and one-pound notes.

Colin stood, his throat dry, and took a step backwards. 'Stay here.'

Jenny's voice squeaked when she spoke. 'Don't leave me.'

'You'll be fine.'

'What if they come back?'

'Scream.' Money had replaced sex as his priority now. If this was what he thought it was, there might be a whacking great reward. 'I won't be long, promise.'

'Where you going, Colin?'

'To call the police.'

The Phoenix pub, off Sussex Gardens, had become the un-official HQ for Jack Slipper's part of the Train Squad. It was not on Tommy Butler's radar – few pubs were – and enabled the lads to discuss the various leads without Tommy jumping in and running off with them. And then claiming the credit.

So each night, Slipper gave an off-the-record briefing to whichever members of his team were in the bar. That night, it was Len and Billy, both already feeling the strain of fifteen hours, seven days a week. Not to mention six pints in the Phoenix every night.

'It'll be nine, ten days before we get definitive results on the prints,' the guv'nor said glumly.

'So much for bloody Quatermass,' muttered Len.

'There's a lot to dust and analyse at that farm,' said Slipper sympathetically. 'Maurice Ray knows he's got to get this right. Or else.'

They were all acutely aware of the pressure on them from above, like a giant cast-iron press with a screw handle, slowly being wound to crush the life out of them. *Find these men. Turn. Charge Them. Turn. Try Them. Turn. Make sure it sticks. Turn.*

'Has Roger Cordrey said anything?' asked Billy.

'Not so as we've heard.' Like all the suspects would, Cordrey had finished up at Aylesbury. 'His mate Boal claims he had nothing to do with the actual tickle. Could be right. But Cordrey, you know, that gives us the possibilities of Jim Hussey and Tommy Wisbey. Both big buggers. If I wanted to scare some sorters, I'd choose to have them along.'

'What about the money in Dorking?'

'Around a hundred grand.'

470

'Any of the right numbers?'

Slipper drank his pint. 'No.'

'But?' asked Len, sensing there was more. 'What else, guv'nor?'

'There was a hotel receipt in the bottom of one of the bags. From Germany. Made out to a Herr and Frau Field. Brian Field.'

Len spilled his drink down his front. 'What, Brian Field – the solicitor? The one with the German wife?'

'That's the one.'

Slipper had clearly already made the next connection, but he let Len say it anyway. 'The one who put together the defence for Gordon Goody on the airport job?'

'The very same.'

'Bugger me sideways.' Len was beside himself. 'I knew it was Goody. I just fucking knew it.'

'Drink up, lads. First thing tomorrow, I want you down knockin' on his old lady's place in Putney, see if she knows where her little Gordy is.'

'What about Field?' asked Billy.

'Malcolm Fewtrell is scooping him up, don't you worry.'

'So the dominoes have started tumbling.'

'Aye, lad,' said Slipper triumphantly. 'And we haven't even got the fingerprints back yet.'

The Chief Warden of Norwich Prison poked his head around the battered metal door of the visiting room.

'Gentlemen, it's nine o'clock. Visiting hours finish at nine-fifteen and I need to get home. If you will hurry it along.'

'We'll be as quick as we can,' said George Hatherill meekly. 'Thank you.'

He turned back to Geoff Barrow, sitting on his Remploy chair opposite himself and Ernie Millen. He was scratching at the chipped enamel on the table. 'They don't know who you are?' he asked nervously.

Millen shook his head. 'Told you, son. Anonymous. We were dropped off in town, we'll be picked up in town. Nobody will know who we are or what we wanted.'

'And this will help me?'

'Geoff, we'll do our best. All be on the QT though, won't it? We can't very well stand up in court and say: "Mitigating circumstances – Geoff Barrow gave us some right ripe names". Not unless you want to come out of the shower room with an extra arsehole.'

Millen looked at Hatherill with distaste. 'It won't come to that, George. Will it, Geoff?'

'I fuckin' hope not.'

'We have only ten minutes left.'

'And we won't be coming back next week,' said Hatherill. 'It's not like *Beat the Clock*.'

'I can't tell you where I got these names.'

'Of course.'

Geoff took a deep breath. The two detectives waited.

It was like a dive off the high board. The nerve could go at any point up to the launch. After that, it was too late to turn back. 'Bruce someone. Begins with R,' Marie had actually told him the full name, but he wanted to hold some things back. They were meant to be detectives, after all. 'You know him? You going to write this down?'

Hatherill shook his head. 'Ernie has a phonographic memory.'

'Oh. Right. Well, they call this bloke the Colonel.'

'Do they indeed?' said George, with a smile. 'But spare us the initials shit, Geoff. Full name.' He scowled. 'Now, or the deal is off.'

Geoff swallowed hard. 'Reynolds, that's it. Bruce Reynolds.'

Hatherill relaxed. Same name as the anonymous caller gave. Which meant Geoff Barrow might be on the level.

'He had a couple of old mates with him, by all accounts. From when he did time.'

'Names?'

'No, sorry.'

Well, Reynolds's known associates were already being checked. It wouldn't be hard to generate a list of likely accomplices. 'Who else?'

'A racing driver. Don't know his name. "The Weasel" is the nickname he goes by.'

'The Weasel? Nobody else?'

'Bits and pieces. Jimmy, an ex-Army bloke. No surname.

473

A fella who has a club in South London. Edward something . . . or something Edward. And someone called Goodman. Or Goodrich. Antique dealer.'

Goody, thought Hatherill, but kept it to himself. Don't lead the witness. 'Half the villains in London are antique dealers, Geoff. You'll have to be more specific than that.'

Geoff went on like this, dropping hints and half-truths, until the warder banged on the door. Most of what he had told them was based on what his sister had spilled, which she had got out of Tony. The other names were from the Clarence Boys, who had big mouths.

At the last minute, he threw in a couple of extra blokes for good measure, men whom he knew had nothing to do with the robbery, but were faces he owed money to. They would have a hard time collecting from inside. Always assuming he didn't spend too long in there and end up at the same nick. 'I don't want any of them sent here.'

'This is a geriatric prison, Geoff. Old men and first-timers.'

'That's me,' said Geoff. 'First offence.'

'More by luck than judgement,' said Hatherill, rising to his feet.

'We'll keep our part, best we can,' said Millen.

'If you can just answer this one last question?' Hatherill added. 'And think hard.'

'What's that?'

'Someone's put your brother-in-law Tony Fortune right

in the frame for this. Any thoughts about that you would
wish to share?'

Billy tried not to stare too hard at the boy's face. It was
covered with pustules, some of them straining with the pressure beneath them, looking as if they could pop at any
moment. They were sitting in the stationmaster's office at
Euston, and Spotty Muldoon was the fourth train enthu-
siast he had interviewed.

It had seemed like a good idea. Surely the robbers would
have cased their target at both ends of its journey? And
on the platform there was a readily available group of
witnesses. That was what they did, didn't they? Hung
around stations, watching. But if the previous trio were
anything to go by, they only had eyes for trains, not human
beings. If someone should fall under a loco, Billy had the
impression they'd be able to tell you the bogey layout of
the fatal engine, but not whether the victim was male or
female.

He passed the boy the bottle of Vimto he had asked for.
'Your name is Bernard . . . ?'

'Harwood.' Billy wrote it down and then the address the
lad volunteered.

'And you come here most evenings?'

'Yes. After school. Monday to Thursday. And Saturday
mornings, too.'

'How long do you spend?'

'Depends. An hour on week days, perhaps four or five on the weekend.'

Christ, how boring, Billy thought.

'Now, I am going to show you some photographs of men and I want you to tell me if you have ever seen any of them down here. Understand?'

'Yes.'

Billy struck gold on the sixth of the smudges. Bernard Harwood bounced up and down in his seat, as if he needed the lavatory. He jabbed at the photograph with a shaking finger. 'Him! Him!'

Billy held it up at chest height. 'You sure?'

'Yes. Said he only collected diesels. Thought it was weird.'

You should know, Billy thought uncharitably. Flipping the photo round, he found himself studying the delicate features of Roy James.

Letter sent to Train Squad, Scotland Yard

Dear Sir,

No doubt you will be surprised to hear from me. Especially after my trial at the Old Bailey for the London Airport Robbery. At the time of writing I am not living at my home address because it seems I am a suspect in the recent train robbery. Two Flying Squad officers recently visited my home address and made a search of the premises, despite not having a warrant. To be honest, I am very worried that they will connect me with this crime.

The reason I write now is because the police always treated me very fairly during the Airport case. That cost me eight months and every penny I had, and to become a suspect in this last big robbery is more than I can stand. So my intention is to keep out of harm's way until the people concerned in the Train Robbery are found.

To some people, even writing this letter would seem like a sign of guilt, but all I am interested in now is keeping my freedom.

Yours Sincerely,

Gordon Goody

Paddy gave Tony the slip of paper with a number on it. He looked up from his desk in the office.

'Called while you were out.'

There was no name next to the number. 'Who was it?'

'Didn't say,' the old man sniffed.

Tony took his jacket from the back of the chair. 'I'm just going out for ten minutes. Get you a sandwich?'

Paddy was frowning down at him, his lined face thrown into even deeper creases. 'That packet you gave me to look after . . .'

Tony looked at the floor as he shrugged on his jacket. 'Yeah?'

'It's all right, is it?'

'I told you. Just hiding it from the taxman.'

'Oh, all the profit from all those cars we've been shifting.' He looked out at the full showroom. 'I'm not stupid, Tony.'

'I know that. Which is why you'll always be able to say, hand on heart, "I thought it was tax money". Understand?'

Paddy nodded. 'I see.'

'But it won't come to that.'

Paddy spoke softly, his voice tinged with regret. 'I robbed a bank once.'

'What?'

'Well, more of a Post Office it was. In Ireland. For some of The Boys, if you know who I mean.'

'I think I do.' Although he wasn't sure whether he meant gangsters or the IRA. Perhaps they were one and the same.

'It was the only way to get my brother off the hook, y'see. So I did it, with a kid's plastic cowboy gun, handed over the money to some fella, and left the country. Never been back. But I'm too old to do much more of that, Tony.'

He put a hand on his shoulder. 'We'll sort something out, very soon.'

'I'd be grateful.'

But where? Was there a foolproof hiding-place for so much cash? 'I'll get you a sandwich.'

'Butter not marge, mind.'

'Of course.'

Tony walked quickly to Warren Street Tube. The scuffed

wooden phone booth just inside the entrance was unoccupied, so he stepped inside and dialled the number.

'Tony?' It was Roy.

'Yup. How are you, Roy?'

'You know. Ducking and diving. You hear about Roger?'

'Yeah.'

'Roger – of all people. You know this bloke they lifted with him? Bill Something?'

'Boal. No.'

'Me neither. And they have Brian, too.'

'I heard.' Tony had pieced together what had happened during his own interviews with the Flying Squad. 'They tied him to the money in the woods, apparently.'

'What was that all about?'

'It was the drinks, left for someone to pick up, I reckon. What else could it be? You don't go dumping that much cash in the bloody forest otherwise, do you?'

'I suppose not,' said Roy. 'Someone's going to be pissed off, aren't they? Talking of which, I just wanted to tell you: Bruce is pretty narked about the farm. Last time we met he asked Charlie to have a word with you and Brian.'

A cold, prickly sweat broke out on Tony's forehead. 'Have a word' could mean several things, depending on Charlie's mood, but even the mildest – an up-close-in-your-face bollocking – was less than pleasant. And at the other end of the spectrum . . .

'Fuck.'

'All I'm sayin' is, watch your back. Bruce will have calmed down by now. To him it's a figure of speech, know what I mean? But Chas . . . What happened anyway?'

'I met Brian. He told me to torch it. I was on my way up and I got a tug. Nothing I could do.'

'Brian left you to do it by yourself?'

'Yeah. Said he had things to sort out.'

'What was more important than the farm?' Roy yelled. '"One big clue", the paper said.'

'I know, Roy, I know. But the Old Bill is on my case. I can't move. They know I was at the farm, God knows how. Keep banging on about it.' Jack Slipper, Len Haslam and Billy Naughton had all interviewed him before they had let him go. They knew he was good for it, but so far had no proof. If they found some, he could wave goodbye to his new son for ten years or more. The thought made him physically ill.

'They've tied you to the farm?' Roy asked.

'Not physically, but they seem certain I was there. They can't get me for the actual tickle, but they want me for some of it at least.' There had also been the sly allusion to 'helping him out' if he were to turn the others in.

'But you kept your gloves on, right?'

'Course I did. Nobody mentioned my dabs being there. Where's Bruce now?'

'Gone to ground. So has Buster. Says he's going abroad. Gordy's off to Spain for a while.'

Tony glanced over his shoulder, half-expecting to see a familiar, and unwelcome face. 'And Charlie?'

'With the family. Look, don't worry about him. It was probably nothing. Be lucky.'

'You too, Roy. You too.'

In the Buckinghamshire Police incident room, Len Haslam and Billy Naughton stood before one of the two enormous blackboards that had been borrowed from the local Aylesbury Adult Education Institute. On them were written the names of all those in the frame for the robbery. The writing covered both boards, more than forty names in all. A code had been devised, updated daily. After each one was a colour-coded letter. S just meant suspect; KAO was Known Associate Of; I stood for Interviewed, with the officer's initials and the date in brackets afterwards; WFQ, Wanted For Questioning; DQ was for Detained for Questioning, with a cipher for which station; and a red C meant the suspect had been charged. So far, only three names had gained the C: Brian Field, Roger Cordrey and Bill Boal.

Jim Hussey, Tommy Wisbey, Ronnie Biggs and Bobby Welch were all 'I' status. Slipper, Williams or Hatherill had interviewed each one. All were suspects by association, either with Cordrey or with the name heading the list, Bruce Reynolds.

Gordon Gordy was up there, despite his letter proclaiming his innocence, since Len had been able to prove he hadn't been in Belfast on the night of the robbery, but had left two days earlier. Ronald 'Buster' Edwards had earned his place because of connections to Roger Cordrey.

Tony Fortune was on a different list, one reserved for those who had in some way aided and abetted the actual robbery. The Squad would get him for accessory before or after the fact, they were sure.

The young PC in charge of updating the board finished adding the last of the morning's abbreviations and turned to the two Squad detectives. His tunic was covered in a coating of multi-coloured chalk dust. He looked as if he had been baking with Technicolor flour.

'I see how these boys fit together, but what tipped the wink about this Reynolds?' he asked, tapping the name he had just written in.

'I don't know,' said Len truthfully – although he had a shrewd idea. George Hatherill and Ernie Millen were adamant he was a key player but would offer no reason. Which meant the confirmation of Reynolds' role came from Geoff Barrow. It was their lead. 'Guv'nor's call.'

They had driven up by car that day to attend the twice-weekly catch-up session with Malcolm Fewtrell, when information was pooled and cross-checked, only because more senior officers were still pulling in every villain in London and putting them through the wringer. The idea was it concentrated the mind when they discovered it wasn't some junior detective facing them, but the heard-it-before expressions of

Hatherill or Millen or Tommy Butler, Jack Slipper or Frank Williams. It was said hotels in Brighton and Eastbourne were booming as every face with form in the capital decided it was a good time for a seaside holiday.

'What's that?' asked Billy, pointing to a bright red question-mark hovering above Bruce's name.

'Mr Big.'

'What?'

'Mr Fewtrell thinks there must be someone behind it. A planner. He says that this is too complex for your average villain. Must be a Mr Big.'

'What, like Dr No?' sneered Len. 'Maybe we should see if Sean Connery is free to lend a hand.'

'Roy James, also known as "the Weasel"?' Billy asked as he read down the board. James was WFQ. Placing him at Euston looking at trains didn't amount to a watertight case – not unless being a weirdo became a crime. 'You ever heard him called that, Len – "Weasel"?'

Len shook his head. 'And he usually drives something faster than Land Rovers.' It was his turn to read aloud. 'Gordon Goody, KAO Brian Field.' He turned to the PC. 'While we're up here, any chance we can take a look at the farm?'

'I think the forensics are finished,' the young man said. 'I'll go and check.'

After he had left, Len turned to Billy with the kind of smile on his face that always made the junior officer uneasy.

'We've got to get back,' Billy said. 'Slipper wants us to talk to Biggs again. We can't hang around.'

Slipper had gone through the OB – the Occurrences Book – in Redhill and discovered Charmian's call about Ronnie and the woodcutting. The wife had blown her husband's alibi wide open. So now they had to ask him where he really was on the seventh and eighth of August.

'Don't you worry, Billy,' Len said with a wink. 'One day, Slipper will thank me for this.'

The farm disappointed the London policemen. Despite themselves, the Squad had come to admire the men behind the crime, if only for their style, bottle and chutzpah. They genuinely disagreed with those who painted them as latterday Robin Hoods – where exactly was the 'give-to-the-poor' part? – but they could accept that the whole job was a cut above the run-of-the-mill. Unlike Leatherslade Farm.

Billy walked around the outside of the house. He had seen photographs, of course, and been surprised then that it wasn't some cute, half-timbered structure, only a dull, suburban dwelling. But with its blistered paintwork and neglected windowboxes, it looked even more down-at-heel than he expected. Hardly the kind of HQ Mr Big would choose. Didn't they operate from flashy penthouse flats with armed minions dressed in black?

'Len? Shall we go inside?' he shouted.

There was no answer.

'Len?'

He found him in one of the garages, kneeling down beside the Austin lorry. In his left hand, he had a brown suede shoe.

'What are you doing?'

'Shut up! Anyone out there?'

'No, they are either inside or at the gate.'

'Gently does it.'

Using a long-bladed screwdriver, he took a dried flake of yellow paint from the can on the floor and pressed it onto the sole of the shoe. Billy noticed he was wearing gloves.

'Len . . .'

Duke stood and looked at his handiwork. 'There.' He slipped the shoe into a large plastic evidence bag and then placed it in his briefcase. 'Do you want to look inside?'

He went to push by, but Billy stepped into his path. 'What are you doing?'

The other man stripped off his gloves and shoved them into his jacket pocket. 'What does it look like I am doing? I'm fucking Gordon Goody.'

'Sir? You in there, sir?'

It was the young copper from the incident room.

'Just coming,' said Len.

When they emerged from the semi-darkness into the light, they could see the PC hopping from foot to foot in excitement.

'What is it?'

'Just come over the radio. They've got the fingerprinting results.'

'And?'

'Hundreds. We've got them all – Reynolds, James, Hussey, Biggs. We should get back. There's a big round-up coming.'

As they followed some distance behind, Len held up the briefcase containing the suede shoe. 'Ah well, Billy. We might not be needing this after all.'

Fifty-three

Goodwood Racing Circuit, 24 August 1963

Roy pulled into Goodwood's cramped, overcrowded paddock, almost slicing off a few toes. It was, as usual, a zoo, but a cracking one. Being invited to race at the Tourist Trophy meet was a big deal. There would be a cocktail party with the Duke of Richmond that evening and the next day a Driver's XI took on the Duke's players. Roy was not much of a batsman although he had a turn of speed as a bowler. But the match meant more than just rubbing elbows with a few nobs. It represented recognition, the tacit nod that you had been noticed, were a coming man, a driver to keep tabs on. Roy James was going up the ladder, to the roof.

As if it knew what rested on its shoulders, his car had performed well, lapping the tricky circuit – actually the perimeter road of a wartime RAF airfield – at close to 100mph. Only Peter Arundell in his Lotus-Ford was quicker.

As he pulled to a stop, hands reached out and patted him on the back. Bobby Pelham, Roy's mechanic, had to push wellwishers aside to lever him out of the cockpit.

'Not bad,' Bobby said, as Roy pulled off his goggles and blinked dust from his eyes.

'Not bad?' Roy protested with a smile. 'A ton, not bad?'

'Lost your line on Woodcote,' Bobby tutted. 'Cost you.'

'Nearly lost the front end at No-name, thanks to bloody Dickie. Still, as you say, not bad.'

A tall, blazered figure pushed through the crowd. It was one of the track stewards, Major Grace – a crusty sort, very much from the right side of the tracks. However, he liked Roy and had always looked out for him at other events, no matter how rough and ready the young man's origins.

'Roy, your mother just phoned the office.'

'My mum? Is she OK?'

'She said you'd had visitors.'

'Visitors?'

'Yes. Wouldn't be more specific. Said you would understand. Insisted I give you the message.' The Major looked nonplussed, like a bawled-out schoolboy. Roy could imagine his mother taking him to task if he had even hesitated to carry out her wishes. She had a tongue like a stiletto when required.

Roy took off his helmet and handed it to Bobby. 'I know what that means. It's my uncle, from Australia. Look, Major,

I've got to do some work on the engine overnight. Need to get it back to the workshop.'

'Can't you do it here?'

'I'd rather use my own tools. You know how it is.'

The Major knew full well that drivers and mechanics liked to cosset their steel and fibreglass babies on their own home turf. 'You'll miss drinks.'

'Well, it's more about the racing than drinking.'

The Major laughed. 'So some say.'

'I'll be back for the cricket.'

'That's more like it.'

As soon as the Major had left, Roy pulled Bobby Pelham aside. 'Can you take the car back to the garage?'

'OK. What's up?'

'That rubbish about "visitors". Means the Old Bill was at my mum's.'

Bobby looked shaken. 'Christ. About you-know-what?'

Bobby knew what Roy had been up to, but not the exact details of how much he had received for the job.

'Well, I doubt if it's because my Road Tax is overdue.'

Roy had been gripped by a sense of urgency. He looked at the crowd in the pits, as if he expected to see Tommy Butler to be shouldering his way through at any moment. He walked to the Jaguar he used as a towing motor and searched in the boot, producing a fat envelope from beneath the toolkit. He handed it to Bobby. 'Wages,' he said. 'That'll keep you going for a while.'

Bobby looked inside and paled. 'Is it . . .'

'Just don't spend it all at once.' Roy slapped Bobby on the upper arm. 'I'm going to use the Mini. I'll call you when I know what's what, OK?'

Bobby could tell from the cast of Roy's face that he didn't expect things to be OK for a long time. 'Yeah – 'course.'

Tommy Butler wanted to do Charlie Wilson himself. Of all the names that had come into the frame with the fingerprints, he knew Charlie could be the most troublesome. He might not have the bulk of Hussey, Wisbey and some of the others, or the brains of Bruce Reynolds or Gordon Goody, but he was cunning. And he had a temper.

There was only one place where he wouldn't kick up a fuss. With his family. His wife and three daughters were Charlie's very own Kryptonite, his weakness. The news had already gone out to all police forces that Charlie, Reynolds and Jimmy White – the first three with confirmed dabs at the farm – were wanted. Butler needed to lift Charlie before the item hit the evening news bulletins and the papers.

So, it was lunchtime when four squad cars pulled up outside Charlie's home in Crescent Lane, Clapham, circling like covered wagons in a Western. Tommy made the officers wait while he strode up to the bright yellow door and rang the bell.

Pat Wilson answered, ashen-faced. She would have seen the cars through the window. 'We're just having lunch,' she said, looking over his shoulder into the street. Neighbours were already appearing to take in the show.

'Can't wait for pudding, I'm afraid. I'll give him a sandwich at the station.'

'It's all right, Pat,' said Charlie from the hallway, grabbing a jacket.

'Charles Wilson?' Butler asked in his most formal voice.

'Mr Butler, please.' Both his eyes and words were pleading.

The policeman could see his three daughters standing at the foot of the stairs. He understood what Charlie meant. This was no time for doing it by the book. He could caution him later.

'Cannon Row, Charlie. Just for a chat.' Although Tommy Butler knew it was likely to be Aylesbury before the day was out.

Charlie slipped his arms into his tweed jacket and kissed Pat goodbye. 'Give my brief a call,' he said. 'He'll have me back home for tea.'

'Mrs Wilson, some of my officers will be around later with a search warrant. Please don't disturb anything in the meantime. Come on, Charlie. Gently does it.'

As they walked to the cars, Butler held tightly to Charlie's upper arm. He should have cuffed him, but there was no point in winding up a man like Charlie Wilson. They tended to respond best to a little respect. 'You know what this is about, don't you, Charlie?'

'Is it the gas bill?'

'Not unless you ran up one for two point six million.'

Charlie smiled at that. 'I suspect someone has made a right balls-up.'

'One of your pals?'

'No, one of yours. You're wasting your time. I've got nothing to do with that. Never been there.'

'Then you have nothing to worry about.'

They reached the car, the door opened and a hand pushed Charlie's head down and folded him into the rear seat, where another detective waited. He produced a pair of handcuffs and snapped them over Charlie's proffered wrists. Tommy Butler leaned in. 'But I think it's you who have been wasting your time, Charlie. I don't think you'll be home for tea any time soon. About fifteen years, unless I am mistaken.'

Bruce Reynolds knew something was up as soon as Franny came back to the flat. She didn't bother to remove her coat; she simply strode up and turned the TV off. She tried to speak, but only tears came, coursing slowly down her cheeks.

Bruce stood. 'What is it? Is it Nick?'

She walked back to the hall and brought in the evening paper. Bruce felt a jolt when he saw his own face staring back at him. *Yard name men wanted in connection with Great Train . . .*

He read the rest in silence. When he reached the end he almost spat his words. 'It's a fuckin' liberty, putting the pictures in the paper. They never do that till after the trial.

How can you get a fair hearing when your face is all over the place, saying you was the bloke who done it? This is bloody Butler.'

He threw the paper down onto the floor.

That was it. It wasn't only the police who would be after him now – every last crook would be milking him for every penny. He was on the run, good and proper. Which meant the rent on any safe house would be enormous, and anyone who knew where he was would demand lots of little 'loans' for their silence. Plus there would be endless 'drinks' for their minders to do some fetching and carrying. It was sheer fucking extortion.

He walked over and gave Franny a hug, wiping away her tears. 'We knew it might come to this. Game's not over yet.'

She found a handkerchief and blew her nose. 'What do we do now, Bruce?'

'Stop using that name for a start.' It was time for new identities, a change of appearance. He glanced in the mirror, wondering what he could do. He stroked his upper lip. A moustache would help. Then he would need new clothes and passports, travel documents. Suddenly a hundred and fifty grand didn't sound like a lot. 'And think of a new one for you, too.'

'What then?'

'Start packing, love. That's what.'

'Where for?'

What did it matter where for? But he could see she was

493

close to tears again, her lower lip quivering. Bruce said the first country that came into his head. 'Mexico.'

Roy was hammering the Mini Cooper back towards London when the news came on the radio. The last song played before it was 'Four Feather Falls' by Michael Holliday. The Bing Crosby-like voice always triggered a loop of his 'I'm going well, I'm going Shell' jingle in Roy's brain. However, the first line of the bulletin banished the tune immediately.

'Police today arrested Londoner Charles Wilson in connection with The Great Train Robbery of two weeks ago. Scotland Yard says they are also keen to interview Bruce Reynolds and Jimmy White. They expect to be able to release further names within the next two days. Meanwhile Jack Mills, the driver . . .'

Roy switched the radio off. His hands were slick on the wheel, but his throat had dried. The A3 was clear ahead, reeling him back into London. And what? Butler or one of his crew, for sure.

He took his foot off the accelerator. An ERF coal lorry beeped him, and pulled out to overtake. He felt the slipstream buffet his little car, watched the black fallout from the sacks settle on his windscreen. He pulled over and rolled to a halt in a lay-by. He needed time to think. After all, he was a man on the run now. They all were.

'And where is the Weasel now?'

'The who?'

'Roy "the Weasel" James.'

'Nobody calls him the Weasel. He had some French—' Bobby Pelham stopped himself. 'Look, he's not called the Weasel, all right?'

Jack Slipper had it on good account – from George Hatherill, no less – that James's nickname *was* the Weasel, but he let it pass. 'Let's just stick with Roy James then, shall we? Where is he?'

As he spoke, Slipper walked around mechanic Bobby Pelham's first-floor flat in Notting Hill. The carpet was threadbare and stained; the furniture sadly mismatched and he could smell chip fat. On the wall was a poster for the Monaco Grand Prix 1932, a garish print of an Oriental woman and the centre pages from an *ABC Film Review*, of Ursula Andress rising from the sea. It was clearly a single man's abode. From outside, he could hear the clash and clanging of Len Haslam and Billy Naughton sorting through the yard, which was full of discarded motor parts and oil cans.

Slipper stopped at the wooden mantel above the gasfire and picked up one of the trophies. It was for a second place that Roy had achieved at Thruxton.

'Shame about his career. To throw it all away like that.' He looked up at Bobby as there came the thump of something heavy being dropped below them. 'They going to find anything down there?'

'Well, if they find the Weber carb I'm missing I'd be grateful.'

495

'Don't be funny, Bobby,' said Slipper, rising to his full ramrod-straight height. 'It isn't a matter for levity any more. We almost had him yesterday, you know. Arrived ten, fifteen minutes after you two had left Goodwood. And he didn't say where he was going?'

'No, Mr Slipper.'

'Missing a big race today, too. You know, Roy will probably be the second most famous no-show in Goodwood's history.'

'How's that?'

'David Blakely, Easter Monday, 1955, didn't turn up for his event. He's the most well-known no-show.'

Jack Slipper could see Bobby was struggling to place the name. 'He practised on the Saturday at Goodwood and Ruth Ellis shot him on the Sunday outside the Magdala pub, Hampstead. Last woman to hang, of course. At least we won't do that to Roy.'

'Guv.' It was Len Haslam, his face streaked in grease, his white shirt spotted with sump oil. He was holding out a thick envelope. 'It was hidden in a spare tyre in the yard.'

Bobby licked his lips like a nervous reptile. The colour had gone from his face. 'Mr Slipper . . .' he croaked.

'Shush.' Slipper knew what was coming next. 'You going to say you never saw it before? That we planted it? But your prints will be on it, Bobby. You know we can get them off the envelope. We can even get them off mailbags, you know. Oh, yes. You bake them in the oven, so Maurice Ray told me. The material goes rock hard and you can lift the dabs off. Ingenious. You look like you want to sit down. Ah, Billy. Fetch Mr Pelham a glass of water, will you?'

Bobby slumped into an armchair. 'I wasn't in on it. I was just looking after that money.'

'I have no doubt lots of people are looking after lots of money as we speak.' The policeman looked down at the contents of the envelope. 'You know we didn't get many serial numbers from that job. But the ones we did get were all one-pound notes, like these. Must be, what, four or five hundred here? Odds are good we'll have a number. Very good.'

It was a lie, but Bobby Pelham wasn't to know that the recorded serial numbers had been scattered at random between the ten-bob, one-pound and five-pound notes.

'These are from the job, aren't they?'

'What if I say yes?'

'Depends how you came by them.'

'Like I said, I wasn't in on it. Honest. I was just . . .'

'Yeah – looking after it. A cush, eh?' A cushion he meant, money for James to fall back on in an emergency. Bobby nodded his agreement, his head heavy, like a lead weight. 'If what you say is true, then it's receiving. A few months inside at most. Perhaps a caution, depending on what's on your docket.' Slipper knew the mechanic had no form.

'Nothing.'

'I can't promise anything, but if I can say you co-operated . . .'

497

Billy came back from the kitchen with a glass of water. He stumbled over a pile of *Autosports* and *Motoring News* left in the middle of the floor. 'Shit. This place could do with a tidy, Bobby.'

Bobby took the glass and gulped half of the water down. 'It's from the train robbery.'

'And it was given to you by Roy James?'

He bit his lower lip before he spoke. 'Yes.'

'And you will make a statement to that effect?' Bobby didn't answer, just stared at the floor in shame. Slipper repeated the question.

'Yes.'

Slipper turned to Billy. 'Get on to the Yard, will you? Tell them we can release Roy James's picture to the press immediately.'

The voice on the line was muffled and urgent. 'Hello? Can I speak to the Train Squad?'

'Who is this?'

'Is that the Train Squad?'

'No, this is the Scotland Yard switchboard.' The operator wrote down a word on the pad. *Irish?* 'I need a name from you, sir.'

'Put me through or I'll hang up. And they'll never know what they are missing.'

The slightest pause, followed by a sigh. 'Very well, hold on, sir.'

There was a delay of ninety seconds before anyone came on. The man sounded bored. 'Detective Sergeant Leonard Haslam.'

'Is that the Train Squad?'

'It is. Who am I speaking to?'

'Black Horse Court, Southwark.'

'What about it?'

'There's a phone box. If you get someone there within ten minutes, yer man might find something of interest.'

'Stay on the line, sir.' A hand went over the mouthpiece. 'Who have we got near Southwark? Phone box at Black Horse Court. Get a car there. Now!' He came back on loud and clear. 'Sir? Hello? Sir? Oh, bugger.'

In the Squad room, Len paced up and down while he waited to hear from the car sent to the phone box. Billy was in charge of noting that morning's calls – there were always at least a dozen – and Len went over the conversation with the anonymous caller while Billy logged it. They were turning into station cats, shiny-arsed coppers who never left the factory, and Len didn't like it. But so much information was coming in it had to be processed and ranked or they would drown.

'Nothing in on Goody?' he asked when they had finished.

'No, for the fifteenth time.' It was strange how each detective seemed to have adopted their own personal *bêtes noires* among the suspects. Len was on Goody's case, of course, while Jack Slipper had been keen to pin something on Ronnie Biggs. Once it transpired that Charmian had blown a wedge of cash in Bond Street and Ronnie's prints had cropped up on a bottle of ketchup and a Pyrex dish at the farm, Biggs was bang to rights. Slipper was in Aylesbury that morning, charging him. Next, Slipper said, he would concentrate on bringing in Roy James.

Millen, though, had a thing for Jimmy White, because they had history going back some years. Frank Williams wanted Buster Edwards because he knew him, had drunk with him over the years, liked him. He thought it would be a friendly gesture to be the one who collared him. Keep it in the family.

Butler had his sights set on Bruce Reynolds, whom he considered the prime mover in the whole affair. The fact that there hadn't been a sniff of him in the past few weeks made him even more of a prize.

There was another character irritating Len. One they still couldn't put at the farm. Even his brother-in-law hadn't given him up. All they had was the anonymous tip-off. 'Can we spin Fortune's drum again?' he asked.

'I'm sure.' Up to a dozen search warrants a day were being issued. The normal caution with such briefs had been thrown to the wind where the robbery was concerned. You only had to mention that the warrant was in connection with Sears Crossing to get your chit signed.

Len bent down and opened a desk drawer. He passed Billy a small plastic phial. Billy went to hold it up to the light but Len grabbed his wrist. 'Keep it down.'

'What is it?'

'Flakes of paint.'

'From what?'

'The lorry at the farm.'

Billy looked at him with uncomprehending eyes.

'Look, I've done enough. Best if I'm not near. It's your turn.'

'For what?'

Len shook his head at Billy's denseness. 'Find some shoes, trousers, whatever, to put them on. Take them to forensics.'

'Len—'

'Fortune was at that farm – you know it and I know it. Whoever the bird was who got Reynolds right also gave us Fortune. Remember?'

'But we have Reynolds's prints. That's watertight. There's none of Fortune's prints at Leatherslade.'

'Gordy never left any prints either. Careful, see?' Len hissed. 'And I reckon most of the prints were left *after* the robbery – when they got money-struck and sloppy. And we are sure Fortune was there before the take, not after. Put the paint in your pocket. Go on – get onto it. Right?'

'DS Haslam, Line Five!'

Len loped over and took the call and came back rubbing his hands together.

'What?' asked Billy.

'Money.'

'In the phone box?'

'Two potato sacks. They've just done a quick count.' Len clapped his hands with glee. 'We've just got about fifty thousand pounds back.'

Gordon Goody was going stir crazy. The small room above the pub on the river near Tower Bridge seemed to shrink by the day. Here he was, rich at last – and with the money well hidden – and he was like some kind of laboratory rat in a shoebox. Now and then he went down to the pub and worked behind the bar, but it was risky. He was a big man, not the kind of character you would forget in a hurry. And he could never stop himself flirting with the girls. Couldn't be helped. Skirts were shorter, tops tighter, eyelashes, for the batting of, longer.

But he couldn't risk a bird up in that room. So far he had been very, very careful. The reason that his smudge wasn't plastered all over the front of the *Daily Sketch* was because they had no dabs at the farm. He had never, ever taken his gloves off. The others had been unlucky. A palm print from where his fabric glove had shrunk got Jim Hussey bang to rights. And Bruce? Mr bloody Sheen himself managed to get dusted. There was something fishy there, Gordy thought. Bruce with his prints on a ketchup bottle? Pretentious sod only ever used Lea & Perrins. Which suggested the Fewtrells and Butlers of this world would stop at nothing to bring them in. The job had proved too big to ignore, too much of a poke in the eye with a blunt cosh.

Bloody Buster and his cosh and that daffy cunt Tiny Dave. If that driver had not been thumped, the hue and cry would be that much less intense. But now they were baying for them.

Gordy looked at his watch. Not yet eleven. The day was crawling by. The pub would open soon and he would hear the noise of the customers through the floor, braying and shouting. He never served at lunchtime. Different crowd, all male, even some lawyers and coppers.

He had to do something though; he would end up topping himself if he had to watch the ceiling cracks for much longer. He reached into the bedside cabinet and found his address book. Locating the number he wanted, Gordy swung his feet off the bed, grabbed a handful of change and padded downstairs to the telephone by the Gents.

While he dialled he shouted to the landlord. 'Reg?'

The ruddy-faced Reg stuck his head out from behind the bar. 'You all right?'

'Can I borrow your car for a couple of days?'

Reg looked unsure.

'There's a nifty in it.'

Reg shrugged. 'Two days.'

Two days, fifty quid. Plus a monkey for the use of the room. Reg wasn't doing too badly. Even got a free barman now and then.

'Thanks,' Gordon said. Then: 'Sue? Is that you? It's me, Gordon. Right. Look, Sue, I know it's short notice, but do

503

you fancy a get-together? Yes, that sort of get-together. At a hotel, on me. The Grand. Sounds perfect. Tomorrow? Well, dump him. You deserve better anyway. Well, me for one. Right. Tomorrow. Book it in your name, will you? And get some champagne on ice. What are we celebrating? Me seeing you again.'

Gordy put the phone down and walked through to Reg, who had unbolted the doors to open for the day's business. There were only a couple of regulars in at that time of day and they didn't even look up from their papers. Gordy's stomach rumbled as he caught the aroma of the homemade pies that the pub dished out at lunchtime. He pulled a couple of pound notes out. 'Reg, can you send your boy to Woolworths? Get me a couple of spectacle frames with plain glass in them.'

Reg took the money. 'OK.'

'And does your missus have any hair-dye?'

Reg had a traditional landlord's build, with sizeable beer belly and a florid complexion. Marjorie was whippet-thin and exuded a blowsy glamour. 'What shade?'

'Not blond.' He pointed at his scalp. 'Darker than this.'

'I'll ask. If she hasn't, I'll tell her to get you some.'

'Thanks.'

'What is it, Gordy?' smirked Reg. 'Fancy dress? Who you going as?'

Gordy smiled back. 'Clark bleedin' Kent.'

*   *   *

Billy Naughton stepped into the rowing boat and the lad from the hire shed pushed them off. Tony dipped the oars and pulled them away, heading out into the centre of the Alexandra Palace boating lake. It was a blustery day, with the sun piercing the cap of white cloud only infrequently. Apart from a couple of schoolboys playing truant to smoke fags, they had no company out on the water. Which was how they both wanted it.

'You know that they kept German civilians here, during the war?' Billy asked.

'No, I didn't, Mr Naughton. Is this to be a history lesson?'

'Recent history, Tony. It was your money, wasn't it?' said Billy.

Tony carried on pulling, settling into a good smooth rhythm. He was enjoying the exertion. 'What was?'

'In the phone box.'

Tony shrugged. 'Don't know.'

'Look, we know you were at the farm. We know you probably got a drink out of it. We know that on the day after we collared Roy's mechanic, someone dumped the money. Panicked, most likely. It's gone toxic.'

Tony laughed at the expression. 'What does that mean?'

'Corrosive. Poisonous. It's like King Midas, except everything it touches turns to shit.' Tony blew out his cheeks, as if accepting this was true. 'Roger Cordrey cops it by flashing too big a roll of money. Charmian Biggs, she spends too much of it and gets herself noticed. The money left in

505

Dorking woods – who was that for? Either way, he or they didn't make it in time, did they? Some guy with his trousers round his ankles found it. Ten-grand reward and a right earful from the wife for going off into the woods in the first place. Bobby Welch. We get a call that he is in a betting shop near London Bridge. Now who would tell us that? Maybe the bloke he left his stash with. Take Bobby out of the game, he can do what he wants with it because Bobby is looking at a fifteen, twenty jolt. Who else? Oh yeah, another Bobby – Bobby Pelham, the mechanic. Done for receiving. And you. I think your man panicked when he heard about Pelham and dumped the cash in the phone booth. What do you reckon?'

Tony had a good view of the ugly palace itself, with the transmitter mast that beamed out the evening BBC news. He began to describe a long, lazy circle around the edge of the lake. 'I reckon I remember you when you were some wet-behind-the-ears tenderfoot. About six months ago, that was. Now here you are lecturing me like you're Tommy Butler.'

Billy ignored that, saying, 'The thing is, you lot don't have much of a choice, do you? You either give your cash to someone who isn't in the life, in which case they are likely to panic. Or you leave it with some villain who, because they are by nature thieving bastards, either takes it all or charges you an extortionate minder's fee. Right Shylocks some of them, so I hear.'

Tony stopped rowing. A duck paddled over, in search of food. It quacked plaintively then moved on. Tony fixed the copper with a hard stare. 'What is this about?'

'I'll tell you another interesting thing. The count written on the wrappers of that stash in the phone box added up to forty-seven thousand pounds. But there weren't forty-seven in notes. Only forty-two. It was five grand light. So whoever dumped it took a little sweetener and skipped. Am I right?'

Tony sighed. He was sure that wasn't the case. Or perhaps it was. Money changed everything. 'Can you blame him? It's a free-for-all.'

So someone had stiffed him, thought Billy. 'Roger, Charlie, Bobby, Ronnie, Tommy, Jim Hussey, Bill Boal—'

'What's this? Some kind of rollcall?'

'All I'm saying is, it's only a matter of time before we get the rest. Bruce, John, Buster, Roy, Jimmy White, Gordy and . . . you.'

Tony began rowing again, pulling deep and hard. Did they have his fingerprints? No. Otherwise he would be in Aylesbury right now, facing Butler, Williams, Fewtrell or Hatherill or at Cannon Row with Slipper or one of the other DIs.

Billy placed a small brown bag, the top rolled over several times, on the seat between them. It looked like someone's packed lunch.

'What's that? A bribe? Doesn't look enough, Mr Naughton.'

'I'm meant to be spinning your place right now. In there are some flakes of yellow paint which, in the course of my perfunctory search, will find its way onto the bottom of a pair of your shoes.'

'Yellow paint?'

'From the garage at Leatherslade.'

Tony stared down at the bag, as if it was radioactive. He nudged it with his foot. 'I don't understand.'

'I'm meant to daub that on the sole of one of your shoes. Tomorrow, under the same warrant, a forensic officer will be sent over. He will discover said paint and take the shoes away for analysis.'

'Why are you telling me this?'

Billy hesitated. He wasn't 100 per cent sure himself. But he wanted to get rid of the temptation to ape Len once and for all. 'I'll just say this. You ever see George Hatherill in a pub, you send him over a drink.'

Gordon Goody parked the borrowed Morris Minor Traveller and checked himself in its mirror. His hair was several shades darker and he now wore tortoiseshell glasses. There was nothing he could do about his height except stoop, but he didn't look like any picture of him they might have circulated. Just because one hadn't appeared in the press didn't mean the police weren't pushing them around to stations throughout the country. Gordy's was one scalp they wanted very, very badly.

Satisfied with his new appearance, he fetched his holdall from the back seat and walked into the Grand Hotel, looking forward to seeing Sue Crosby again. She had been a hostess at Marbles, one of the better London clubs, and then won a Miss Brighton contest and had set up a small clothes shop in her hometown of Leicester. She and Gordy had not seen each other for two years, but they had the kind of relationship that could be picked up – or curtailed – without any recrimination or consequences.

Gordy approached the reception desk and beamed at the young woman behind it. 'Morning.' He couldn't keep the cheeriness from his voice.

'Afternoon, sir.' Well, it was two o'clock he supposed, so technically she was right. The girl had a black beehive with a slight flick at shoulder level and kohl-blackened eyes. She reminded Gordy of Susan Maugham, the singer of 'Bobby's Girl', and if he hadn't been here to see Sue, he might have spent some time on her.

'I believe my wife booked a room. Susan Crosby. I'm Mr Crosby.'

'Let me check, sir. Yes, here we are. Six-oh-two. You are the first to arrive, but I'm afraid it isn't ready as yet.' She pointed to the clock behind her. 'Check-in is at three, but I'll see what I can do to hurry it along. Would you like to take a seat? Or have a drink in the bar?'

Gordy looked at the row of glistening optics he could see through the archway to his left. 'How long?'

'Twenty minutes at most, sir.'

'I'll wait in the bar.'

'Very well, sir.'

As soon as the big man was out of sight, the receptionist burst through the door into the office and began to rummage around on her desk. Peter, the Duty Manager, looked up, perplexed.

'What's wrong?'

'Call the police.'

Peter rose to his feet. 'What's happened, Brenda?'

But Brenda had found the newspaper she was looking for and tore through it. The pictures had long vacated the front page, but often put in an appearance whenever an arrest was made. There, next to a story about Great Train Robbery money being found in a phone box, were the mugshots of the three wanted thieves. The top one stared out at the camera from behind hornrimmed glasses. 'It's him.'

'Who?'

'You won't believe this.' She showed Peter the picture of the bespectacled robber and tried to keep the thrill from her voice, the excitement of having a story she would repeat ad nauseam for the next few days. 'Bruce Reynolds has just checked in!'

Part Three

PROS & CONS

Fifty-four

Bedford Prison, October 1963

Charlie found his prison visits bittersweet. It was wonderful to see Pat, to hear about the kids, but the inevitable moment of separation brought home to him just what might lie ahead: years of being apart from his family. The thought made him angry, but as he stood in the holding pen waiting for his name to be called through to the visitors' room, he tried to contain the fury building in him. There had almost been an incident in the kitchen that morning, a temptation with a pan of boiling water and a sneering screw, but Charlie had just smiled and walked away.

'Fourteen years,' the cunt had whispered in his ear. 'Fourteen on the Forty-Four.'

Special Order 44 was used to stop known associates

gathering and communicating in prison, just in case they got up to their old tricks. Or new ones, such as prison breaks. The screw was suggesting he would get fourteen years and never see his old mates again. As if the latter part worried him.

'Charles Wilson, table seven.' At least, being on remand, he had no number for them to bark out and he was wearing his own clothes. He still felt at least partially human. More so than the institutionalised screws, he thought as he glared at one of those sad bastards who slashed the peak of his hat so it came down partially over the eyes. You aren't in the Guards, mate, he thought. You are just a grown-up babysitter in a shitty gaol.

He passed through the gate and into the depressingly bare visitors' room, where he expected to see John Matthew, his brief. As he recognised who it really was sitting at the other side of the table, Charlie kept his face impassive. He was good at that. Hadn't so much as glanced at Ronnie Biggs when they crossed in the exercise yard.

He sat down and, in a ritual repeated at tables across the room, the two men leaned in close, foreheads almost touching, voices low.

'Fuck me,' said Charlie.

'I registered as Joe Gray.'

'Gordy, what are you doing here?'

'I came to tell you what's going on. I got picked up because some silly bitch thought I was Bruce. How fucking ironic is that? I was blond, then brunette, but underneath, I was a natural dickhead. Butler interviewed me, then I got released. On bail.'

'I heard.'

'Thought you might have thought it . . . you know, iffy.'

Charlie frowned, but said nothing.

'Butler had a pair of my shoes with yellow paint on them, from the garage at the farm. I'm on remand while tests are carried out.'

'No prints?'

'At Leatherslade? Nothing. I was worse than Bruce with the gloves.'

'What about the shoes?'

Gordy leaned in closer, until he could smell Charlie's sour breath. 'I never took them with me to the farm, Charlie. I'm sure of it. Butler's done me up like a kipper. I just wanted you to know I didn't do any kind of deal.'

'You silly cunt.' Charlie's face darkened. He made fists and the knuckles turned white. 'I know you're all right. Jesus, I'm not worried about anyone grassing. Not in our firm. That bleedin' driver of Ronnie's maybe, but not us.' Charlie thought for a minute, considering all he had just heard. His expression relaxed and his fists uncurled. 'You sure this is Butler's style? He might verbal you a bit, like he did me, but planting evidence? Not sure.'

'Doesn't matter if it's Butler or one of the others. That paint ties me to the farm, I'm cooked.'

Charlie didn't disagree.

'How you holding up?'

Charlie rubbed his forehead. 'So far, OK. They're talking about double-digits for it.'

'Come on,' said Gordy. 'It was a tickle. You only get that for murder now.'

Charlie shook his head. 'We didn't think what we was robbing, mate. We thought it was a train, didn't we?'

'It *was* a train.'

'Ah, but it wasn't British Rail. It was the Royal Mail.' He said it again, emphasising the first word. 'The ROYAL Mail. We nobbled the Establishment. The Establishment will want to nobble us back. Even if it does mean painting your shoes yellow.'

'Christ. What are we going to do?'

Charlie came in very close and spoke in a murmur. 'Ronnie and me passed a couple of messages back and forth. We get fourteen years?' His eyes darted right. 'We're goin' over that fuckin' wall.'

Bruce returned to the flat in buoyant mood. It was the first time for weeks he had been out, but the smart moustache he had grown had given him confidence, as if it was a full-face mask. He had risked taking Franny into town, where he treated himself to a new haircut at Trumper's in Curzon Street, as well as a trim for the face furniture, followed by lunch at the Mirabelle, which cost a whopping fourteen pounds.

Afterwards, slightly tipsy on a nice Fleurie, he had called at Coombs & Dobbie in Jermyn Street and ordered a pair of handmade shoes – under an alias, of course. They were twenty-six pounds. It would take two months to complete the order, the master cobbler reckoned. So he told them he would forward an address abroad where they could be sent when they were ready. The afternoon ended with champagne cocktails at the Ritz, reminding him of happier times when they had celebrated the acquittal of Gordy and Charlie.

One day, well over fifty pounds down. But it was worth every penny: he had become used to sending Franny out with an 'escort'. She was a young woman, and needed to get out of doors, so Bruce had arranged a series of 'chaperones'. And anyway, even a hundred quid was nothing compared to what was being leeched off him by 'friends' and 'associates' keeping him in hiding till he and Fran could skip.

So, pleased and still buzzing, he hailed a cab all the way back to the new place at Croydon. As soon as they opened the door, they knew something was wrong. An unfamiliar breeze was blowing through the flat.

'Did you leave a window open, Fran?'

'No.'

'Neither did I.'

The draught was coming from upstairs. Bruce took the steps two at a time, and found the open window in the spare bedroom. As he went to close it, he spotted the ladder that had been propped against the wall outside. He looked around the room with fresh eyes. It had been turned over, cases pushed aside, cupboards opened.

Burgled.

The bloody cheek of it. How fuckin' dare they?

'Coo-ee. Hello.'

Bruce looked out of the window, at the neighbour waving from the garden next door. 'Are you all right?' the woman called. 'I saw it happen.'

'What, love?'

'The thief. I called the police. They should be here any minute.'

You interfering old cow. He bit his tongue. 'Thank you. Very kind of you. I don't think anything has been taken.'

'He was only in there five minutes. You must have disturbed him.'

Just then he heard the doorbell ring.

Shit.

Franny was behind him, wide-eyed with fear. He watched as she took a grip on herself. 'Get into bed, Bruce.'

Unused to taking orders from her, he hesitated. 'What?'

'Get your kit off and get into bed. Leave this to me.'

By the time she reached the bottom of the stairs, Franny had undone her blouse and ruffled her hair. She yanked the front door open to reveal two uniformed constables.

'Sorry to disturb you, miss.' The one who had spoken caught sight of her wedding ring and corrected himself. 'Madam. We had a report of a burglary at this address.'

'Yes, Officer. I mean, no. Someone did come in, but well, we made a bit of a racket and I think he got frightened. Nothing has been taken.'

'Do you mind if we take a look?' asked the older of the two coppers.

'Well . . .' She glanced nervously up the stairs, but snapped her head back when she realised her mistake.

'When you say "we",' asked the other one before she could formulate a decent excuse, 'who exactly do you mean?'

'Your husband?'

Right bloody Tweedledee and Tweedledumb, Franny thought. 'Not exactly.' She took a deep breath. 'Come in, Officers. We have the top two floors.'

They removed their helmets and entered, their boots thumping as they climbed the stairs.

'Second bedroom. Down the corridor at the end.'

Only one of them went into the spare room. The other hovered outside as she came up. He pointed down the corridor. 'What's in there, madam?'

'The master bedroom.'

'Mind if I take a look?'

He was in before she could object and she heard his exclamation of surprise at the sight of a naked man in bed at five in the afternoon.

'Blimey,' said Bruce. 'Is sex with a woman against the law now?'

The policeman laughed. 'Not yet, sir. And you are?'

'He's not my husband,' said Franny, blushing a deep red. 'We were in here when we heard a noise. Thought nothing of it, so we carried on.'

Bruce nodded to confirm her story. 'That's right. Then we heard a crash, I got up, but whoever it was had scarpered.'

The policeman looked puzzled. 'And you came back to bed?'

It was Bruce's turn to look baffled. 'We hadn't finished.'

'Right.' The officer put his helmet down. 'And your husband?'

'Works on the ferries. To the continent.'

'I'll take a name if I may, sir,' the copper said, with all the disapproval he could manage.

'Cassavetes,' Bruce said, blurting out the first name that came into his head. 'John Cassavetes.'

'Cassa-what? Can you spell that?'

Bruce did so.

'Address?'

'Forty-eight Margrove Close, Purley.'

The younger policeman poked his head into the room. Bruce sank further into the bed, feeling very vulnerable in only his underpants. 'You sure nothing was taken?'

'No, Officer,' said Franny. 'It's only junk in there.'

'Very well,' said the copper, closing his book. 'We may send someone round to dust for fingerprints, just in case.'

'Good idea,' said Bruce. 'You can catch a lot of villains with prints, so I hear. Those that make a career out of it, I mean.'

The copper just frowned at him. 'And your name, madam?'

'Frances Craddock.'

'But her friends call her Fanny. Obviously,' said Bruce. 'Do you mind if I get dressed?'

'Of course, sir. You might be hearing from us. We will need your prints too.'

'Oh?'

'Just to eliminate you from any at the scene.'

'Only too happy to oblige,' said Bruce.

When she had shown them out, Franny rushed back upstairs and leaped onto the bed next to Bruce. The pair of them burst out laughing.

'Fanny Craddock?' he asked.

'John Cassavetes??'

'I almost said Stirling Moss.'

'You pushed your luck there. What if he had been a film fan?' She watched as Bruce's smile gradually faded. 'What is it?'

He jumped out of the covers, knelt down and pulled out the attaché case from under the bed. He opened it and looked inside. The money was untouched. It was only what Franny called pin money, about three grand, but still, its loss would have hurt. 'I haven't been out for weeks,' he said bitterly. 'The one time I do, someone turns the place over. Too much of a coincidence, you ask me.' The money was a magnet. Some idiot obviously thought he slept with a hundred and fifty grand under the mattress.

'Does this mean we've got to move again?'

He nodded. 'It does. Especially as they'll be back for dabs, Mrs Craddock.'

'Not for a while, Mr Cassavetes.'

'No, indeed.'

Franny yanked the partially unbuttoned blouse over her head and Bruce slid back under the covers. 'Brilliant bit of acting,' he said, reaching round to undo her bra as she struggled with her skirt's zip. 'I'll tell you what, Mrs Craddock.'

'What's that?'

'Now you're cooking with gas.'

Fifty-five

Frank Williams wasn't sure why Buster had chosen Sidney Dart as his go-between on this one. Sidney was as slippery as an eel in a bucket of snot. An electric eel, at that, because he could always give you a sly shock. He was six-foot two and was so wide he appeared to be made of two men compressed into one. They met at the Royal, a pub on Denmark Hill, neutral ground for both of them. After pleasantries and beer, Sidney got down to it.

'How much would Buster have to deliver? If he was to get consideration for it?'

'All of it,' said Frank as he took the first third of the beer down in one large gulp.

523

Sidney found something to work at in his ear. 'There isn't all of it left.'

'Can you stop that, it's disgusting.' Sidney extracted his finger and examined the end of it, as if expecting to find a gold nugget stuck to the nail. 'I know he'll have expenses, but there's got to be over a hundred left. Unless you are charging him by the hour.'

'I'm just the go-between, Mr Williams. A friend. What Buster is worried about is someone – not you – stitching him up for something he had no part of.'

'Nobody is doing any fitting-up.'

Stanley didn't look convinced. 'That's not what Gordon Goody is saying.'

'Oh, right. Gordon Goody wasn't there, is that what you are trying to tell me? That we have the wrong man?'

Sidney took a slug of his beer and said nothing.

'Spare me the bleating about him. Gordy is overdue and you all know it. Now, what is Buster worried about?'

'The driver.'

'Jack Mills? Buster coshed the driver?'

'No, but he knows who did. Says you haven't got him yet.'

'And he'd give us this man?'

Sidney ripped open the bag of crisps he had bought. 'Oh no. He's no snitch – you know that, Mr Williams. He just doesn't want to have it put on him.'

Which suggested he did have something to do with it, but Frank knew they could sort this out later. 'Get me all the money, at least a hundred and twenty grand, and I give him my word he will be prosecuted according to the evidence.'

Sidney chewed through a handful of crisps. 'He won't take it. He'll flee the country, as you lot like to put it.'

'Christ, they stink.' Frank waved away the blast of cheese and onion that washed over his face. 'Let him be the judge of that, eh? Offer it to him. Buster knows I like him. And I'm not the only one on his tail. Tell him this is a gypsy's whisper from me. Butler is thinking about him. Thinking a lot.'

'OK. I will.' Sidney slapped his palms together to get rid of the crumbs. Normally, at this point, he would slip away. There was something else on his grubby mind.

'You after a few extra bob, Sidney?'

'Well, I've got something.'

Yes, the morals of a fucking sewer rat, Frank thought. 'What is it?'

'Roy James.'

Stay calm, Frank. 'The Weasel?'

'So you lot keep calling him. It was Ferret for a while. Ferret up a drainpipe, you know? But Weasel – never heard him called that.'

'But we are talking about Roy James, the racing driver?'

'Yes.'

'What have you got?'

'He was holed up with a bookie, but he got into a bit of bother.'

'What kind of bother?'

'Wife wanted a bit of comfort while Hubbie was at the dogs. Roy didn't fancy this particular bitch, she caused a fuss, he had to scarper.'

'To?'

'St John's Wood.'

'Address?'

Sidney looked down at his glass. 'That's all I know.'

'St John's Wood? That's the best you can do? What are we meant to do, house-to-house searches?'

'Narrows it down.'

'I'll narrow you down one of these days, Sidney.' Frank shook his head in mock disgust. 'For cryin' out loud.'

'Not worth anything, then?'

'Piss off, no. Get Buster in and the cash and you'll get a finder's fee.'

Sidney looked crestfallen and after a few moments Frank took out his wallet. Under the table he counted out three fives and passed them across.

'I'm going to put that down on my tax return as a charitable donation, right next to Battersea Dogs' Home. Now trot along and speak to Buster. Tell him it's a one-off offer. It's that or he'd better book a place in the sun a long way away.'

Sidney palmed the cash and stood. 'Yes, Mr Williams.'

Frank gave a thin smile and watched him go. Roy James. St John's Wood. Not bad for fifteen quid. Then he shuddered.

As he always did after dealing with the likes of Sidney, Frank Williams felt as if he needed a long, hot bath.

'Inconclusive? What does *that* mean?' Len was virtually shouting into Billy Naughton's face, spraying spittle around the Public Bar of the Phoenix pub. Jack Slipper looked on, impassive.

'It means that they can't say for sure—'

'I know what it means, Billy. I'm not illiterate. But let me get this straight.' He banged his forehead, as if trying to hammer information in. 'The paint on Gordon Goody's shoes puts him at the crime scene. At Leatherslade Farm.'

'Along with some of the khaki from the Land Rover,' added Slipper.

Len looked at Slipper, as if he had forgotten he was even in the room. 'Yes, Skip. But yellow paint on Tony Fortune's shoes is "incon-fucking-clusive". Yet it's exactly the same paint.'

'We don't know that,' said Slipper softly.

Oh yes we do, thought Billy. At least, Len thinks we do.

'Bit of a bloody coincidence, guv,' Len said, 'him having yellow paint on the shoes at all. But not from the farm.'

'Tony Fortune deals in cars. He paints them sometimes. Some people even like yellow cars,' said Billy.

Len glared at him, as if he suspected some treachery on his part. Billy began to sweat under the gaze, and hid behind his drink.

'Ah lads, I was hoping to find you here.' It was Frank Williams, rubbing his hands together. 'Who's buying?'

'My shout,' said Slipper. 'What'll it be?'

'Just a Teacher's,' he replied. 'A double.'

The long-suffering landlord raised his eyebrows in mild protest – it was well past closing time – but he replenished everyone's drinks and they chinked glasses. 'What is it, Frank? You look like you've got feather underpants on.'

'I hear a whisper that you've been asked to concentrate on Buster Edwards. True?'

'Tommy did suggest we might switch to Buster, having drawn a blank on James.' It had been many weeks since the near-miss at Goodwood; there hadn't been a sniff of the driver since. Tommy Butler, newly appointed to the top Squad slot, had decided to shake things up. 'Is that a problem, Frank?'

'See, I have a contact with Buster. A friend of a friend. We've opened lines of communication.'

Slipper looked unfazed. Frank always had the best contacts at gutter level.

'I'd like a free hand to see how that runs. Without Tommy knowing too much.'

'How do we explain that, guv?' asked Len. 'When he's asked us to find him?'

'Because you have a fresh lead on Roy James to concentrate on.'

'But we—' Len began.

'Shush,' snapped Slipper, knowing how Williams operated. 'What have you got for us, Frank?'

'He's in St John's Wood. Before you say anything, I know how big it is. But, last time I looked, it was smaller than London, which is all you have at the moment. And at least you know he hasn't skipped completely. Is that something you can work with?'

Slipper didn't take long to make up his mind. 'I believe it is, Frank. Good luck with Buster.'

'And the tip didn't come from me, right? Anonymous bird phoned it into the Yard.' They all laughed. There had been plenty of those calls.

'That's fine by me.'

Frank Williams downed his drink and left with a spring in his step.

'What's his game?' asked Len after he had left the pub.

'I thought he'd be pissed off about Tommy Butler,' Billy suggested. The recent reorganisation put Butler as the new head of the Squad, with Millen kicked upstairs and Frank Williams stalled at deputy.

Slipper shook his head. 'No. Frank will never get head of Flying Squad. He knows that. Too many toes trodden on over the years.' He didn't offer any further explanation, just turned to them and said, 'So? Any thoughts on St John's Wood?'

The trio frowned into their glasses for a few minutes. Billy spoke first. 'You remember when we were at Bobby Pelham's – Roy's mechanic?'

'Yup,' said Len. 'What about it?'

'All those copies of *Motoring News* and *Autosports* I nearly broke my neck on? There were stacks of them.'

'Go on,' prompted Jack Slipper, leaning his long skinny frame forward, eager to hear the next line.

'Well, Roy is still likely to want to know what's going on in racing, especially as he can't go to any meetings.'

'That's true,' Len agreed. 'So what do we do?'

Jack Slipper spoke for Billy, showing his gap-toothed smile. 'We go around all the newsagents in the area. See if anyone has put in an order for either *Motoring News* or *Autosport* recently.'

Len reached over and pinched Billy's cheek between forefinger and thumb. 'You little beauty,' he said. 'If you were a woman I'd let you suck my cock as a reward for that.'

Before Billy could come up with a smart answer to the remark, Len went over to the jukebox and put on the Chiffons' 'He's So Fine' and began to dance around the empty pub.

'Well done, son,' said Slipper. 'Proper police thinking. You all right? You look tired.'

'So do you.'

Slipper had come out in some ugly boils over the past weeks, scattered across his neck. Some jokers claimed each one represented a train robber still free, but it was the stress and the long days and nights taking their toll. 'Used to it. So's the missus. You don't get much chance of a love-life in the Squad if you don't have one before you begin.'

Billy smiled. He had given up free samples from the Soho girls – he would have anyway, even if the train robbery weren't all-consuming – and there had been a few tentative starts with WPCs, but all those had fizzled out, again because of the train. It was the same with his stable girl, scuppered by the distance involved. The newspapers were telling them that promiscuous sex was bursting out all over, what with Kinsey, *Lady Chatterley*, saucy pop music and the Pill, but not for him, it seemed. At least, not while some of the robbers were free. 'That's me and Cliff Richard, then. Bachelor Boys together.'

'And Tommy Butler,' Slipper reminded him. Detectives with families, like Jack Slipper, sometimes resented Butler's work-all-hours mentality, arguing that because he wasn't married, he didn't understand how difficult it was to keep family life going, particularly with kids, unless you had some time off. 'This business with the yellow paint, Billy. That's all above board, is it?'

'Yes, sir,' he said formally. 'Gordy's right for this one.'

The big man stood up, towering over Billy on his stool. Foam from his beer was stuck to his thin moustache. 'That wasn't what I asked.'

Billy almost crossed his fingers when he replied. Hatherill's example had made him hesitate in fitting up Tony Fortune, but that didn't mean he was going to drop Len in it. 'It's GOFC.' It stood for Good Old-Fashioned Coppering, one of Slipper's favourite phrases.

Slipper wiped the beer froth from his mouth and showed his gappy grin once more. 'In which case, we won't be seeing Gordon Goody for a long, long time.' He pointed to an angry lump on his neck. 'That'll be another of these buggers gone.' And then he swayed off towards the Gents, whistling the tune that had just finished on the jukebox.

'Oi'll give it foive,' Len said, as he came over and draped an arm around Billy, imitating the Brummie tones of Janice Nicholls from *Thank Your Lucky Stars*. Billy wondered if he'd ever get to see that, or any other TV programme, again.

Then Len came close to his ear, his hot beery breath filling it. 'You screwed me up with Tony Fortune, didn't you? *Didn't you?* I know you did. I don't know how and I don't know why.' He stood up. 'Well, no hard feelings, Billy.' Len slapped his cheek lightly with the ends of his fingers, in rhythm with his words. 'Because I am going to make sure that fucker goes down for this, one way or another.'

Tony Fortune stood at the window of his showroom, his left foot tapping out a jittery rhythm, although he had no idea what it was. Some kind of modern jazz, he assumed. Nothing else was quite so jagged. Stravinsky, perhaps.

He normally watched the pavement for punters, the window-shoppers and tyre-kickers who might be enticed in to buy a nice, low-mileage run-around or prestige saloon. Men and women who might be open to flattery

('You'd look great behind the wheel') or bluster ('I had a bloke in here at lunchtime who was interested. He's coming back at four').

Today, he was watching the winter sky darkening and the strange clouds being jostled across it by the unimaginable winds of the upper atmosphere. They had been drawn out into peculiar shapes by the stratospheric forces, one a Zeppelin, its neighbour a graceful dolphin, another a praying mantis, poised to strike.

He was seeing signs and portents everywhere, he realised. Why had that copper given him the yellow paint? Why on earth had he believed his story and applied a substitute – Ford Signal Yellow – to his own shoes? Mischievousness, he supposed. It also stopped them planting anything else, because they had thought they had him with the Hush Puppies.

One thing was for sure, he was right about Paddy. There had been a break-in at the showroom the previous night, the back door jimmied. Nothing was taken except Paddy's precious transistor radio. True, it was the most portable thing in the place and it might have been kids looking for something to sell. But his heart told him it was Paddy, a farewell visit. So, if the coppers were to be believed, the old fella had skimmed five grand for himself before dumping the loot in the phone box. Good on him.

But he had lost a good friend when the old man bolted. And now he had lost Marie, too. When he told her what had happened, she had raged and cursed. Failed car salesman, failed getaway driver, failed robber and now failed husband, apparently. Oh, and failed to give Geoff a part in the tickle, which caused all his problems to begin with. So, failed brother-in-law.

She had taken little, barely formed Alfie off to her mother's, embracing once more the family she had vehemently disowned.

He felt a stab of ice into his heart. He had hardly got to know Alfie, only got used to that strange, warm, milky smell, and he had been snatched away. Well, she would get over it. Women went a bit strange after giving birth, so he had heard. He would go and find them and hold his son again. The alternative was too grim to contemplate.

The next twisted cloud scudded into view. A hooded monk. Ah well, he thought, he could always retreat to a monastery and take a vow of silence. He had precious few people left he could talk to anyway. No wife, no son to coo over, no mechanic to confide in, no dodgy friends who weren't running scared.

In the meantime, there was a lock and clasp to fix on the back door. He tore himself away from the window and turned to go out back to repair the damage.

The entrance to the showroom clanged open and he stopped in his tracks. It was John, the newsagent opposite. 'You had the radio on, Tony?'

'No.'

'They've shot Kennedy. In Dallas.'

'Fuckin' hell. Is he dead?'

'Not sure.'

Ah well, he thought, at least that's one they can't pin on me.

Fifty-six

Scotland Yard, December 1963

'We're pretty sure he's at fourteen, Ryder's Terrace,' announced Billy to Jack Slipper. He placed an *A-Z* on the desk. 'St John's Wood. Would you believe it, the very last newsagent we try. It's a mews, virtually a cul-de-sac, with only an alley leading off from the rear. We can block it off at both ends easily enough.'

Slipper took a look at the map, peering at the dense lines and tiny writing. Billy waited for a commendation, but nothing came. He was used to that with Butler, whose idea of praise was two grunts instead of one, but Slipper normally indulged his detectives.

'OK, Billy. You and Len get some Ordnance Survey maps of the area. Then get down there and poke around.'

'There's only those two exits, guv. A couple of cars each end'll bottle him up.'

Slipper shook his head. 'You've read his docket?'

'Of course.'

'He used to be a first-floor man, didn't he?'

Billy knew what was coming.

'Then if we come knocking at the front door, what is he likely to do?'

'Out through a skylight?'

'If there is one. We should find out. Go and look it over, on the QT, let me know what you find. Take Patricia Waring with you.'

'Why?' Waring was one of the small number of WPCs that the Squad called upon when a woman was the best, or only, option. She had posed as barmaids, toms, landladies and even a fruit-picker living in a caravan in Kent. For the Train Squad she had shared a Derry & Toms changing room with Charmian Biggs to monitor her spending behaviour. They got on so well they had moved on to cocktails at the Roof Garden. Billy had no problem with Waring; she just seemed an unnecessary encumbrance.

'Because a couple sniffing around an area for a house to buy or rent is a lot less suspicious than a lone bloke who looks like he's casing the joint. Think of her as Arm Meat,' he said, using the slang for West End escort girls who didn't go the whole way with clients. Or, at least, claimed not to. 'Spend a day or two on it, come back, and we'll make sure we get the bastard.'

Billy turned to leave, but he sensed Slipper wasn't done and paused. Slipper looked up at him and spoke slowly and softly.

'I just got off the blower with Butler. The DPP has been leaned on from on high. We don't wait until we've got James, Reynolds, Edwards and White, we go with who and what we have. Which means pulling everything together, pronto. All hands to the pumps on evidence prep, which means we let Reynolds and the others slide for now.' Billy could tell this didn't please him. They had almost caught Jimmy White after his missus went on a spending spree in Reigate. They tracked him to a caravan where they found £30,000 hidden in the walls, and White's fingerprints. But no Jimmy. 'Trial will be early next year at Aylesbury. I'm going to claim the call came *after* I sent you after our laddie in St John's Wood. So, Billy, come January, make sure Roy James is in the dock as well, won't you?'

The estate agents on Blenheim Terrace was a holdover from the 1940s, with a heavily wooded front and thick frosted glass designed to keep natural light out of the place. What little managed to enter simply highlighted the volume of dust floating in the air, thrown up whenever a document was inadvertently disturbed. At the rear, under spluttering fluorescent lights, two elderly men were writing in ledgers, and they sent their apprentice forward to deal with the inconvenient interlopers.

The young clerk listened to Billy and WPC Waring as they explained they were looking to move into the area and how much they could afford. Apparently two thousand pounds was not enough to get them anything other than a garage in need of decoration, so they upped it to three and were rewarded with a thin folder of possibilities, mostly one-bedroom flats. One of them, however, was a tiny cottage in Ryder's Terrace. They took the single sheet description and left the gloom of the office before they developed rickets.

Holding the paper before them, they walked around the corner into the mews. WPC Waring slid her arm through Billy's as if snuggling for warmth. It was a cold, bright day, the sky blue and diamond-hard, the sun low enough to hurt the eyes.

'Relax,' she said, as she felt him stiffen when she pulled him closer. 'Newly engaged couple looking for a house for marital bliss. What could be more natural?'

'What's GCH?' he asked.

'Gas Central Heating.'

'Right. T and G?'

'Don't know.'

He glanced down at her. Under an A-line topcoat she was wearing a grey woollen dress, sleeveless, with a cream chiffon blouse underneath. She had on knee-high boots, white tights or stockings, and a small beret on the back of her hair. It was certainly a change from the unflattering uniform and clunky shoes she was forced to wear most days. 'What made you join the Force, Patricia?'

'My dad.'

'Really?' It was hard to imagine any father wanting to put his daughter into the rough and tumble of the all-male, unforgiving world of the Met.

'He was a DS in Brighton for twenty years. Didn't want me to go in, but it's his own fault for telling so many good stories. And yes, he was right, you do get treated either like a dyke or a whore. It's Patti, by the way.'

'What?'

'My name. Patricia in uniform, Patti at all other times, William.'

'Billy.'

She rolled her eyes. 'I know. I was teasing. Shouldn't detectives be a bit quicker on the uptake?'

They had reached Ryder's Terrace and looked along the row of houses. There were two rows of cottages. Number 14 was on their left, on the plainer side of the street, flat-fronted and painted white. The ones opposite had fancier doorways and bowed windows.

The apparently happy couple stopped outside number 18, which contained the flat for sale, and looked up at it.

'Windows need painting,' he said. 'And look at that guttering.'

'Billy.'

He turned to look at her and she pushed onto her tiptoes

and planted a kiss on his lips. 'Try and look pleased,' she whispered. 'Someone's just come out of number fourteen.'

He gave a smile.

'You look like you've got constipation. Show me the property details.'

He was aware of someone passing behind them as he looked from page to house, reading out some of the features.

'He's gone,' Patti said.

'Was it him?' Billy asked, stepping back from her and looking down the passage that led back to Blenheim Terrace.

'Right height. Beard, though. And hat. Hard to be sure. Sorry about the kiss.'

'All in the line of duty.'

'Well, I'd wipe off the lippie before you get back, for both our sakes.'

Billy took out his handkerchief and dabbed away the pink lipstick from the corner of his mouth. 'Nice shade.'

'Pale Fire,' she said. 'Come on, let's take a look.'

They strolled past number 14. It was a two-storey house, with large windows on the first floor, protected by railings, like a small, impractical balcony. Two doorbells showed it was also split into flats, although judging by the exterior dimension they must be exceedingly compact.

'The bottom one says Mrs King,' said Patti, squinting. 'I doubt if he's gone that far to disguise himself.'

'What good eyes you have,' Billy said, unable to read the names for himself. 'Let's take a stroll around the back.'

541

They walked the neighbouring streets, alert for a likely escape route. Number 14 butted against the walled yards of Blenheim Terrace. Jumping into one of those would trap you. One end of the row meant a drop into the access alley directly onto the pavement. You'd break a leg or ankle. At the western end of the cottages, the terrace gave onto rough waste, its ground level higher than that of the street. The distance from the roof to earth was still daunting.

'He'd need a parachute,' said Billy, turning away.

'Hold on.'

Patti picked her way gingerly across the rubble and broken glass, careful not to snap her spike heels. She hesitated at the foot of the wall and crouched down.

'What is it?'

She stood up and retraced her steps just as carefully. Then held up a hand blackened with dark soil. 'An allotment, apparently.'

'DC Naughton. A word.'

It was George Hatherill, looking terribly drawn, his usually immaculate tie askew. Billy guessed the Train Squad weren't the only ones working all the hours God and the devil sent.

'Sir.'

'In here.' He shuffled Billy into an unused interview room. 'You've heard, I suppose? About the DPP?'

'Yes. Trial to go ahead.'

Hatherill took out a cigarette and offered Billy one.

They lit up. 'Well, the PM, Home Secretary and Postmaster General all had a hand in it. I want to know whether things are watertight this end.'

'Sir?'

'You know what I mean. Has anyone been unduly enthusiastic? I don't want any nasty surprises in court.'

Billy thought about Gordon Goody and the paint. Len had certainly been 'enthusiastic', but he wasn't going to reveal that to Hatherill, just as he hadn't to Slipper. 'Not that I know of, sir.'

'Because these blokes have the cash to hire some of the best briefs in town. Speed, Finch and Salmon, among others. One of them has that bastard Miles Cokely who would get Hitler off if the money was right.'

'There's one thing worrying me, sir.'

Hatherill smoked furiously. 'What's that – Frank Williams?'

'No. We've got the robbers at the farm, right?'

'Yes. Conclusively.'

Billy didn't think so. 'Many of the prints are on items that could be moved. Monopoly, for instance.'

'I am aware of that. They'll claim they played elsewhere. We'll be prepared for it.'

'And we have nothing at all to place anyone at the robbery. Nobody at Bridego Bridge or Sears Crossing. Not a single print, fibre or hair. Everything depends on that farm and the jury believing that if you were at the farm you were part of the team.'

Hatherill dismissed that with a wave of his Senior Service. 'Well, it's common sense.'

'Will that bastard Cokely think so? Or will he sow some seeds of doubt? You might have been at the farm, you might even have money, but does that mean you were at the train? He could go for accessory after the fact or receiving.'

'That's true,' the Commander conceded. 'But we've got Arthur James and Neil MacDermot for the prosecution. They are no pushovers. Receiving might do for some of them, but the main blaggers I want done for conspiracy to rob the mail and armed robbery. Which brings me back to my main point. I know time is running out, but I don't want to see anyone in the dock who will embarrass us. Is that clear? If you have any doubts about how anyone is proceeding, the veracity of the evidence, dates, times, forensics, anything at all, then come straight to me. Not Slipper or Butler or Williams. *Me*. You understand?

Oh yes, sir. You want your Last Big Case to go off without a hitch. And you want me as you own little snout.

'Perfectly.'

'Good.' He clapped him on the shoulder and left, puffing smoke behind him like a corpulent steam engine.

Billy stubbed out his own cigarette and followed, his feet dragging a little more than when he entered the room.

Roy James heard the doorbell downstairs ring and froze. He wasn't expecting anyone. Nobody came round at night and he never went out. Who would come calling? The only people who knew where he was were his mum, who didn't do visits in the dead of winter, and Dennis, a friend who had the rest of his train money well hidden. Before that he had entrusted it to an 'associate' of Charlie's and the Richardsons, but that bastard had started to spend it. When he'd tried to get it back he had been forced to drop the names of some of Charlie's even heavier friends who might assist in its recovery. Using mallets and nails. He'd got the lump back, minus seven grand 'expenses and minder's fee'.

Dennis, though, wasn't a gangster, and Roy was confident he wouldn't take advantage. He was equally certain that Dennis wouldn't come round unannounced, ringing his doorbell.

Roy was aware that whoever was at the door would know somebody was in the flat. He was playing Ray Charles loud enough to be heard outside and the lights were on in the first-floor living room and hallway.

From the bedroom he heard the tinkle of breaking glass and leaped to his feet. His 'cush' was stashed in the low cupboard next to the mantelpiece. He yanked the door open, grabbed the BEA vinyl bag and ran into the hallway. There was a key in the lock of the bedroom, which he turned, buying himself a few seconds. In a well-practised move, he then climbed onto the stair banister and pushed open the fanlight.

He tossed the bag onto the roof and hauled himself

through. Below him came the sound of hammering and splintering as the bedroom door was shattered.

It was bitterly cold outside and he shivered as, jacketless, he clambered onto the low-pitched roof. The stars were out, with but a sliver of a moon, but even in that light he could see the roof was sparkling with frost. It was going to be slippy, getting over the tiles.

He picked up the bag and crept forward, bent almost double, walking like Max Wall, his feet slithering and the slates splitting underfoot with a series of loud cracks, until he reached the end of the terrace. Below him, he could hear raised voices in the street. Police and neighbours, bellowing at each other.

Roy peeked over into the blackness, a void not penetrated either by the feeble starlight or the distant street-lamps. He had to visualise the landing pad he had prepared – a six-inch deep strip of soft, yielding soil amid the broken bottles and scrap metal. He dropped the bag over, wincing as it thudded to earth. It was quite some drop.

Counting to three, Roy followed it, launching himself into space, his legs slightly bent, ready to absorb the impact, cold air streaking past him, flapping his shirt. His feet sank into the soft soil and he pitched forward, landing heavily on one shoulder and partially winding himself. He took a couple of deep breaths, waiting for the pain to subside, then sprang up. He swept to the left where he was sure the bag had fallen.

Nothing.

He moved to the right, hands scything low over the soil, until something sharp caught one of his fingers. 'Shit.' He sucked it and tasted coppery blood.

'Looking for this, Roy?'

The torch beam snapped on, illuminating a woman holding his BEA shoulder bag.

'That? That's not mine,' he said quickly, standing upright. 'Never seen it before.'

'Oh, Roy,' said Billy Naughton, his voice full of regret at such a feeble lie. 'The prints placed you at the farm – what do you think these will do?' The cylinder of light turned on him and Roy held up his arm to shield his eyes from the glare. As he did so, someone grabbed his wrist and snapped a handcuff bracelet round it.

'Four months since you gave us the slip at Goodwood,' said Duke Haslam, as he squeezed the second steel circle shut on the left wrist and gave him a poke in the kidneys for good measure. 'Hope you enjoyed it. It's the last bit of freedom you'll have for a while.'

Billy looked over at a beaming Patti Waring. He hoped she got credit for working out that the bit of urban 'gardening' on the bombsite was, in fact, a soft landing pad for a quick, daring escape, dug by the wily racing driver. She probably wouldn't, though. Both Butler and Slipper were at the front of 14 Ryder's Terrace and one or both would doubtless scoop all the kudos.

As Len Haslam led a disconsolate Roy James around to one of the waiting Squad cars, Billy took the bag from Patti and tucked it under his arm. She deserved a drink if nothing else.

'And then there were twelve,' he said, having added up who was behind bars now.

'Best go for the round number then,' shouted Len over his shoulder. 'A nice fat baker's dozen.'

For the moment, Billy didn't appreciate what he meant. But he would soon enough.

Fifty-seven

Scotland Yard, December 1963

In the small room put aside for them, the two Bank of England officials examined the contents of Roy's holdall while Frank Williams and a bleary-eyed but happy Billy Naughton watched. After depositing Roy James and the money at Cannon Row, he and Patti had gone out for that drink, which became seven or eight. He had avoided the Dive Bar and the Phoenix, instead using one off Charlotte Street she knew. It had been a better-than-pleasant evening, and had ended with a kiss that was the genuine article, rather than a means of distraction. Or, at least, he hoped so.

The Senior Clerk examined the piles of cash before him and said, with evident satisfaction, 'Twelve thousand, five hundred pounds exactly.'

'What are those?' asked Billy, pointing at the smallest pile.

'These have serial numbers that match the money on the train.'

'*Yesss*,' hissed Frank, punching the air. 'Got the weaselly bastard. If that doesn't give Tommy a hard-on, his dick has died and gone to heaven.' He caught the expression on the bankers' faces. 'Sorry, gents.'

'And there is this. At the bottom of the bag.' The clerk's cotton-gloved hands smoothed out a piece of paper. It was a list of figures.

£22,400–£5
£15,000–£1
£18,200– £1
£14,000– £5
£10,000– ?
£5,000–10s
FRA– £1,000
Flat – £2,000
Car – £1,000
£12,500 – Dennis
£1,500 – Brab

The Senior Clerk watched the policemen's lips moving as they performed the mental arithmetic. 'In case you are wondering,' he said, 'it comes to one hundred and nine thousand and five hundred pounds.'

'It must be his share,' said Billy. 'Although it doesn't seem enough.'

Frank snorted. 'It'd do me. Maybe minus some expenses or drinks. Bobby Pelham's lot isn't there, is it?' He read it one more time. 'What's a Brab?'

'Brabham,' said Billy. 'Might be a new engine or something. You can't buy a Brabham car for that.'

'And Dennis?'

Billy thought, sifting through the dozens, no, scores of names which had been linked to the robbery. 'Can't recall a Dennis ever coming up.'

'FRA?'

'Nope. Franny? Bruce Reynolds's wife?'

'Unlikely. A Frank somebody, perhaps. I'm sure Tommy will get to the bottom of it when he questions the lad. Well, we'll bag the list and get it to Aylesbury for him. Yet another exhibit. Must be like the bloody V and A in their evidence room.'

There were already more than a thousand items that could be used as evidence, and the witness list – which included virtually anyone who had come across the accused – had passed two hundred. It was going to be a very big number indeed.

'Thank you, gentlemen,' he said. 'We'll take it from here.'

'You have to sign our count,' replied the Senior Clerk, pushing a document over to Frank.

The detective fished a pen from his jacket pocket and scrawled his name on the three sheets. 'I'm certain we'll be seeing you again.'

'Yes,' drawled the Senior Clerk, picking up his briefcase and hat. 'Just another two million or so to locate, I believe.'

'Piss off,' muttered Frank under his breath as they closed the door behind them.

'Where's Len, by the way?' he asked Williams. Duke rarely missed a chance to be at the finale of any collar, and they also had their notes for the previous evening to write up, in case they were called into the box to refute James's claim that he had never seen the BEA bag before.

Frank was busy wriggling his fingers into a set of the white gloves with which he would handle the compromising evidence. 'Len? He's got that warrant.'

It was the first Billy had heard about it. 'What warrant?'

'To turn over Tony Fortune.'

Billy swore softly. 'Home or showroom?'

'I don't know. Be in the Duty Book.'

Billy was out the door before he had finished. Frank's voice echoed down the linoleumed corridor as Billy skidded along it.

'Oi! I need a hand here. Where are you going?'

But Billy's mind was too occupied to even register the question. *A baker's dozen*, he had said. Len Haslam was going to take Tony Fortune down.

Buster Edwards risked going up top from the airless cabin he had been assigned on the stubby little freighter, but he took his case of money on deck with him. He positioned it between his feet and leaned on the rail. The ship was old, it stank of diesel and greasy food. His cabin was close to the engines, noisy and hot. He could have had one on the *Canberra* for the price he was paying for this crossing. And there would be food then. He was starving; all he had eaten while hiding in the cargo area in the shadow of the Custom House had been one cheese sandwich.

He let the chill breeze clear his airways, enjoying even the scent of the molasses factory by the Blackwall Tunnel which it carried. It reminded him of a brewery, rich and hoppy. The wind whipped at his hair and he leaned forward and looked down at the dirty old river churning beneath the hull.

The freighter steamed away from St Katharine's Docks, vibrating its way downriver, passing the first saw-toothed outline of the still-derelict warehouses of Wapping. Buster watched Tower Bridge shrink and then disappear as the ship rounded a bend in the river. Would he ever look upon that bridge, or any other Thames crossing, again?

He had seriously considered giving himself up, but such was the frenzy about the Train, he was certain they would get double-digit sentences. He trusted Frank Williams, as much as he trusted any copper, but there was only so much the man could deliver on any promise. So, there had been no real choice. Buster could wait for them to come and get him or he could leave.

It had meant abandoning June, which pained him, but

she would be all right. She had instructions to go to Williams once he was clear and tell him he had gone and to leave her alone. He was sure Frank would. None of the Squad cared much for prosecuting wives.

He had also left Bruce in London, still planning the details of his own escape and waiting for his fake documents. Buster was bound for Antwerp and then Germany.

'Mr Miller.' It was the captain, a hawk-faced Dutchman with a scraggly blond beard, standing behind him. 'You should go below. Stay out of sight. I'll call you for meals.'

'In a second. Just saying goodbye.'

'Don't be long. The crew get curious about passengers who carry their cases with them everywhere. If you understand me.'

Buster looked down at the cash between his feet. 'Thanks. Yeah.'

Mr Miller. He had to remember that he was no longer Buster Edwards, he was Jack Miller. Different name, then different face – Brian Field had friends of friends in Germany who could arrange plastic surgery. Then he would send for June and they would settle somewhere in the world, far away from Butler and Co. Mexico, Bruce had said he fancied. Mexico sounded pretty good, Buster thought. And then a little voice in his head said, *But not as good as London*.

The weather was changing; the wind strengthened, moving from chilly to biting, and the sky darkened ominously, but Buster waited until they were level with Greenwich, and he

SIGNAL RED

admired the lines of the *Cutty Sark* and the beauty of Sir Christopher Wren's Naval College one last time, before he went below to his temporary prison, feeling dark clouds of his own gathering.

Tony Fortune was under a TR4, fitting a new clutch without the benefit of an aligning tool – Paddy seeming to have either hidden it or taken it – when he became aware of someone standing next to the car.

'Be with you in a mo'.'

'Take your time, Tony. No rush. We put the Closed sign up for you.'

Tony pushed himself out from beneath the chassis using the wheeled trolley underneath him. He was looking up at a grinning Len Haslam. He could hear car doors being opened and shut, out in the showroom. 'What's this?'

Len flipped open a piece of paper. 'I have here a search warrant to execute.'

Tony jumped to his feet, wiping his hands on his overalls. 'For what, exactly?'

'We have reason to believe that proceeds from the Sears Crossing Train Robbery—'

Tony grabbed a rag from the bench and wiped the last of the grease from his fingers as he walked to the front of his premises. Three uniformed police officers were examining each car in turn.

'They won't find anything.'

Len folded his arms, the smirk still on his face. 'Let's see.'

He watched as the three coppers gave the little Goggomobil bubble car the once over and came up clean. Len's smile began to fade. 'Do it again.'

After ten more minutes, the copper shook his head. 'Shall we rip out the seats and panels?'

'You could,' said Tony. 'Then you'd have to pay me for the damage. There's nothing to find.'

Len took a deep breath. His skin had turned mottled, aflame with patches of red. 'Well, Mr Fortune.'

'Well, Mr Haslam.'

'Come on, lads. We'll be back.'

As he walked by the tiny German car he gave it a hefty kick, and the door dented. 'Built of tinfoil, these things,' he muttered.

A breathless Billy Naughton was waiting for him outside. Len sent the uniforms back to the cars and turned to Billy, a scowl where the smile had been minutes before. 'You fuckin' little pissbag of a shit cunt.'

'No luck, Len?'

'What did you do?'

'I asked Tony if he had had a break-in recently. He said he had. Nothing taken but a radio. No log books or MOTs or other stuff a real criminal might take. What was it you planted? A skim from the phone-box money? Because that didn't quite add up, did it? When the bankers counted it, it was light a few grand.'

'I tell you, Goody-two-shoes, Hatherill won't save you this time. When Tommy Butler hears what you did—'

'What, stopped you fabricating evidence? I should have shopped you for Goody.'

'What's stoppin' you?'

Billy shrugged. 'It's not the way it should be.'

The punch surprised him, a sharp uppercut that clashed his teeth together and sent him bouncing off the showroom window. He slithered down to a crouching position, waiting for the stars he was seeing to fade. A powerful kick to the ribs finished him off, and through sparking tunnel vision, he watched Duke stride off, still muttering obscenities.

He must have blacked out, because the next thing he knew Tony was feeding him sweet tea and he was sitting in the workshop.

'You all right?'

Billy touched his jaw and winced. When he spoke, his tongue felt too big for his mouth, as if he'd traded places with an ox. 'Think I need a dentist.'

'And a new opo.'

'That, too. Where's the money?'

'Safe, well away from here. You'll want it back, I assume.'

Billy shook his head, then regretted it. 'Right now, I can't explain where it came from. It hasn't been missed. It might be more trouble than it's worth. How much was there?'

Tony sipped his own tea. 'I didn't stop to count it. You called to say the cossers were coming with a warrant and that

557

you suspected something incriminating had been planted. I was lucky it was in the second car I searched. The Goggomobil. Under the wheel arch.'

Billy looked around at the workshop, the faded calendars on the wall, the half-empty tins of oil, the mounds of spare or discarded parts. 'You got anything keeping you here?'

'London? No. Just the stock out there.'

'Will the train money cover it?'

'A good part.'

'Shut the place up then. Go and lie low till the scream dies down.'

Tony's eyes narrowed, his voice full of suspicion. 'Why would you do that? Let me walk away – again?'

'Did you do the train, Tony?'

'No,' he was able to answer truthfully.

'I thought not. But they aren't going to care about details. They're building a bloody great steamroller and everyone in its path is going to get flattened.'

'I would've though,' the other man said softly. 'I bloody would have.'

'And where would you be now?'

Tony ran a hand through his hair. 'Is that your crime-doesn't-pay-speech?'

'Perhaps. The closest to one you're going to get, anyway.'

Tony stood and went over to the pegboard where the keys for the cars dangled from hooks. He picked off a set and tossed them to Billy. 'If you were a certain kind of copper,

I would recommend the Ace. Best motor in the shop. I straightened the chassis. It'll need bushes on the back axle within six months, is all. Log book is in the desk drawer. Signal Red, very eye-catching.'

Billy stared at the ignition key in his hand, imagining driving down through country lanes, to a pub in Kent perhaps, with Patti at his side. And he wondered how he would explain to Patti – or Hatherill, for that matter – how he came by such a racy machine. 'If I was that kind of copper I'd take it.' He sighed and threw the keys back to Tony.

Tony snatched them from the air. 'And you're not?'

'Apparently,' Billy said, as if he were baffled himself.

'I don't understand.'

'No. I expect you don't. Thanks for the offer of the car anyway. I'd best get back.'

'You said something about a steamroller. What do you think they'll do? To the ones they've caught?'

Billy finished the tea and placed the mug on the bench. 'The Train Robbers? They'll throw the book at them.'

Fifty-eight

From The Times, *17 April 1964*

GREAT PUNISHMENT FOR TRAIN ROBBERS

OBVIOUS MOTIVE OF GREED

SEVEN SENTENCED TO 30 YEARS' IMPRISONMENT

The heaviest series of sentences in modern British criminal history were imposed at Aylesbury, Buckinghamshire, yesterday on the 12 men guilty of being involved in last August's £2,600,000 mail train robbery. The effective total amounts to 307 years. Seven of the accused were each sentenced to 30 years' imprisonment. Earlier in the trial one of the defendants, John Daly, was found to have 'no case to answer', despite his fingerprints being found on a Monopoly board at the gang's hideout. Daly claimed to have played with his brother-in-law, Bruce Reynolds, still wanted in connection with the crime, some weeks before the robbery.

Passing sentence, the Judge, Mr Justice Edmund-Davies, said it would be positively evil if leniency were exercised. A great crime called for great punishment, not for mere retribution but to show others that crime did not pay – that the game was not worth even the most alluring candle.

FIRST AND LAST

As well as the seven who received sentences of 30 years, two more men were sent to prison for 25 years, one for 24, another for 20 and the twelfth man received 3 years.

Passing judgement on the twelve men, the Judge said that the crime, in its enormity, was the first of its kind in this country. 'I propose to do all within my power to ensure it will also be the last of its kind.

'Your outrageous conduct constitutes an intolerable menace to the well-being of society. Let us clear out of the way any romantic notion. This is nothing less than a sordid crime of violence, which was inspired by vast greed.

'The motive of greed is obvious. As to violence, anybody who has seen that nerve-shattered engine driver can have no doubt of the terrifying effect on law-abiding citizens of a concerted assault by armed robbers.'

All with the exception of Wheater (see table below) were found Guilty of conspiring together with other persons not in custody to stop the mail train with intent to rob the mail. All with the exception of Wheater, Cordrey and the two Fields (who are not related) were found Guilty of being armed with offensive weapons, robbing Frank Dewhurst, Post Office official on the train, of 120 mail bags.

Cordrey pleaded Guilty to three charges of receiving £78,983, £56,047 and £5,901.

Wheater and the two Fields were found Guilty of conspiring together to conceal the identity of the person who agreed to purchase Leatherslade Farm by making false statements to police officers, and thereby obstructing the course of justice.

In a separate trial, which ended on Wednesday, Ronald Arthur Biggs was found Guilty of conspiring to stop the train to rob it, and also of taking part in the armed robbery. Like the majority of the defendants, he had pleaded Not Guilty.

Police still wish to interview Bruce Reynolds, Ronald Edwards and James White in connection with the robbery.

THE MEN AND THE SENTENCES

The men sentenced to 30 years were:

Ronald Arthur Biggs, aged 34, carpenter, of Alpine Road, Redhill, Surrey;

Douglas Gordon Goody, aged 34, hairdresser, of Commondale, Putney, S.W.;

Charles Frederick Wilson, aged 31, market trader, of Crescent Lane, Clapham, S.W.;

Thomas William Wisbey, aged 33, bookmaker, of Ayton House, Camberwell, S.E.;

Robert Welch, aged 34, club proprietor, of Benyon Rd, Islington, N.;

James Hussey, aged 34, painter, of Eridge House, Dog Kennel Hill, East Dulwich, S.E.;

Roy John James, aged 28, racing motorist and silversmith, of Nell Gwynn House, Sloane Avenue, S.W.

The other sentences were:

William Boal, aged 50, engineer, of Burnthwaite Road, Fulham, S.W. – 24 years
Roger John Cordrey, aged 42, florist, of Hurst Road, East Molesey, Surrey – 20 years
Brian Arthur Field, aged 29, solicitor's managing clerk, of Kabri, Bridge Road, Whitchurch Hill, Oxfordshire – 25 years
Leonard Denis Field, aged 31, merchant seaman, of Green Lanes, Haringay, N. – 25 years
John Denby Wheater, aged 41, solicitor, of Otways Lane, Ashtead, Surrey – three years

Fifty-nine

Surrey, May 1992

Our feet crunched on the gravel as we opened the gate and I started my second journey up the drive to the house. Above us the moon was sagging in the sky, as if tired of the effort of staying aloft. I knew how it felt.

'How is he?' Bill Naughton asked, huffing slightly, his cheeks glowing from the cold night air.

'Roy? Up and down.'

'Personally, I don't think he was ever the same once he came out. I think that thirty-year jolt disturbed the balance of his mind,' Naughton said. 'Roy's, I mean. Even though none of them served the full whack, it must've been a psychological blow.'

'Devastating.' I remembered the outrage at the sentences

– including my own numb sense of shock, especially as I could so nearly have been in that dock – and the instinctive, widespread feeling that they were disproportionate to the crime, the coshed driver notwithstanding. The Judge had intended to show the public that the country wouldn't tolerate such banditry, that there was no room for Robin Hoods. But it had the opposite effect to the one intended: it created a wave of sympathy for the robbers that a ten- or fifteen-year term would not have generated. The thirty years made them martyrs.

The Establishment, of course, must have felt besieged from all sides at that point in history, and the hefty sentences were part of it blindly lashing out at changes it couldn't understand. The *ancien régime* didn't know it, but the full force of the 1960s was about to burst over them. The robbery must have seemed just yet another worrying signifier – along with Peter Cook and the contraceptive Pill, Mick Jagger and miniskirts, Marlon Brando and Lenny Bruce – of a descent into anarchy. Baffled, out-of-touch authorities would make similar mistakes a few years later and over-react by busting the Rolling Stones and prosecuting gormless hippy magazines.

'Of course,' Bill continued, 'those with wives or girlfriends who stood by them managed the best. Roy never had that.'

'You ever get married, Mr Naughton?' I asked as we walked nearer the entrance.

'Yes. To a WPC. Patti. She passed away last year.'

'Sorry to hear that.'

'Yeah. Good while it lasted, though. Very good. What about you? Your missus ever come back?'

We reached the front door of Roy's house, which I had left open. 'Only us. Don't shoot!' I shouted, only half-joking, then turned back to the copper who had once saved my bacon. 'No. She was disgusted that I couldn't even manage thieving properly. Divorced me. I've got a son out there somewhere who I last saw when he was just a couple of months old. Alfie.'

'Must hurt.'

It was a lot worse than that, but the pain had numbed over the years. It was a wicked thing to do though, to keep me away from my boy. I sometimes felt I'd been punished worse than the train robbers for not doing the crime. I had heard that Marie had recently moved to Dubai or some other Godforsaken sandbox.

'Yeah, but I remarried,' I sighed. 'Did a Bruce and Roy. Chose a younger woman.'

Naughton dropped his voice as we neared the kitchen. 'Bruce struck lucky with Franny, but I hope you made a better job of it than Roy.'

I thought of Jane, still in bed at that hour, curled up, the echo of her perfume still on my skin. 'I did, I think.'

Bill walked ahead of me into the kitchen and sniffed the air. 'Ah, still a menace to society I see, gentlemen. Should I call the Drugs Squad?'

'Not unless we need fresh supplies. Those bastards are

the biggest dealers in London. You want some first?' Bruce asked, holding out the joint. He had moved to sit next to Roy, at the opposite side of the table from where I was standing with Bill Naughton.

Bill shook his head. 'No, not for me. I'll have a drop of whisky, though.'

I poured him one and handed it over. His eyes went to the gun on the table, still lying in front of Roy. 'Cheers.'

'Bruce here wanted the griff on who grassed them up, Bill,' I said.

'Well, as you know, lads, I never did get to see it through to the end. I was taken off the Flying Squad well before the trial and moved to CID Uxbridge. Didn't get back on the Sweeney for another – oh, twelve years.'

'They shift you because you was too clean?' Bruce asked. 'Because you wouldn't bundle us up like the others?'

Bill sighed. 'Not that old tune, Bruce. You were done fair and square.'

'I was.' Bruce had been caught in Torquay, down on his luck and with the remaining money dwindling fast, after five years on the run following spells in the South of France and Mexico. Rumour had it he simply shrugged when Tommy Butler had turned up at the door, as if he had been expecting him, almost relieved it was over. He had just three grand to give back. He received twenty-five years.

'But Bill Boal was just a mug who helped Roger out after the event and he died in prison, the poor sod. And Charlie never said anything about "poppy" when arrested. Butler made that up.'

'I can't say,' said Bill, as if reluctant to speak ill of the Squad that had disowned him. I wondered if they had done so because he would have no part in fitting me up. 'It's Butler's word against Wilson's.'

Charlie Wilson always maintained that the line he was meant to have spoken to Butler, 'I don't see how you can make it stick without the poppy and you won't find that' – the 'poppy red' (bread) being a convoluted rhyming slang for money – was a total fabrication. Maybe. I, for one, had never heard any of them use that particular phrase. But Butler didn't need to make anything up; he had prints at the farm.

'OK.' Bruce wagged a finger at the policeman. 'And you lot fitted up Gordy, good and proper.'

'He was there, Bruce,' Bill said. 'Gordy was at it, you all were. It was all part of the game back then.'

'Not for you,' I reminded him.

His face drooped a little. Did he regret once being quite so right and proper? 'I was out of step.'

'What happened to your mate? Haslam, was it?' I asked, knowing full well it was.

'Len? Went in one of the anti-corruption purges in the early seventies. Jumped before he was pushed. Frank Williams was head of security for Qantas by then. Gave him a job, I believe.'

'All right for some,' muttered Bruce.

The robbers had not fared well. Most were broke or dead, like Charlie, who escaped, was recaptured by Butler, served his time, then ended up in the drugs trade that killed him. Ronnie escaped from Wandsworth and was still at large in Rio, despite Jack Slipper's various attempts over the years to get him back. But everyone knew that what Ronnie craved most of all was a pint in Redhill, not cocktails on the Copacabana. He was not so much a fugitive as an exile, banished from his beloved homeland.

Roy spoke up for the first time. 'So – was there a grass?'

My heart began to beat a little faster. Geoff's role in this – and Marie's – had never come to light. It wasn't my fault, not really, although I had stupidly broken the rule about keeping the wives in the dark. Between them, Geoff and my missus had helped put Butler onto Bruce.

'Ah, that'd be telling. Was there a Mr Big?' Bill asked mockingly.

Bruce laughed. 'Now who is playing an old tune?' Bruce maintained he had never denied the Mr Big concept simply because it helpfully diminished his own role in things. He had hoped for a lighter sentence or earlier release if they thought he was a mere lieutenant. It might have helped, too; he only served nine of his twenty-five. Or perhaps attitudes had changed by the time he came to do his time. 'You can tell me now, Bill. If there was a snitch, it's not like I am in a position to do anything about it.'

Naughton sighed. 'You know we had anonymous calls. About you.'

Bruce's head snapped round and he glared at him. 'Who from?'

'Anonymous people. By definition we don't know who they are. One of them mentioned you, Bruce. And you, Tony. That's why we were so sure you'd had something to do with setting it up.'

Me? This was the first I had heard about that. Who could or would finger me?

But really, I knew immediately. Janie Riley. Beautiful, sexy, unstable Janie Riley.

Bill saw certainty forming on my face and moved quickly on. 'But we were already onto both of you. There was no big grass in the firm, Bruce, there didn't need to be. Just a lot of little mistakes on your part. I don't believe there was a Mr Big, either. Only some bloke on the inside we never caught. Eh, Bruce?'

Bruce remained impassive, brooding on it all. I hoped he didn't come up with Janie as the snitch. Not after all this time.

Then he surprised us all by saying, apparently à propos of nothing: 'You know Janie Riley topped herself? Pills. Well, pills and a bottle of vodka. It happened while Jack and I were in Mexico. Buster, I mean. He was Jack in Mexico. Shame.'

Nobody spoke until Roy put his head in his hands. 'What jolt will I get for all this, Mr Naughton?'

'I don't know, Roy. Four? Six, tops.'

He groaned. 'Don't talk to me about six. I can't do six.'

'Course you can,' said Bruce, placing a hand on his shoulder. 'You're still a young bloke.'

The movement was so quick, the arm a blur, it was as if Roy was demonstrating that he still had the reflexes of a twenty-eight year old. He snatched up the pistol and had it in his mouth before any of us could stop him

'No!' I managed to shout as I lunged forward, but Bruce was there before me, grappling with Roy. I threw myself backwards as the gun went off, the discharge filling the room and traumatising my eardrums. A slow trickle of plaster came down from the ceiling, as if it had escaped from a snow-globe.

A graceful curl of blue smoke spiralled slowly above the table. We all watched it, transfixed, for a moment.

Bruce stared down at the weapon in his hands and tossed it to Bill, who caught it and slotted it into his overcoat pocket.

We all then looked at Roy, and at the thin trickle of blood running from the corner of his mouth. Bruce must have caught the foresight on the skin as he wrenched it from his mouth.

'I fuckin' hate guns,' said Bruce, handing him an immaculate, folded handkerchief. 'What you doin' with one, Roy? You could hurt yourself, you know?'

Roy dabbed at the wound and gave a small, hollow laugh. 'I bought that from a mate of Charlie's when I got out. I was going to shoot Dennis for pissing all my money away.

Good, solid Dennis, stand-up bloke, developed a taste for the gee-gees and bimbo women. Who would have thought it?' He looked up at Bill. 'Only thing I got to show for the whole kit and caboodle was a house for my mum.'

'Must be easier ways of getting one of those,' said Bill.

'I should have stuck to motor-racing.'

'We all should have,' said Bruce. 'You're still bleeding, mate. Sorry about that. Keep the handkerchief.'

'We have to go,' said Bill. 'Someone outside will have heard the shot. They'll be in here like Bruce bloody Willis any minute.'

I shook my head and my ears popped and I was fully back in the room. 'We'll lock up,' I promised. 'Turn out the lights.'

'Thanks. And can you leave a dish of milk outside for next door's cat?' Roy asked.

This tickled Bruce and his thin frame shook as he laughed. 'Fuck me, Roy. Don't you ever learn?'

I remembered then that one of the prints that incriminated Roy had been on the cat's bowl at the farm.

Roy gave a lascivious wink. 'You haven't seen the neighbour.'

He stood, and first I, then Bruce shook his hand, a solemn moment with a strange feeling of finality, of the curtain coming down one last time.

'Thank you for your time, gents,' said Bill. 'I'll be in touch.'

'I'll always stand character witness,' said Bruce, breaking the gloomy atmosphere. 'I'm good for it.'

'Christ, only if Peter Sutcliffe's not free,' said Roy, with a grin that seemed to come from the old Roy James.

Bill Naughton smiled, placed a hand on the small of Roy's back and propelled him into the hallway. As they headed for the front door, Roy's arms were already going up above his head in the traditional gesture of surrender.

Bruce and I stood in silence for a few minutes. I poured the remains of Bill's whisky into my own glass and pulled back the curtains. The sky was growing lighter now, a very tentative dawn, no more than a few spirals of burnished copper in the east.

'How are you really, Bruce?' I asked, turning back to him.

A wave of weariness seemed to wash over him. For the first time, he looked his age. I probably did too. Staying up till first light was a young man's game. We needed our beauty sleep.

'Me?' he said. 'Since I got home, I'm an old crook living on handouts from other old crooks.' He began to build himself another joint. 'You know, when I got back from Mexico and put the word out, I thought there'd be dozens of young guns wanting to get involved with the famous Great Train Robber. Not a bit of it. They were like – "whoa, thirty years? I'm not having any of that". Still the same, even now. I guess that fuckin' judge knew what he was doing, after all.'

I suddenly remembered I needed a lift back home and that the cops owed me one. I didn't want to walk out to an empty road. 'We should go, too.'

He looked at the joint, made to light it and thought better of it. He tucked it into an inside pocket. 'And then there are those twats who think I'm still loaded. That I live in Croydon because I'm an eccentric millionaire. They only got about three hundred grand back, so they reckon we still have the rest. They have no idea. There's some right fuckin' villains out there, including the lawyers. They should look at how much those cunts charged us all.'

'I can do you a good deal on a BMW.' I handed over a card. 'Give me a bell.'

He took it and examined it. 'My BMW days are over, but thanks. If I get a second wind, I'll come down for one of those nice old Sixes. You must be doing OK.' He ran a thumb over the printing. 'Embossed and everything.'

I explained to him that after my run-in with Len Haslam, I'd gone to Germany with the money he had intended to plant on me, where I had bought ex-Post Office yellow VW vans and shipped them back to England. They soon became the favoured transport of the hippie generation, and I made enough, eventually, to come back and open a BMW and NSU franchise, one of which, at least, came good.

'So you landed on your feet, after all? You know, the only one of the rest of us who really did all right was Gordy. Served his time, came out, got his money, a hundred and sixty grand, and buggered off. Hardly a sniff since, apart from the odd wish-you-were here card from Spain. He did OK, did Gordy.'

'Him and Tiny Dave.'

'Ah, yes. The one who really coshed the driver.'

Jack Mills was dead now, killed by leukemia, although there were those – his family amongst them – who still reckoned it was the robbery that really did for him.

'It was Dave who hit him?' I asked. 'I always wondered.'

A shrug. 'I wasn't on the train. Bloody chaos it was, by all accounts. But yeah, that's how it went. With a lot of encouragement from Buster, so I hear. And if Dave hadn't done it, Buster would have. Like a bloody little Jack Russell with that cosh, he was.'

'Whatever happened to Tiny Dave?' I asked.

'Ah. Talk about *Tales of Mystery and Imagination*. Tiny Dave was last seen walking off into the night with his whack, thirty years ago.'

'Never heard anything?'

'Of Dave? Not a dicky bird.'

I remembered him talking about going to Bangkok. I wondered if he'd made it. 'Which means he is either the legendary One Who Got Away. Or . . .'

'Someone killed him and took the money. Wouldn't surprise me. That cash never brought anything but bad luck.'

I recalled Billy Naughton had said much the same thing when we were out on the rowing lake. 'Toxic', he had called it.

Bruce mistook my silence for disbelief. 'Look at the facts. Charlie dead, Brian Field dead, Bill Boal dead. Buster and Roy bloody basket cases. Ralph was coming back to give himself up a few years ago. Been lying low in Belgium. Got a ferry back. *The Spirit of Free Enterprise*.' I shook my head at the bad luck. The boat had capsized, killing 193 people. Clearly, Ralph, the dwarf signal man, had been among them. 'And Tommy Wisbey's in a bad way. You hear that? Strokes. Never the same after his sixteen-year-old daughter died in a car accident. And Bobby Welch a cripple. And for what? It was an eye-opener when I realised the poor sod of a train driver ended up with more than me in the end, after the great British public had a whip-round for him.'

That wasn't strictly true; Mills hadn't received anything like a hundred and fifty grand. More like thirty, as I recalled. But it was a fact that he held on to more of it than Bruce.

'You know the young fireman died too?' I asked.

'Who?'

'The co-driver. David something.' Anything to do with the robbery had always caught my eye, often triggered a what-if moment, where I thought about how close I came to being in that dock. 'Heart-attack. Thirty-three or four, he was.'

'Shit. That's a tough break.' Then, with a twinkle in his eye, 'They blame that one on me as well?'

'Not that I heard.'

Bruce stood, pulled on his overcoat, picked up the glasses and cups from the table and took them to the sink. 'Ah, well,' he said with a rueful smile as he rinsed them. 'As the old Sinatra song has it, you might be on top of the world in April, but you'll crash and burn in May.'

We stood staring at each other, pondering this pearl of wisdom from Ol' Blue Eyes. 'Wasn't he back on top in June?' I asked.

Bruce put a quarter-inch of milk in a saucer and placed it outside the kitchen door, then locked and bolted it. Placing a bony, veined hand on my shoulder, he steered me towards the front door, flicking off lights as he went. When he spoke, the jaunty sing-song tone had disappeared, replaced by a melancholy whisper.

'Ask Roy. He'll tell you. Sometimes June is a fuck of a long time coming.'

Aftermath

Bruce Reynolds: after moving around various safe houses in London, he fled abroad (France, Mexico) but, once the money ran low, he came back to the UK. He was caught by Tommy Butler in Torquay in 1968, given a twenty-five-year sentence but released in 1978. Reynolds and his wife divorced while he was inside, but were reconciled upon his release. He did time in the early 1980s for dealing in amphetamine sulphate, which he still contests. Reynolds is the author of a very successful and readable autobiography (see Acknowledgements).

Ronald Biggs: the most famous/notorious of the robbers, but one who played only a small part in the robbery itself. After his escape from Wandsworth in 1965, he moved around the world before settling in Rio, where he fathered a child who saved him from extradition by Jack Slipper. In 2001, he returned to England, a very sick man, having been on the run for a total of thirty-eight years. He was released on compassionate grounds in 2009 so he could die a free man.

Ronald 'Buster' Edwards: on the run, he joined Bruce Reynolds in Mexico but, homesick, he eventually returned to the UK and gave himself up. He was sentenced to fifteen years in 1966 and was released in 1975. Despite being portrayed as a lovable cockney rogue by Phil Collins in the movie *Buster*, there are those who still believe he was the one who coshed driver Jack Mills. Found hanged in his garage in 1994, at the age of 62.

Charlie Wilson: sentenced to thirty years, he escaped from Winson Green Prison after four months. He was tracked down in 1968 by Tommy Butler in Canada, brought home, and served twelve years. Wilson was shot dead outside his Marbella home in April 1990.

Roy James: the talented racing driver was jailed for thirty years; he served twelve. An attempt to pick up his driving career failed and for a while he ran a gold VAT scam with Charlie Wilson, narrowly avoiding jail. In early 1993, he was sentenced to six years after shooting his father-in-law and hitting his wife with a pistol butt. He died of a heart-attack in 1997.

Brian Field: the solicitor was released in 1969. His wife Karin divorced him while he was in prison, and married a German journalist. He died in a motorway accident in 1979.

Thomas Wisbey: another thirty-year man, he was released in 1976. However, after a period as a car dealer, he fell back into crime and was jailed for ten years in 1989 for cocaine dealing. Now retired.

Robert Welch: sentenced to thirty years and released in 1976. Crippled by a bungled leg operation in prison, he ran clubs when released. Now retired.

Gordon Goody: sentenced to thirty years and released in 1975, he claimed in the Carlton TV programme *I Was A Great Train Robber* that he spent most of his share of the money on lawyers and was 'ripped off' for much of the rest.

James Hussey: sentenced to thirty years, he was released in 1975. He became a car dealer (in Warren Street) but was jailed for seven years in 1989 for cocaine dealing. Retired.

Roger Cordrey: sentenced to twenty years for rigging railway signals but served fourteen after an appeal. Returned to being a florist in the West Country.

James White: was on the run for three years, but eventually gave himself up and was sentenced to eighteen years in 1966. Released in 1975 and opted for a quiet life in Sussex.

William Boal: died of a brain tumour in 1970 while serving his sentence. Bruce Reynolds always maintained he was never part of the gang.

Leonard Field: involved in the purchase of Leatherslade Farm. Sentenced to twenty-five years for conspiring to obstruct the course of justice, later reduced to five. Released in 1967.

John Wheater: a solicitor jailed for three years in 1964 for conspiring to pervert the course of justice. He was released in 1966.

There are persistent rumours that between one and three robbers were never arrested or prosecuted. The man identified as 'The Ulsterman' in several accounts ('Jock' here) has also never been traced, nor has the mysterious Mark who acted as go-between. Stan (sometimes called Peter), the retired train driver, also disappeared without trace.

Acknowledgements

This novel is a work of fiction. It uses real characters and situations, but I have treated them as a novelist, not a historian. Many characters are entirely fictitious, and any resemblance between them and persons living or dead is entirely fictitious. Nevertheless, the arc of the story, from airport job to train robbery and subsequent capture and prosecution, is an accurate representation of the gang's operations.

I would like to thank Mike Lawrence, motor-racing guru and author of many fine books on the sport, including *The Glory of Goodwood* (with Simon Taylor and Doug Nye), who was my very first port of call. I knew I wanted to avoid building the story around the two most well-known train robbers, Ronnie Biggs and Buster Edwards. Roy James (there is some confusion over whether he was ever consistently called 'the Weasel', or if the police got it wrong and the name stuck)

582

seemed to me one of the most tragic of the thieves. Whether he was as outrageously talented as some suggest, I'm not convinced, but he was certainly a more than capable driver, on and off the track.

Mike not only knew the Roy James story intimately, he knew Roy himself: he raced against him in his karting days, and thought highly of his skill. The early scenes on the air base came from Mike's memory, but, of course, filtered through my distorting lens.

Thank you to Holly Groom for additional research on the trial of the robbers and to Sinead Porter of the News International syndication department for allowing me to use part of Colin MacInnes' article *An Honest Citizen's Guide to the Criminal Classes* and extracts from *The Times* newspaper. Thanks also to Duncan Campbell, ace crime reporter and author of the excellent novel *If It Bleeds*, which features a walk-on by Bruce Reynolds.

As initial source material I used the memoirs of Jack Slipper (*Slipper of the Yard*), George Hatherill (*A Detective's Story*, which contains the story of the headless corpse in Cornwall), and Ernest Millen (*Specialist in Crime*, wherein Millen claims the big tip-off came from an interview with a snitch in prison), as well as Bruce Reynolds's highly readable *Autobiography of a Thief*, Piers Paul Read's *The Train Robbers*, Wensley Clarkson's *Killing Charlie*, Ronnie Biggs's *Odd Man Out* and *Keep on Running*, and Peta Fordham's *The Robbers' Tale*.

But if you want a concise, authoritative overview of the truth – all the previous titles being unreliable in one aspect or another – I would point you to Peter Guttridge. His *The Great Train Robbery* for the Crime Archives series of the National Archives is a skilfully condensed version of the whole saga, including the unanswered questions. Chief among these is, was there a Mr Big? (We'll never know, but it's unlikely.) Where did the money dumped in Dorking woods and Black Horse Court come from? Again, we'll probably never know, but it was alleged in the Carlton TV programme *I Was A Great Train Robber* that Brian Field's parents got rid of the Dorking cash when they realised it was ill-gotten gains. But that was never substantiated.

Also useful was *Villains' Paradise* by Donald Thomas, *Gangland Soho* by James Morton, *The Flying Squad* by Norman Lucas and Bernard Scarlett, and *The Underworld* by Duncan Campbell. For some of Bruce's answers to Colin Thirkell (a fictionalised version of Colin MacInnes), I dipped into *The Courage of His Convictions* by Tony Parker and 'Robert Allerton', a series of interviews with a career criminal in the early 1960s. Plus the News International archives provided many contemporary accounts, as did the Colindale Newspaper Library.

For the scenes at Ronnie Scott's, I relied on *Jazz Man: The Amazing Story of Ronnie Scott and His Club* by the always-excellent John Fordham.

Part of Chapter 42, the police car chase, is inspired by the opening scenes of *Robbery*, Peter 'Bullitt' Yates's 1967 film that also fictionalises the events of August 1963. Star and producer Stanley Baker was a well-known face in the clubs and pubs frequented by the underworld, and Peta Fordham, who wrote *The Robbers' Tale*, was an adviser, so the core planning and robbery is very well portrayed – far better than in the later *Buster*.

Paul Wilson of the Kent & East Sussex Railway (*www.kesr.org.uk*) took me through how to start and drive diesels large and small, as well as the signal warnings that sound in the cab. Any errors in that department are mine alone.

The majority of events in this novel are true, although some of the dates have been shifted, but the details of the airport and train robberies and incidents such as Gordon Goody being arrested because he had managed to disguise himself as Bruce Reynolds; the two Jags being stolen before the first train robbery; Charmian Biggs telephoning the police to help find Ronnie; the burglary of Bruce Reynolds's hideout; the capture of Roy James; the find of money in Dorking and the phone box – are genuine occurrences. Len Haslam, Billy Naughton, Tony Fortune and Tiny Dave Thompson, however, are totally fictitious characters (and any resemblance to real police and thieves is entirely coincidental), although they are often slotted into actual events. 'Ralph' is also a fiction. No train robber died on *The Spirit of Free Enterprise*.

I would like to thank Bruce Reynolds for reading a version

of the book and treating it kindly. We had a very convivial lunch together, since we share an interest in cars, planes, guns, the war, film noir, tailors and jazz; however, those who want Bruce's viewpoint should consult his autobiography. This is a fictional account and he is in no way responsible for any of the content.

I am particularly and eternally grateful to Rowland Cordery, who broke a long stalemate by dreaming up the title *Signal Red*, which was just so perfect it made all the many suggested alternatives – most of them mine – look feeble in comparison.

Finally my gratitude goes, as always, to David Miller, Jo Stansall, Katie Haines, Sheila David, and, of course, my editor for eleven books now – does that make him eligible for the prefix 'long-suffering'? – Martin Fletcher.

Robert Ryan, London.
www.robert-ryan.net

Afterword by
Bruce Reynolds

At 8 a.m. on 8 August, 1963, the BBC broadcast a news item that made the whole country sit up and take notice. The gist of it was that a Glasgow to London mail train had been stopped and robbed at Cheddington, near Tring, Buckinghamshire. Details were sketchy. It had happened at about 3 a.m. that morning; the driver and the fireman had been attacked and injured and the front two coaches of the train had been detached. Senior police officers were already at the scene. Although it was clear that a large number of men had taken part and that they had stolen a considerable amount of cash, nobody was certain of the amount involved. I, of course, knew by then how much it was, because we had counted it. We had taken the Royal Mail for just over

£2.6 million in used notes (the best part of £40 million now). Staggering – the stuff of dreams.

The heist was known during those first few frenzied hours as The Cheddington Mail Train Robbery, but this was soon deemed not snappy enough. Instead, the media lifted the title of The Great Train Robbery from an American film dating back to 1903. With massive public interest in the event, the authorities became angry and agitated. There were questions in parliament, and reverberations spread through the country and across the globe like a distant but persistent drumbeat. The words echoed down the corridors of power: 'They must be caught and convicted'.

The police were given carte blanche, and the 'big boys' were called in, notably the Flying Squad, with Tommy Butler as Thieftaker General. It was a job he was admirably suited for, as he remarked with conviction to his colleague 'Nipper' Read: 'We'll get the bastards'. The hunt was on.

Rumours were rife. Informed sources said the organiser of the robbery was an ex-commando; others claimed that Billy Hill, the self-proclaimed King of the Underworld, was involved. Both wrong, of course. Names were bandied about, reputations besmirched, with plenty of winners and losers in the media frenzy that surrounded the robbery. The biggest losers, of course, were the men who robbed the train.

None of the actual robbers appreciated the full consequences of their actions; it only became apparent at a later date just how determined the authorities were. The scale of the manhunt, the size of the rewards offered and, especially, the eventual sentences were all unprecedented. Thirty years was unheard of, even for terrorist bombers.

But 'stone walls don't a prison make, nor iron bars a cage'. And so it proved to be. Charlie Wilson and Ronnie Biggs refused to accept their dire situation and promptly escaped. The media revelled in this turn of events and the hunt stepped up a gear. As did the whole story of The Great Train Robbery, which went through peaks and troughs of public interest, subsiding when the chase went quiet, thrusting its way back into the limelight with Ronnie's rip-roaring adventures in Rio. The public applauded this cheeky chappy, their emotions switching from curiosity, through admiration to envy: who wouldn't want to live a free and easy life in Rio?

The story has been told many times now, but continues to fascinate the media and readers, perhaps because it all begins with intrigue and ends in mystery.

Now Robert Ryan has fictionalised the tale based on known facts but using imagined situations and dialogue, a technique he has employed before in his novel *Death on the Ice*, about Captain Scott, and with Lawrence of Arabia in *Empire of Sand*. They were both key characters from my boyhood days, which is what attracted me to his work. The story he tells in *Signal Red* is impeccably researched and the salient facts are all there. For his characterisation, however, he had to rely on contemporary accounts, memoirs, other writers' descriptions and conclusions (many of the major figures on both sides of the law being deceased) and his own interpretations, and that doesn't always fit with my own memories of some of the personalities involved.

That is not to say he is wrong. In fact, he could be correct. At the time I might well have been blinkered: the light that he shines illuminates some dark corners whilst throwing shadows on others. But while my memory and his version don't always see eye-to-eye, he captures the times perfectly and particularly the essence of camaraderie which existed and flourished under the banner of crime, specifically robbery. When a group of men embark on a nefarious series of enterprises that will, almost certainly, see some of them in prison, losing everything, then your relationships with your fellow robbers become the most important element of the undertaking. Being able to trust them is of paramount importance (and remember, none of the robbers turned Queen's Evidence or co-operated with the police in any way).

Ultimately, as a robber, you face losing your freedom, but I don't think you can fully appreciate what this means until it is taken away from you. That realisation comes too late, even though you are aware every time you go to 'work', it might be your last job. Your mind plays tricks on you about the consequences of your actions and the chances of being caught. *Is it worth the risk?* you might ask yourself. But if you're a grafter, you'll dismiss the risk factor and go for the adrenaline. That's the addiction.

True, old-fashioned greed is also a motivating factor, whether it is for money, power or reputation. I guess we all craved one or more of those things, and some of us embraced them all. Upon reflection, I realise that at the time of the robbery I never questioned people's motivation for being 'at it'. In fact, I hardly know them now.

Charlie Wilson lived in the next street to mine in Battersea and we went to school together. He was younger than me and we were pals without being bosom buddies; I only really got to know him in his twenties. In my eyes, he never changed: always cheerful, game for a lark and totally reliable. A very sound man.

I was shocked to hear of Charlie's death, shot by the side of his swimming pool at his home in Marbella, evoking the end of Fitzgerald's Gatsby. The theft of his life only led to retribution and further theft of lives. The moral there is, no matter how big you are, there is always someone bigger and with more power.

Charlie was buried in Earlsfield, local to us Battersea Boys. The service closed with a final flourish of bravado, as the coffin was accompanied by Sinatra doing his version of 'My Way'. That was Chas all right.

Roy James had one ambition when he received his thirty-year sentence: to get out of prison and pursue his motor-racing career and ultimately his dream of becoming World Champion. He embraced Seneca and the Stoics' principle, as defined by prison doggerel: 'If you can't do the time, don't do the crime', or my favourite, 'Eat your porridge every day and do your bird the easy way.' Nice constructive sentiments, but nobody serves a decade inside without physical and mental damage.

In spite of Roy's pursuit of physical fitness, something had gone when he finally got out. He transferred his ambitions in other directions, and was very successful financially, but perhaps less so emotionally. He had a long-term relationship that broke up and eventually ended up marrying a younger woman and fathered two daughters. It appeared he had made it: he had the country house, complete with ponies and stables, an attractive young wife and lovely daughters. But somehow, it was not enough. Nothing satisfied him. Probably because the grand ambition – to win the World Championship – was lost and gone for ever.

What caused his confrontation with his wife and father-in-law and the events that followed is a mystery, yet such events are all too common in the real world of domestic discord. Ignominiously Roy (forever saddled with the media-invented, or at least media-popularised, nickname of the Weasel, which he hated) went back to prison.

Inside, his physical condition declined. He had seen Bill Boal – innocent of the crime, yet convicted – die inside. He had seen Biggsy kidnapped from Rio and promptly stolen back by the Brazilian authorities. He had seen Buster's tragic suicide. He must have asked himself, as most of us of a certain age do – what is it all about?

He died in hospital of a heart-attack. He was 62.

Roy's mantra was best expressed as pitting yourself against the world, going to the extreme to see if you can hack it. Will you match up? It's a hard code to live by. There is a consolation: I now know you don't recognise success unless you have first experienced abject failure. Your ambition to drive to the edge of the abyss, to seek the impossible and make it possible, certainly invites failure. But if you do fail, it's an honourable failure.

Bruce Reynolds, author of *Autobiography of a Thief*

ROBERT RYAN

Empire of Sand

The First World War rages in Europe, but intelligence officer Thomas Edward Lawrence has been consigned to the Map Room at GHQ in Cairo. Yet, spurred on by personal tragedy, he is about to unlock a secret that will alter the course of history.

Lawrence is convinced that an Arab revolt is the only way to remove the Ottoman presence and achieve a free Arabia. But through his network of spies, alarming reports reach him of a tribal uprising against the British, orchestrated by infamous German agent Wilhelm Wassmuss. Hostages have been taken and the War Office in London immediately despatch government assassin Captain Harold Quinn to Cairo on a deadly mission.

With a shared purpose, Quinn and Lawrence begin the hazardous journey to the deserts of Persia. They soon discover that their German nemesis is an experienced master of stealth and deception. But has he finally met his match when he confronts the shrewd and resourceful tactician, Lawrence of Arabia?

Praise for *EMPIRE OF SAND*:

'Plenty of action, sharp dialogue and swift characterisation. The whole is intelligently structured so that this is absorbing and thoughtful as well as tense and exciting' *Daily Telegraph*

978 0 7553 2926 7

headline
review

ROBERT RYAN

Death on the Ice

January 18, 1912: Captain Robert Falcon Scott's expedition reaches the South Pole. Just a few weeks later, trapped in one of the worst blizzards Antarctica has ever known, Scott and his four companions perish in sub-zero temperatures.

How did the icy conditions overwhelm Scott, Captain Oates and their party on the fateful return journey? Both experienced explorers, neither Scott nor Oates was prepared for the disappointment of losing their polar race against Norwegian Roald Amundsen. Nor could they have known that the accretion of a few small mistakes would ultimately cost them their lives.

The story of Scott and Oates, their incredible journey and their tragic final day is one of the most captivating and endlessly fascinating tales from the Golden Age of Exploration.

Praise for ROBERT RYAN:

'Stirring, a true epic' *Daily Telegraph*

'A superb writer' *Independent on Sunday*

'A hugely enjoyable speculative novel' *The Sunday Times*

978 0 7553 4722 3

headline
review

Now you can buy any of these bestselling books by **Robert Ryan** from your bookshop or *direct from his publisher*.

FREE P&P AND UK DELIVERY
(Overseas and Ireland £3.50 per book)

1007469103 PLAN

Underdogs	£7.99
Nine Mil	£7.99
Trans Am	£7.99
Early One Morning	£6.99
The Blue Noon	£6.99
Night Crossing	£6.99
After Midnight	£6.99
The Last Sunrise	£6.99
Dying Day	£6.99
Empire of Sand	£6.99
Death on the Ice	£6.99
Signal Red	£6.99

TO ORDER SIMPLY CALL THIS NUMBER

01235 400 414

or visit our website: www.headline.co.uk
Prices and availability subject to change without notice.